Volume One

by
Jen Lee Quick

HAMBURG // LONDON // LOS ANGELES // TOKYO

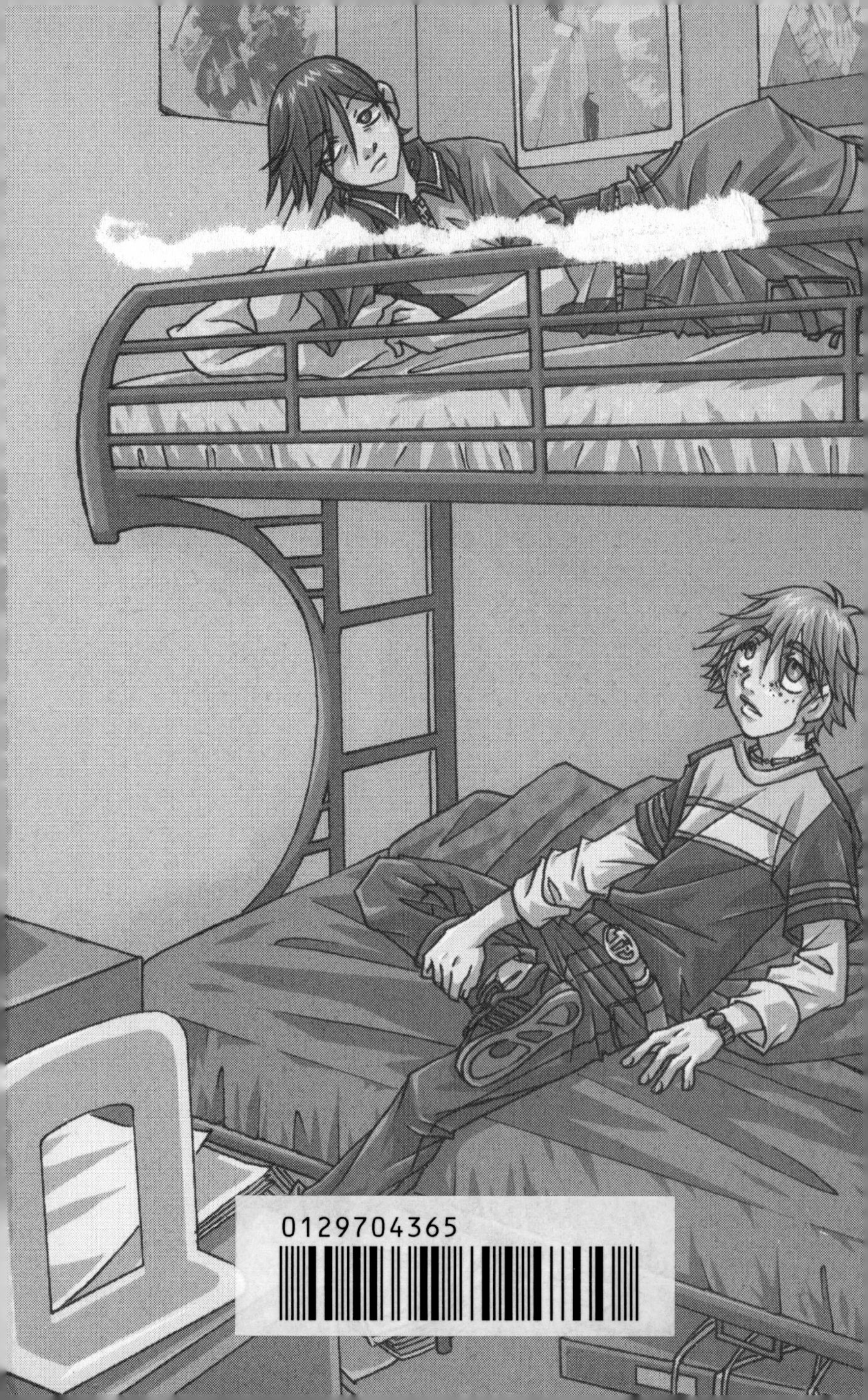

Off *Beat vol. 1
written and illustrated by Jen Lee Quick

Layout Artist - Vanessa Satore
Production Artist - James Dashiell
Cover Design - Seth Cable

Editor - Lillian Diaz-Przybyl & Jodi Bryson
Digital Imaging Manager - Chris Buford
Production Managers - Jennifer Miller and Mutsumi Miyazaki
Managing Editor - Jill Freshney
Editorial Director - Jeremy Ross
VP of Production - Ron Klamert
Publisher and E.I.C. - Mike Kiley
President and C.O.O. - John Parker
C.E.O. - Stuart Levy

A  Manga

TOKYOPOP Inc.
5900 Wilshire Blvd. Suite 2000
Los Angeles, CA 90036

E-mail: info@TOKYOPOP.com
Come visit us online at www.TOKYOPOP.com

ISBN: 1-59816-132-6

First TOKYOPOP printing: September 2005
10 9 8 7 6 5 4 3 2 1
Printed in Canada

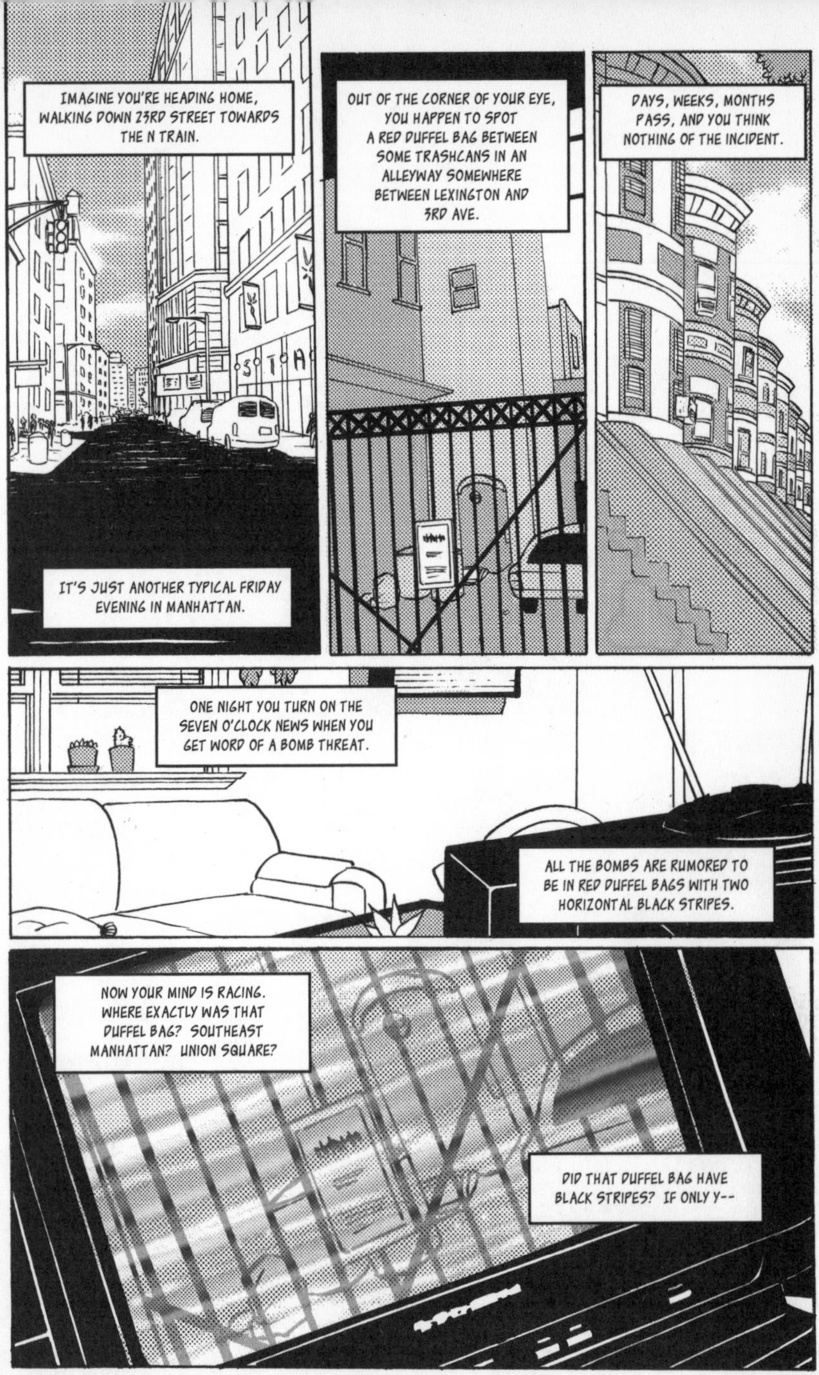
IMAGINE YOU'RE HEADING HOME, WALKING DOWN 23RD STREET TOWARDS THE N TRAIN.
IT'S JUST ANOTHER TYPICAL FRIDAY EVENING IN MANHATTAN.
OUT OF THE CORNER OF YOUR EYE, YOU HAPPEN TO SPOT A RED DUFFEL BAG BETWEEN SOME TRASHCANS IN AN ALLEYWAY SOMEWHERE BETWEEN LEXINGTON AND 3RD AVE.
DAYS, WEEKS, MONTHS PASS, AND YOU THINK NOTHING OF THE INCIDENT.
ONE NIGHT YOU TURN ON THE SEVEN O'CLOCK NEWS WHEN YOU GET WORD OF A BOMB THREAT.
ALL THE BOMBS ARE RUMORED TO BE IN RED DUFFEL BAGS WITH TWO HORIZONTAL BLACK STRIPES.
NOW YOUR MIND IS RACING. WHERE EXACTLY WAS THAT DUFFEL BAG? SOUTHEAST MANHATTAN? UNION SQUARE?
DID THAT DUFFEL BAG HAVE BLACK STRIPES? IF ONLY Y--

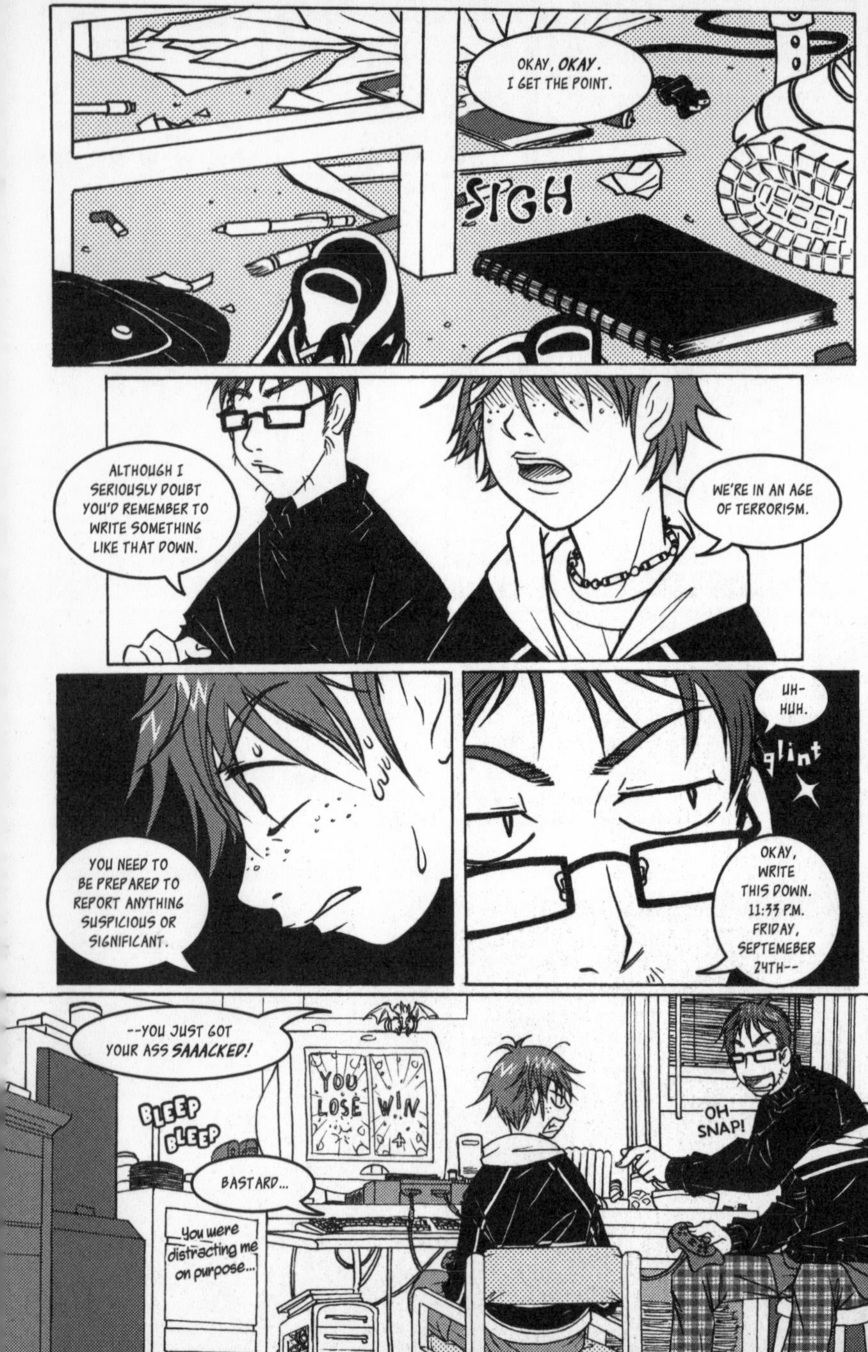
OKAY, OKAY.
I GET THE POINT.
SIGH
ALTHOUGH I SERIOUSLY DOUBT YOU'D REMEMBER TO WRITE SOMETHING LIKE THAT DOWN.
WE'RE IN AN AGE OF TERRORISM.
YOU NEED TO BE PREPARED TO REPORT ANYTHING SUSPICIOUS OR SIGNIFICANT.
UH-HUH.
glint
OKAY, WRITE THIS DOWN. 11:33 P.M. FRIDAY, SEPTEMEBER 24TH--
--YOU JUST GOT YOUR ASS SAAACKED!
YOU LOSE
WIN
BLEEP BLEEP
OH SNAP!
BASTARD...
You were distracting me on purpose...

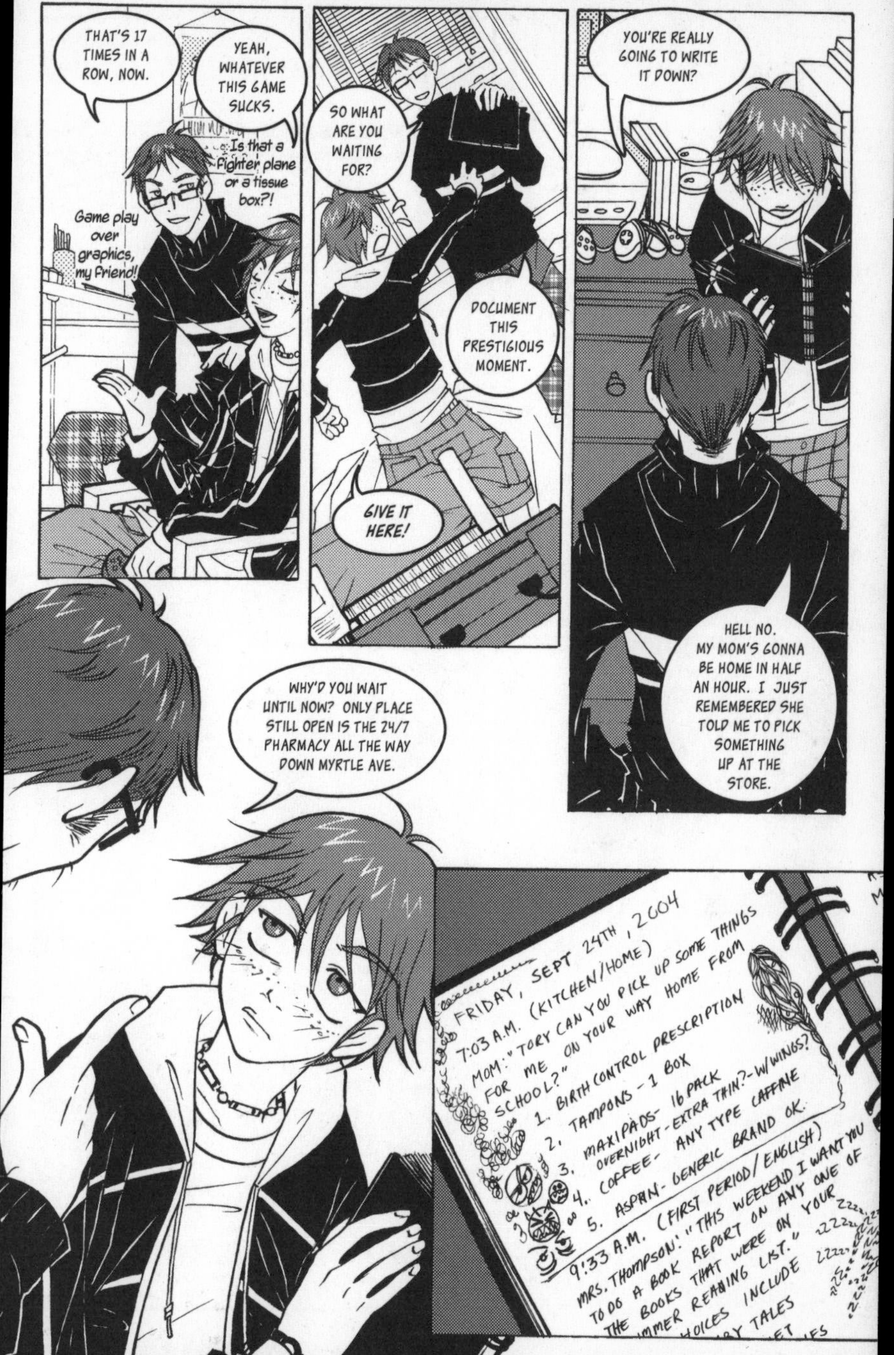
THAT'S 17 TIMES IN A ROW, NOW.
YEAH, WHATEVER THIS GAME SUCKS.
Is that a fighter plane or a tissue box?!
Game play over graphics, my friend!
SO WHAT ARE YOU WAITING FOR?
DOCUMENT THIS PRESTIGIOUS MOMENT.
GIVE IT HERE!
YOU'RE REALLY GOING TO WRITE IT DOWN?
HELL NO. MY MOM'S GONNA BE HOME IN HALF AN HOUR. I JUST REMEMBERED SHE TOLD ME TO PICK SOMETHING UP AT THE STORE.
WHY'D YOU WAIT UNTIL NOW? ONLY PLACE STILL OPEN IS THE 24/7 PHARMACY ALL THE WAY DOWN MYRTLE AVE.
FRIDAY, SEPT 24TH, 2004
7:03 A.M. (KITCHEN/HOME)
MOM: "TORY CAN YOU PICK UP SOME THINGS FOR ME ON YOUR WAY HOME FROM SCHOOL?"
1. BIRTH CONTROL PRESCRIPTION
2. TAMPONS - 1 BOX
3. MAXIPADS- 16 PACK OVERNIGHT-EXTRA THIN?-W/WINGS?
4. COFFEE- ANY TYPE CAFFINE
5. ASPRIN- GENERIC BRAND OK.
9:33 A.M. (FIRST PERIOD/ENGLISH)
MRS. THOMPSON: "THIS WEEKEND I WANT YOU TO DO A BOOK REPORT ON ANY ONE OF THE BOOKS THAT WERE ON YOUR
READING LIST."
INCLUDE
ZZZZ

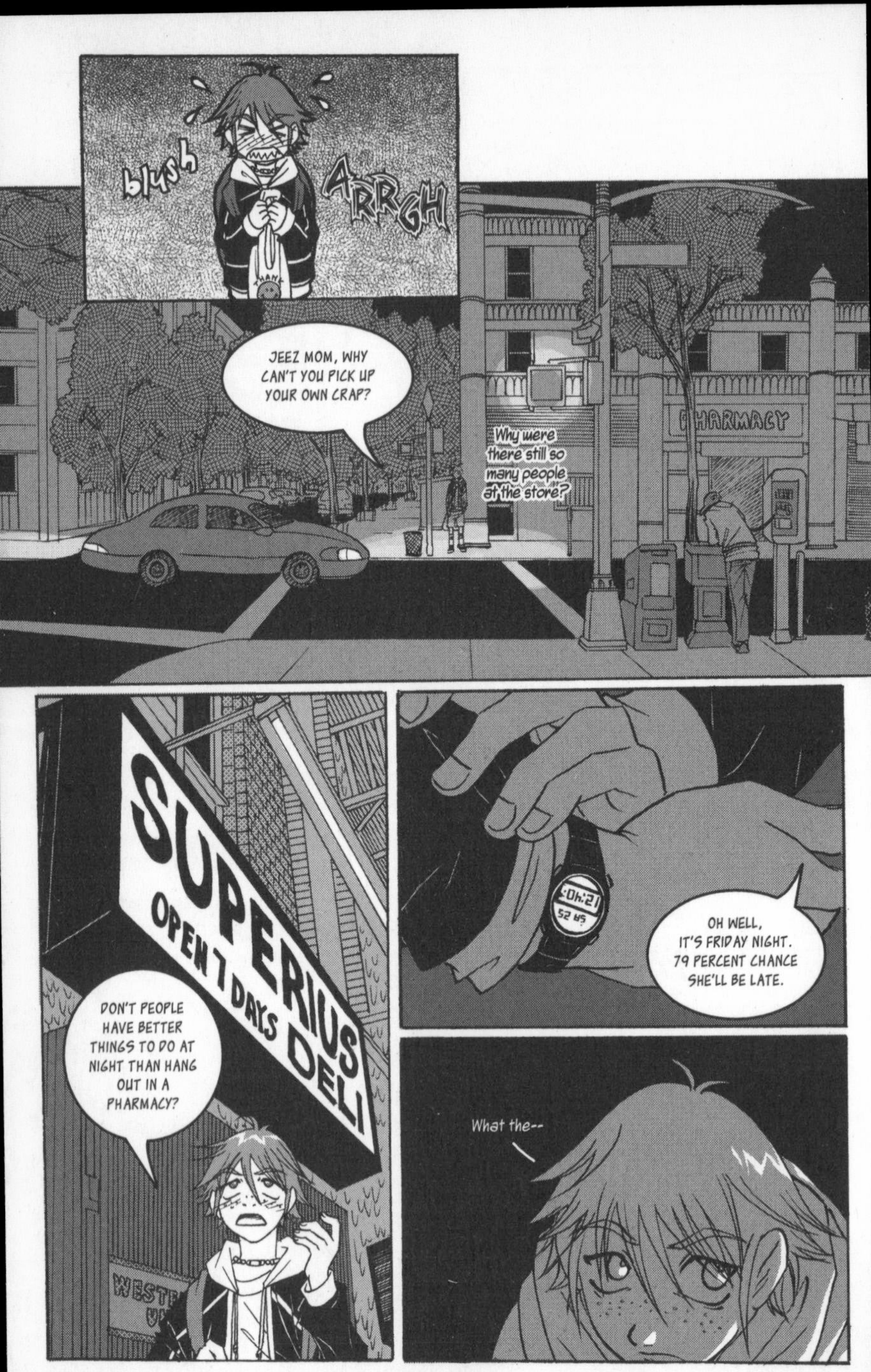
blush
ARRGH
JEEZ MOM, WHY CAN'T YOU PICK UP YOUR OWN CRAP?
PHARMACY
Why were there still so many people at the store?
SUPERIUS
OPEN 7 DAYS DELI
DON'T PEOPLE HAVE BETTER THINGS TO DO AT NIGHT THAN HANG OUT IN A PHARMACY?
OH WELL, IT'S FRIDAY NIGHT. 79 PERCENT CHANCE SHE'LL BE LATE.
What the--

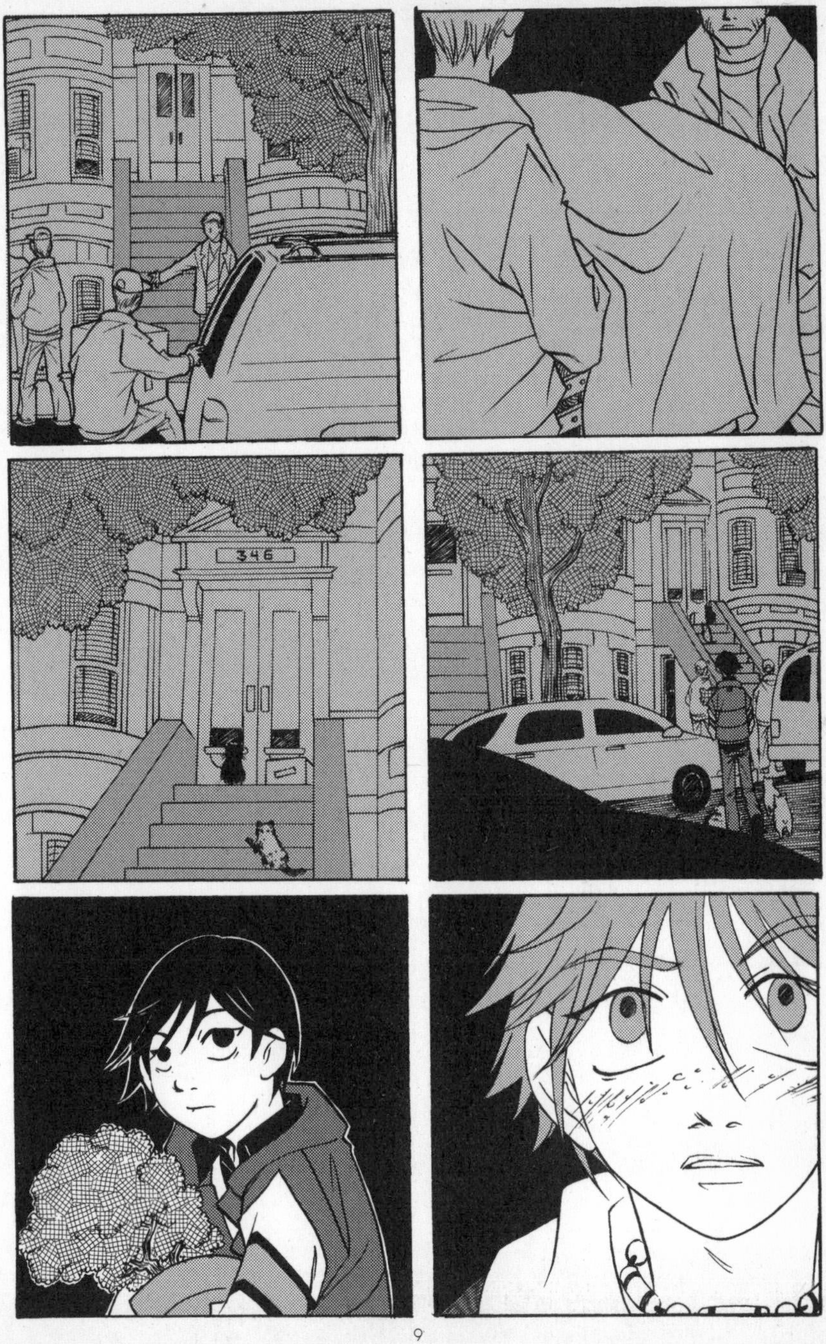
346

SATURDAY, SEPTEMBER 29TH, 2004 SOMEWHERE IN THE VICINITY OF 12:41 A.M. TO 1:25 A.M. COLIN STEPHENS MOVED TO 346 68TH ST, WOODRIDGE, QUEENS, NY...

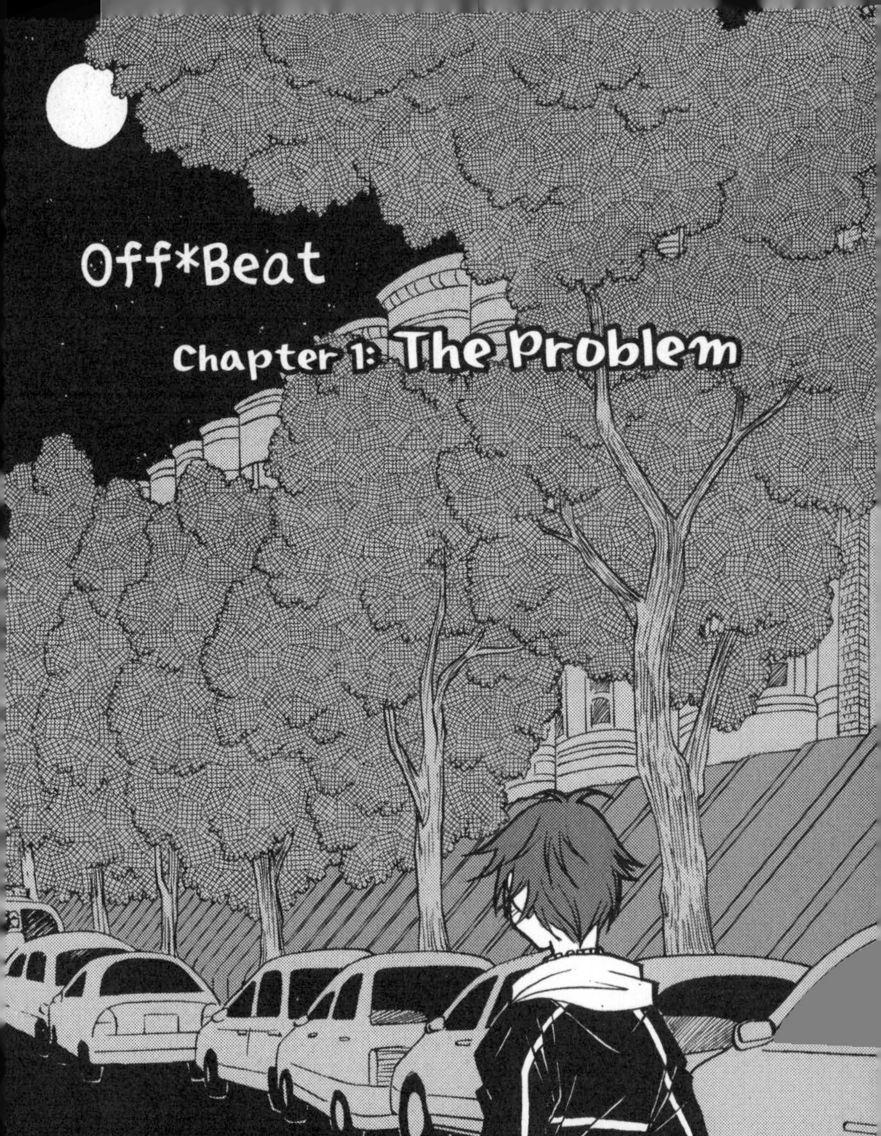
Off*Beat
Chapter 1: The Problem

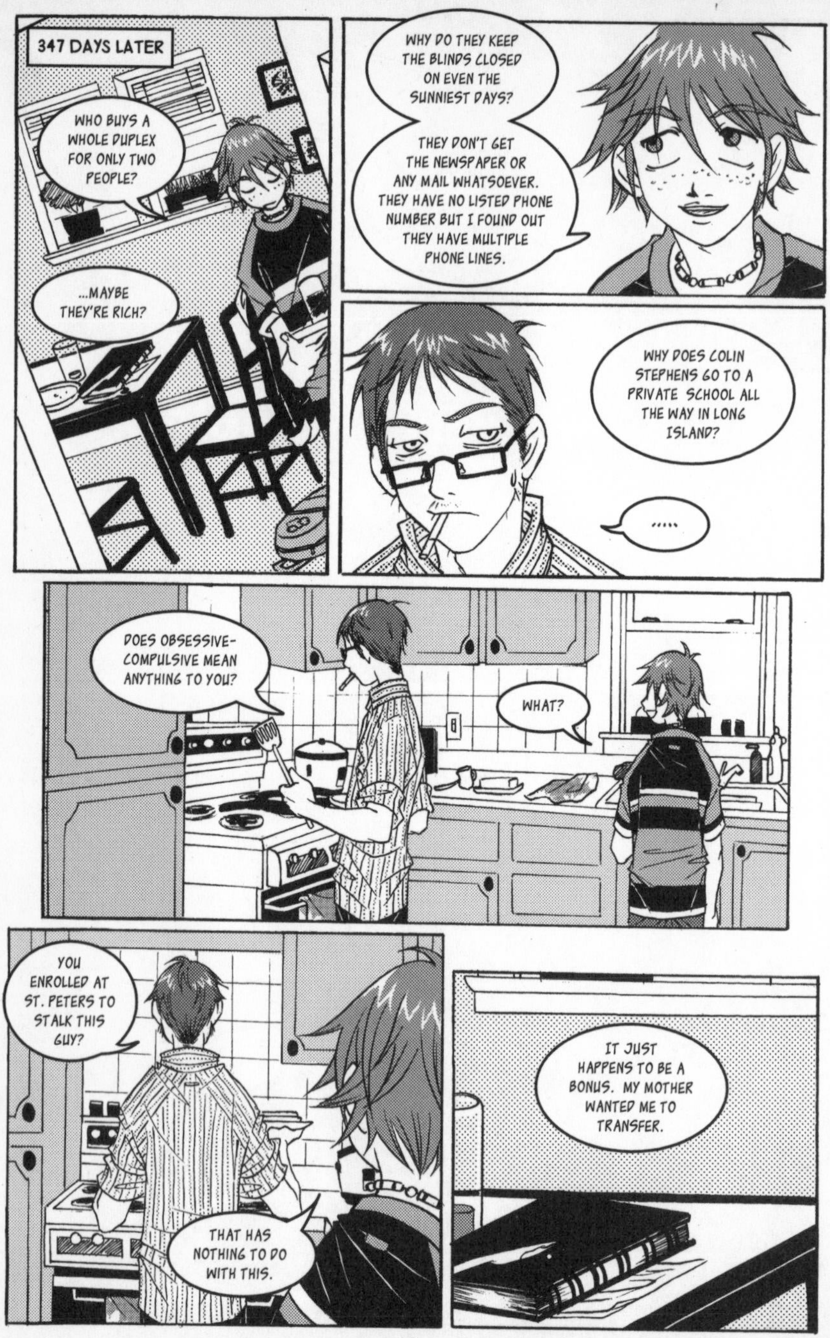
347 DAYS LATER
WHO BUYS A WHOLE DUPLEX FOR ONLY TWO PEOPLE?
...MAYBE THEY'RE RICH?
WHY DO THEY KEEP THE BLINDS CLOSED ON EVEN THE SUNNIEST DAYS?
THEY DON'T GET THE NEWSPAPER OR ANY MAIL WHATSOEVER. THEY HAVE NO LISTED PHONE NUMBER BUT I FOUND OUT THEY HAVE MULTIPLE PHONE LINES.
WHY DOES COLIN STEPHENS GO TO A PRIVATE SCHOOL ALL THE WAY IN LONG ISLAND?
.....
DOES OBSESSIVE-COMPULSIVE MEAN ANYTHING TO YOU?
WHAT?
YOU ENROLLED AT ST. PETERS TO STALK THIS GUY?
THAT HAS NOTHING TO DO WITH THIS.
IT JUST HAPPENS TO BE A BONUS. MY MOTHER WANTED ME TO TRANSFER.

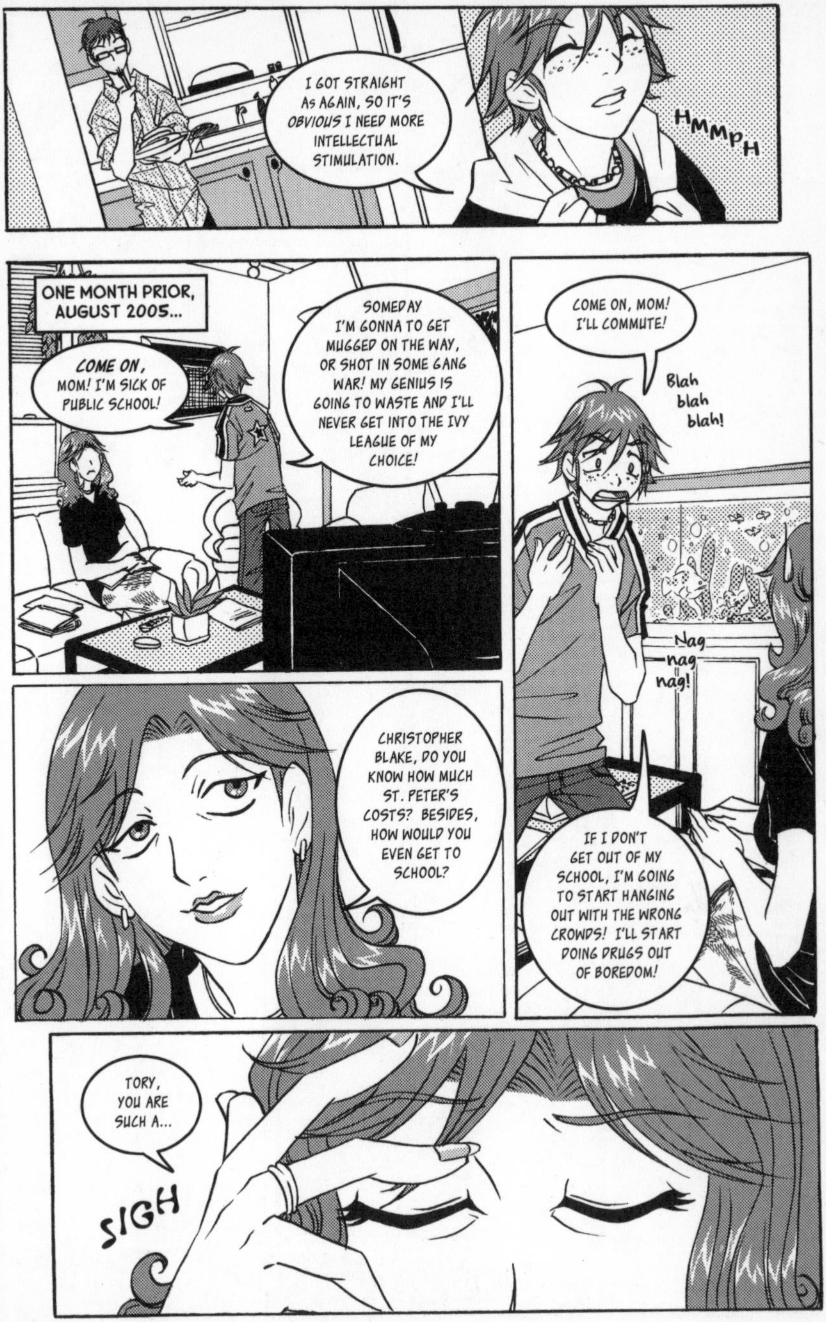
I GOT STRAIGHT As AGAIN, SO IT'S OBVIOUS I NEED MORE INTELLECTUAL STIMULATION.
HMMPH
ONE MONTH PRIOR, AUGUST 2005...
COME ON, MOM! I'M SICK OF PUBLIC SCHOOL!
SOMEDAY I'M GONNA TO GET MUGGED ON THE WAY, OR SHOT IN SOME GANG WAR! MY GENIUS IS GOING TO WASTE AND I'LL NEVER GET INTO THE IVY LEAGUE OF MY CHOICE!
CHRISTOPHER BLAKE, DO YOU KNOW HOW MUCH ST. PETER'S COSTS? BESIDES, HOW WOULD YOU EVEN GET TO SCHOOL?
COME ON, MOM! I'LL COMMUTE!
Blah blah blah!
Nag nag nag!
IF I DON'T GET OUT OF MY SCHOOL, I'M GOING TO START HANGING OUT WITH THE WRONG CROWDS! I'LL START DOING DRUGS OUT OF BOREDOM!
TORY, YOU ARE SUCH A...
SIGH

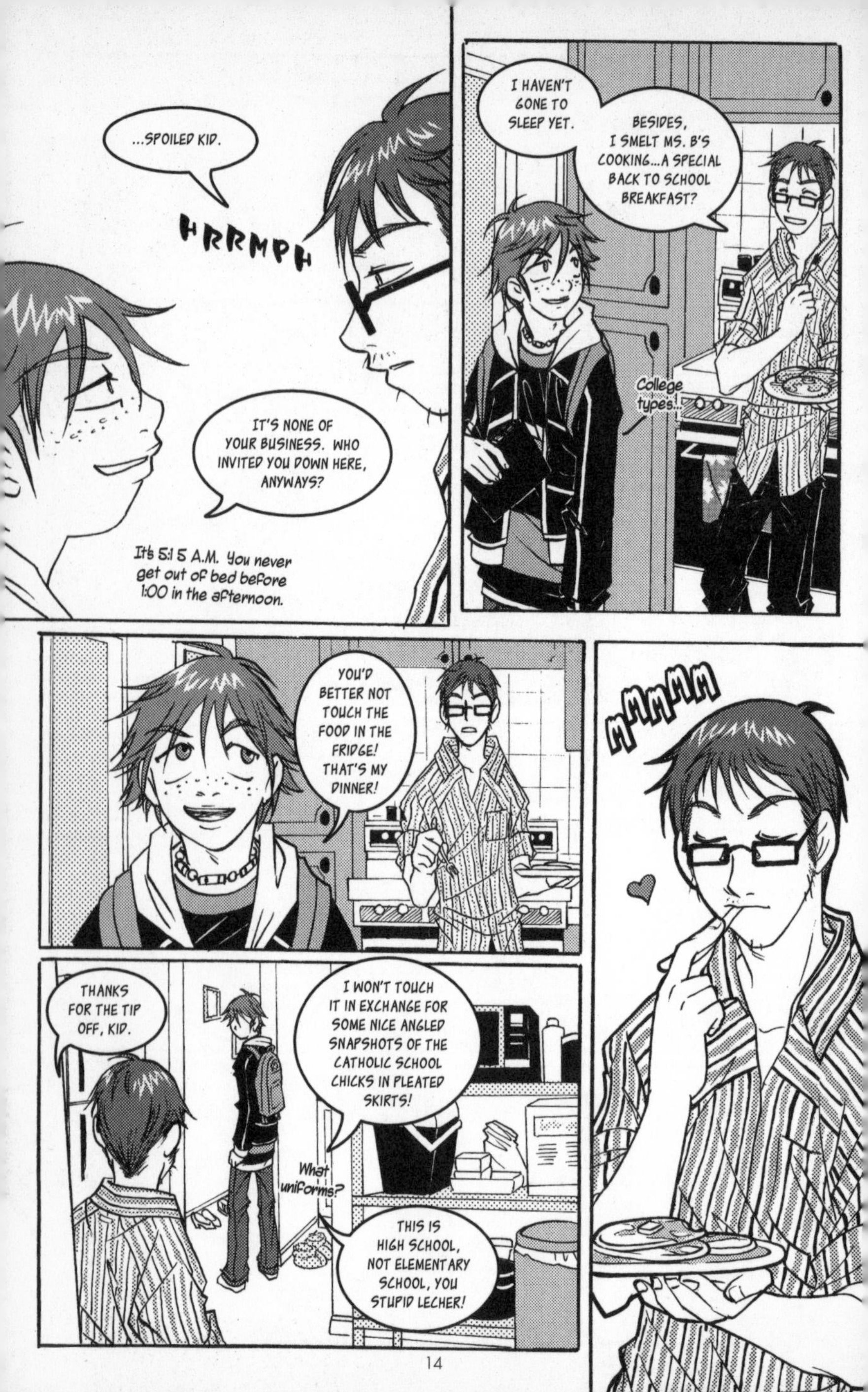
...SPOILED KID.
HRRMPH
IT'S NONE OF YOUR BUSINESS. WHO INVITED YOU DOWN HERE, ANYWAYS?
It's 5:15 A.M. You never get out of bed before 1:00 in the afternoon.
I HAVEN'T GONE TO SLEEP YET.
BESIDES, I SMELT MS. B'S COOKING...A SPECIAL BACK TO SCHOOL BREAKFAST?
College types...
YOU'D BETTER NOT TOUCH THE FOOD IN THE FRIDGE! THAT'S MY DINNER!
THANKS FOR THE TIP OFF, KID.
I WON'T TOUCH IT IN EXCHANGE FOR SOME NICE ANGLED SNAPSHOTS OF THE CATHOLIC SCHOOL CHICKS IN PLEATED SKIRTS!
What uniforms?
THIS IS HIGH SCHOOL, NOT ELEMENTARY SCHOOL, YOU STUPID LECHER!
mMMMM

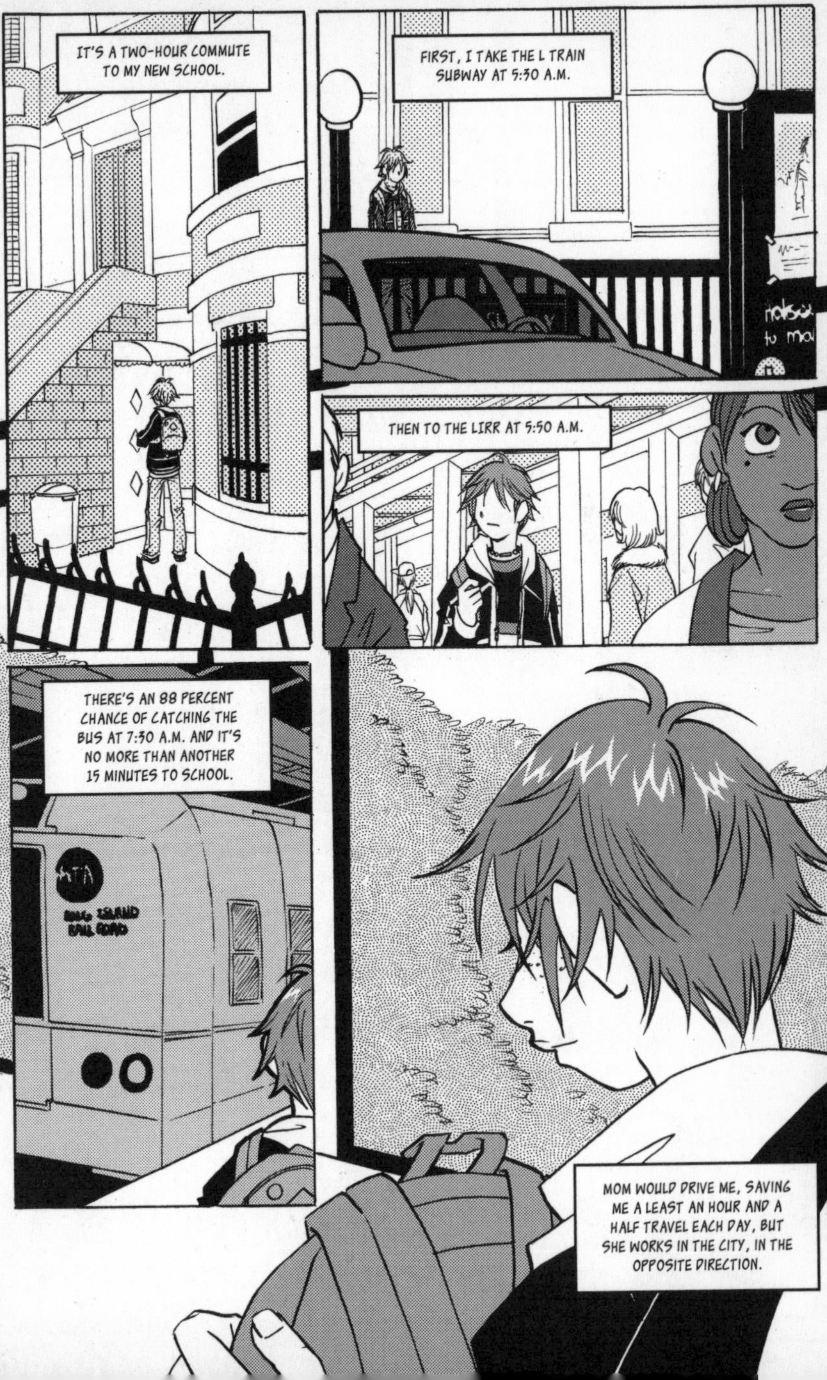
IT'S A TWO-HOUR COMMUTE TO MY NEW SCHOOL.
FIRST, I TAKE THE L TRAIN SUBWAY AT 5:30 A.M.
THEN TO THE LIRR AT 5:50 A.M.
THERE'S AN 88 PERCENT CHANCE OF CATCHING THE BUS AT 7:30 A.M. AND IT'S NO MORE THAN ANOTHER 15 MINUTES TO SCHOOL.
MOM WOULD DRIVE ME, SAVING ME A LEAST AN HOUR AND A HALF TRAVEL EACH DAY, BUT SHE WORKS IN THE CITY, IN THE OPPOSITE DIRECTION.

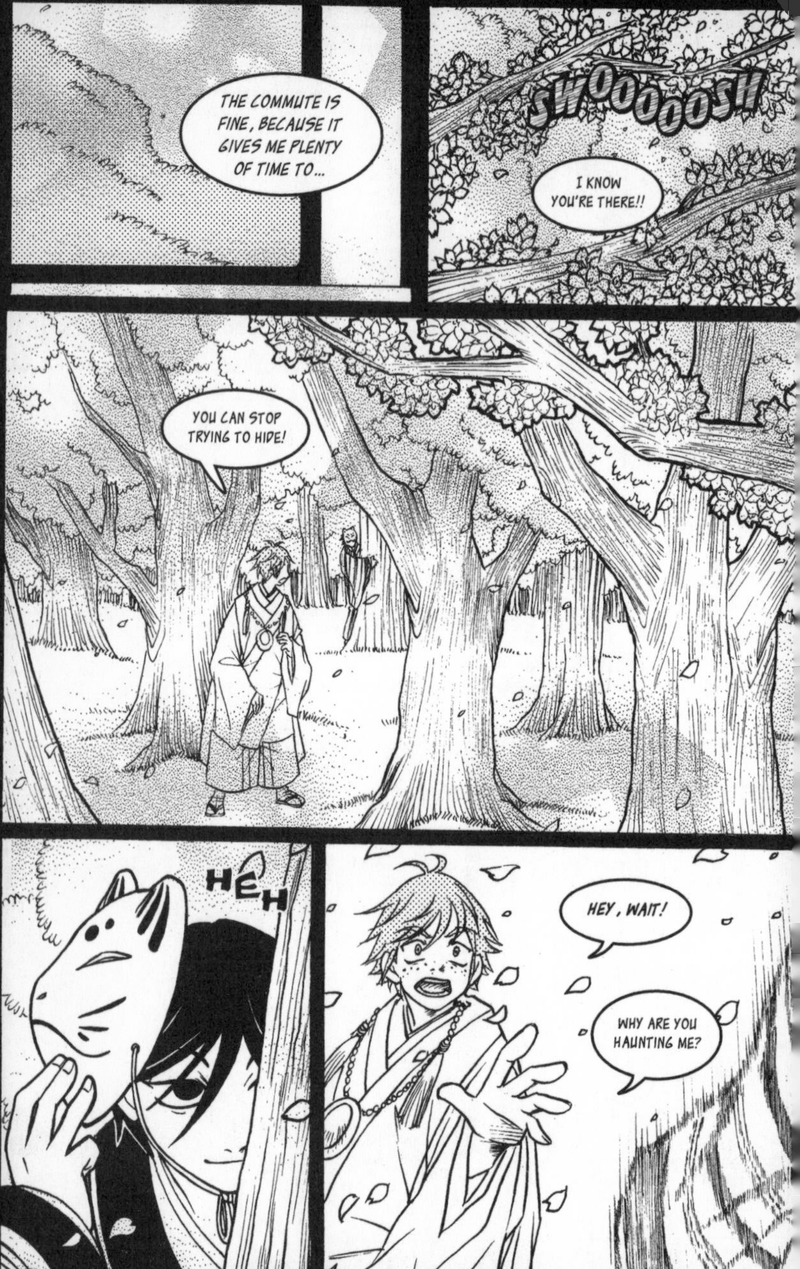
THE COMMUTE IS FINE, BECAUSE IT GIVES ME PLENTY OF TIME TO...
SWOOOOOOSH
I KNOW YOU'RE THERE!!
YOU CAN STOP TRYING TO HIDE!
HEH
HEY, WAIT!
WHY ARE YOU HAUNTING ME?

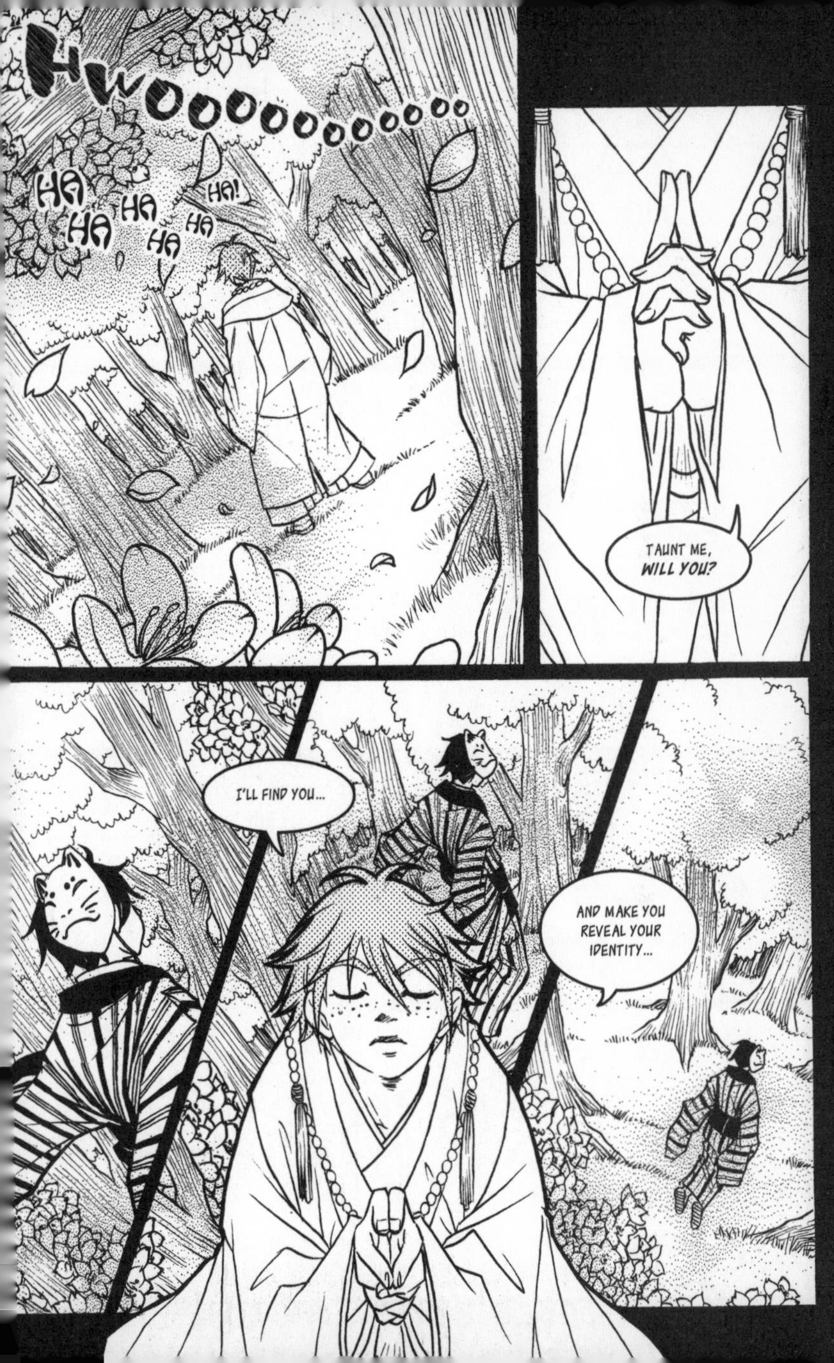
HWOOOOOOOOOOO
HA HA HA HA HA HA!
TAUNT ME, WILL YOU?
I'LL FIND YOU...
AND MAKE YOU REVEAL YOUR IDENTITY...

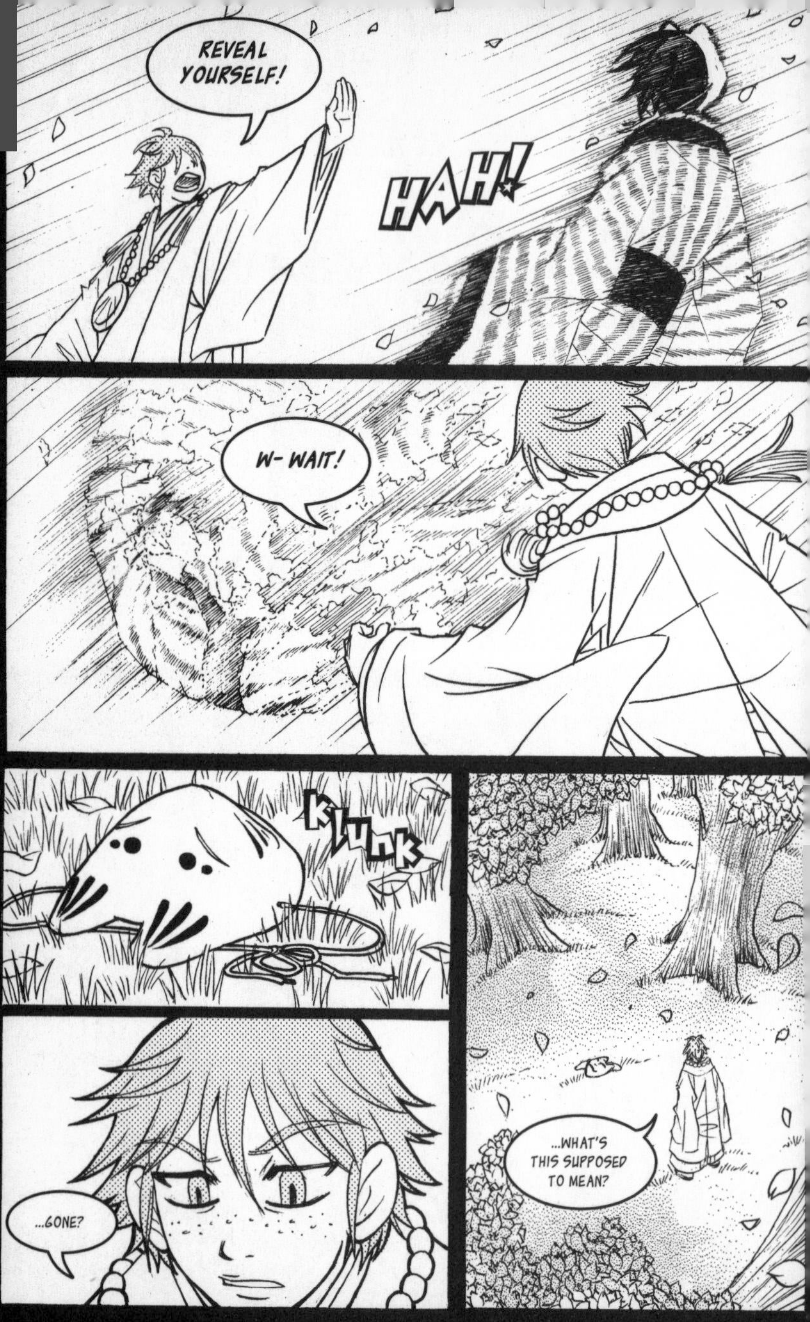
REVEAL YOURSELF!
HAH!
W- WAIT!
KLUNK
...GONE?
...WHAT'S THIS SUPPOSED TO MEAN?

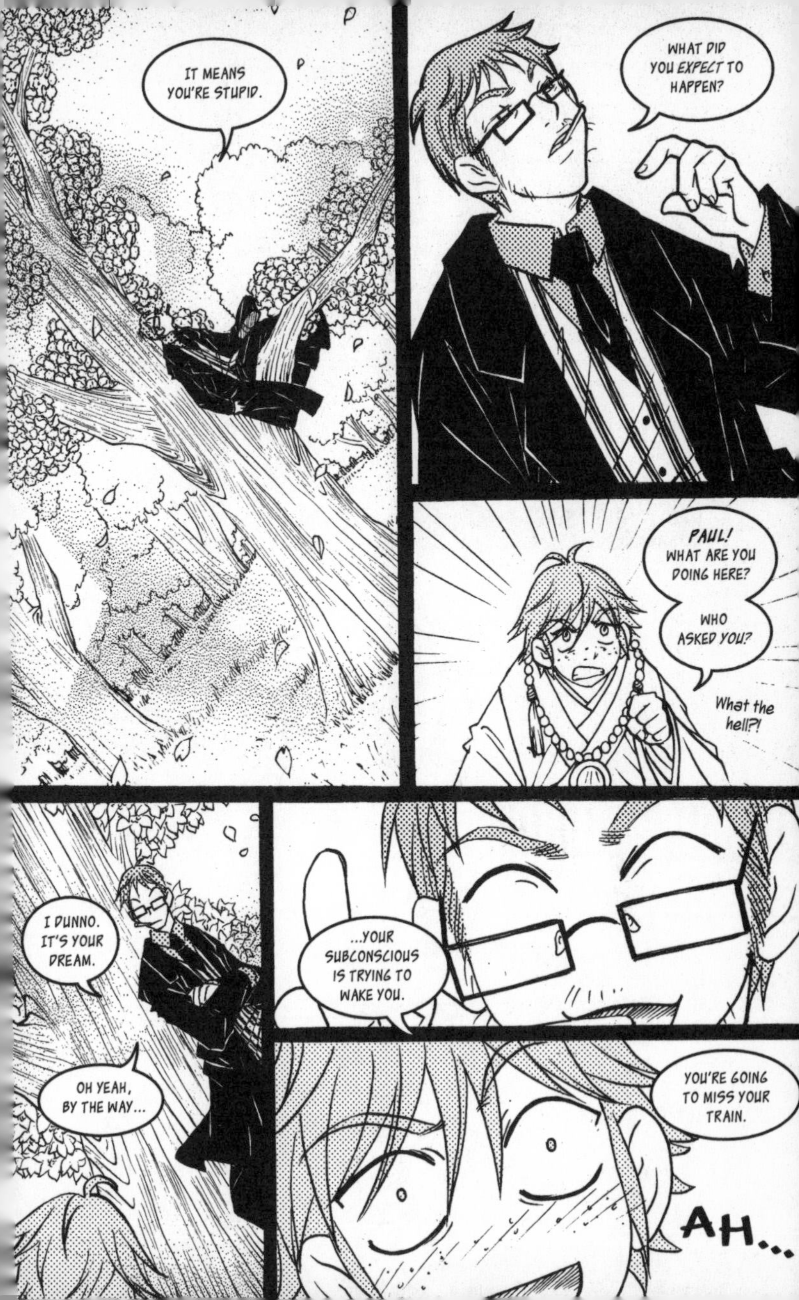
IT MEANS YOU'RE STUPID.
WHAT DID YOU *EXPECT* TO HAPPEN?
PAUL! WHAT ARE YOU DOING HERE?
WHO ASKED YOU?
What the hell?!
I DUNNO. IT'S YOUR DREAM.
OH YEAH, BY THE WAY...
...YOUR SUBCONSCIOUS IS TRYING TO WAKE YOU.
YOU'RE GOING TO MISS YOUR TRAIN.
AH...

NEXT STOP, FINAL DESTINATION, ROOSEVELT PARK!

OH, *CRAP!*

HUFF HUFF

MADE IT...

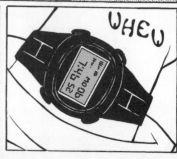

WHEW

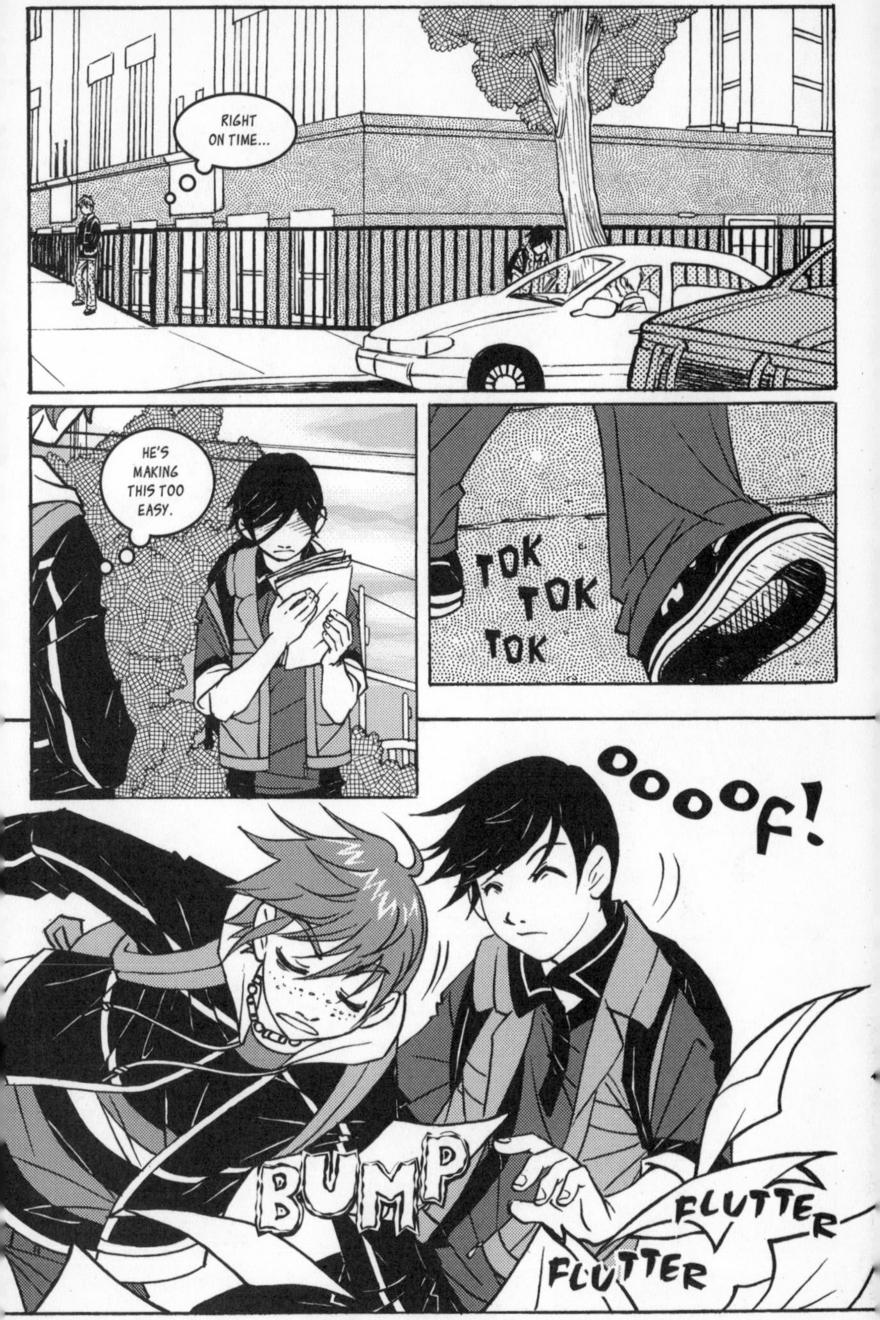
RIGHT ON TIME...
HE'S MAKING THIS TOO EASY.
TOK TOK TOK
OOOOF!
BUMP
FLUTTER
FLUTTER

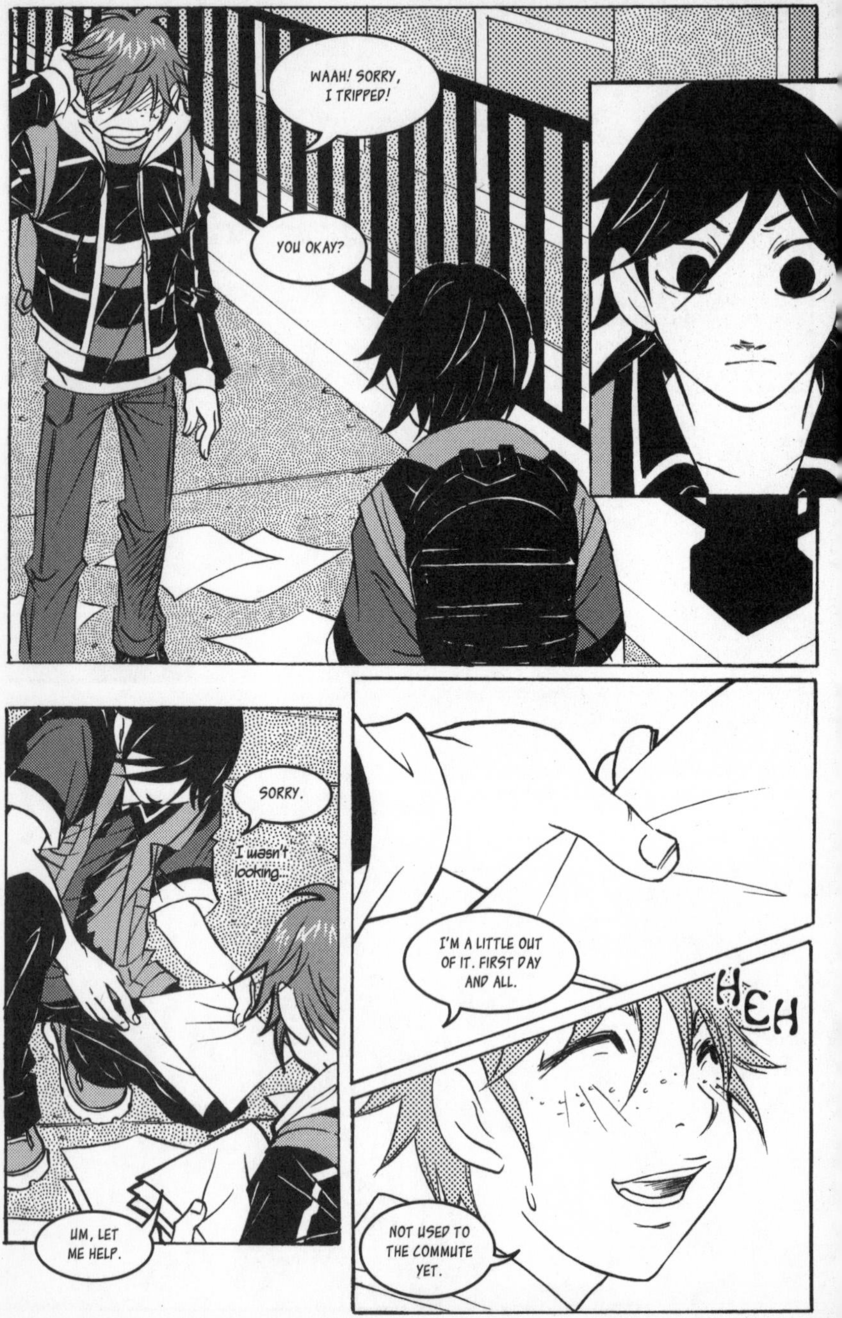
WAAH! SORRY, I TRIPPED!
YOU OKAY?
SORRY.
I wasn't looking...
UM, LET ME HELP.
I'M A LITTLE OUT OF IT. FIRST DAY AND ALL.
HEH
NOT USED TO THE COMMUTE YET.

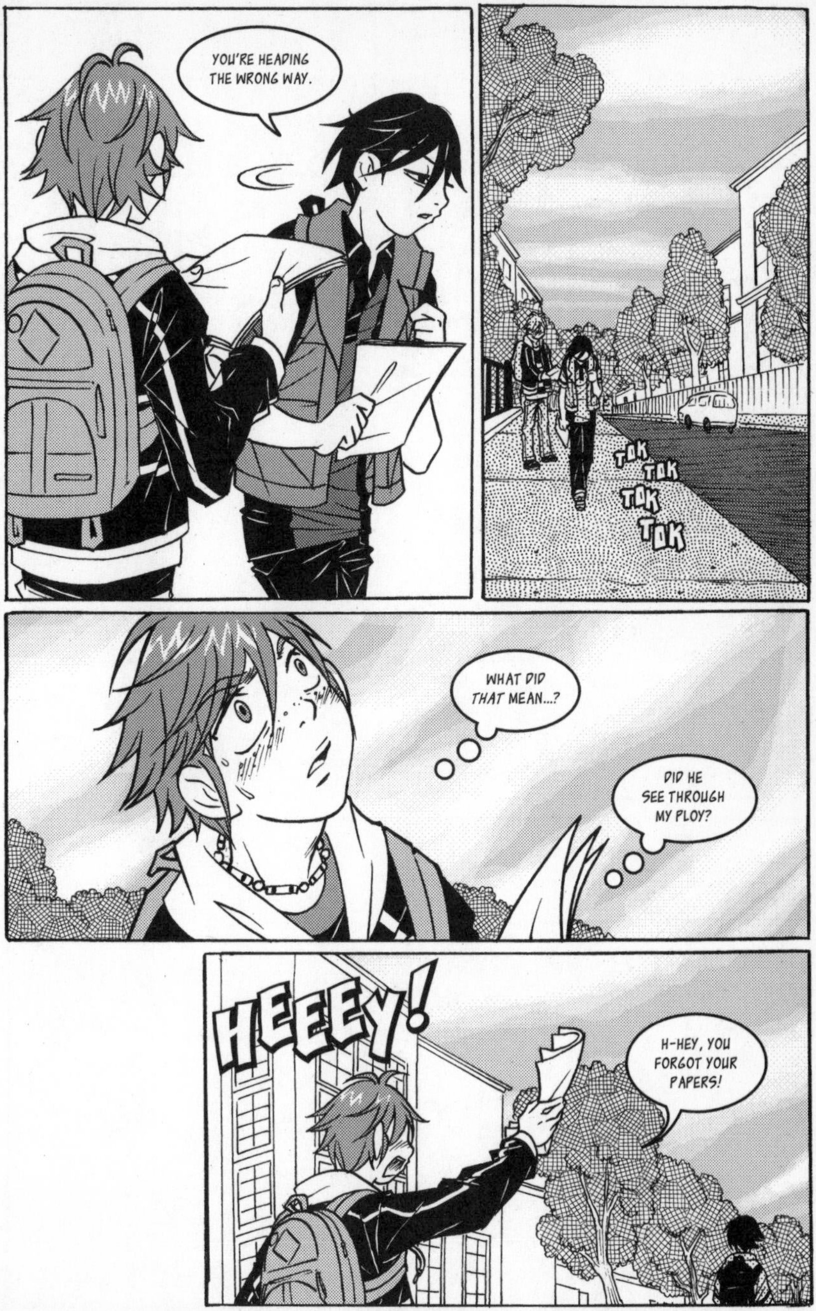
YOU'RE HEADING THE WRONG WAY.
TOK TOK TOK TOK
WHAT DID THAT MEAN...?
DID HE SEE THROUGH MY PLOY?
HEEEY!
H-HEY, YOU FORGOT YOUR PAPERS!

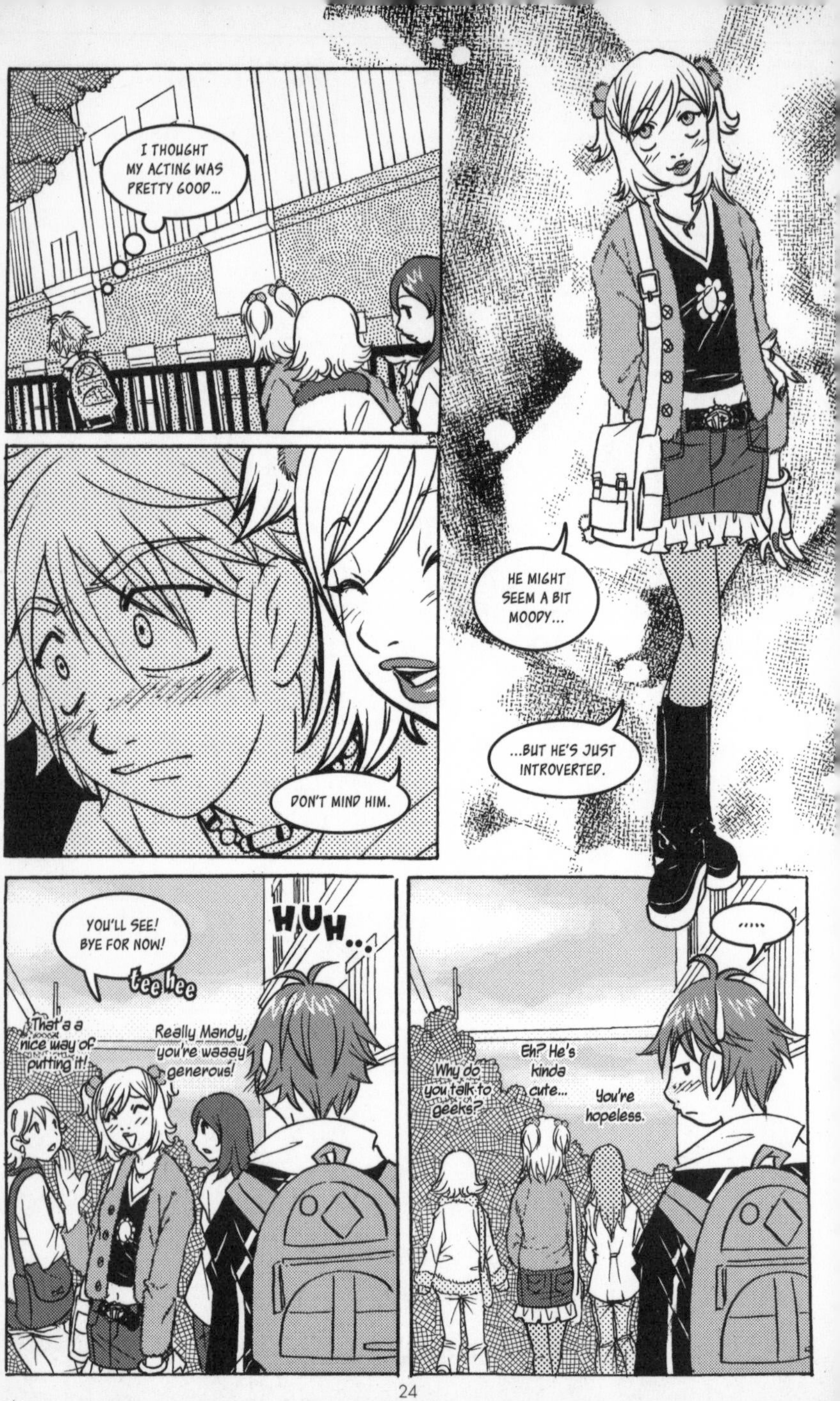
I THOUGHT MY ACTING WAS PRETTY GOOD...
DON'T MIND HIM.
HE MIGHT SEEM A BIT MOODY...
...BUT HE'S JUST INTROVERTED.
YOU'LL SEE! BYE FOR NOW!
tee hee
HUH...
That'a a nice way of putting it!
Really Mandy, you're waaay generous!
.....
Why do you talk to geeks?
Eh? He's kinda cute...
You're hopeless.

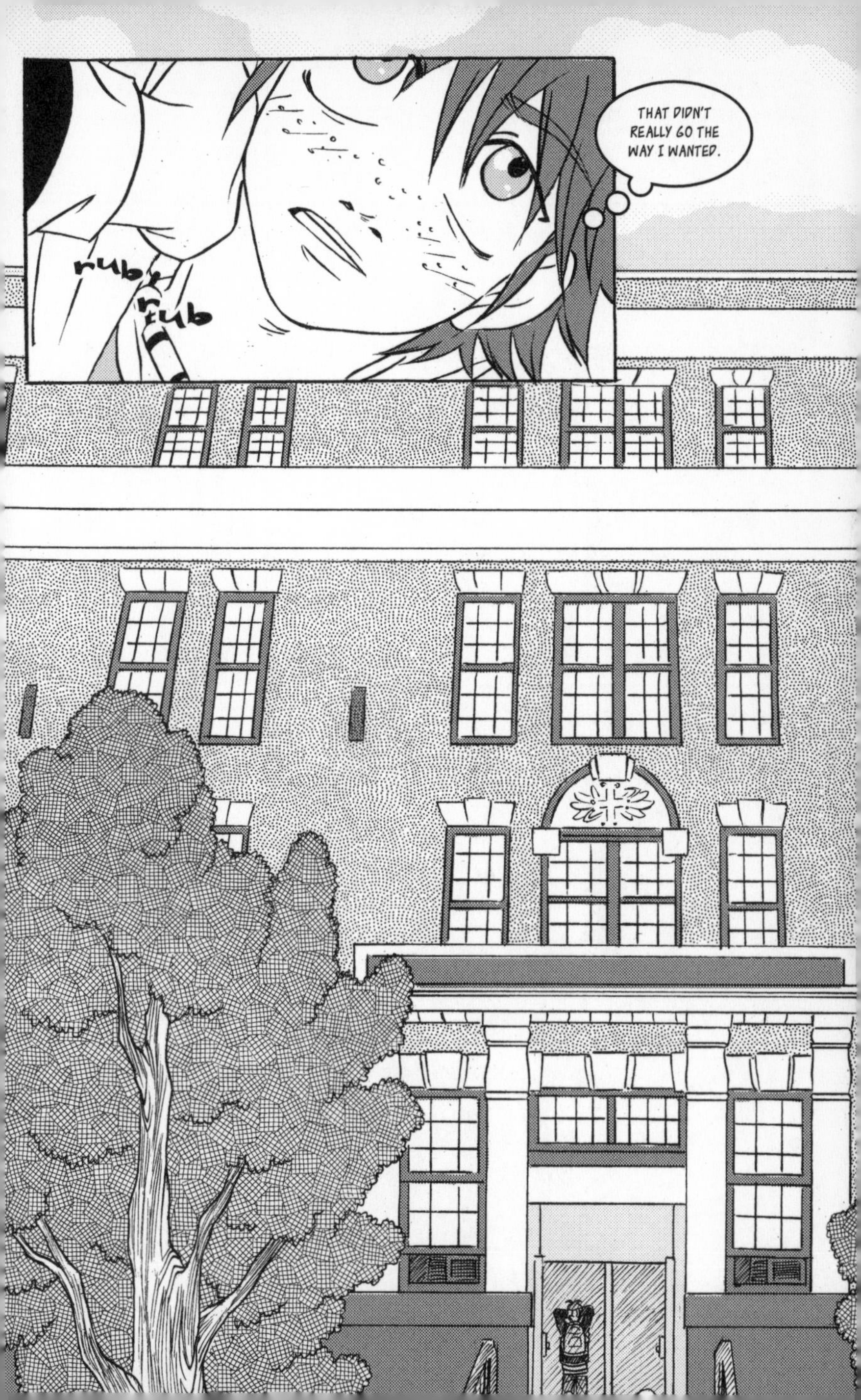
rub rub
THAT DIDN'T REALLY GO THE WAY I WANTED.

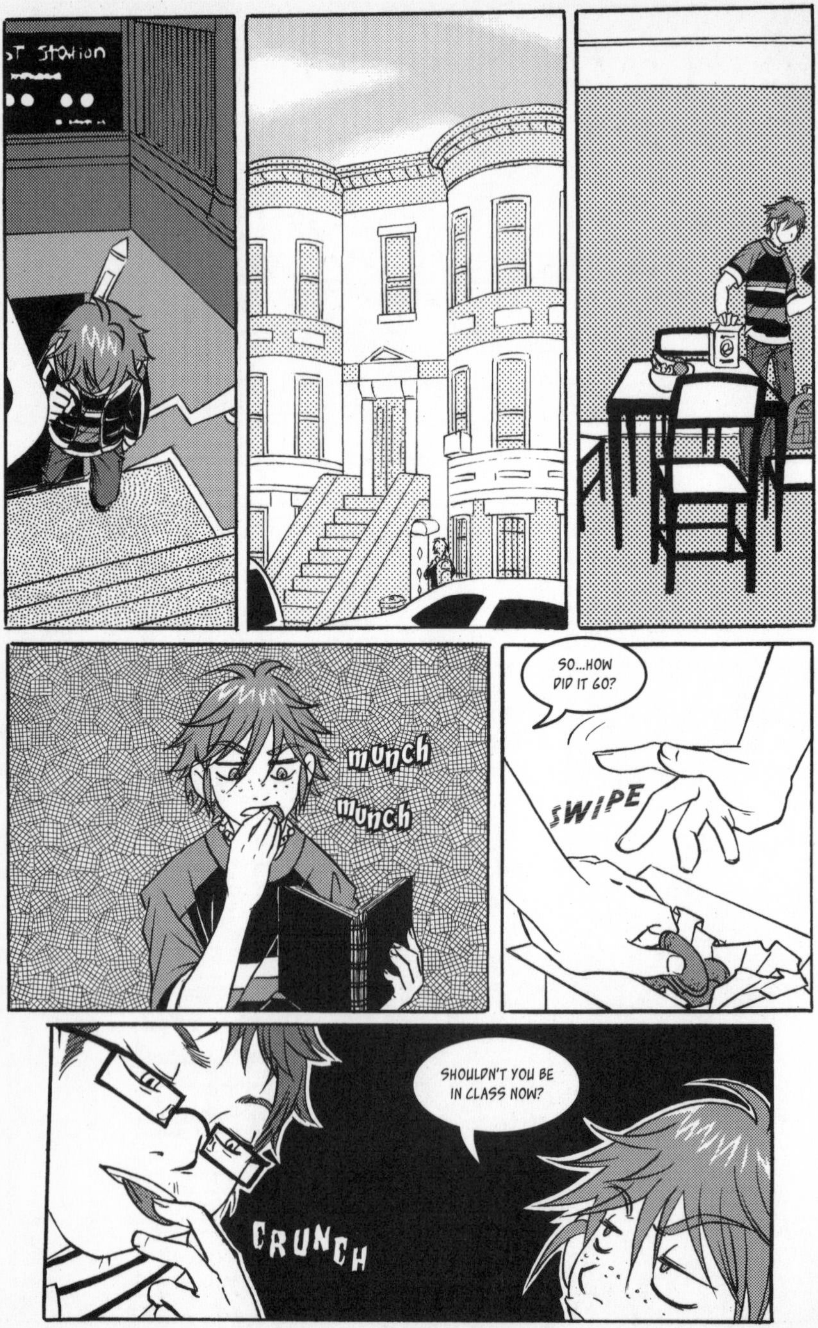
ST STATION
MUNCH
MUNCH
SO...HOW DID IT GO?
SWIPE
SHOULDN'T YOU BE IN CLASS NOW?
CRUNCH

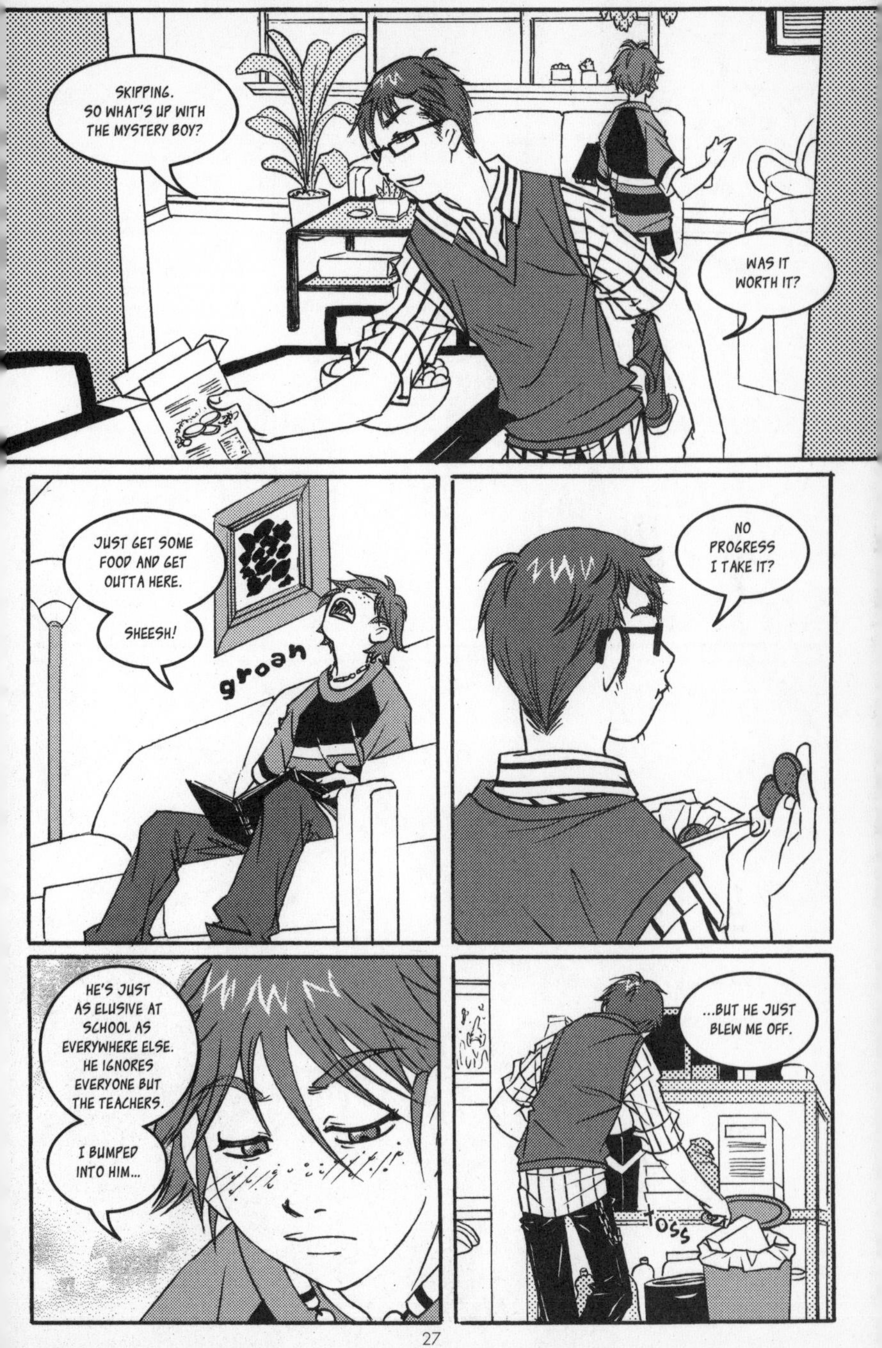
SKIPPING. SO WHAT'S UP WITH THE MYSTERY BOY?
WAS IT WORTH IT?
JUST GET SOME FOOD AND GET OUTTA HERE.
SHEESH!
groan
NO PROGRESS I TAKE IT?
HE'S JUST AS ELUSIVE AT SCHOOL AS EVERYWHERE ELSE. HE IGNORES EVERYONE BUT THE TEACHERS.
I BUMPED INTO HIM...
...BUT HE JUST BLEW ME OFF.
toss

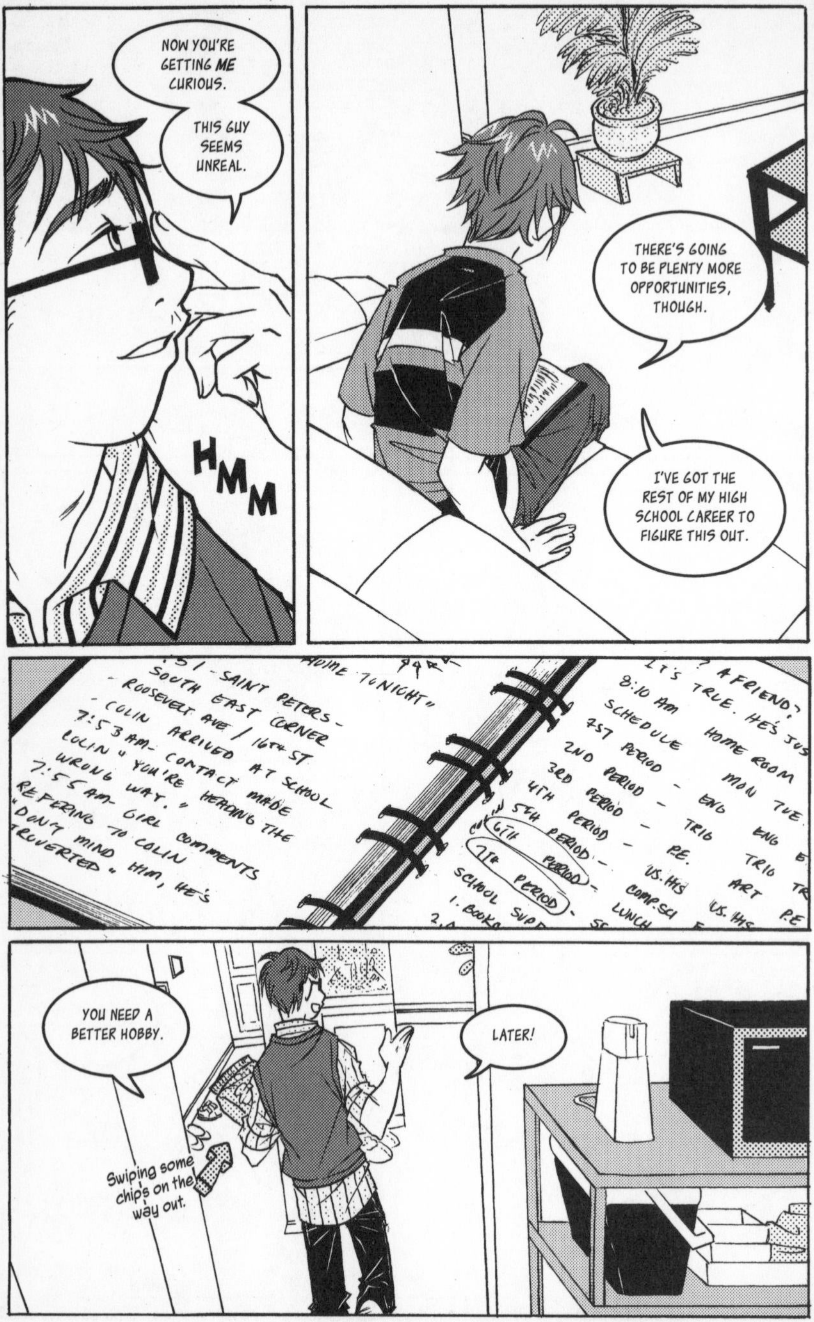
NOW YOU'RE GETTING ***ME*** CURIOUS.
THIS GUY SEEMS UNREAL.
HMM
THERE'S GOING TO BE PLENTY MORE OPPORTUNITIES, THOUGH.
I'VE GOT THE REST OF MY HIGH SCHOOL CAREER TO FIGURE THIS OUT.
SOUTH EAST CORNER
ROOSEVELT AVE / 16TH ST
- COLIN ARRIVED AT SCHOOL
7:53 AM - CONTACT MADE
COLIN "YOU'RE HEADING THE WRONG WAY."
7:55 AM - GIRL COMMENTS
REFERING TO COLIN
"DON'T MIND HIM, HE'S INVERTED."
8:10 AM HOME ROOM
SCHEDULE MON TUE
YOU NEED A BETTER HOBBY.
LATER!
Swiping some chips on the way out.

HMM...

ACCORDING TO MY RECORDS, I THINK I CAN SAFELY CALCULATE THAT THE CHANCES OF ANYTHING HAPPENING TONIGHT ARE LESS THAN 10 TO 1.

First Monday of the month is always quiet...

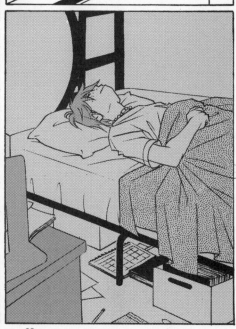

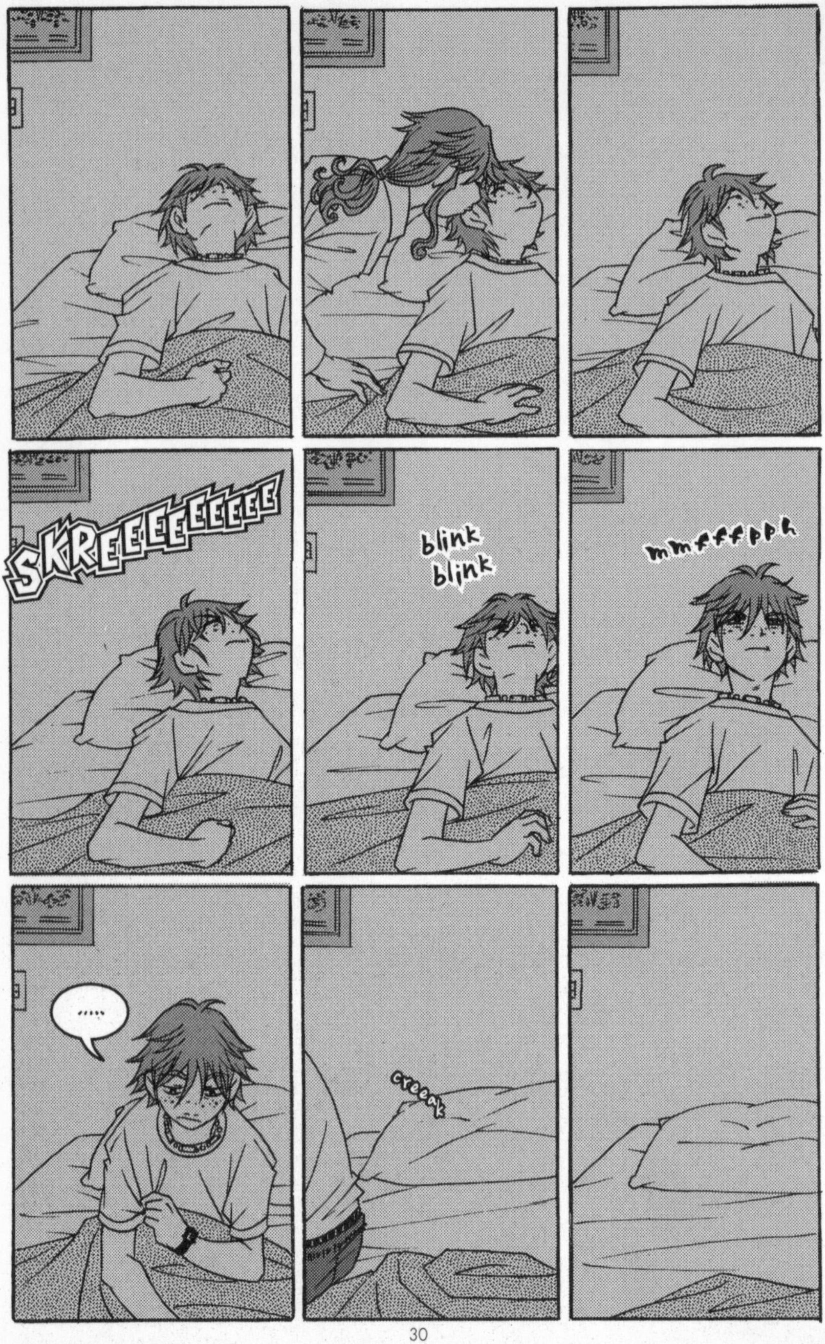
SKREEEEEEEEE
blink
blink
mmfffpph
.....
creeak

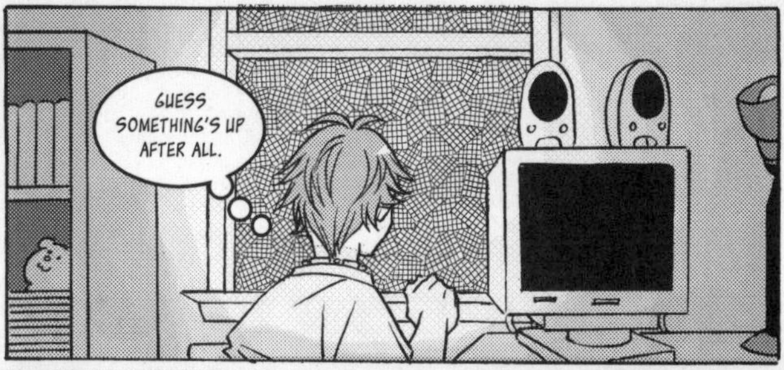
GUESS SOMETHING'S UP AFTER ALL.

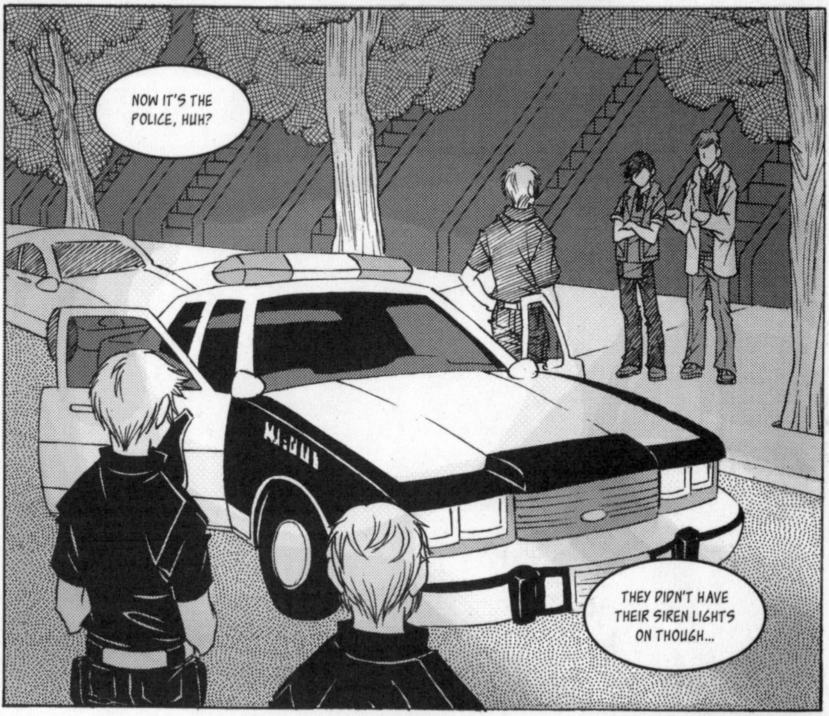
NOW IT'S THE POLICE, HUH?
THEY DIDN'T HAVE THEIR SIREN LIGHTS ON THOUGH...

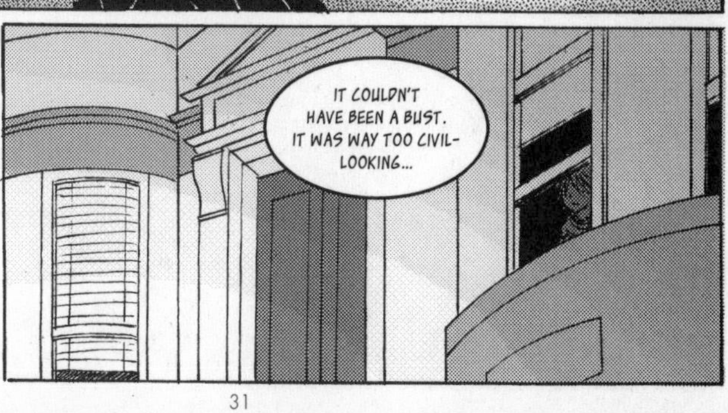
IT COULDN'T HAVE BEEN A BUST. IT WAS WAY TOO CIVIL-LOOKING...

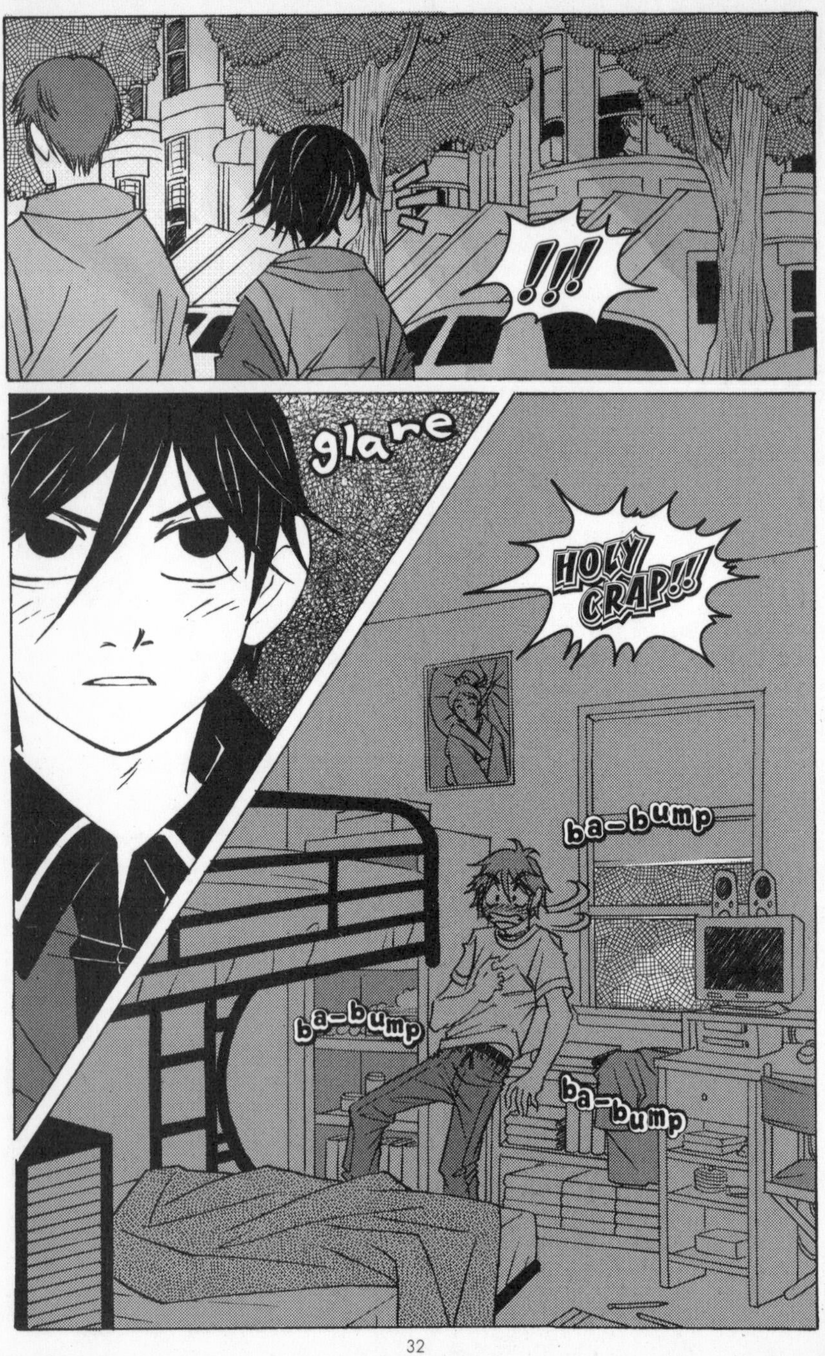
!!!
glare
HOLY CRAP!!
ba-bump
ba-bump
ba-bump

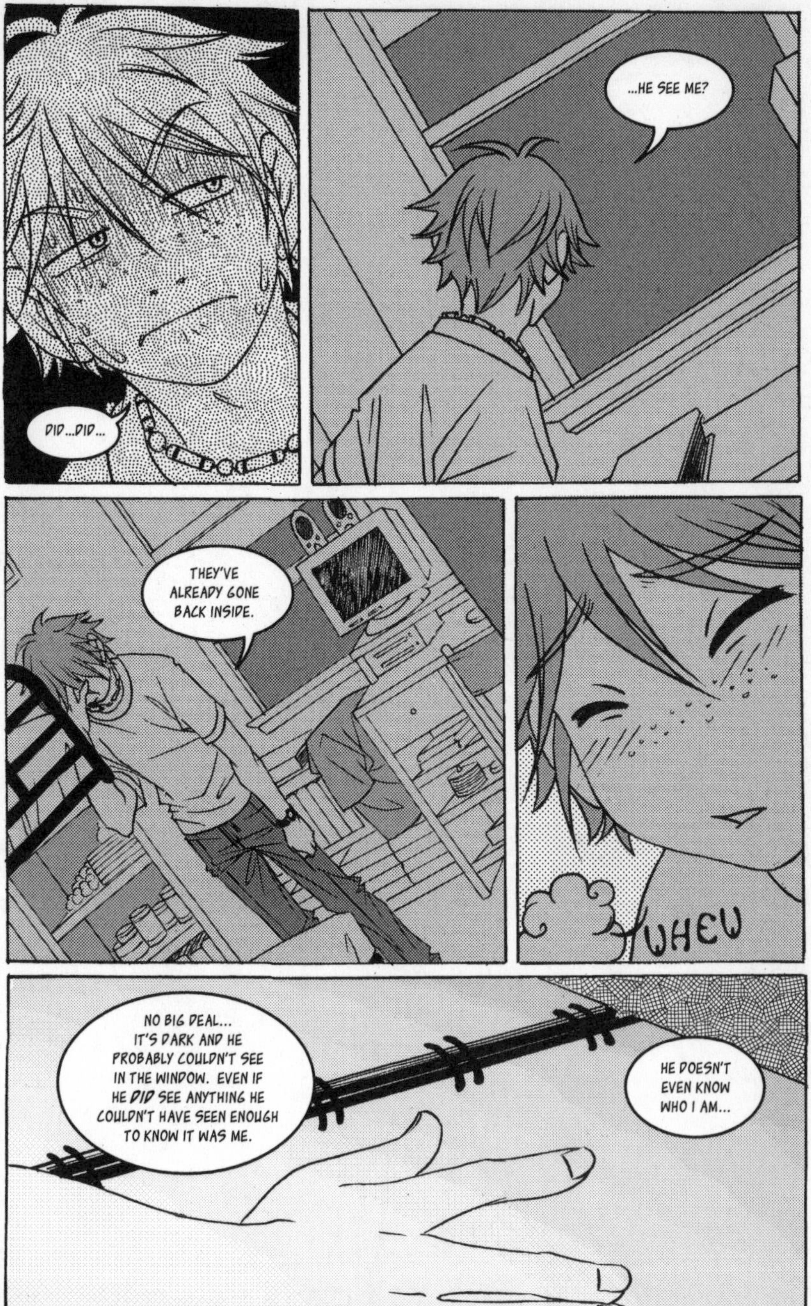
DID...DID...
...HE SEE ME?
THEY'VE ALREADY GONE BACK INSIDE.
WHEW
NO BIG DEAL... IT'S DARK AND HE PROBABLY COULDN'T SEE IN THE WINDOW. EVEN IF HE *DID* SEE ANYTHING HE COULDN'T HAVE SEEN ENOUGH TO KNOW IT WAS ME.
HE DOESN'T EVEN KNOW WHO I AM...

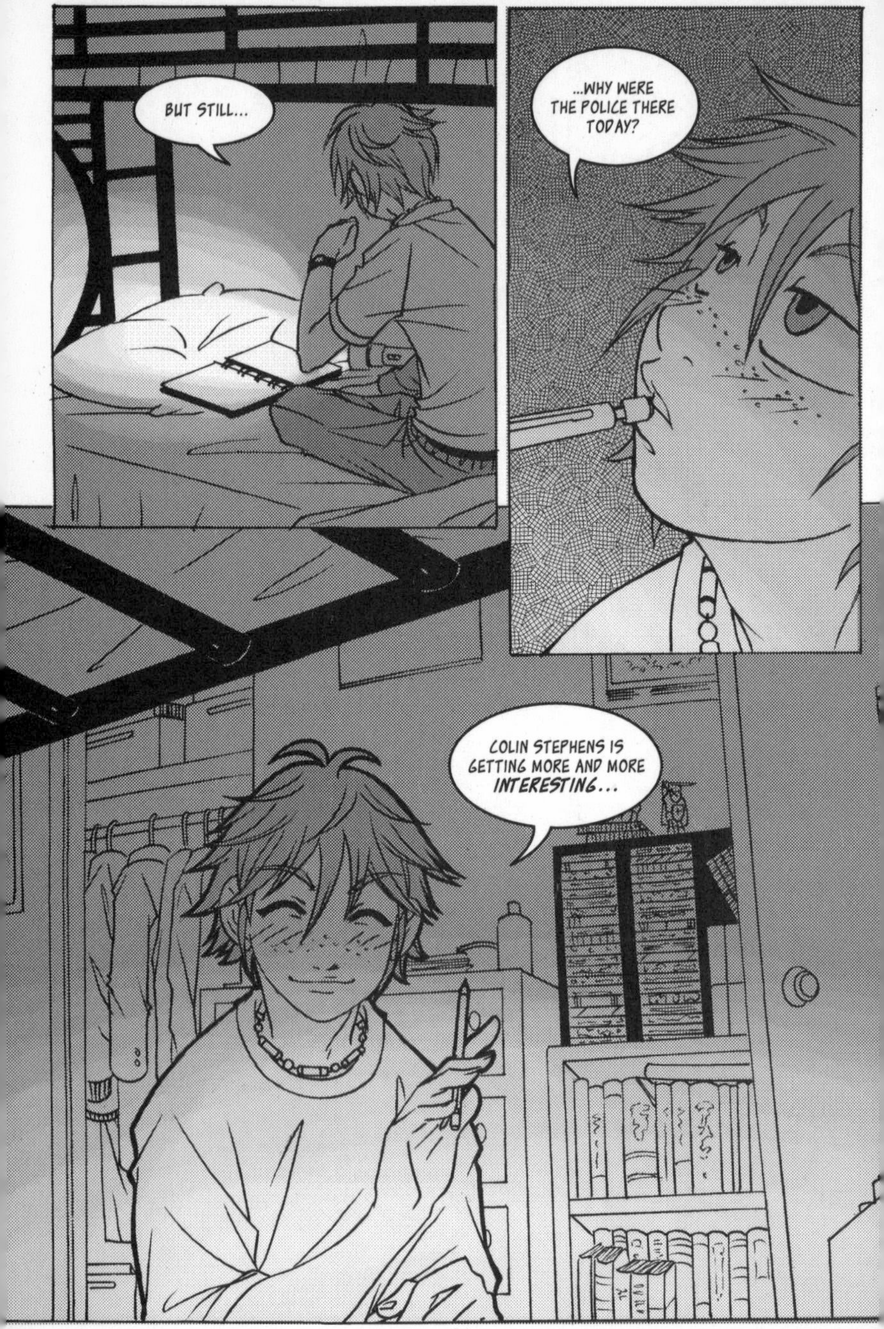
BUT STILL...
...WHY WERE THE POLICE THERE TODAY?
COLIN STEPHENS IS GETTING MORE AND MORE *INTERESTING*...

Off*Beat

Chapter 2: The Investigation

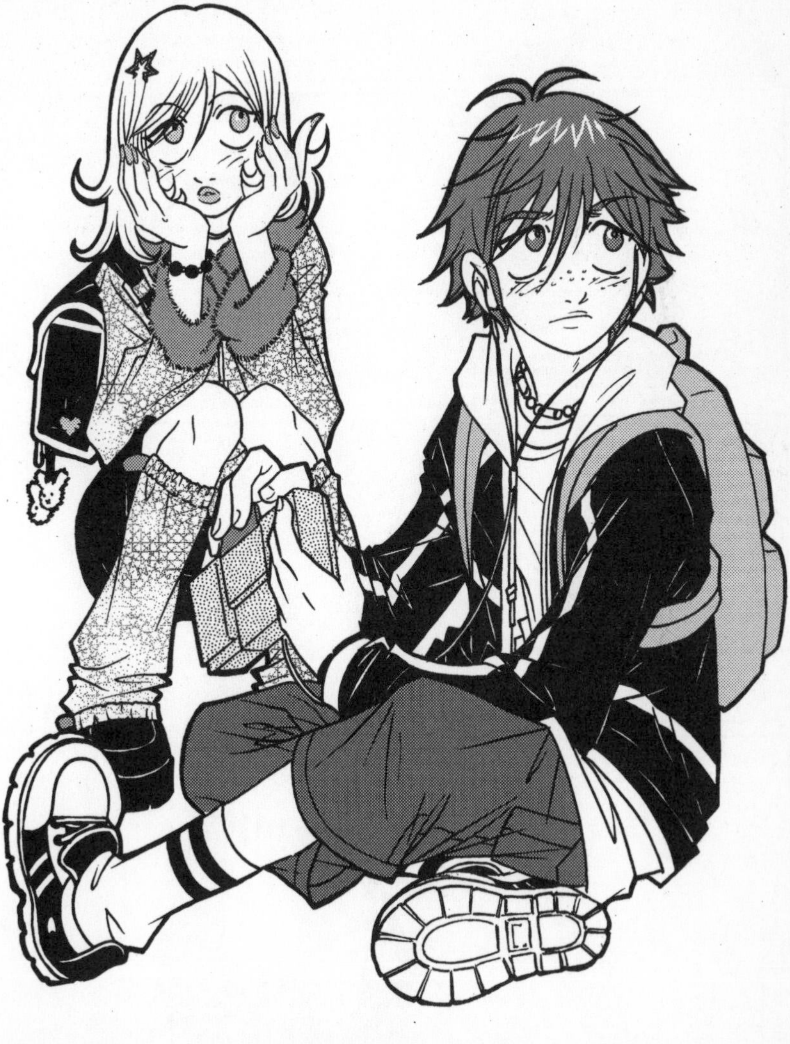

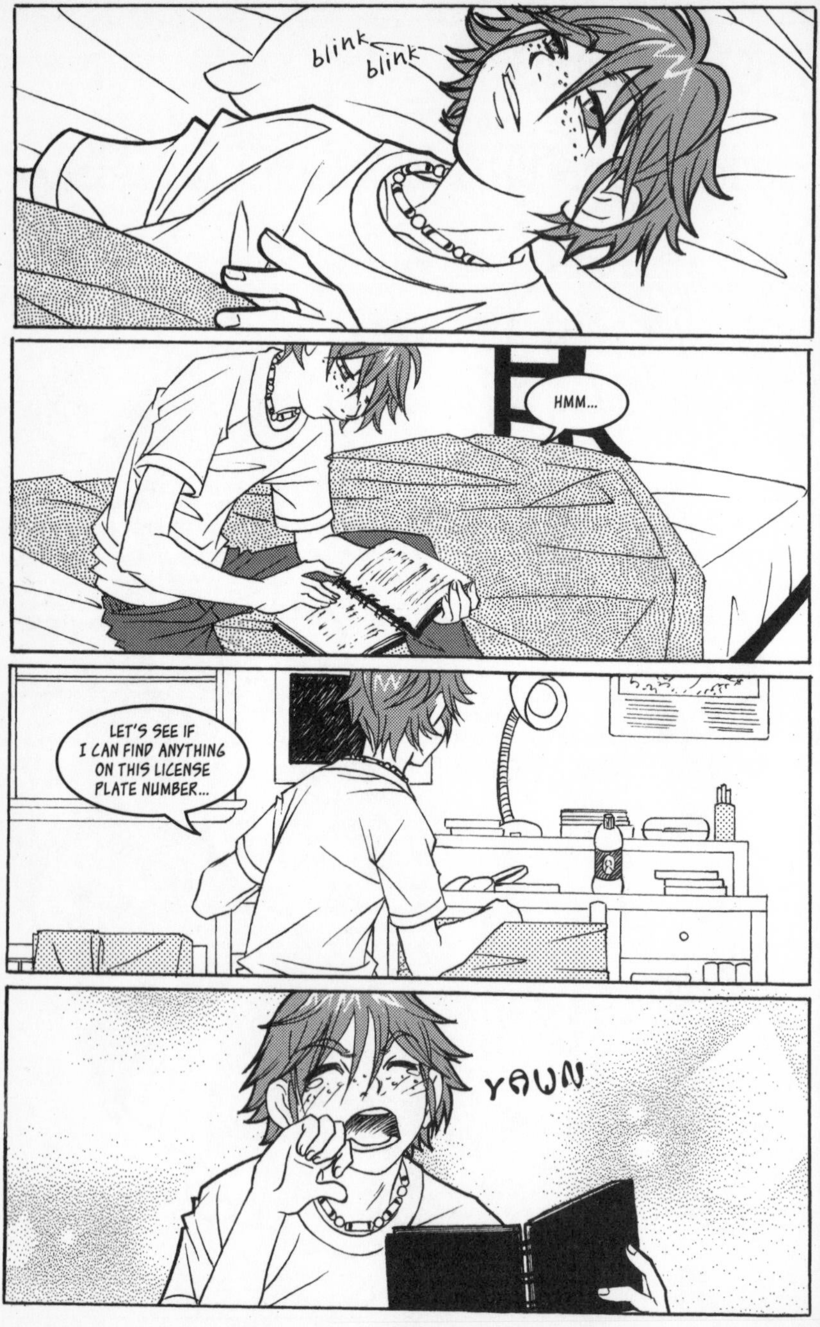
blink
blink
HMM...
LET'S SEE IF I CAN FIND ANYTHING ON THIS LICENSE PLATE NUMBER...
YAWN

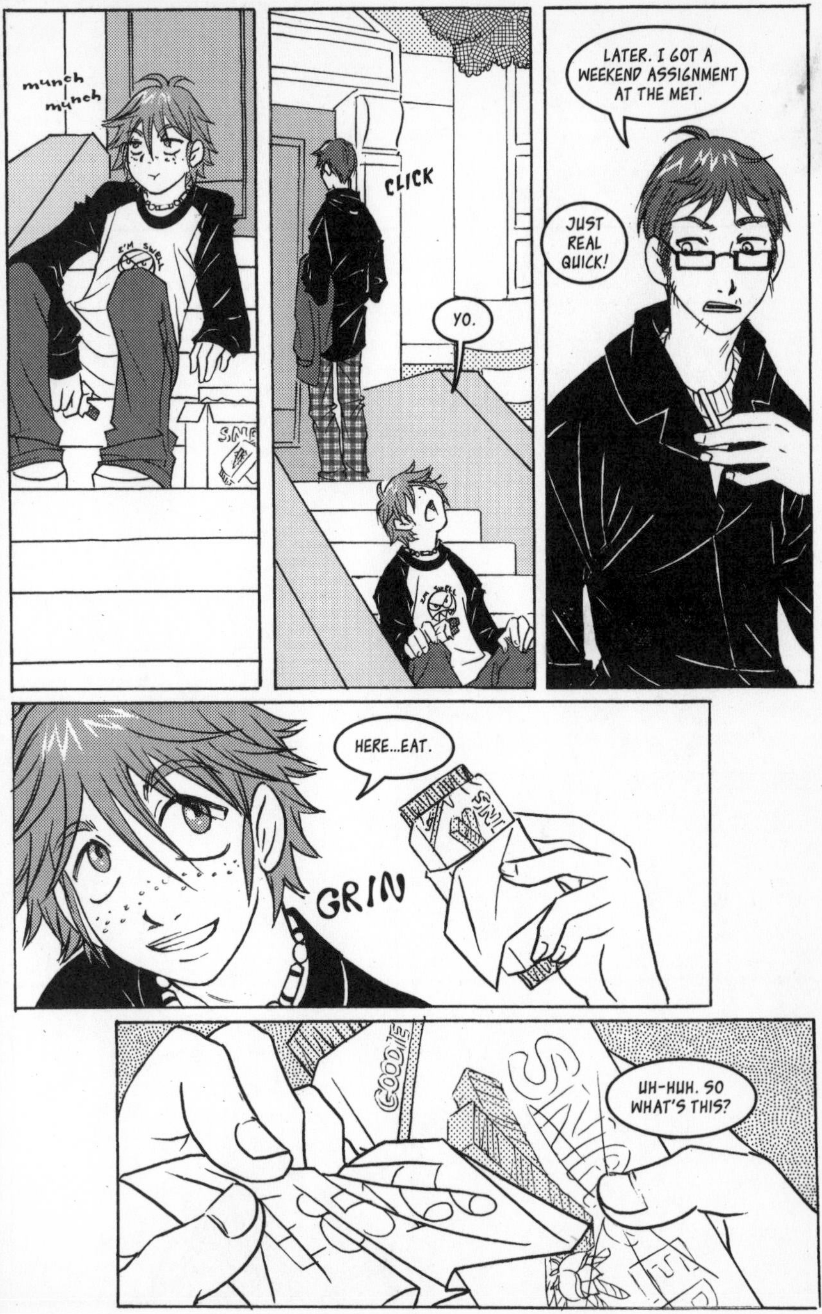
munch
munch
I'M SWELL
CLICK
YO.
LATER. I GOT A WEEKEND ASSIGNMENT AT THE MET.
JUST REAL QUICK!
HERE...EAT.
GRIN
UH-HUH. SO WHAT'S THIS?
GOODIE

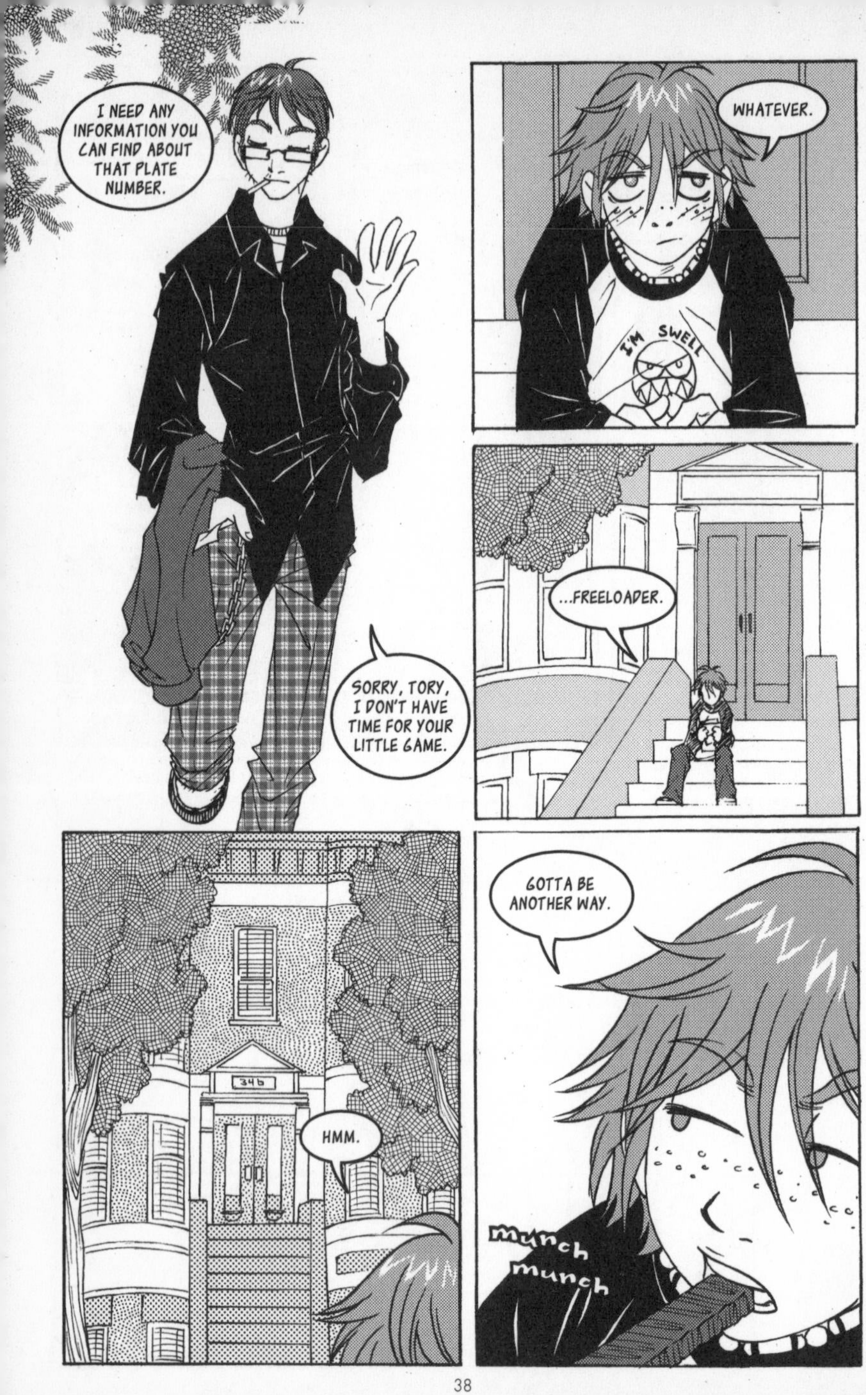

I NEED ANY INFORMATION YOU CAN FIND ABOUT THAT PLATE NUMBER.
SORRY, TORY, I DON'T HAVE TIME FOR YOUR LITTLE GAME.
WHATEVER.
I'M SWELL
...FREELOADER.
HMM.
346
GOTTA BE ANOTHER WAY.
munch munch

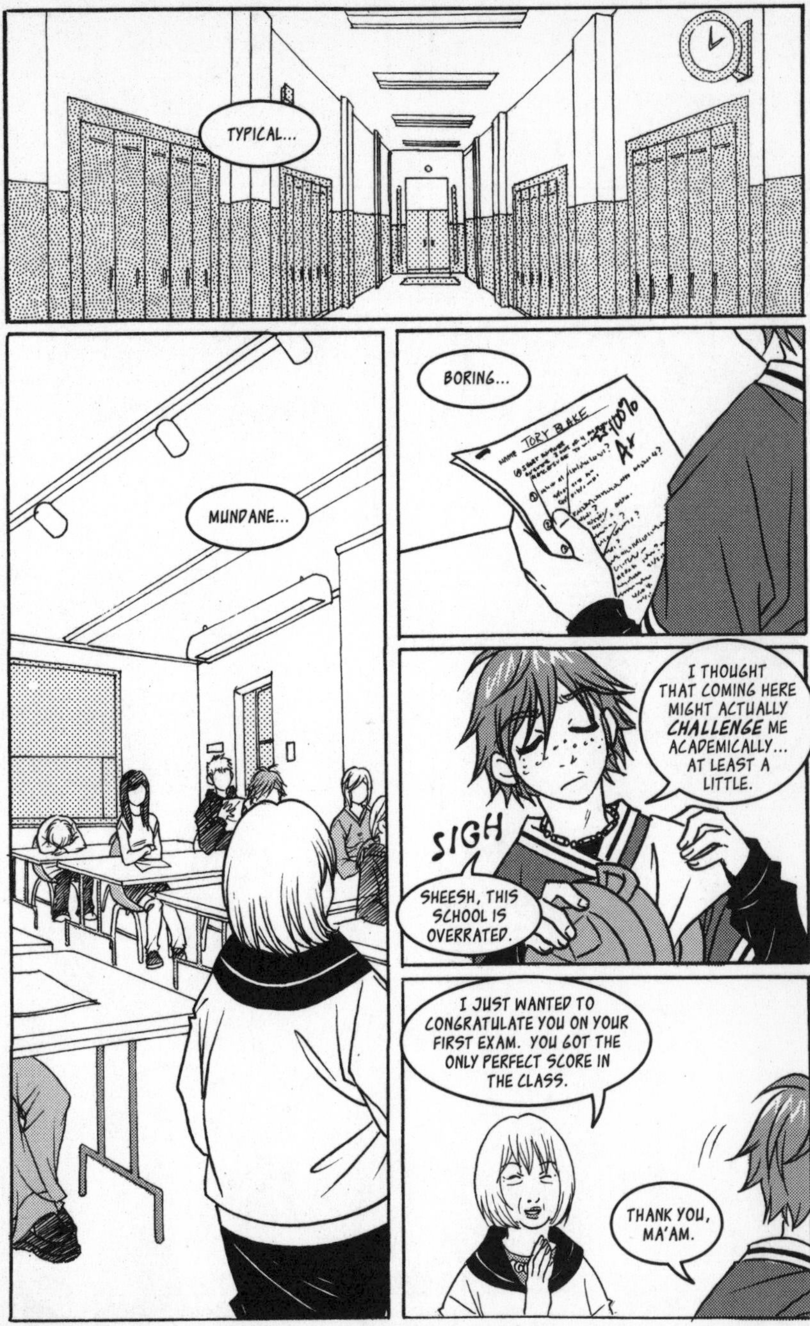
TYPICAL...
MUNDANE...
BORING...
TORY BLAKE
100%
A+
I THOUGHT THAT COMING HERE MIGHT ACTUALLY CHALLENGE ME ACADEMICALLY... AT LEAST A LITTLE.
SIGH
SHEESH, THIS SCHOOL IS OVERRATED.
I JUST WANTED TO CONGRATULATE YOU ON YOUR FIRST EXAM. YOU GOT THE ONLY PERFECT SCORE IN THE CLASS.
THANK YOU, MA'AM.

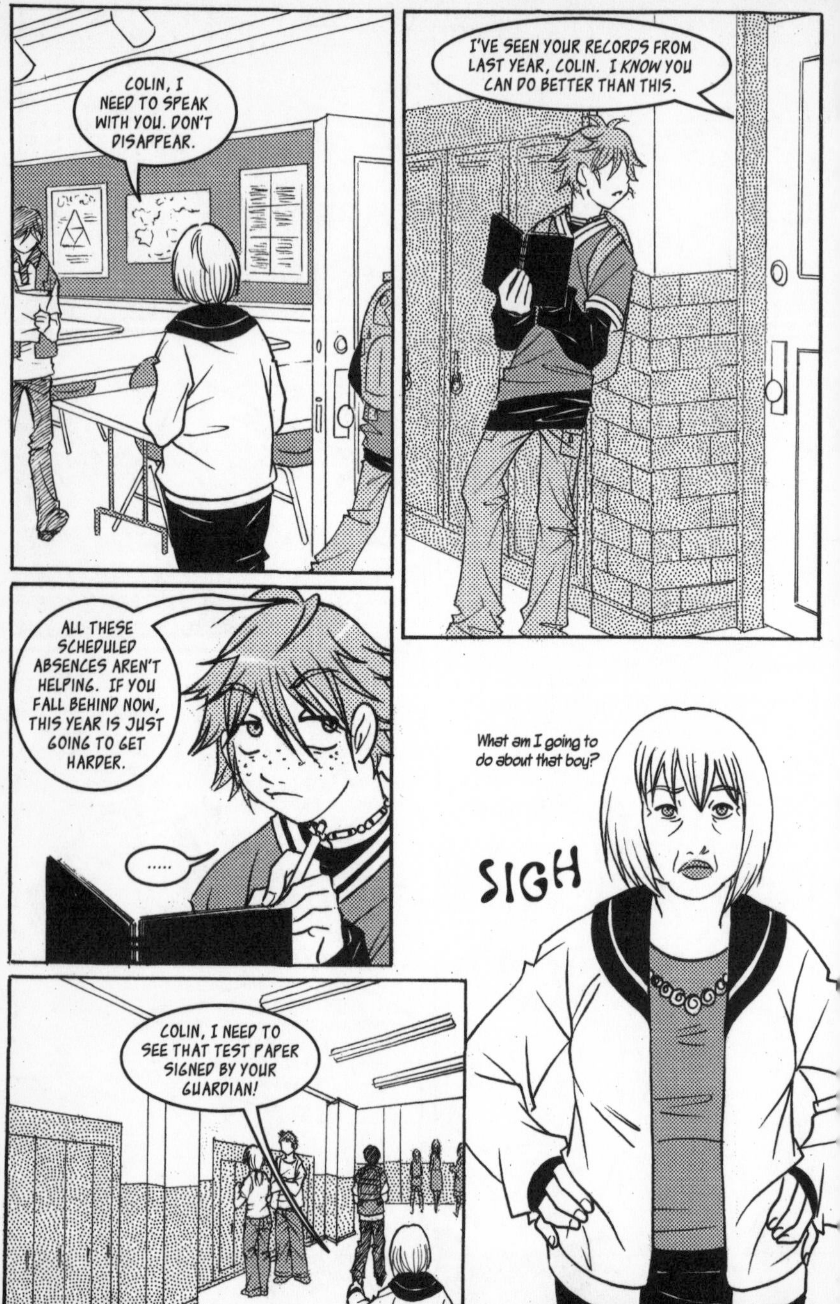
COLIN, I NEED TO SPEAK WITH YOU. DON'T DISAPPEAR.
I'VE SEEN YOUR RECORDS FROM LAST YEAR, COLIN. I *KNOW* YOU CAN DO BETTER THAN THIS.
ALL THESE SCHEDULED ABSENCES AREN'T HELPING. IF YOU FALL BEHIND NOW, THIS YEAR IS JUST GOING TO GET HARDER.
......
COLIN, I NEED TO SEE THAT TEST PAPER SIGNED BY YOUR GUARDIAN!
What am I going to do about that boy?
SIGH

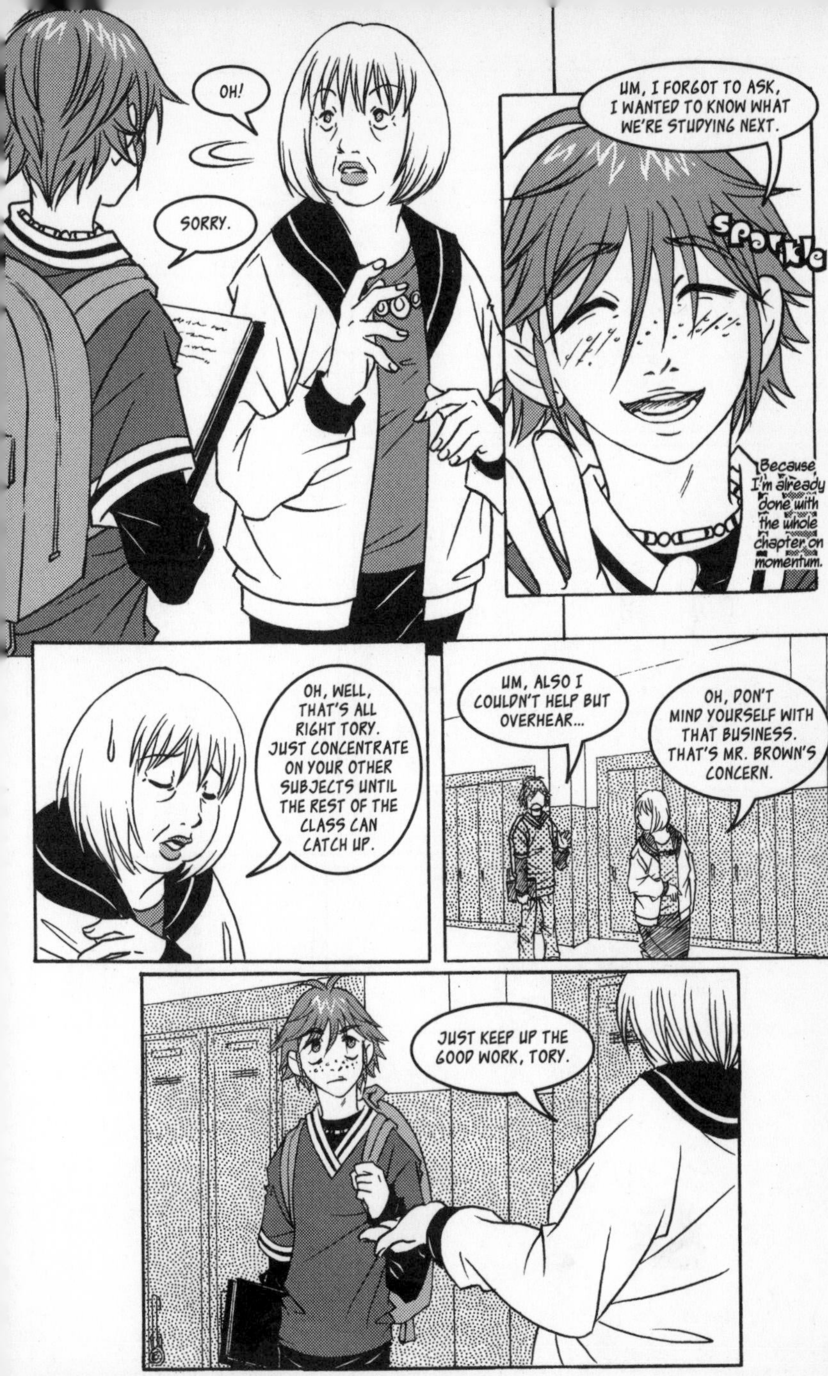
OH!
SORRY.
UM, I FORGOT TO ASK, I WANTED TO KNOW WHAT WE'RE STUDYING NEXT.
sparkle
Because, I'm already done with the whole chapter on momentum.
OH, WELL, THAT'S ALL RIGHT TORY. JUST CONCENTRATE ON YOUR OTHER SUBJECTS UNTIL THE REST OF THE CLASS CAN CATCH UP.
UM, ALSO I COULDN'T HELP BUT OVERHEAR...
OH, DON'T MIND YOURSELF WITH THAT BUSINESS. THAT'S MR. BROWN'S CONCERN.
JUST KEEP UP THE GOOD WORK, TORY.

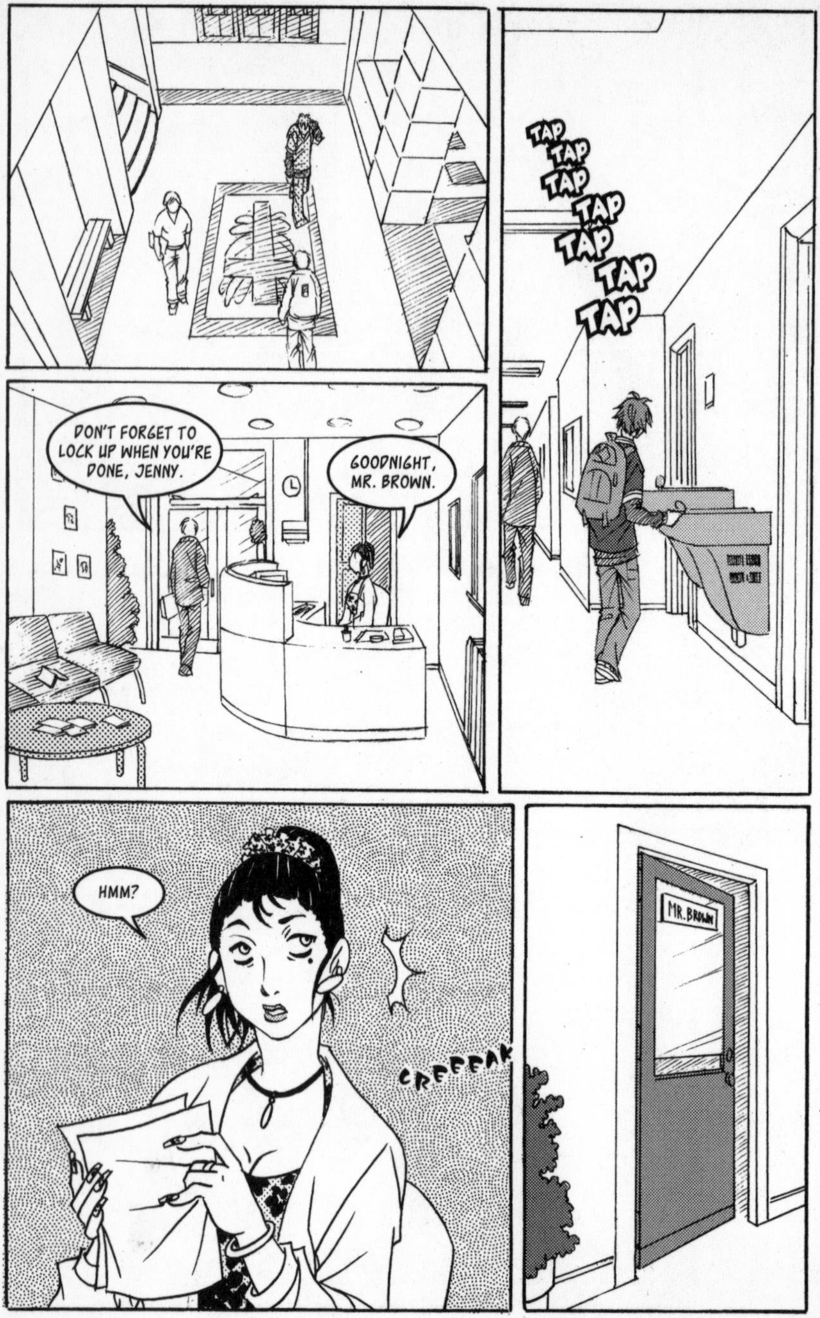
DON'T FORGET TO LOCK UP WHEN YOU'RE DONE, JENNY.
GOODNIGHT, MR. BROWN.
TAP TAP TAP TAP TAP TAP TAP
HMM?
CREEEAK
MR. BROWN

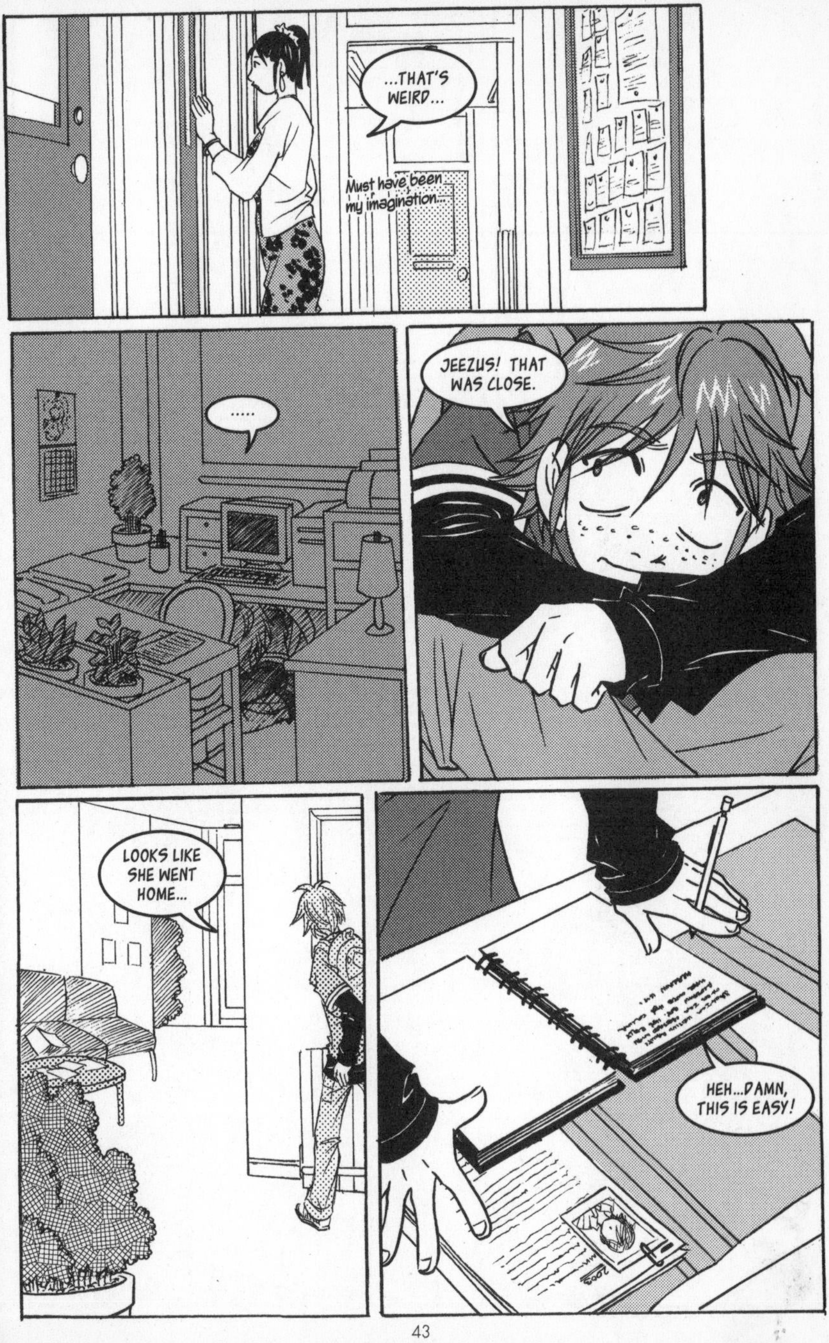
...THAT'S WEIRD...
Must have been my imagination...
......
JEEZUS! THAT WAS CLOSE.
LOOKS LIKE SHE WENT HOME...
HEH...DAMN, THIS IS EASY!

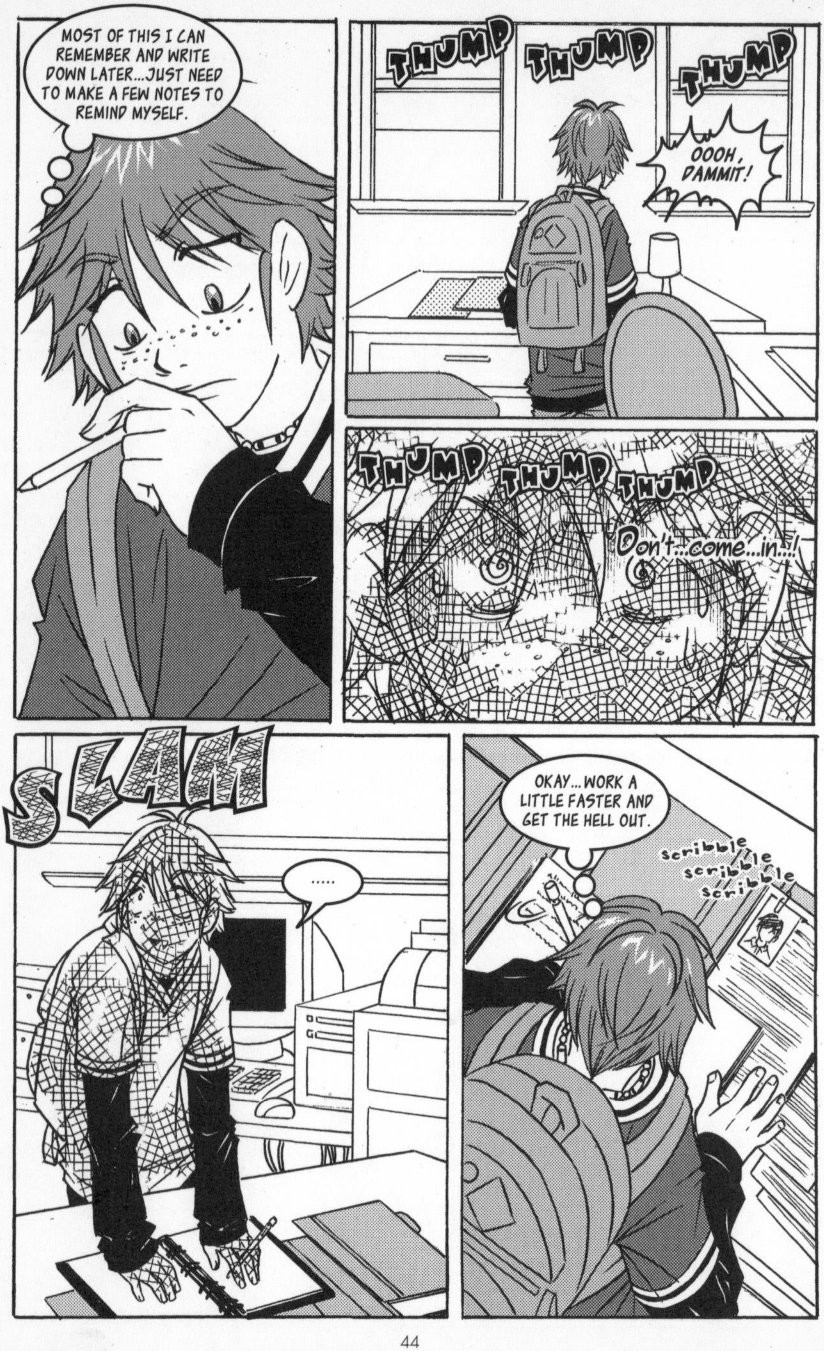
MOST OF THIS I CAN REMEMBER AND WRITE DOWN LATER...JUST NEED TO MAKE A FEW NOTES TO REMIND MYSELF.
THUMP THUMP THUMP
OOOH, DAMMIT!
THUMP THUMP THUMP
Don't...come...in...!
SLAM
.....
OKAY...WORK A LITTLE FASTER AND GET THE HELL OUT.
scribble scribble scribble

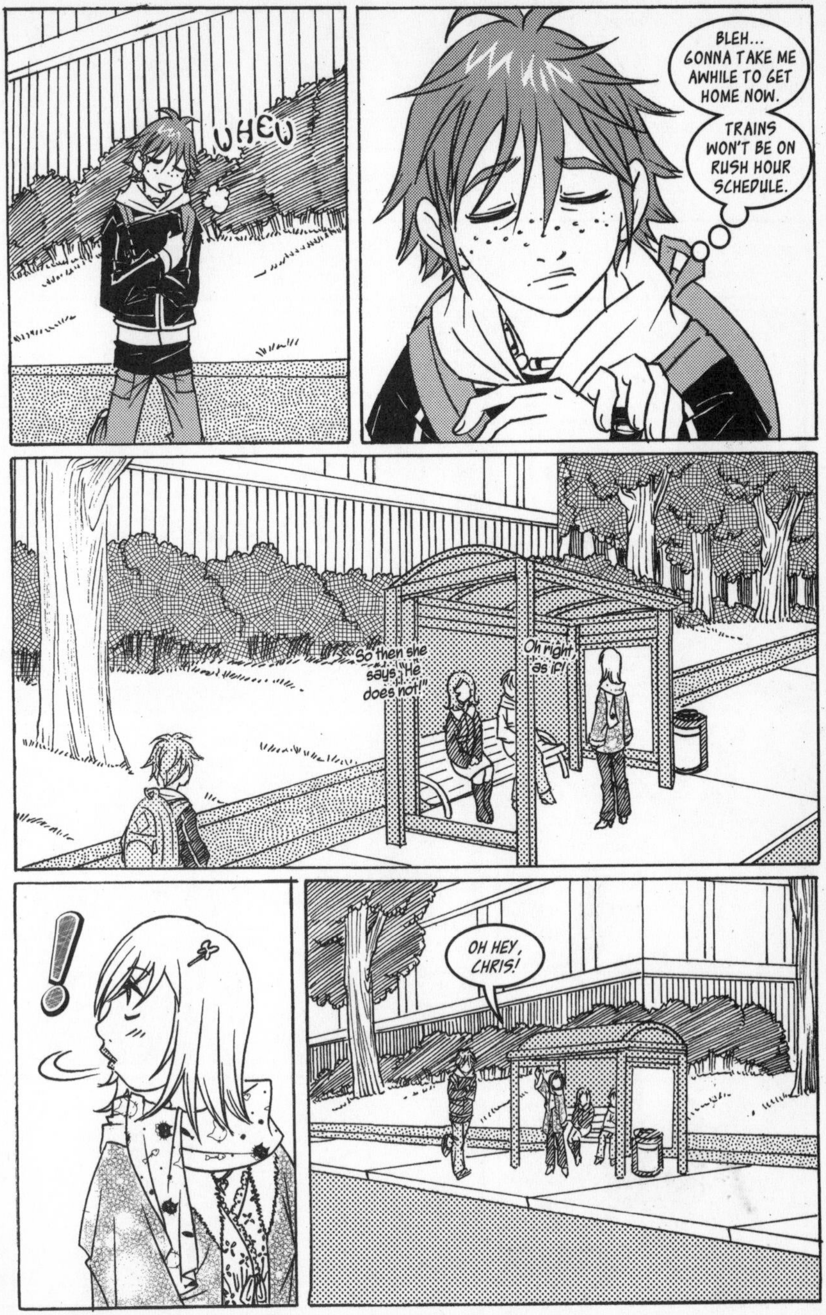
WHEW
BLEH... GONNA TAKE ME AWHILE TO GET HOME NOW.
TRAINS WON'T BE ON RUSH HOUR SCHEDULE.
So then she says "He does not!"
Oh right, as if!
!
OH HEY, CHRIS!

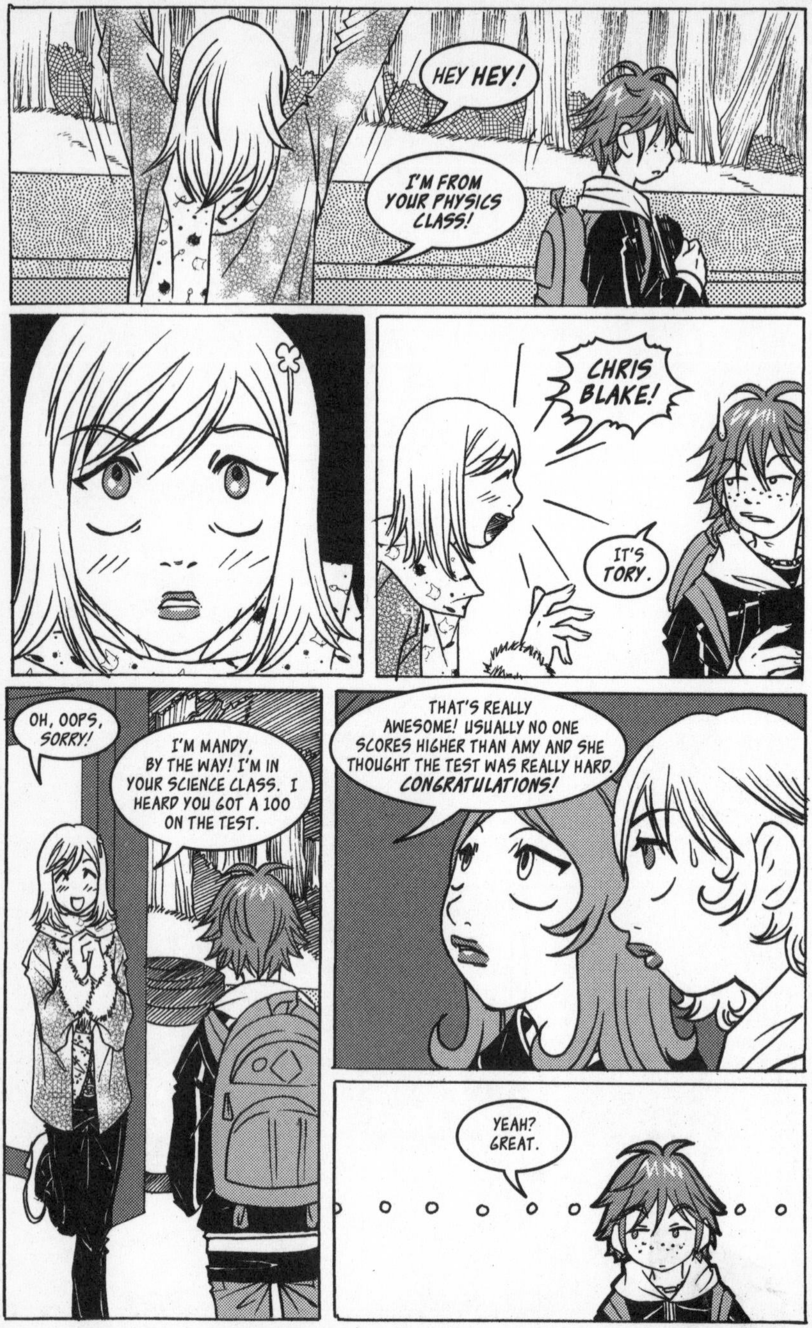
HEY HEY!
I'M FROM YOUR PHYSICS CLASS!
CHRIS BLAKE!
IT'S TORY.
OH, OOPS, SORRY!
I'M MANDY, BY THE WAY! I'M IN YOUR SCIENCE CLASS. I HEARD YOU GOT A 100 ON THE TEST.
THAT'S REALLY AWESOME! USUALLY NO ONE SCORES HIGHER THAN AMY AND SHE THOUGHT THE TEST WAS REALLY HARD. CONGRATULATIONS!
YEAH? GREAT.

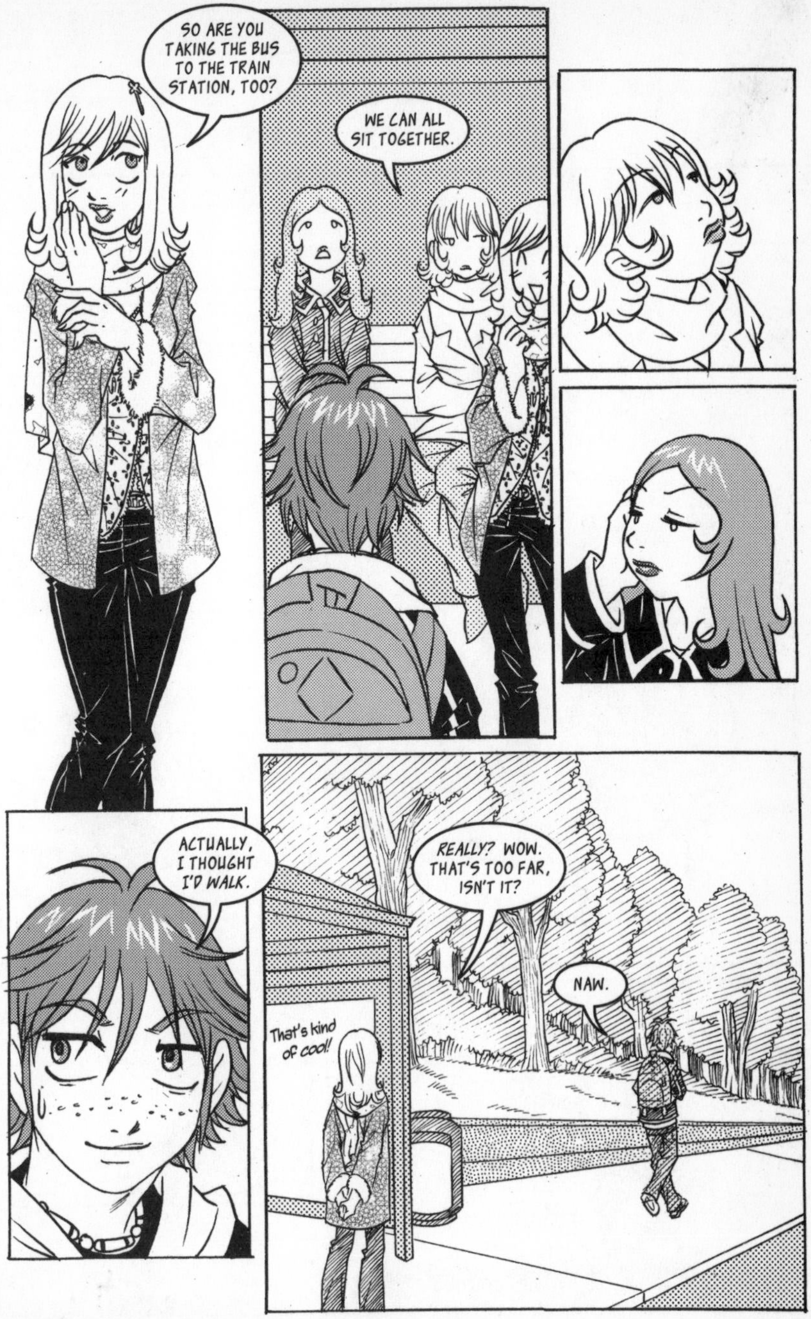
SO ARE YOU TAKING THE BUS TO THE TRAIN STATION, TOO?
WE CAN ALL SIT TOGETHER.
ACTUALLY, I THOUGHT I'D WALK.
REALLY? WOW. THAT'S TOO FAR, ISN'T IT?
NAW.
That's kind of cool!

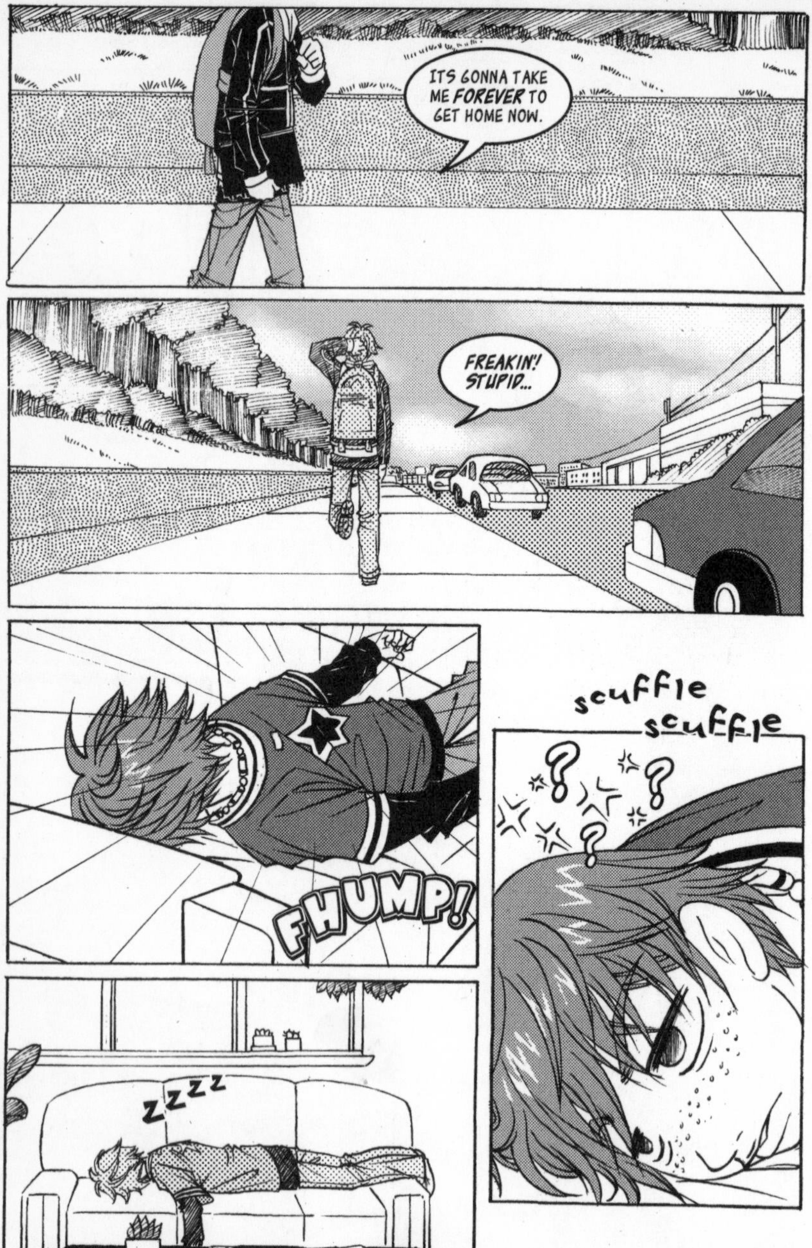
ITS GONNA TAKE ME **FOREVER** TO GET HOME NOW.
FREAKIN'! STUPID...
FHUMP!
scuffle
scuffle
ZZZZ

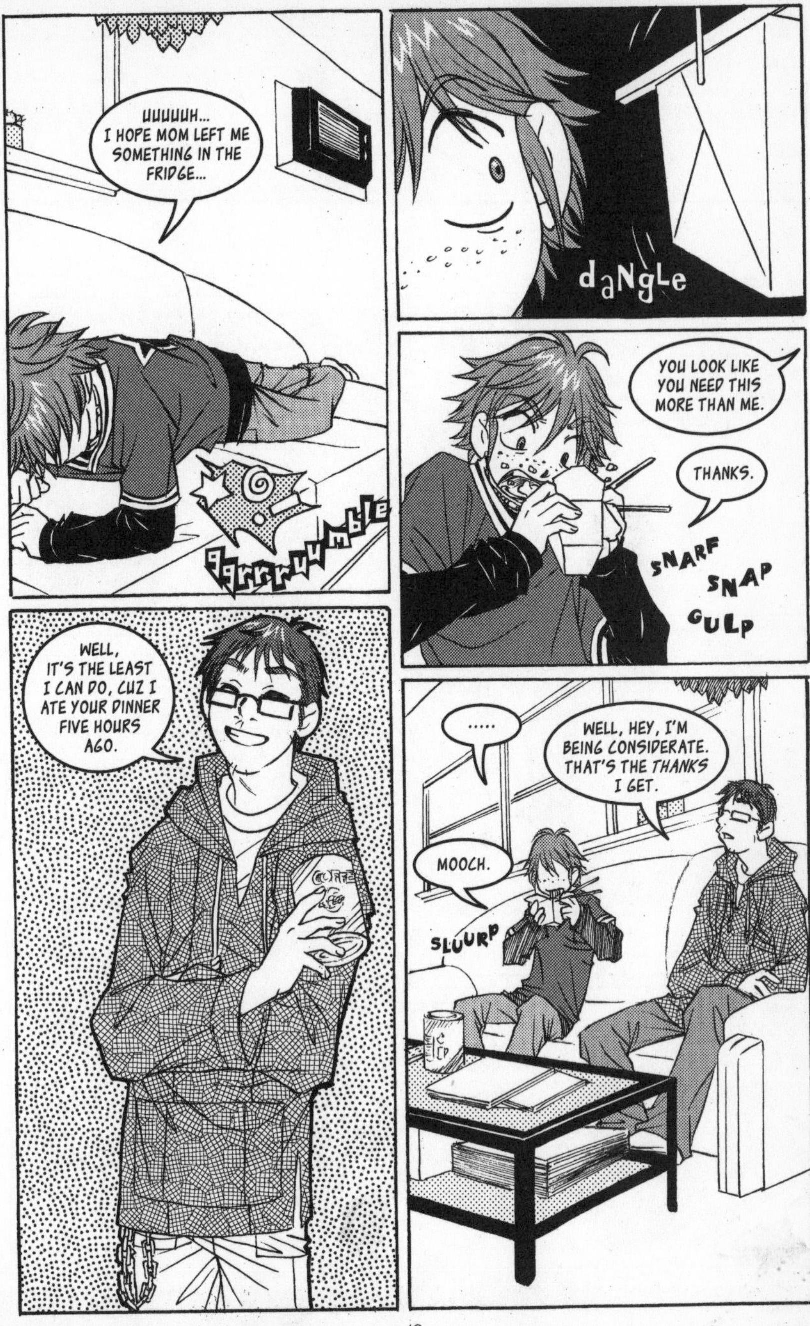
UUUUUH... I HOPE MOM LEFT ME SOMETHING IN THE FRIDGE...
GGRRRRUUMBLE
dangle
YOU LOOK LIKE YOU NEED THIS MORE THAN ME.
THANKS.
SNARF
SNAP
GULP
WELL, IT'S THE LEAST I CAN DO, CUZ I ATE YOUR DINNER FIVE HOURS AGO.
.....
WELL, HEY, I'M BEING CONSIDERATE. THAT'S THE *THANKS* I GET.
MOOCH.
SLUURP

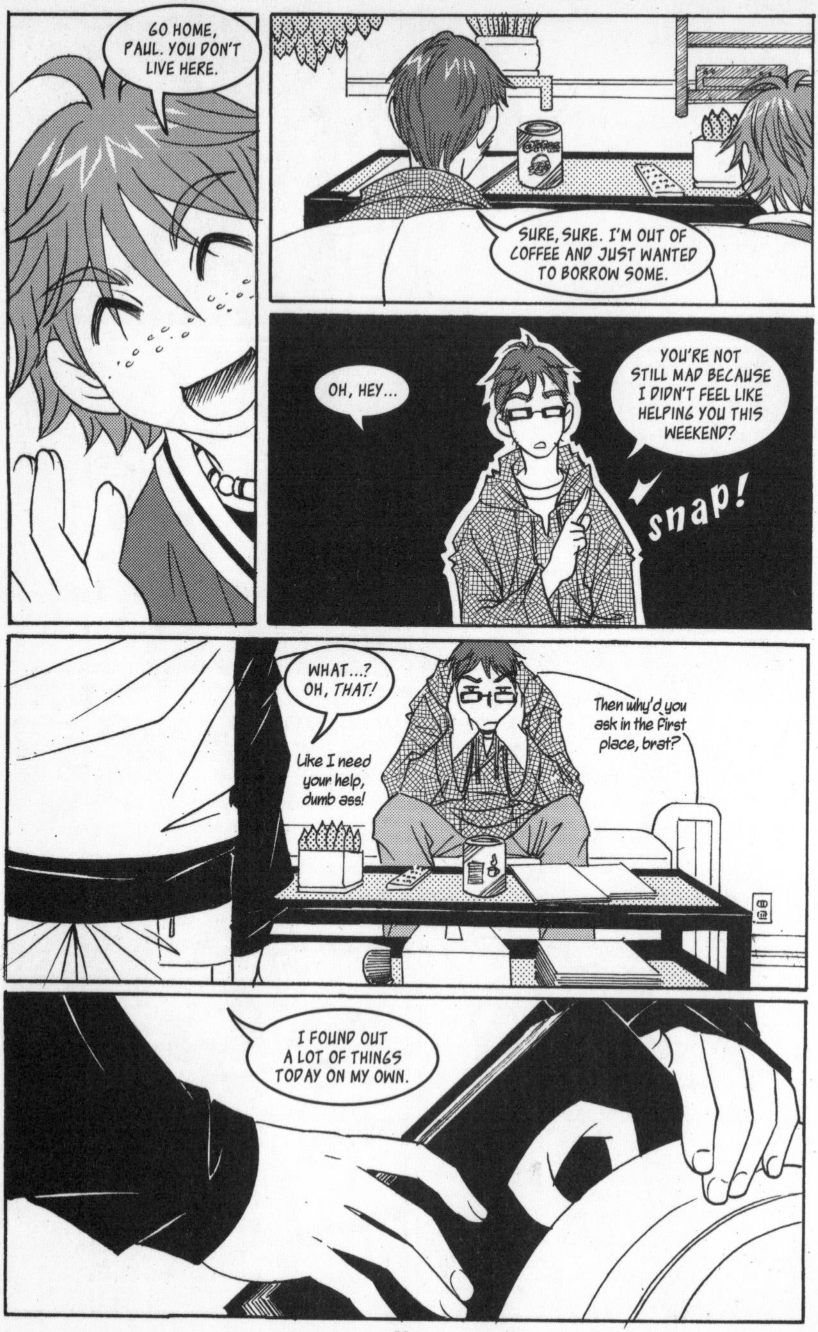
GO HOME, PAUL. YOU DON'T LIVE HERE.
SURE, SURE. I'M OUT OF COFFEE AND JUST WANTED TO BORROW SOME.
OH, HEY...
YOU'RE NOT STILL MAD BECAUSE I DIDN'T FEEL LIKE HELPING YOU THIS WEEKEND?
snap!
WHAT...? OH, *THAT!*
Like I need your help, dumb ass!
Then why'd you ask in the first place, brat?
I FOUND OUT A LOT OF THINGS TODAY ON MY OWN.

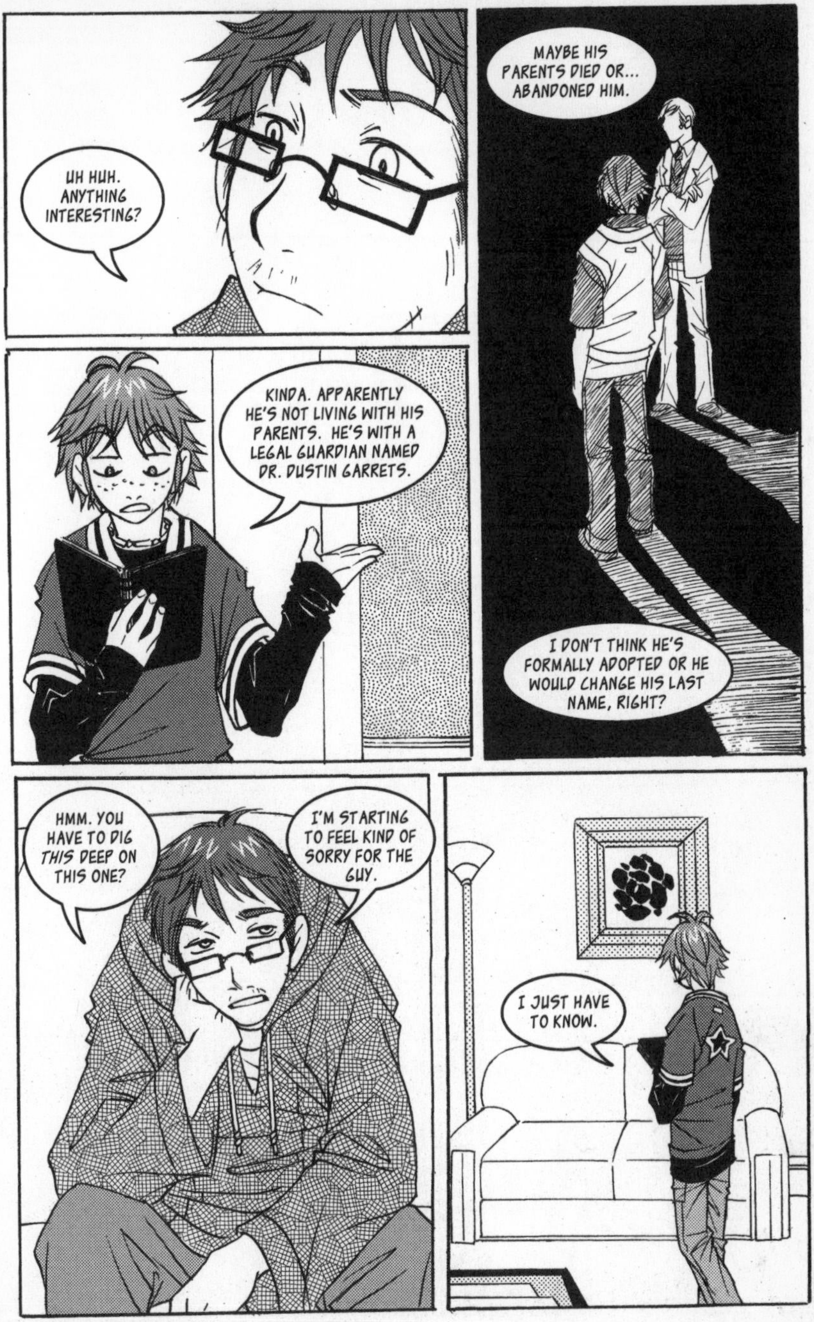
UH HUH. ANYTHING INTERESTING?
MAYBE HIS PARENTS DIED OR... ABANDONED HIM.
KINDA. APPARENTLY HE'S NOT LIVING WITH HIS PARENTS. HE'S WITH A LEGAL GUARDIAN NAMED DR. DUSTIN GARRETS.
I DON'T THINK HE'S FORMALLY ADOPTED OR HE WOULD CHANGE HIS LAST NAME, RIGHT?
HMM. YOU HAVE TO DIG *THIS* DEEP ON THIS ONE?
I'M STARTING TO FEEL KIND OF SORRY FOR THE GUY.
I JUST HAVE TO KNOW.

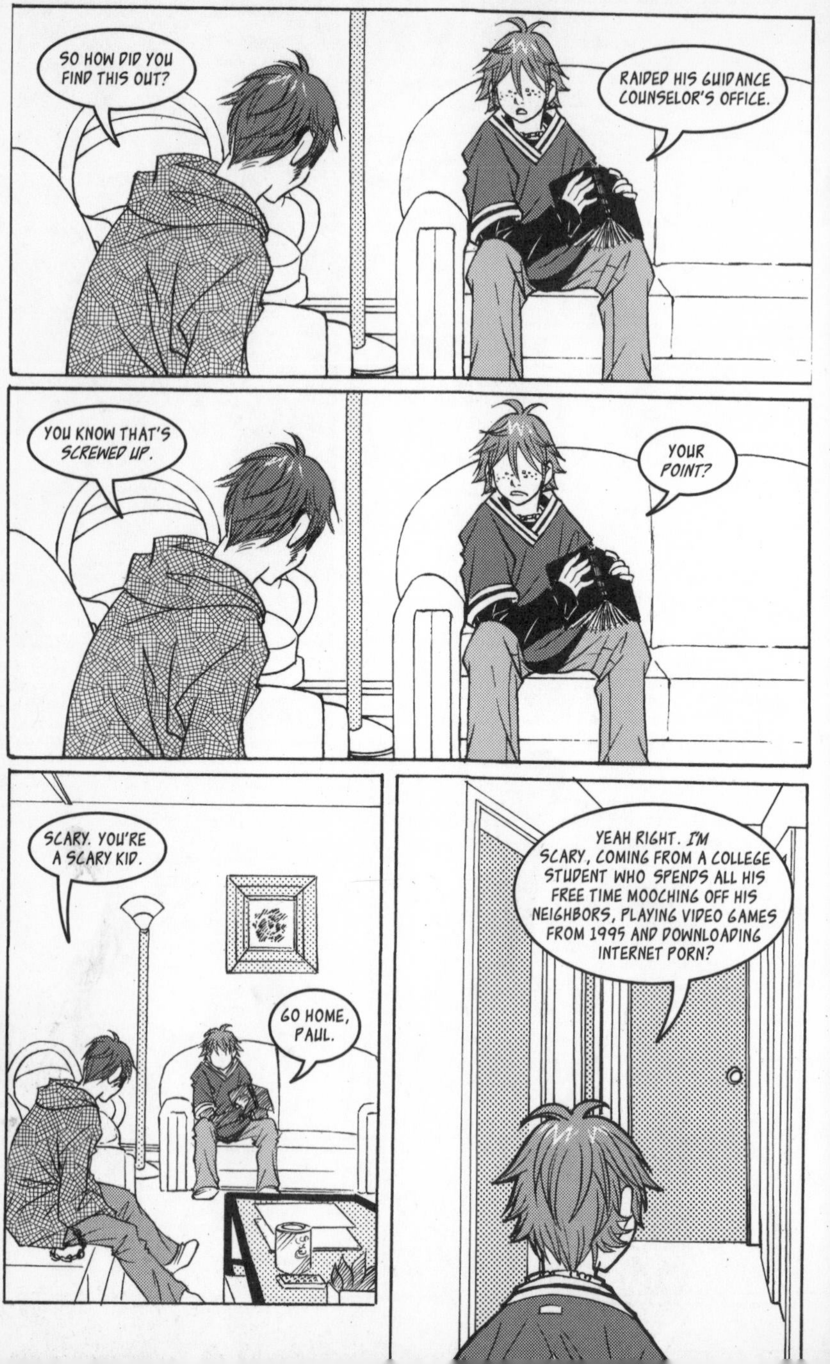
SO HOW DID YOU FIND THIS OUT?
RAIDED HIS GUIDANCE COUNSELOR'S OFFICE.
YOU KNOW THAT'S SCREWED UP.
YOUR POINT?
SCARY. YOU'RE A SCARY KID.
GO HOME, PAUL.
YEAH RIGHT. I'M SCARY, COMING FROM A COLLEGE STUDENT WHO SPENDS ALL HIS FREE TIME MOOCHING OFF HIS NEIGHBORS, PLAYING VIDEO GAMES FROM 1995 AND DOWNLOADING INTERNET PORN?

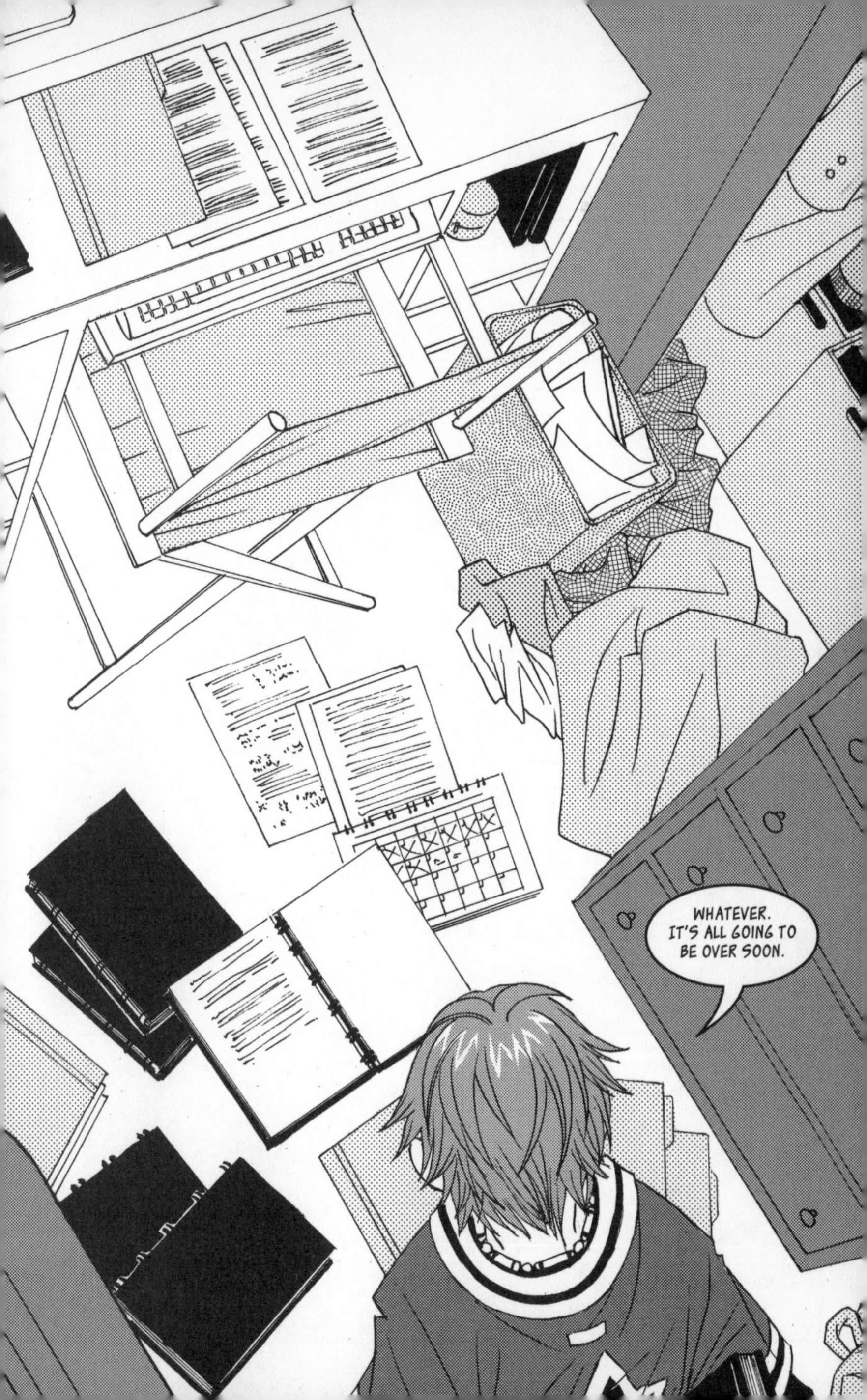
WHATEVER. IT'S ALL GOING TO BE OVER SOON.

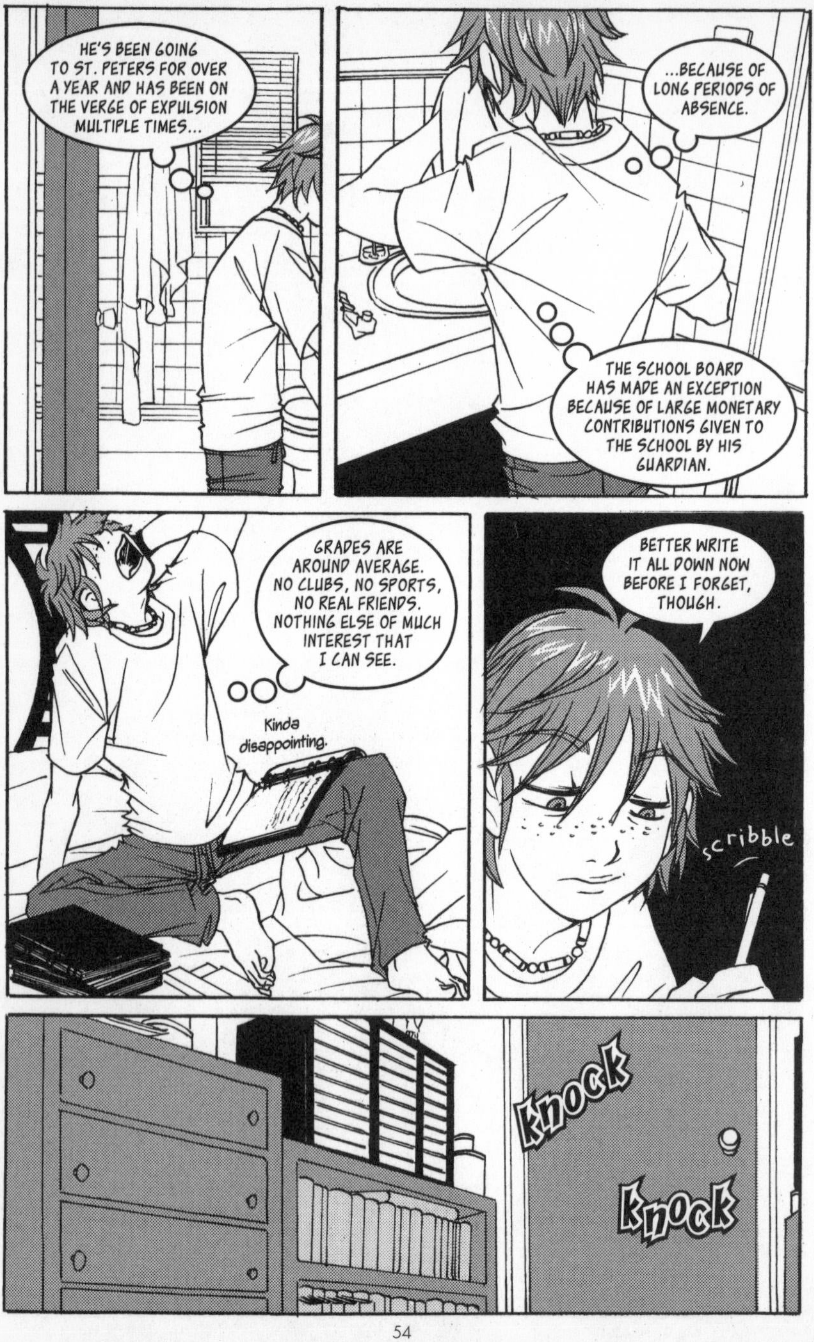
HE'S BEEN GOING TO ST. PETERS FOR OVER A YEAR AND HAS BEEN ON THE VERGE OF EXPULSION MULTIPLE TIMES...
...BECAUSE OF LONG PERIODS OF ABSENCE.
THE SCHOOL BOARD HAS MADE AN EXCEPTION BECAUSE OF LARGE MONETARY CONTRIBUTIONS GIVEN TO THE SCHOOL BY HIS GUARDIAN.
GRADES ARE AROUND AVERAGE. NO CLUBS, NO SPORTS, NO REAL FRIENDS. NOTHING ELSE OF MUCH INTEREST THAT I CAN SEE.
Kinda disappointing.
BETTER WRITE IT ALL DOWN NOW BEFORE I FORGET, THOUGH.
scribble
knock
knock

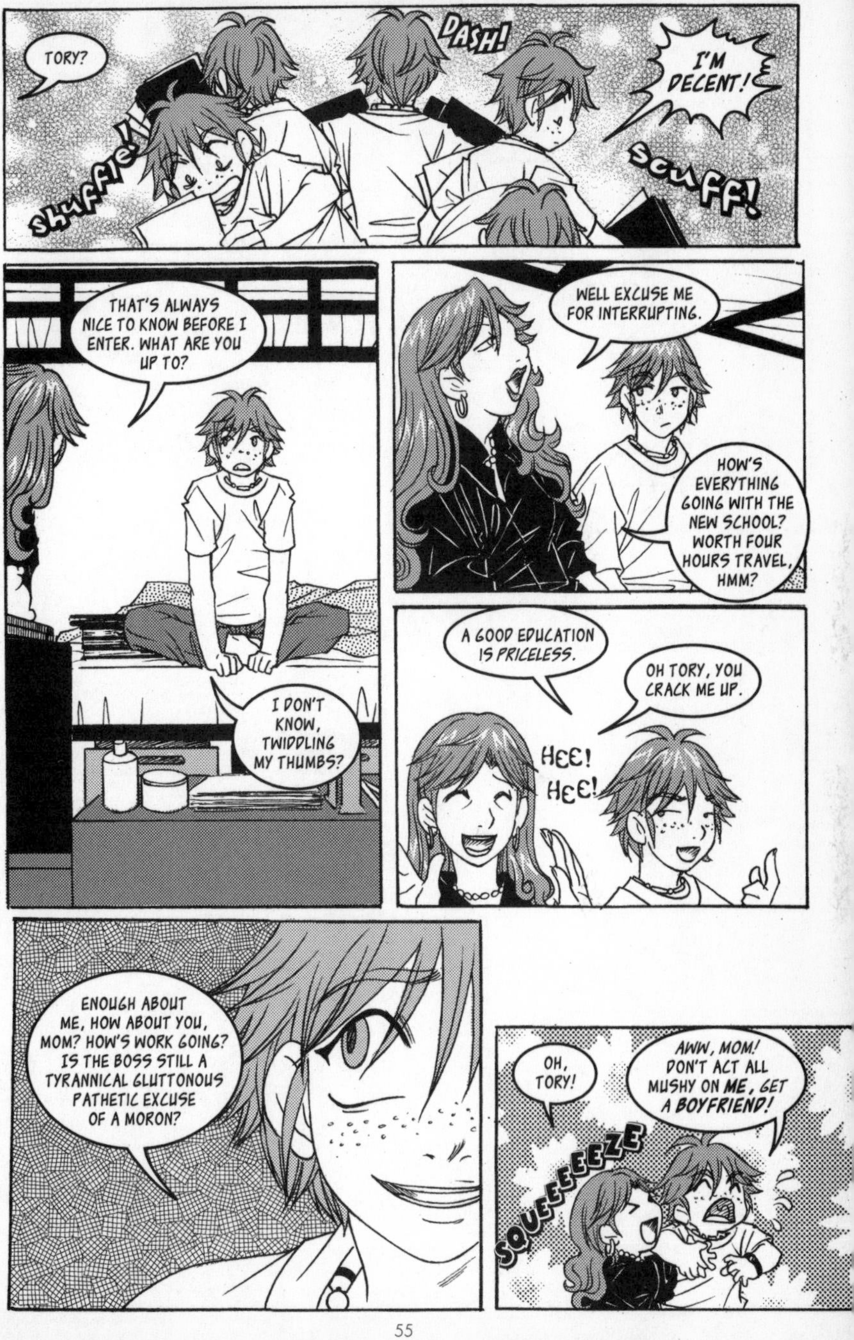
TORY?
shuffle!
DASH!
I'M DECENT!
scuff!
THAT'S ALWAYS NICE TO KNOW BEFORE I ENTER. WHAT ARE YOU UP TO?
I DON'T KNOW, TWIDDLING MY THUMBS?
WELL EXCUSE ME FOR INTERRUPTING.
HOW'S EVERYTHING GOING WITH THE NEW SCHOOL? WORTH FOUR HOURS TRAVEL, HMM?
A GOOD EDUCATION IS *PRICELESS.*
OH TORY, YOU CRACK ME UP.
HEE! HEE!
ENOUGH ABOUT ME, HOW ABOUT YOU, MOM? HOW'S WORK GOING? IS THE BOSS STILL A TYRANNICAL GLUTTONOUS PATHETIC EXCUSE OF A MORON?
OH, TORY!
AWW, MOM! DON'T ACT ALL MUSHY ON **ME**, GET A **BOYFRIEND!**
SQUEEEEEEZE

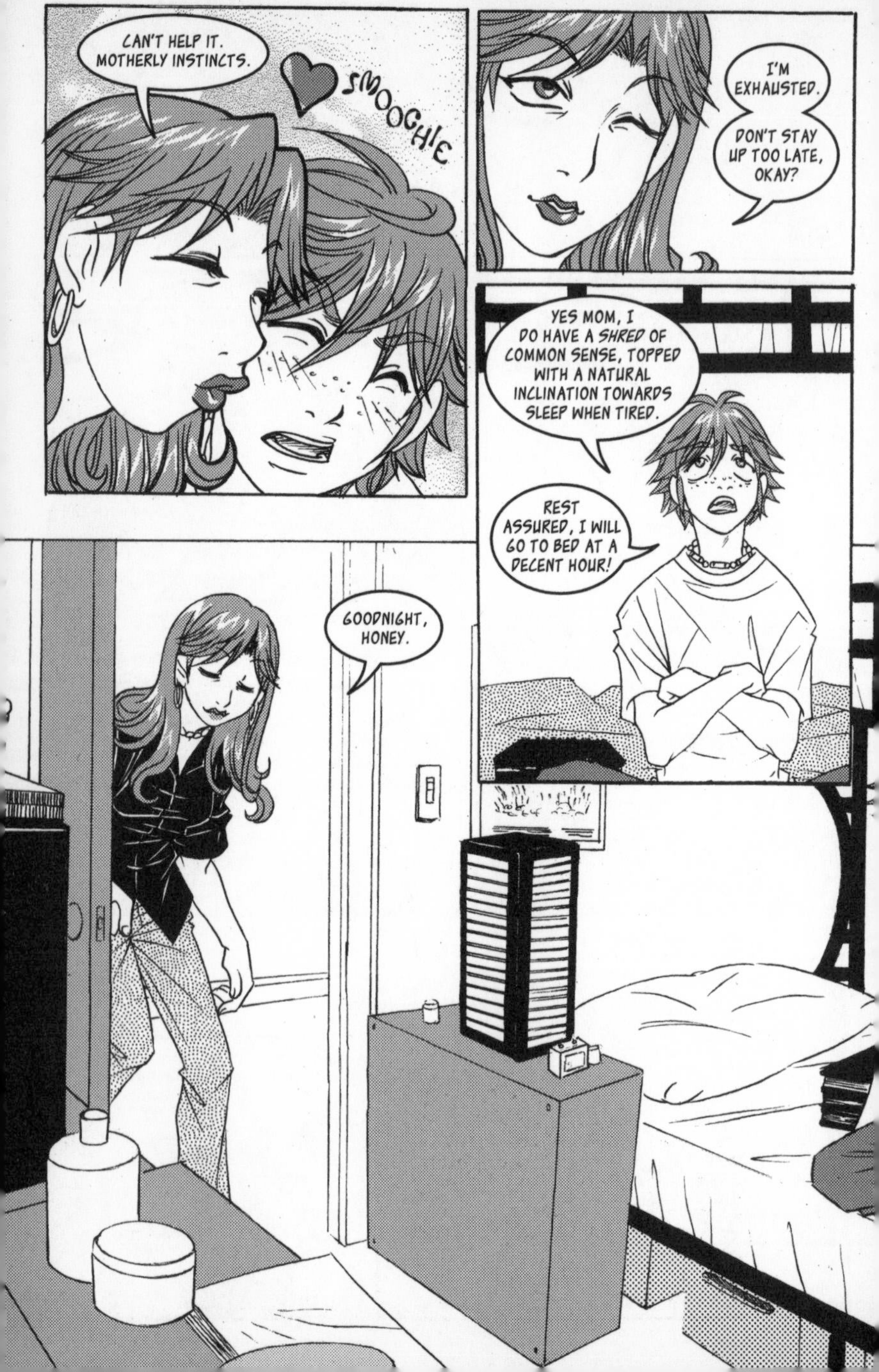
CAN'T HELP IT. MOTHERLY INSTINCTS.
SMOOCHIE
I'M EXHAUSTED.
DON'T STAY UP TOO LATE, OKAY?
YES MOM, I DO HAVE A *SHRED* OF COMMON SENSE, TOPPED WITH A NATURAL INCLINATION TOWARDS SLEEP WHEN TIRED.
REST ASSURED, I WILL GO TO BED AT A DECENT HOUR!
GOODNIGHT, HONEY.

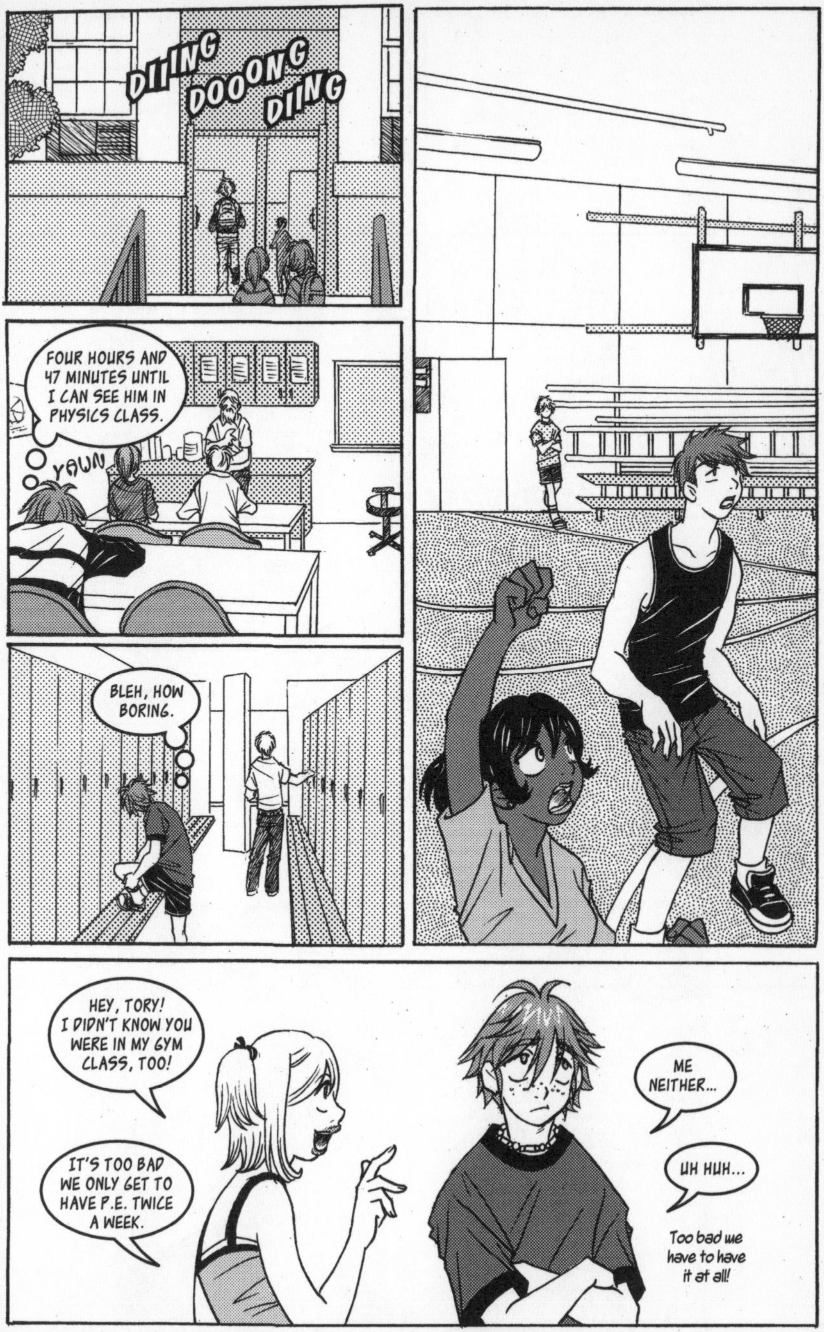
DIIING DOOONG DIING
FOUR HOURS AND 47 MINUTES UNTIL I CAN SEE HIM IN PHYSICS CLASS.
YAWN
BLEH, HOW BORING.
HEY, TORY! I DIDN'T KNOW YOU WERE IN MY GYM CLASS, TOO!
IT'S TOO BAD WE ONLY GET TO HAVE P.E. TWICE A WEEK.
ME NEITHER...
UH HUH...
Too bad we have to have it at all!

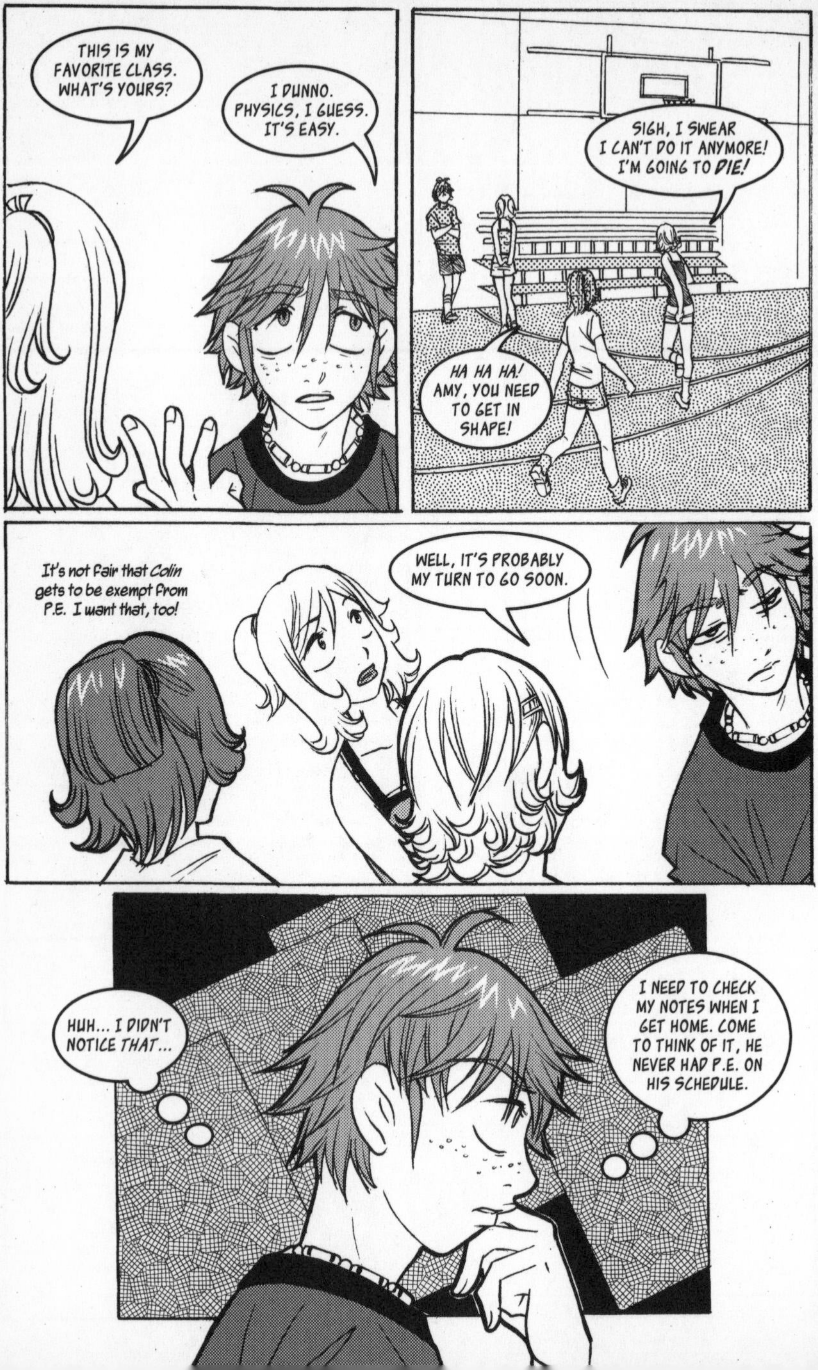
THIS IS MY FAVORITE CLASS. WHAT'S YOURS?
I DUNNO. PHYSICS, I GUESS. IT'S EASY.
SIGH, I SWEAR I CAN'T DO IT ANYMORE! I'M GOING TO DIE!
HA HA HA! AMY, YOU NEED TO GET IN SHAPE!
It's not fair that Colin gets to be exempt from P.E. I want that, too!
WELL, IT'S PROBABLY MY TURN TO GO SOON.
HUH... I DIDN'T NOTICE THAT...
I NEED TO CHECK MY NOTES WHEN I GET HOME. COME TO THINK OF IT, HE NEVER HAD P.E. ON HIS SCHEDULE.

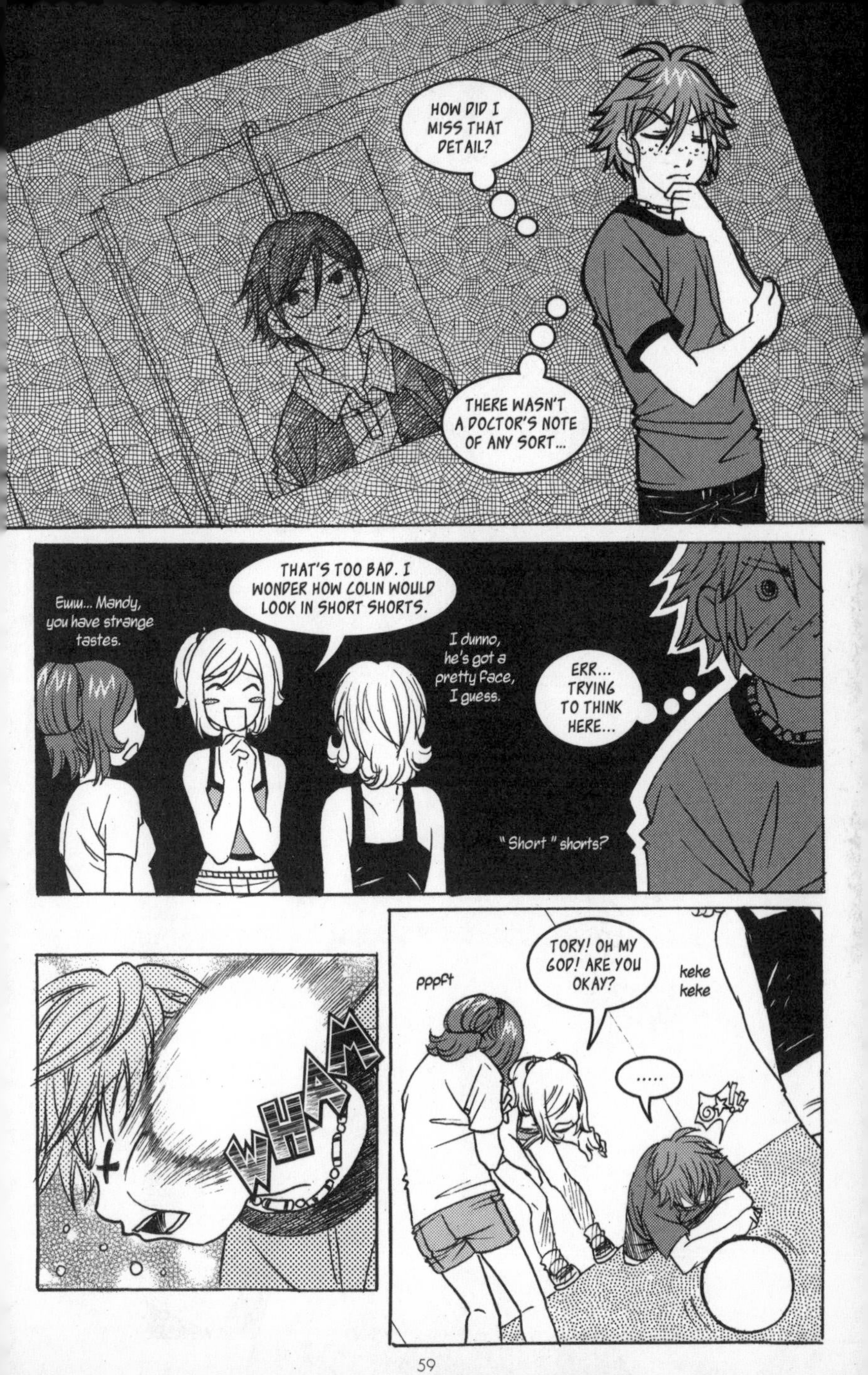
HOW DID I MISS THAT DETAIL?
THERE WASN'T A DOCTOR'S NOTE OF ANY SORT...
Ewww... Mandy, you have strange tastes.
THAT'S TOO BAD. I WONDER HOW COLIN WOULD LOOK IN SHORT SHORTS.
I dunno, he's got a pretty face, I guess.
ERR... TRYING TO THINK HERE...
"Short" shorts?
WHAM
TORY! OH MY GOD! ARE YOU OKAY?
pppft
keke keke
.....

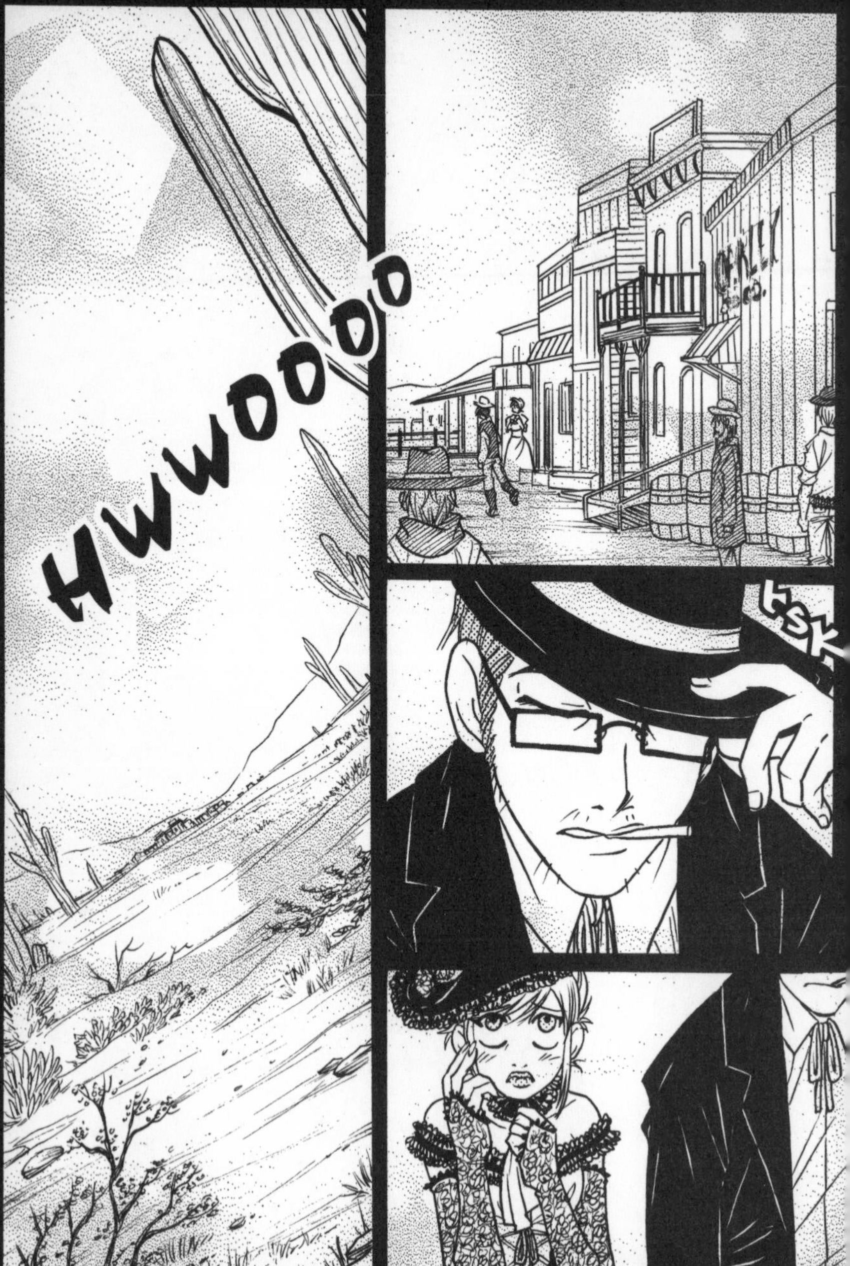
HWWOOOO
tsk

Off*Beat

Chapter 3: The Contact

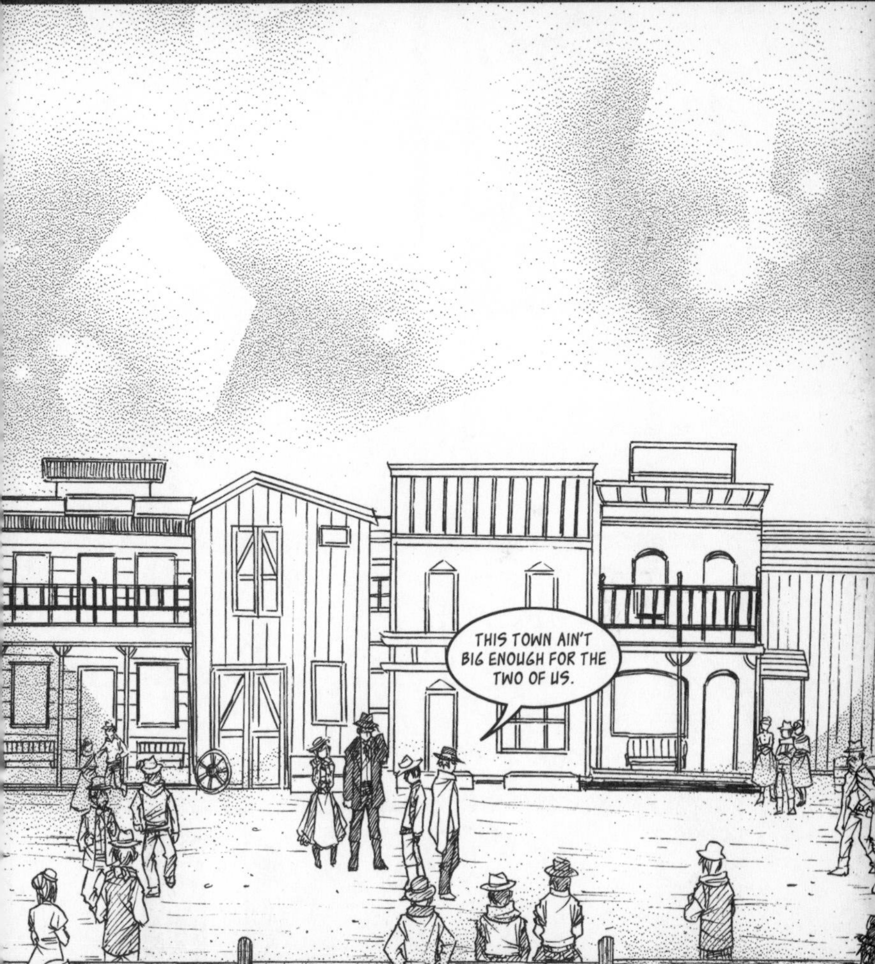
THIS TOWN AIN'T BIG ENOUGH FOR THE TWO OF US.

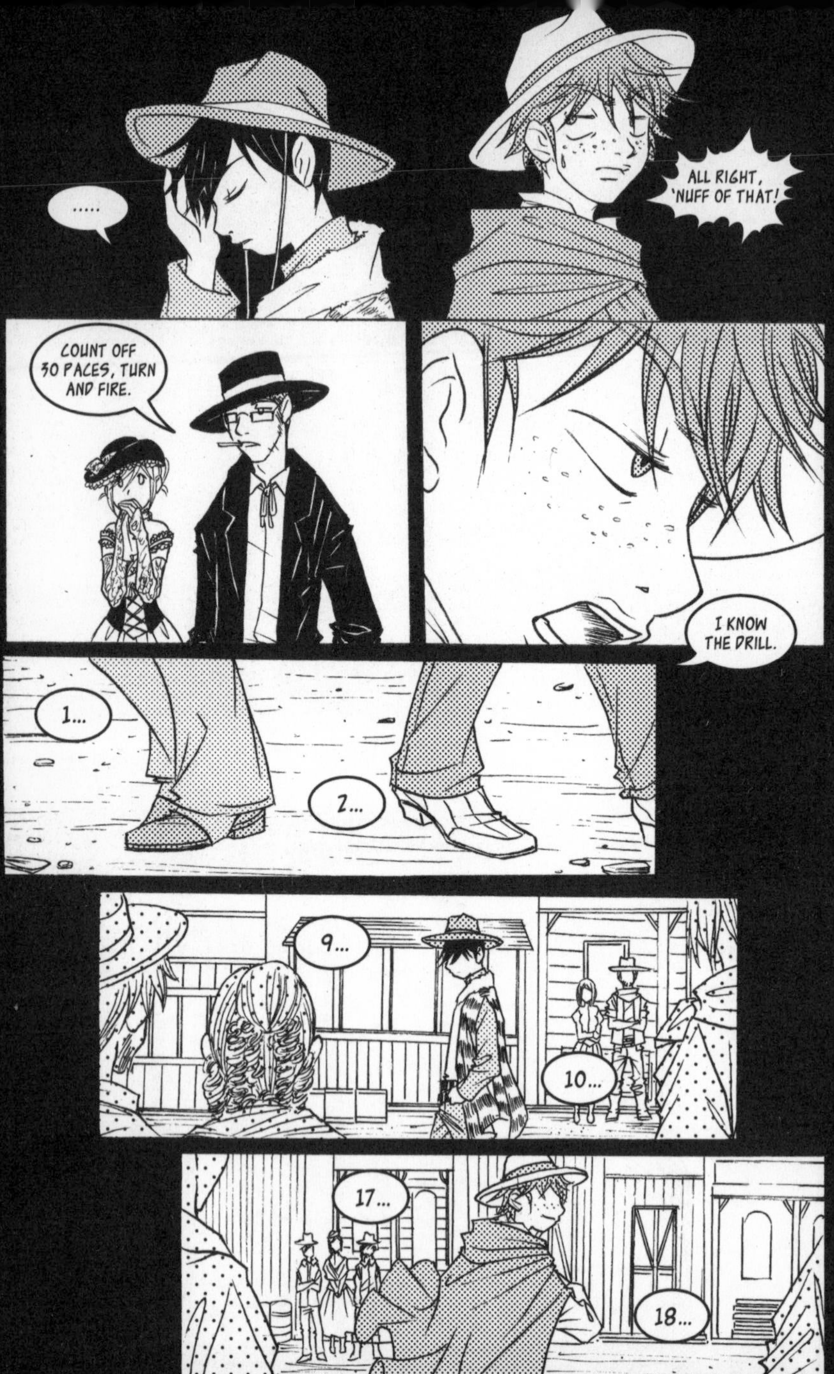
.....
ALL RIGHT, 'NUFF OF THAT!
COUNT OFF 30 PACES, TURN AND FIRE.
I KNOW THE DRILL.
1...
2...
9...
10...
17...
18...

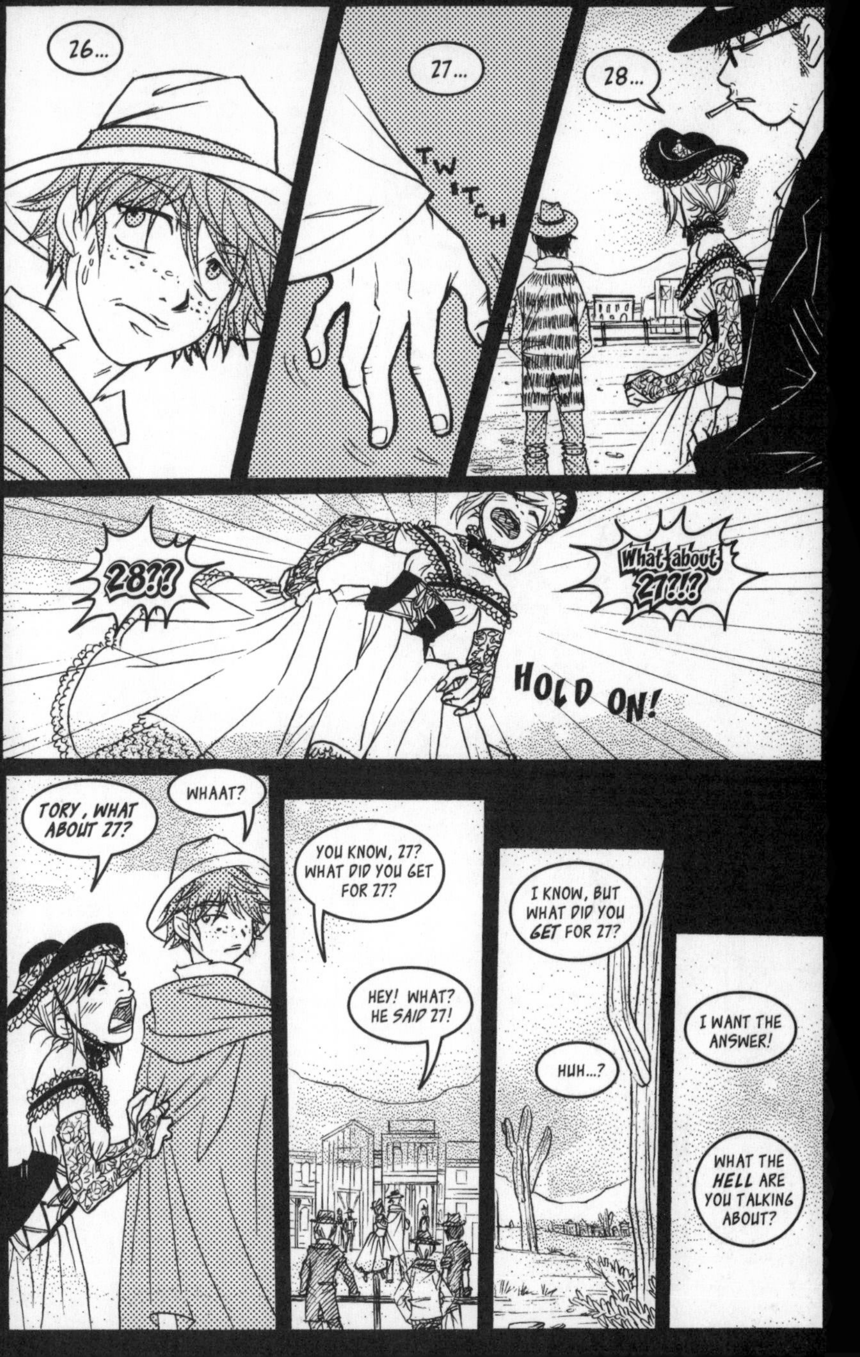
26...
27...
TWITCH
28...
28?!?
What about 27?!?
HOLD ON!
TORY, WHAT ABOUT 27?
WHAAT?
YOU KNOW, 27? WHAT DID YOU GET FOR 27?
HEY! WHAT? HE SAID 27!
I KNOW, BUT WHAT DID YOU GET FOR 27?
HUH...?
I WANT THE ANSWER!
WHAT THE HELL ARE YOU TALKING ABOUT?

TORY?

YOU SEEM REALLY OUT OF IT.

YEAH... I GUESS I DOZED OFF...

ARE YOU EVEN PAYING ATTENTION AT ALL?

HUH... UH...

OH MY GOD! YOU SLEEP WITH YOUR EYES OPEN?

SMACK

Good grief...

HEHE!

THAT'S SO FUNNY! YOU DO SO WELL WHEN YOU'RE NOT EVEN AWAKE IN CLASS...

EH... WHATEVER.

ANYWAYS, SO WHAT DID YOU GET FOR NUMBER 27?

HEY!

Don't just take other people's stuff!

SNATCH

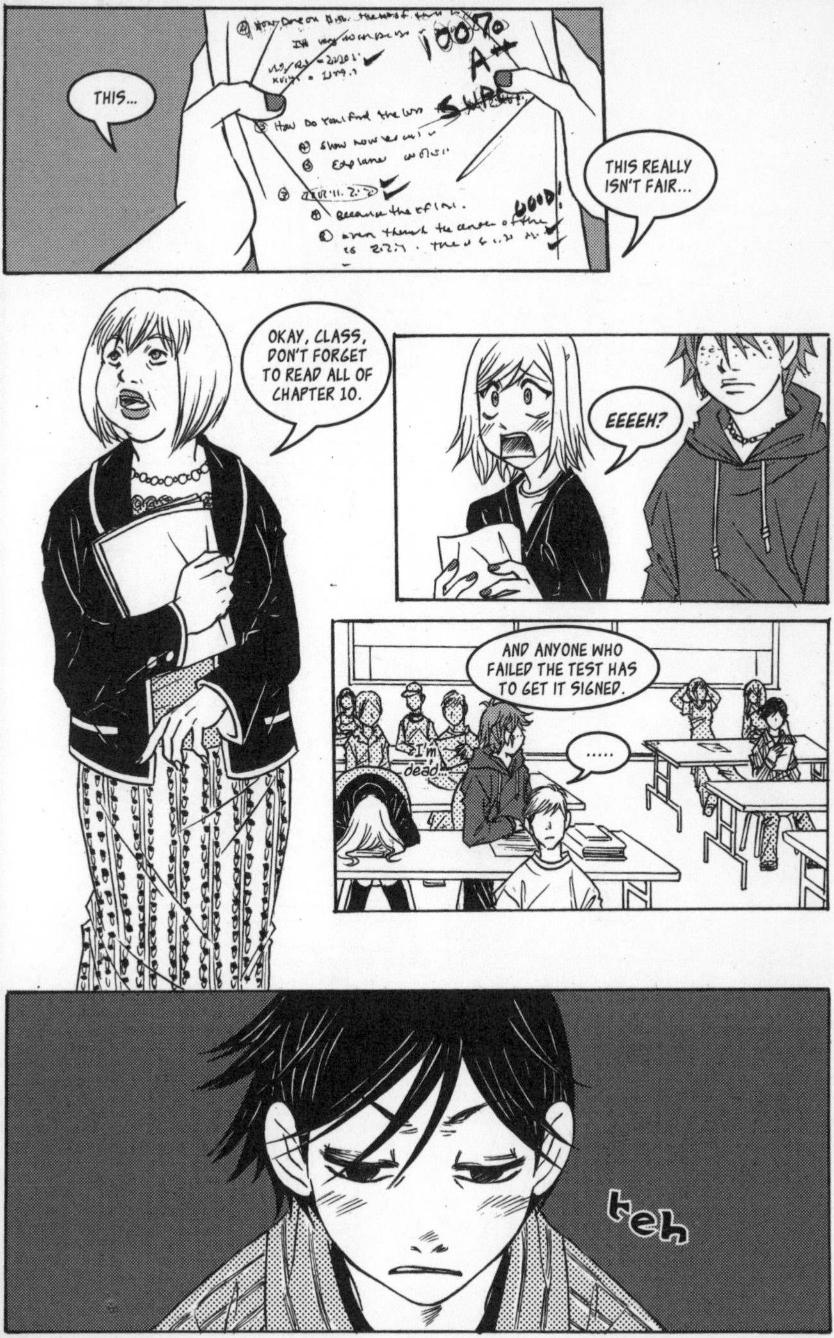
THIS...
THIS REALLY ISN'T FAIR...
OKAY, CLASS, DON'T FORGET TO READ ALL OF CHAPTER 10.
EEEEH?
AND ANYONE WHO FAILED THE TEST HAS TO GET IT SIGNED.
I'm dead
.....
teh

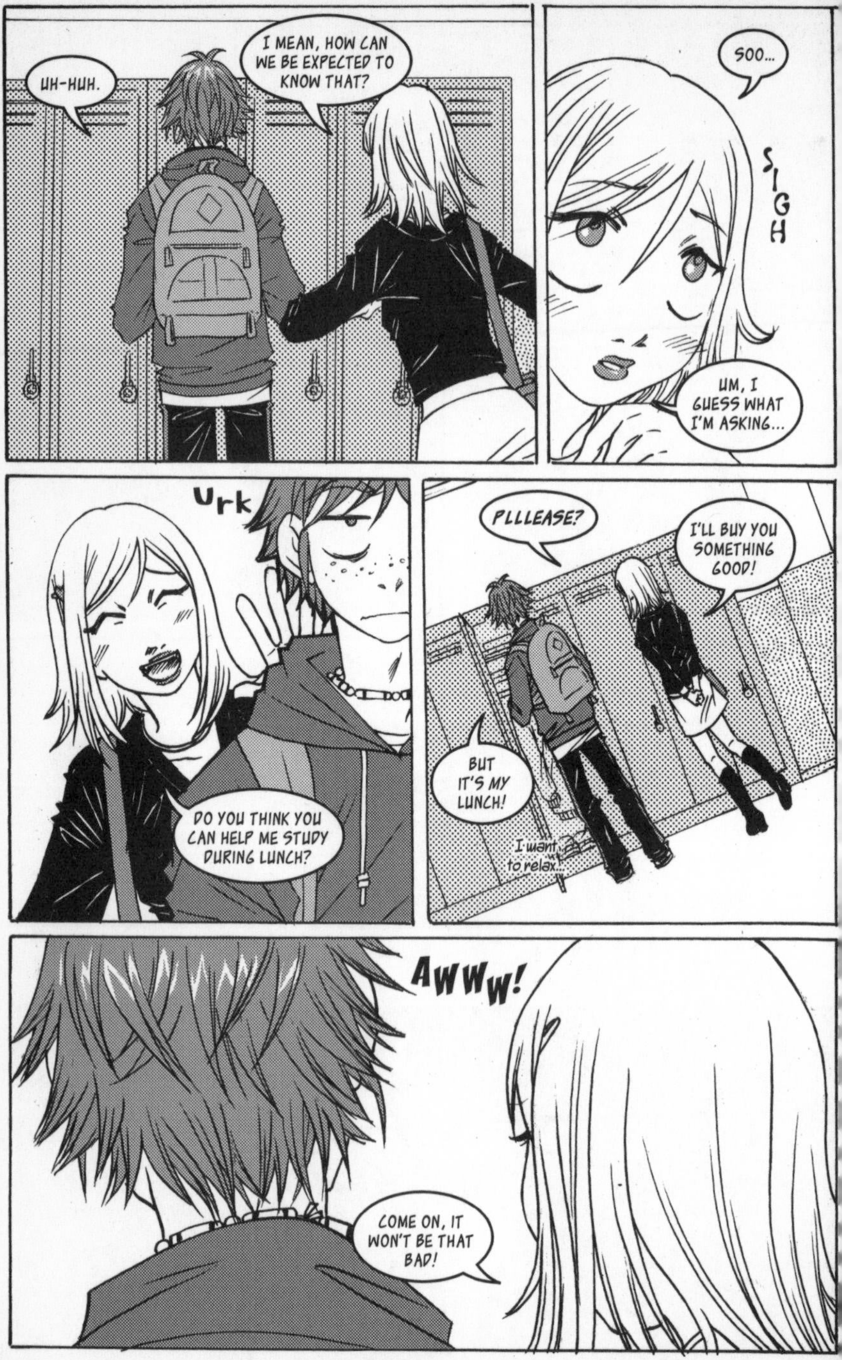
UH-HUH.
I MEAN, HOW CAN WE BE EXPECTED TO KNOW THAT?
SOO...
SIGH
UM, I GUESS WHAT I'M ASKING...
URK
DO YOU THINK YOU CAN HELP ME STUDY DURING LUNCH?
PLLLEASE?
I'LL BUY YOU SOMETHING GOOD!
BUT IT'S MY LUNCH!
I want to relax...
AWWW!
COME ON, IT WON'T BE THAT BAD!

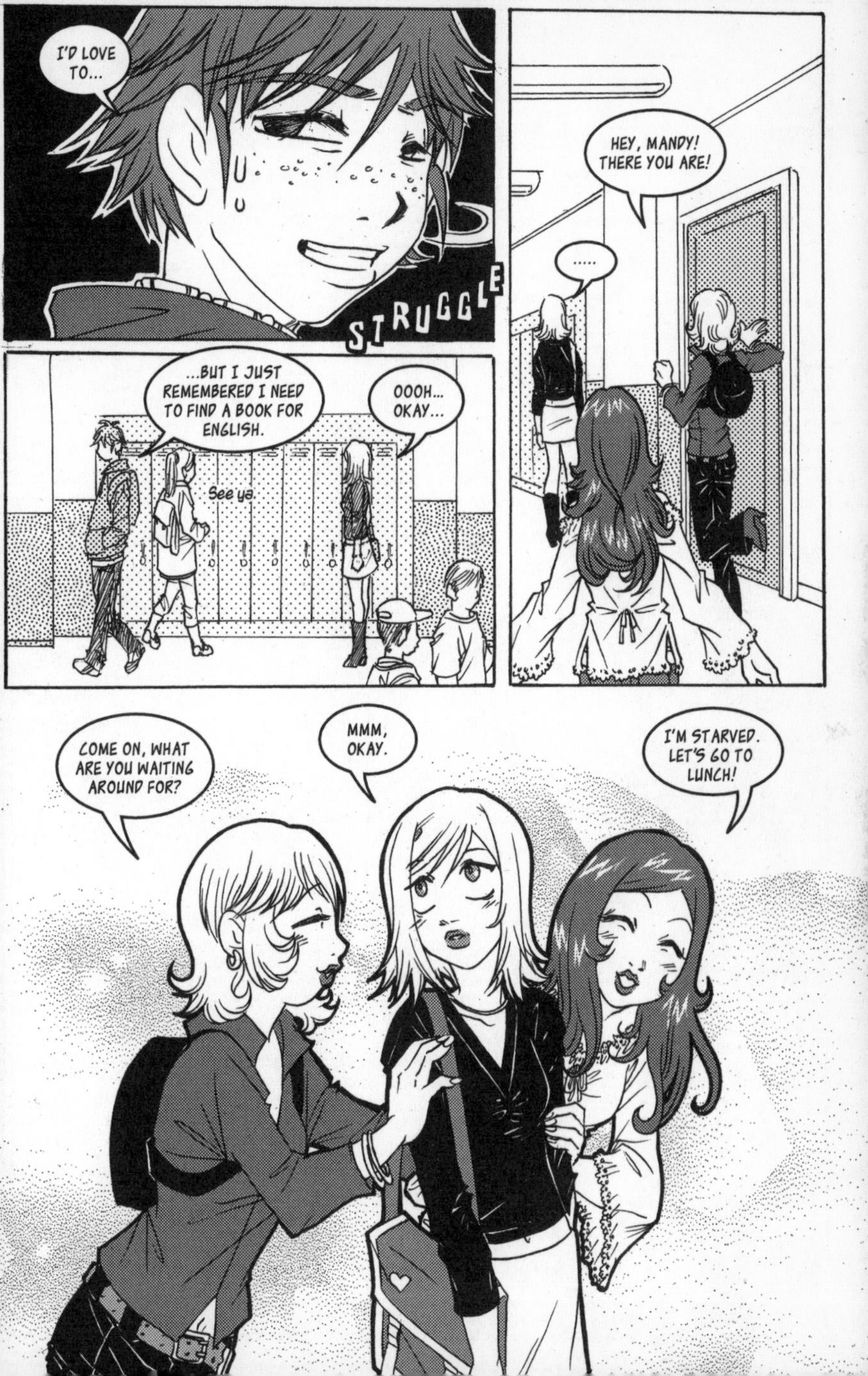
I'D LOVE TO...
STRUGGLE
...BUT I JUST REMEMBERED I NEED TO FIND A BOOK FOR ENGLISH.
See ya.
OOOH... OKAY...
HEY, MANDY! THERE YOU ARE!
.....
COME ON, WHAT ARE YOU WAITING AROUND FOR?
MMM, OKAY.
I'M STARVED. LET'S GO TO LUNCH!

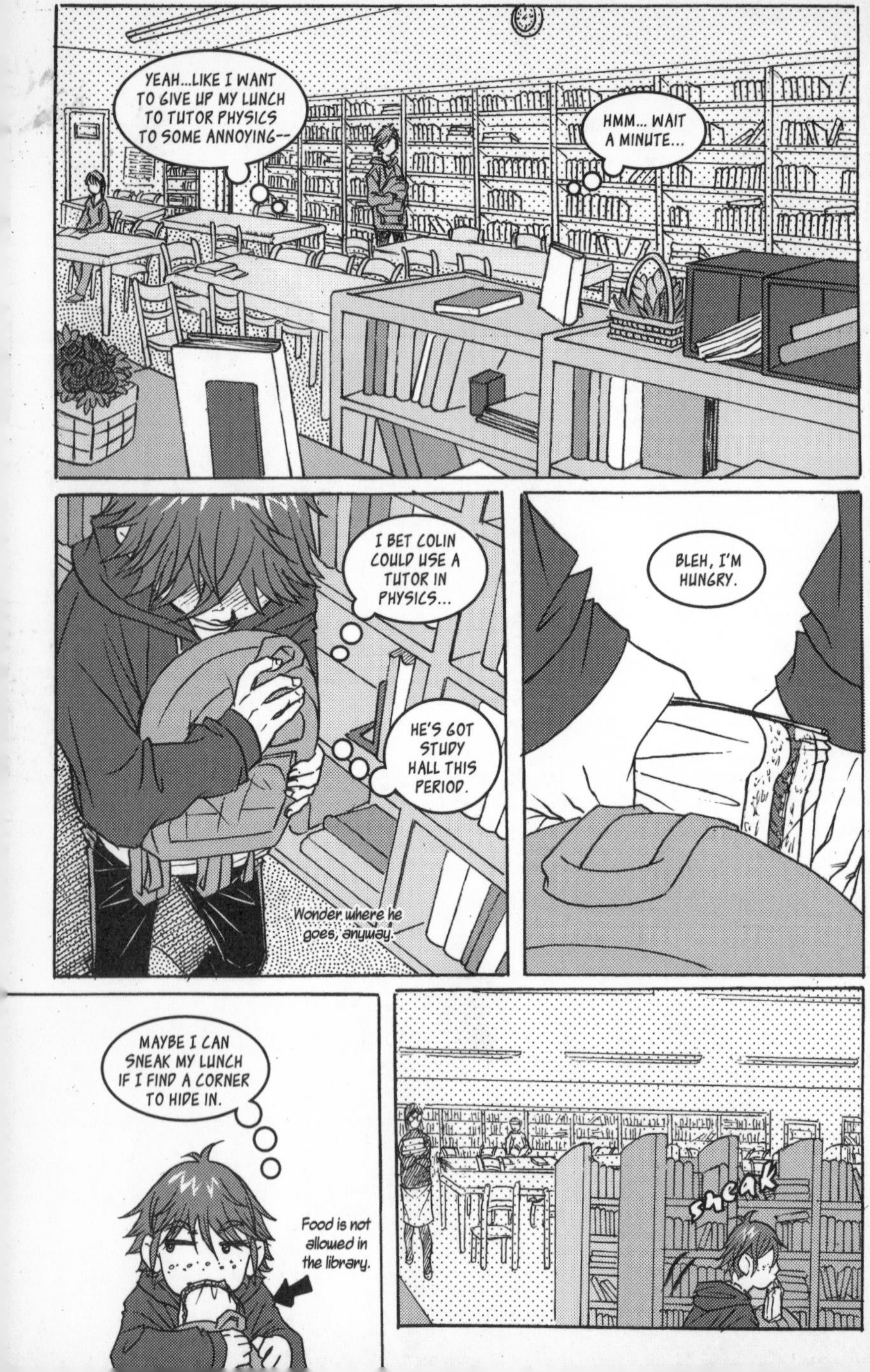
YEAH...LIKE I WANT TO GIVE UP MY LUNCH TO TUTOR PHYSICS TO SOME ANNOYING--
HMM... WAIT A MINUTE...
I BET COLIN COULD USE A TUTOR IN PHYSICS...
HE'S GOT STUDY HALL THIS PERIOD.
Wonder where he goes, anyway.
BLEH, I'M HUNGRY.
MAYBE I CAN SNEAK MY LUNCH IF I FIND A CORNER TO HIDE IN.
Food is not allowed in the library.
sneak

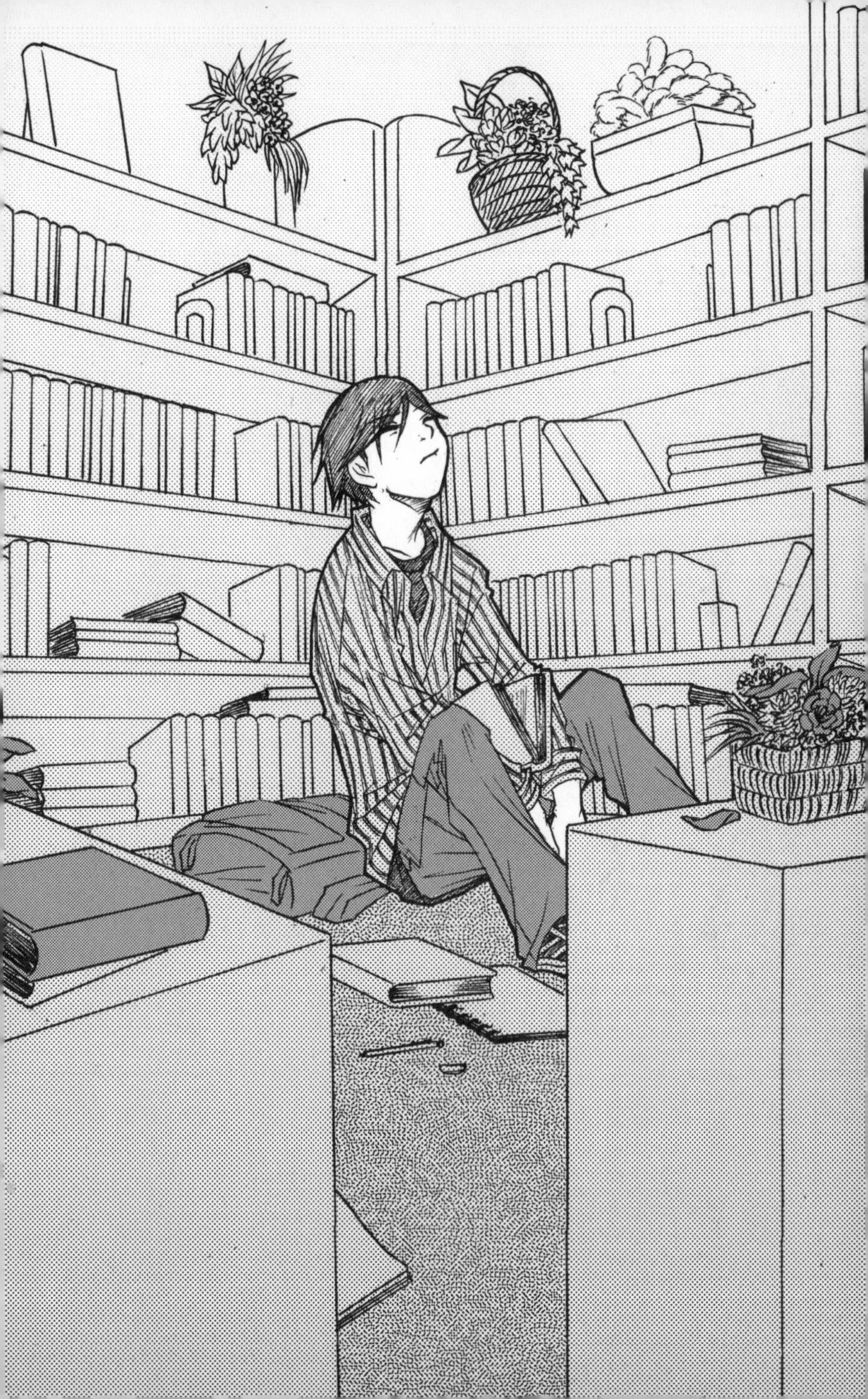

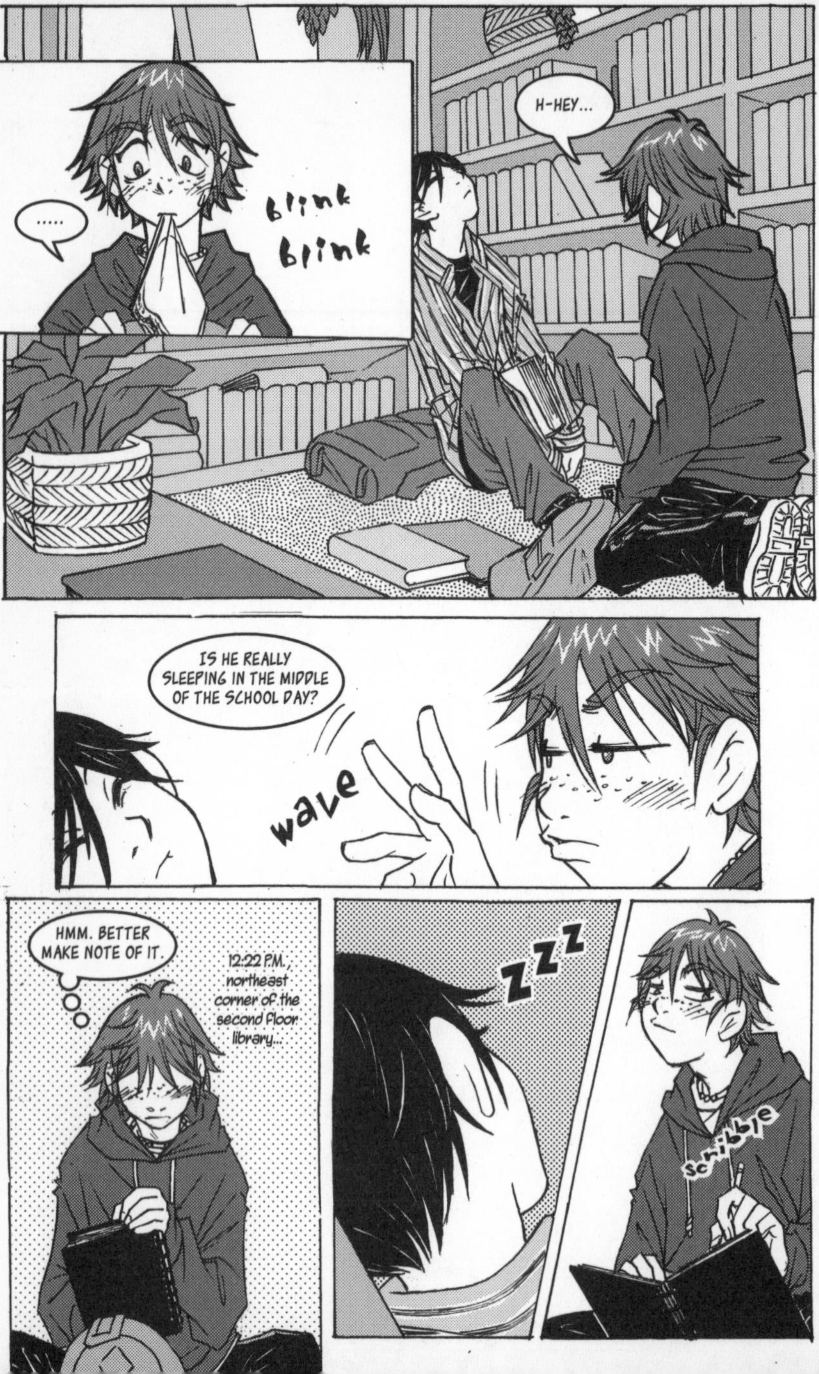
H-HEY...
.....
blink
blink
IS HE REALLY SLEEPING IN THE MIDDLE OF THE SCHOOL DAY?
wave
HMM. BETTER MAKE NOTE OF IT.
12:22 P.M., northeast corner of the second floor library...
ZZZ
scribble

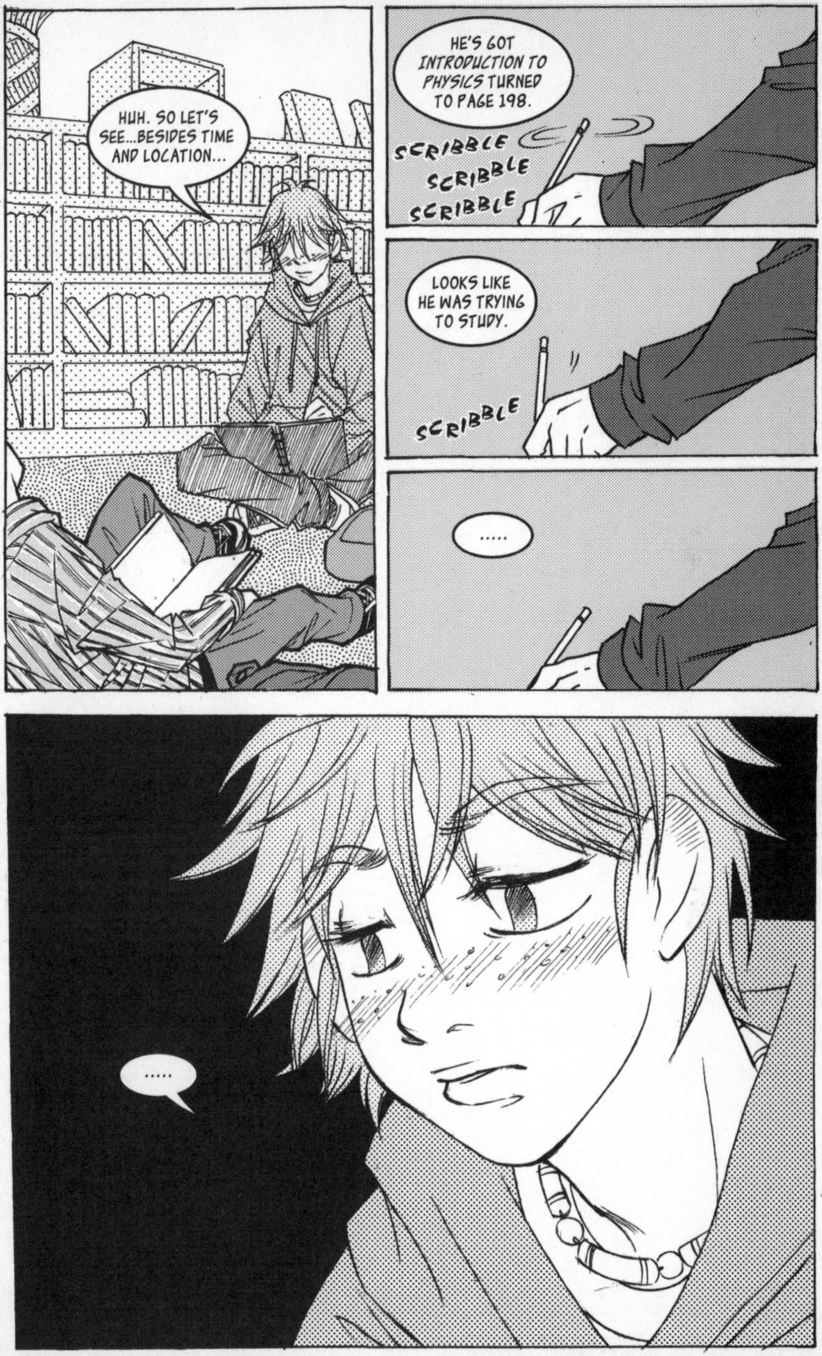
HUH. SO LET'S SEE...BESIDES TIME AND LOCATION...
HE'S GOT INTRODUCTION TO PHYSICS TURNED TO PAGE 198.
SCRIBBLE
SCRIBBLE
SCRIBBLE
LOOKS LIKE HE WAS TRYING TO STUDY.
SCRIBBLE
.....
.....

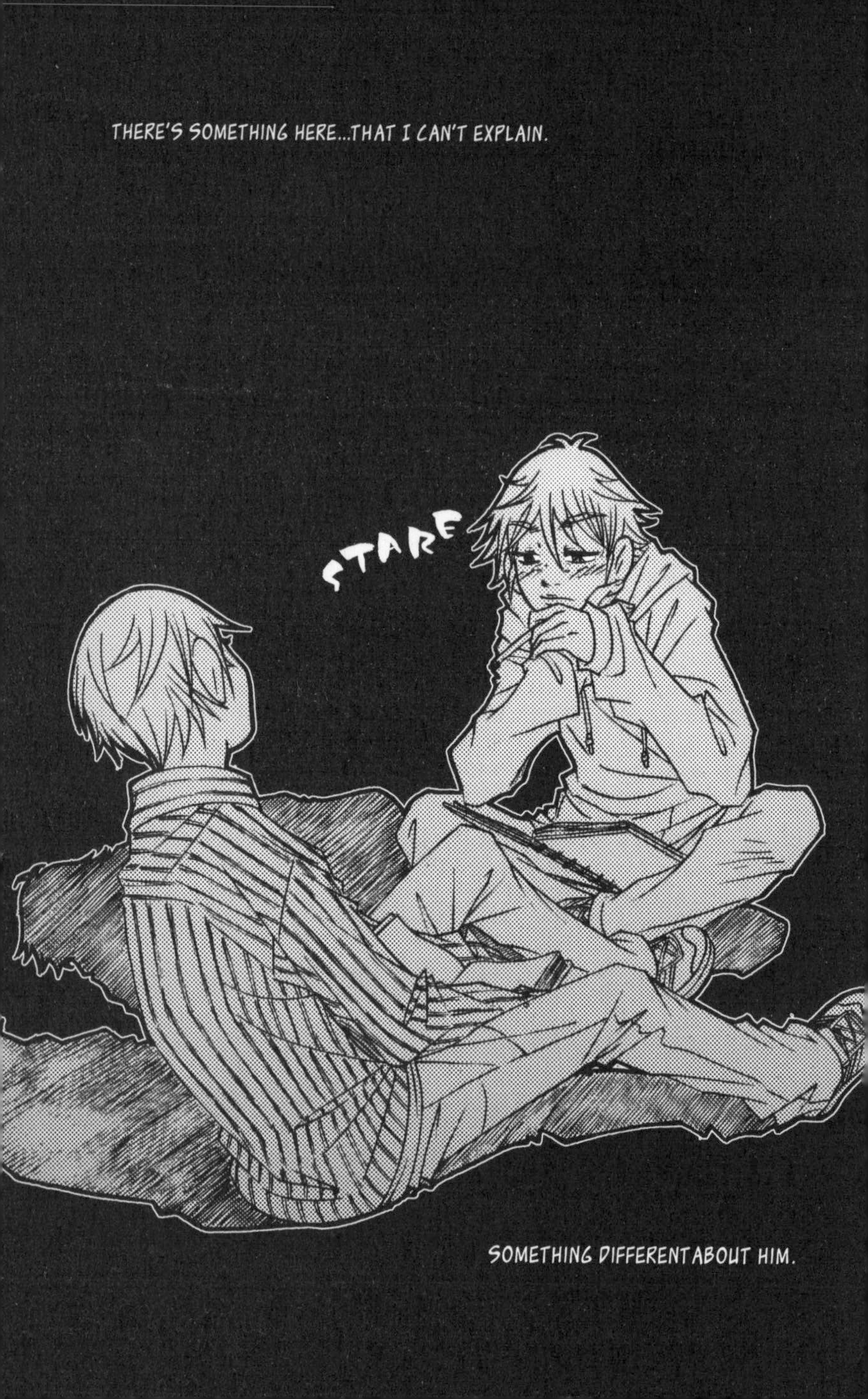
THERE'S SOMETHING HERE...THAT I CAN'T EXPLAIN.
STARE
SOMETHING DIFFERENT ABOUT HIM.

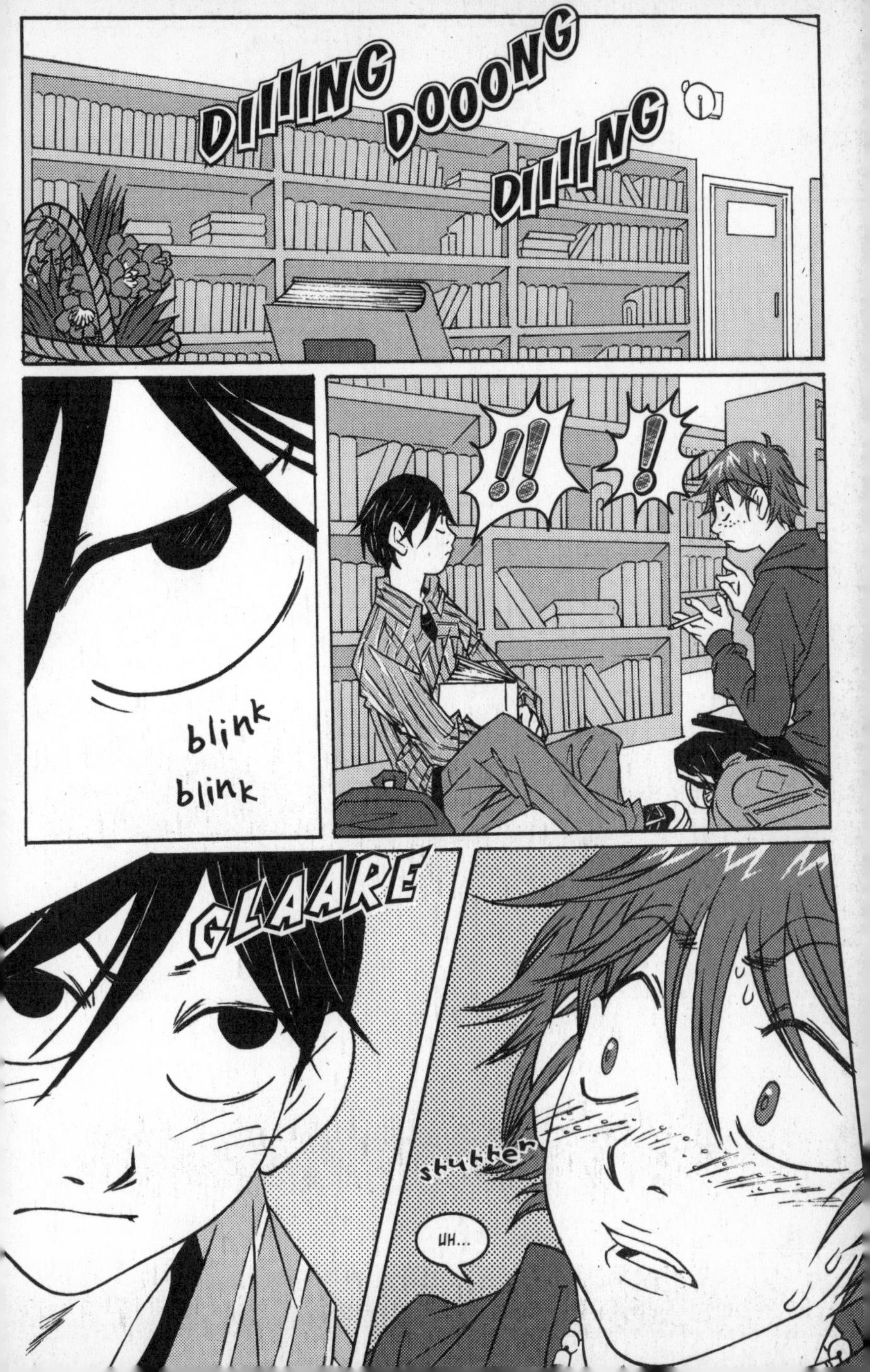
DIIING
DOOONG
DIIING
blink
blink
!!
!
GLAARE
stutter
UH...

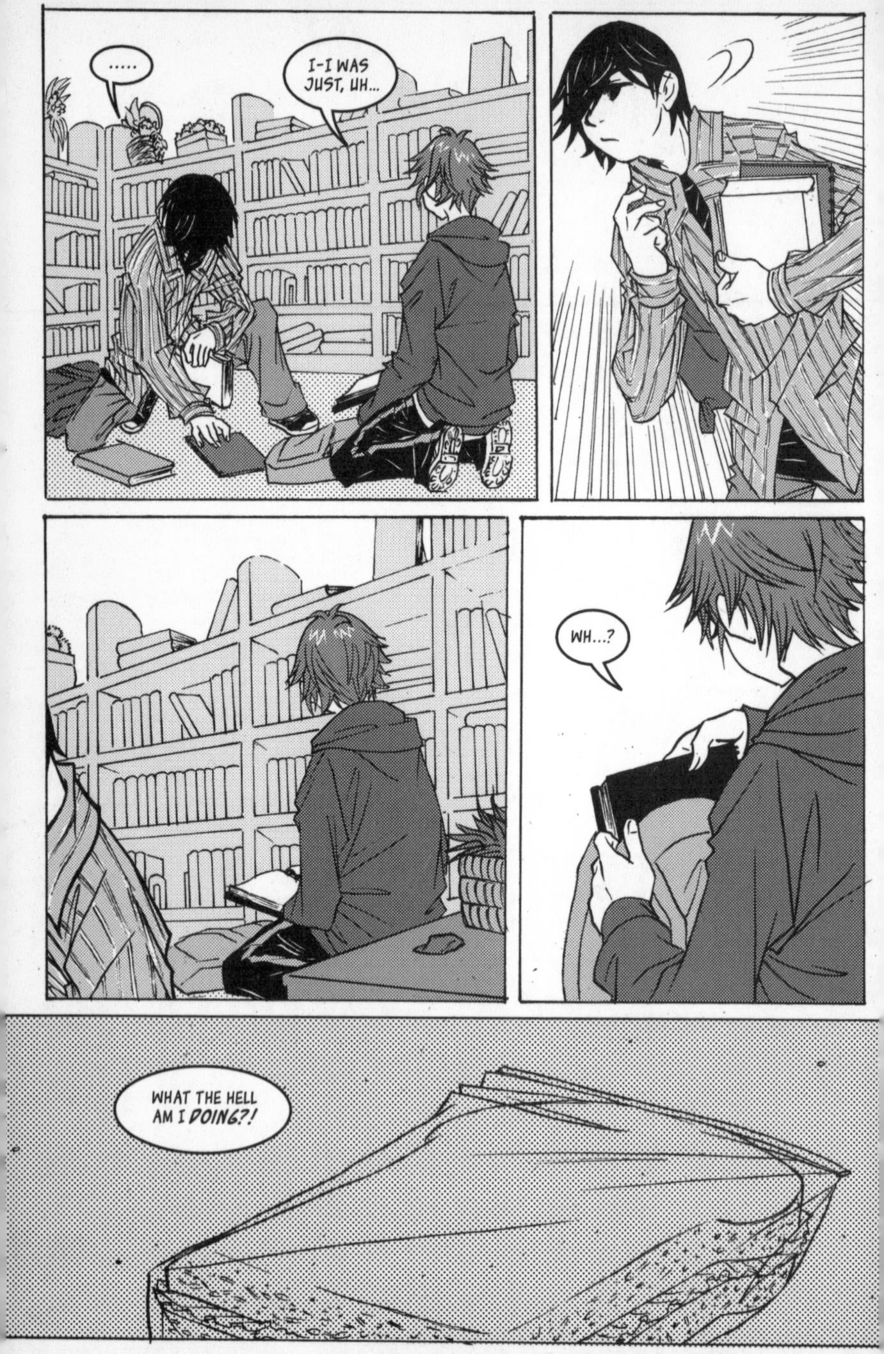
.....
I-I WAS JUST, UH...
WH...?
WHAT THE HELL AM I *DOING?!*

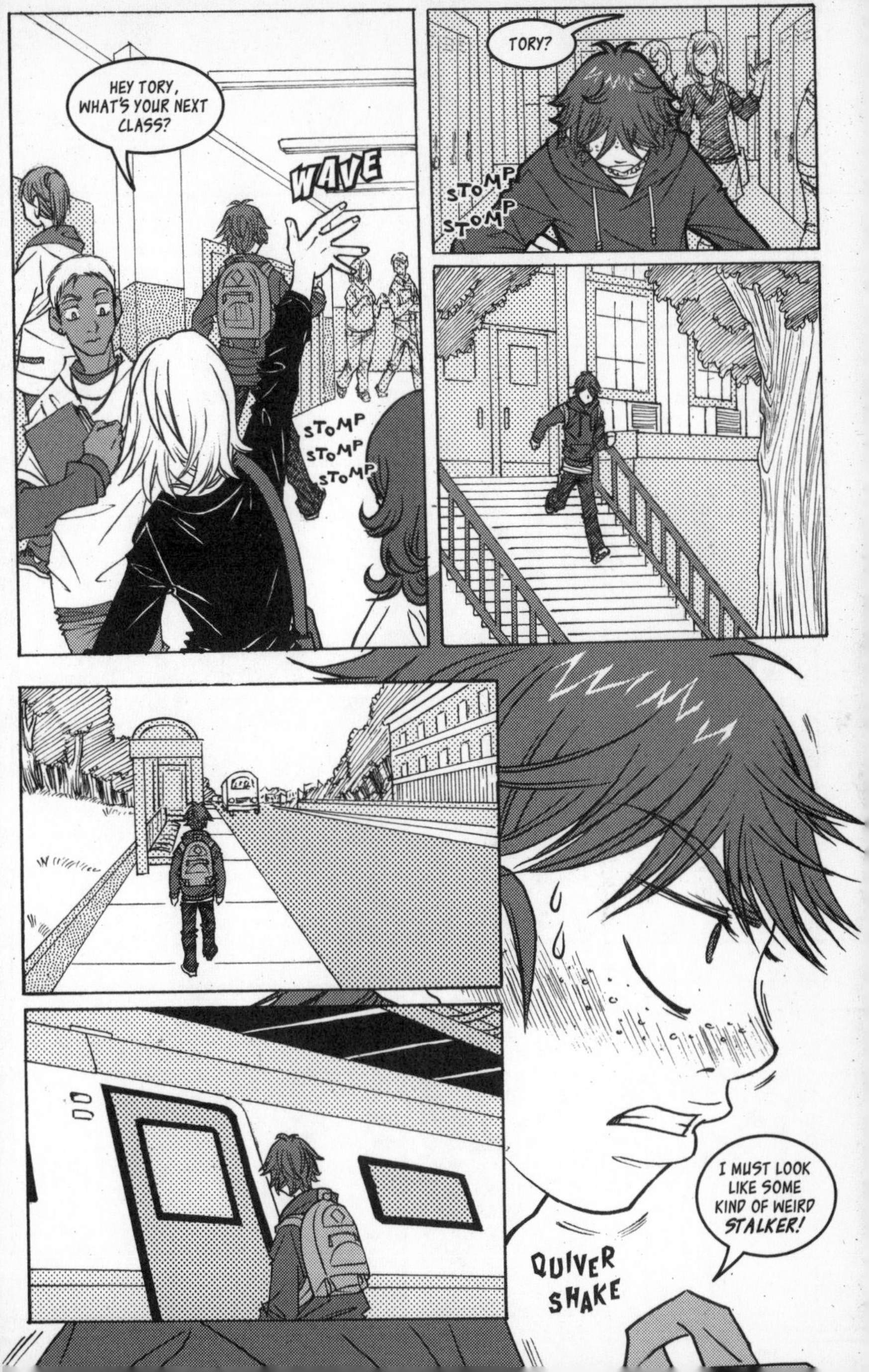
HEY TORY, WHAT'S YOUR NEXT CLASS?
WAVE
STOMP
STOMP
STOMP
TORY?
STOMP
STOMP
I MUST LOOK LIKE SOME KIND OF WEIRD *STALKER!*
QUIVER
SHAKE

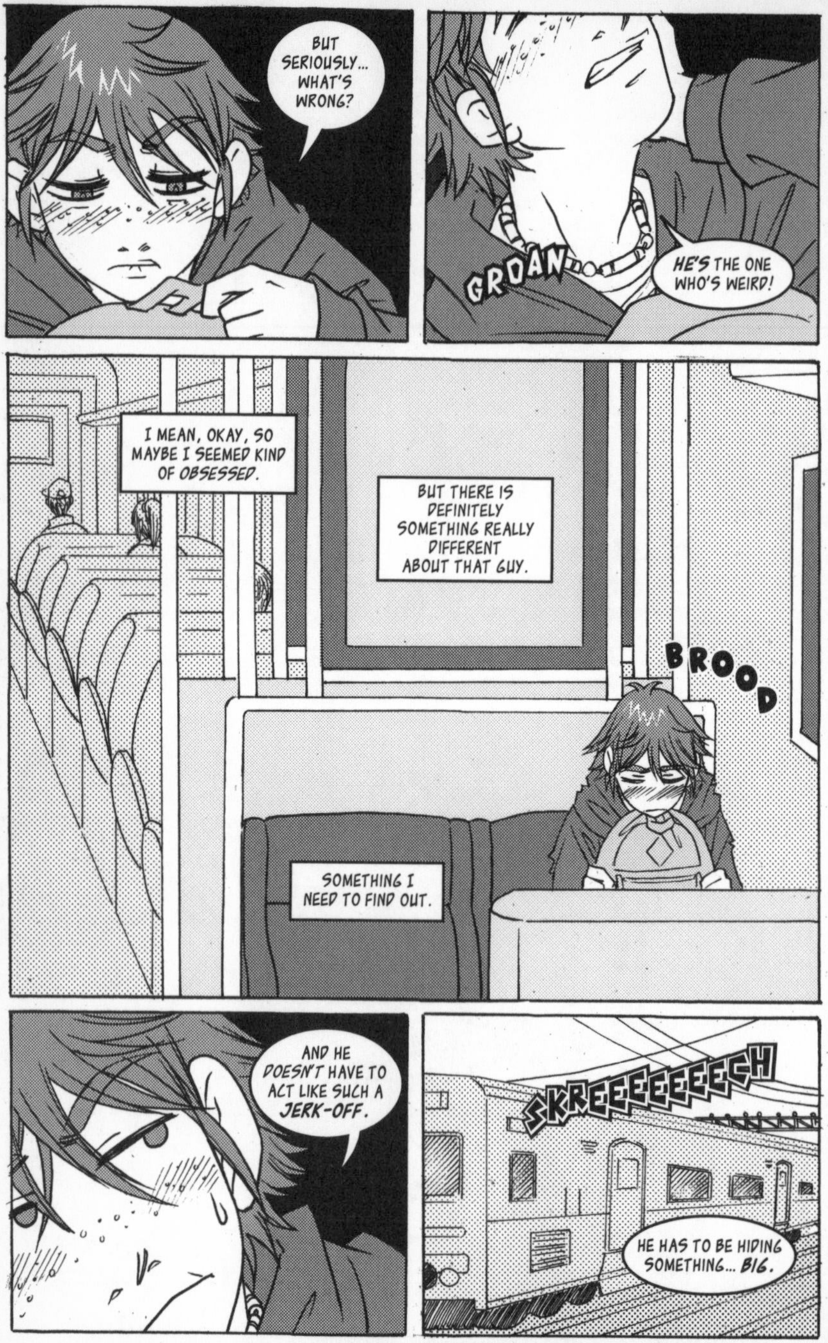

BUT SERIOUSLY... WHAT'S WRONG?
GROAN
HE'S THE ONE WHO'S WEIRD!
I MEAN, OKAY, SO MAYBE I SEEMED KIND OF OBSESSED.
BUT THERE IS DEFINITELY SOMETHING REALLY DIFFERENT ABOUT THAT GUY.
BROOD
SOMETHING I NEED TO FIND OUT.
AND HE DOESN'T HAVE TO ACT LIKE SUCH A JERK-OFF.
SKREEEEEEECH
HE HAS TO BE HIDING SOMETHING... BIG.

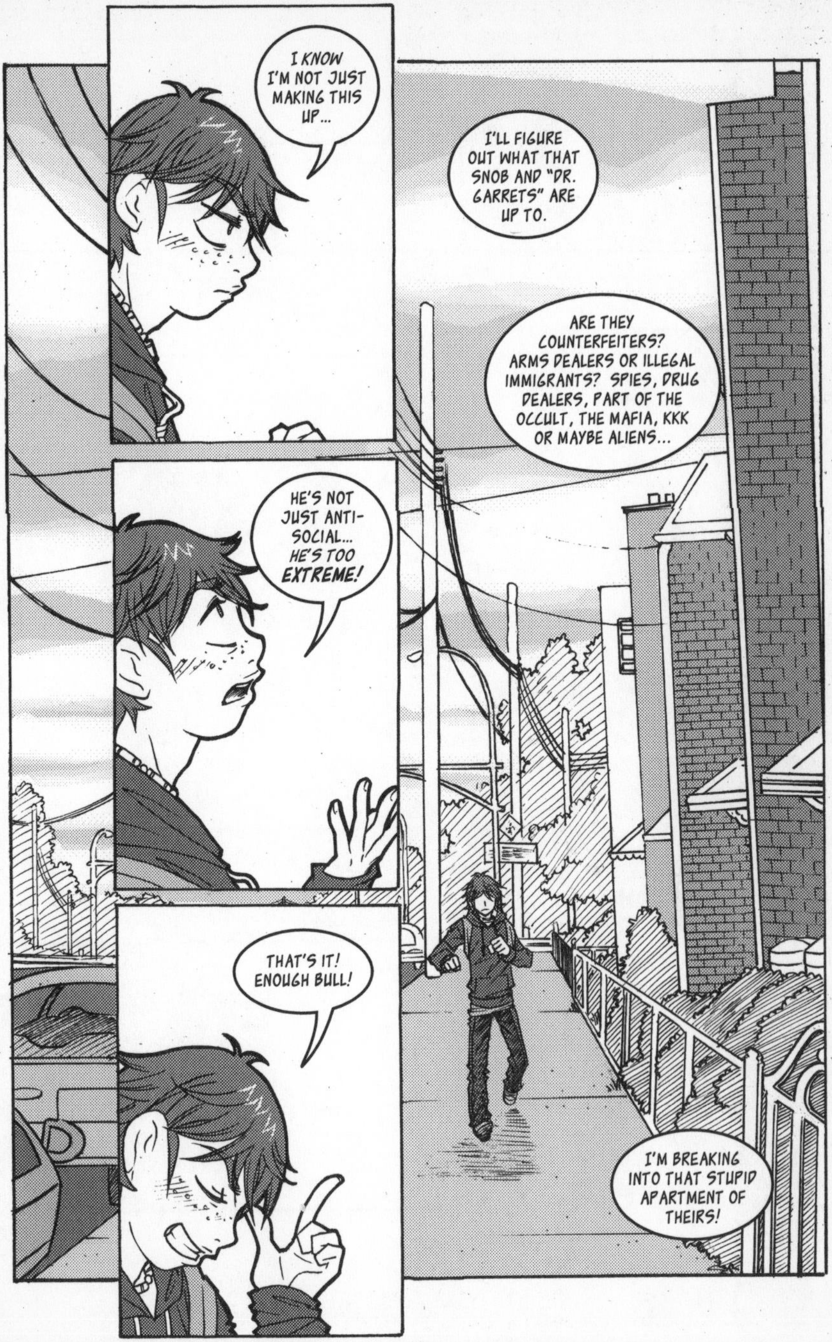
I KNOW I'M NOT JUST MAKING THIS UP...
HE'S NOT JUST ANTI-SOCIAL... HE'S TOO EXTREME!
THAT'S IT! ENOUGH BULL!
I'LL FIGURE OUT WHAT THAT SNOB AND "DR. GARRETS" ARE UP TO.
ARE THEY COUNTERFEITERS? ARMS DEALERS OR ILLEGAL IMMIGRANTS? SPIES, DRUG DEALERS, PART OF THE OCCULT, THE MAFIA, KKK OR MAYBE ALIENS...
I'M BREAKING INTO THAT STUPID APARTMENT OF THEIRS!

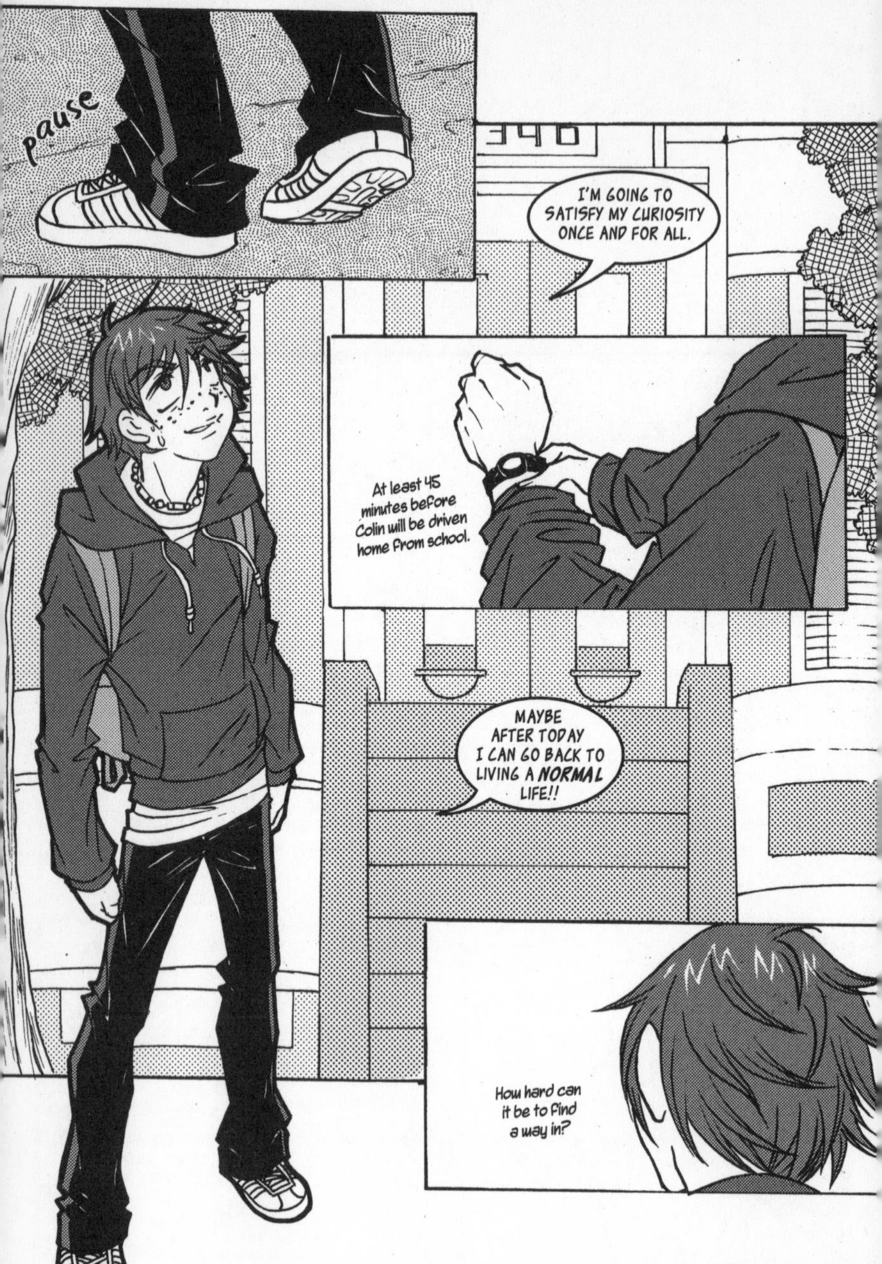
pause
340
I'M GOING TO SATISFY MY CURIOSITY ONCE AND FOR ALL.
At least 45 minutes before Colin will be driven home from school.
MAYBE AFTER TODAY I CAN GO BACK TO LIVING A **NORMAL** LIFE!!
How hard can it be to find a way in?

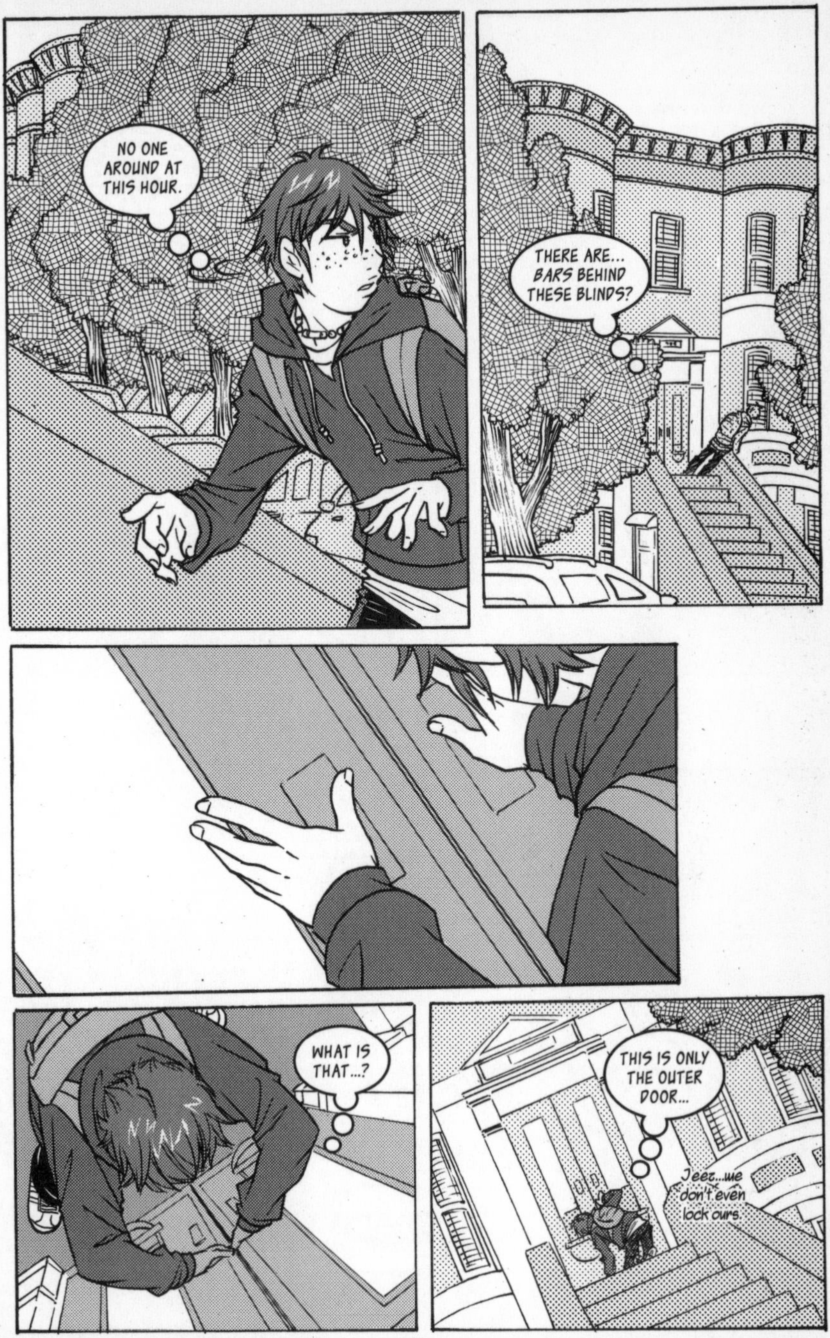
NO ONE AROUND AT THIS HOUR.
THERE ARE... BARS BEHIND THESE BLINDS?
WHAT IS THAT...?
THIS IS ONLY THE OUTER DOOR...
Jeez...we don't even lock ours.

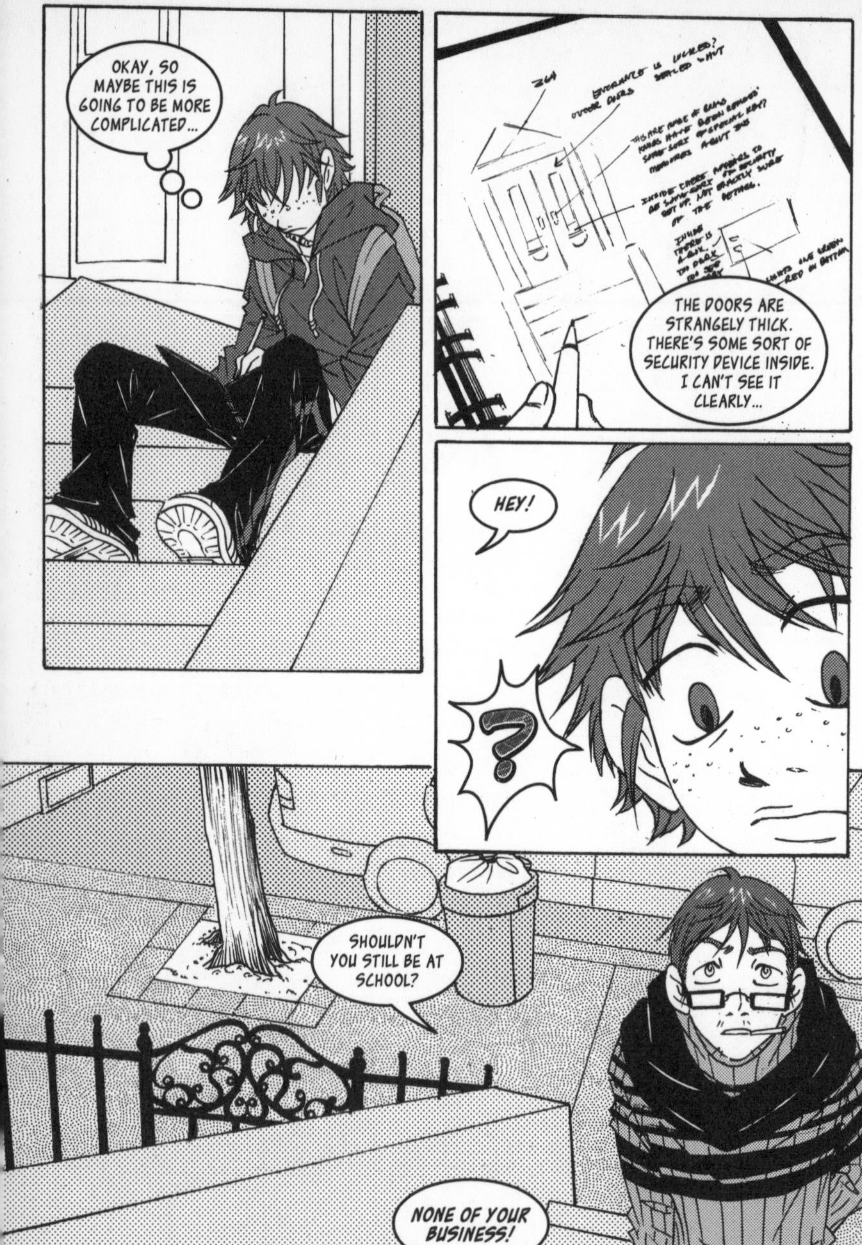
OKAY, SO MAYBE THIS IS GOING TO BE MORE COMPLICATED...
THE DOORS ARE STRANGELY THICK. THERE'S SOME SORT OF SECURITY DEVICE INSIDE. I CAN'T SEE IT CLEARLY...
HEY!
?
SHOULDN'T YOU STILL BE AT SCHOOL?
NONE OF YOUR BUSINESS!

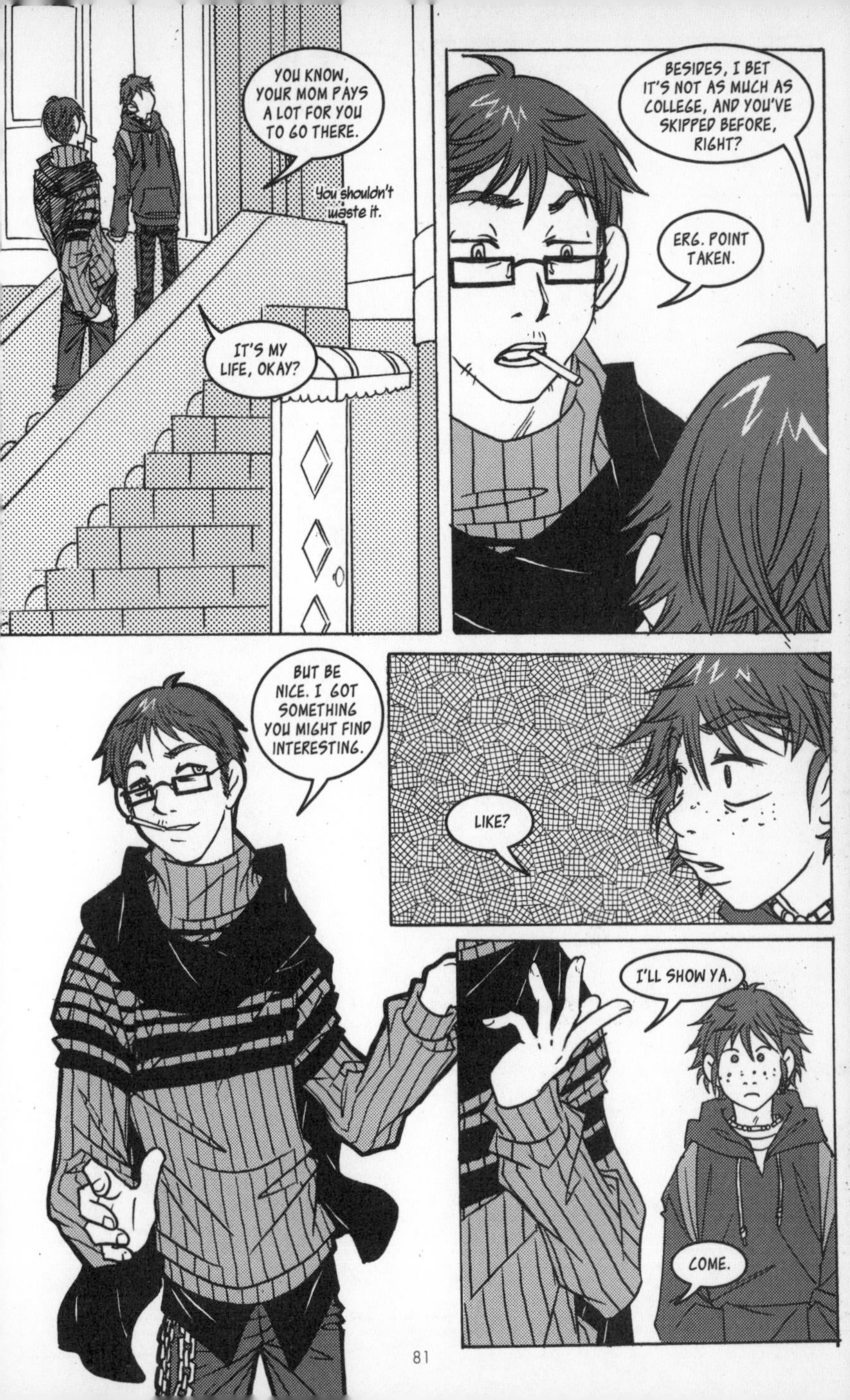

YOU KNOW, YOUR MOM PAYS A LOT FOR YOU TO GO THERE.
You shouldn't waste it.
IT'S MY LIFE, OKAY?
BESIDES, I BET IT'S NOT AS MUCH AS COLLEGE, AND YOU'VE SKIPPED BEFORE, RIGHT?
ERG. POINT TAKEN.
BUT BE NICE. I GOT SOMETHING YOU MIGHT FIND INTERESTING.
LIKE?
I'LL SHOW YA.
COME.

WHAT'S THIS SUPPOSED TO MEAN?

IT MEANS YOU OWE ME DINNER FOR A MONTH.

FUNNY.

THESE ARE THE RECORDS AND THE FILES ATTACHED TO THE LICENSE PLATE YOU HAD ME LOOK UP.

123454684543446
654546823313213
212131312313212
21321321300113
6765434
4321
32
212132
5487654356545

EH? YOU SAID YOU DIDN'T HAVE TIME!

AND THIS IS JUST A BUNCH OF RANDOM WORDS AND NUMBERS.

...Doesn't make sense...

And it's definitely not worth a month of meals, mooch!

OH, BUT IT DOES!

SO WHAT'S IT MEAN?

PATIENCE, I'M GETTING THERE.

tappa
tap
tap
tap

THESE WORDS WERE ENCRYPTED; TAKEN FROM CLASSIFIED FILES ASSOCIATED WITH THE OWNERS OF THIS VEHICLE.

WAIT A SECOND. THAT PHRASE STANDS OUT.

Who's the scary one, here? Huh?

"THE GAIA PROJECT...?"

I NOTICED THAT TOO.

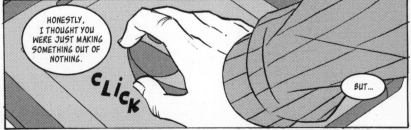

HONESTLY, I THOUGHT YOU WERE JUST MAKING SOMETHING OUT OF NOTHING.

CLICK

BUT...

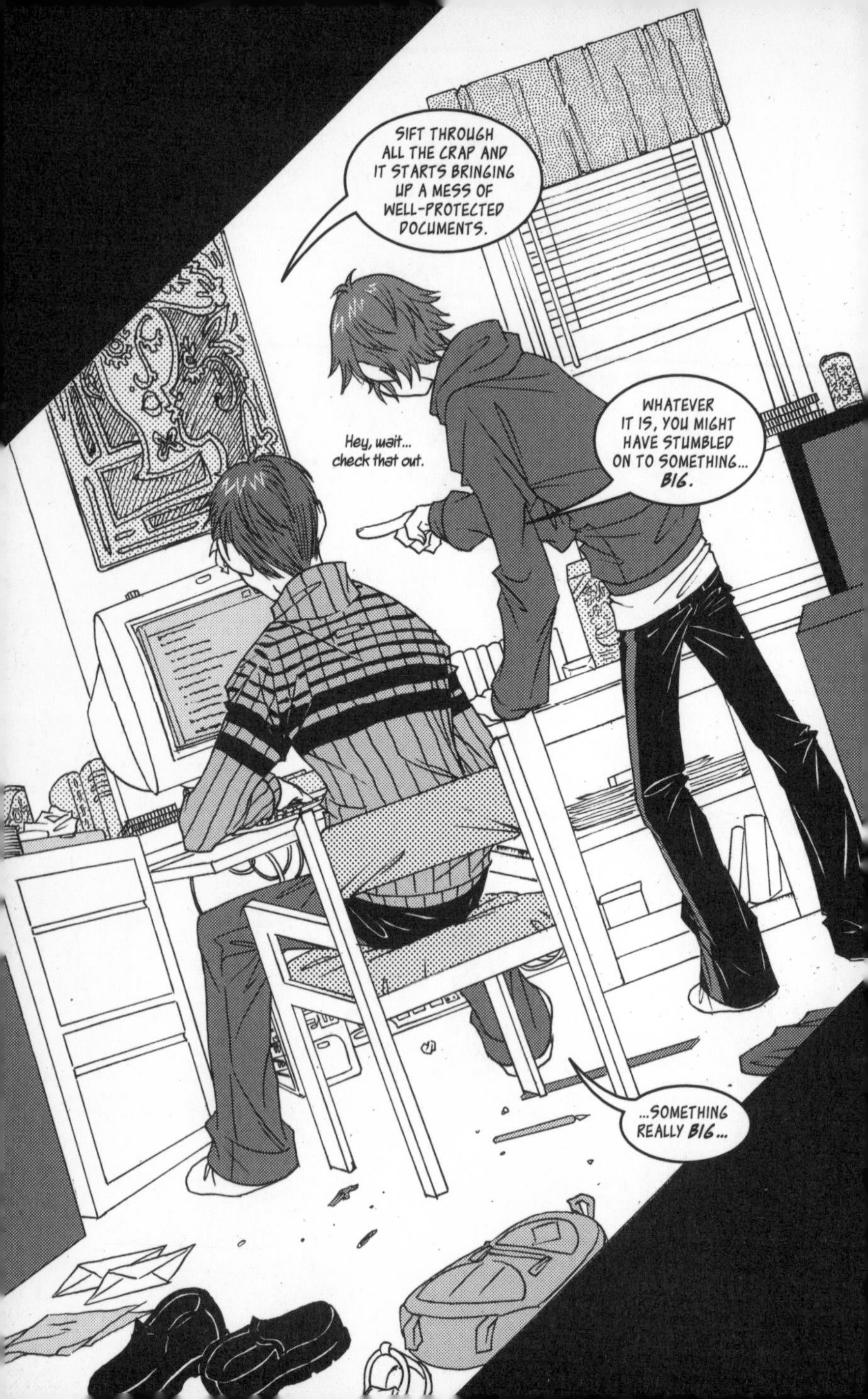
SIFT THROUGH ALL THE CRAP AND IT STARTS BRINGING UP A MESS OF WELL-PROTECTED DOCUMENTS.
Hey, wait... check that out.
WHATEVER IT IS, YOU MIGHT HAVE STUMBLED ON TO SOMETHING... BIG.
...SOMETHING REALLY BIG...

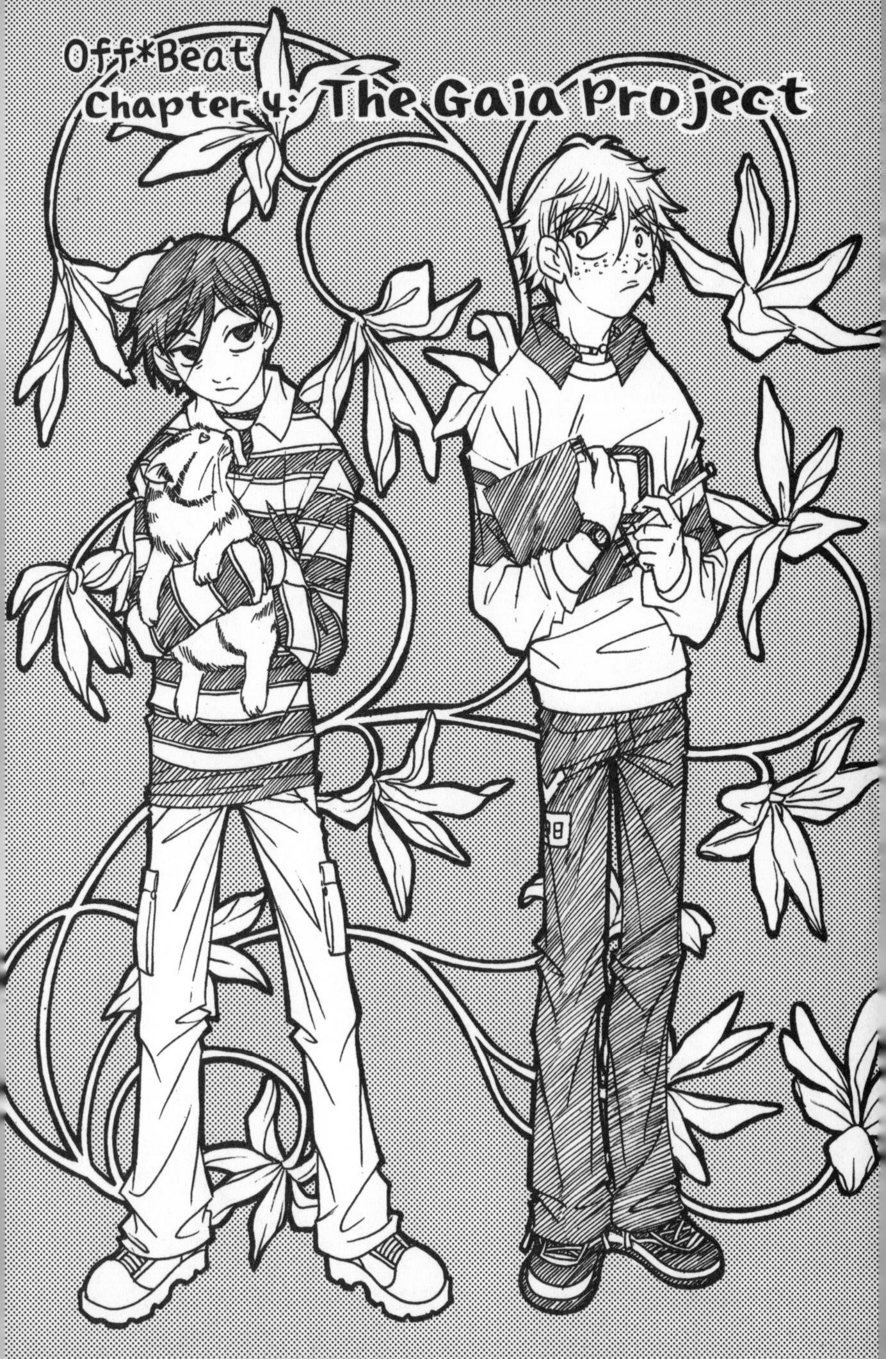
Off*Beat
Chapter 4: The Gaia Project

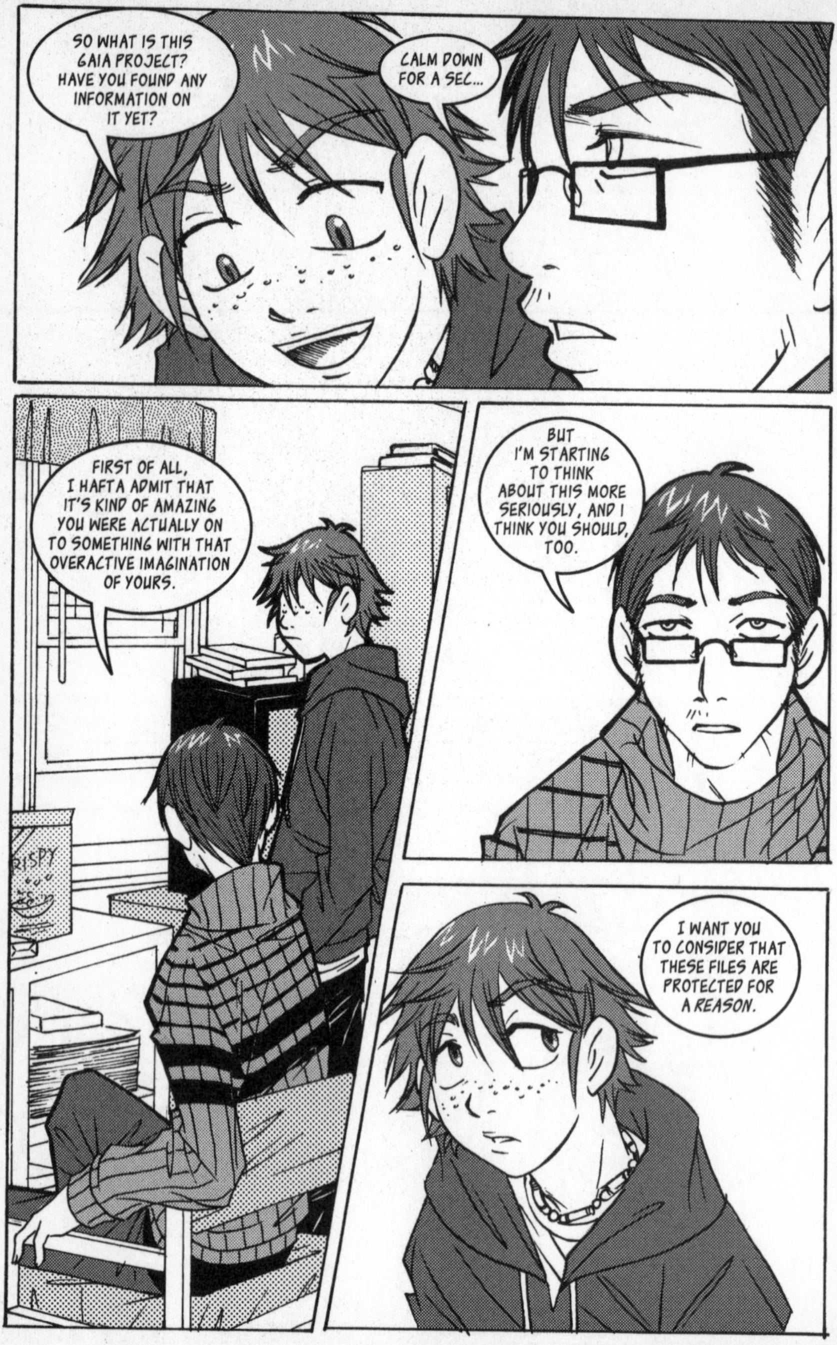
SO WHAT IS THIS GAIA PROJECT? HAVE YOU FOUND ANY INFORMATION ON IT YET?
CALM DOWN FOR A SEC...
FIRST OF ALL, I HAFTA ADMIT THAT IT'S KIND OF AMAZING YOU WERE ACTUALLY ON TO SOMETHING WITH THAT OVERACTIVE IMAGINATION OF YOURS.
BUT I'M STARTING TO THINK ABOUT THIS MORE SERIOUSLY, AND I THINK YOU SHOULD, TOO.
I WANT YOU TO CONSIDER THAT THESE FILES ARE PROTECTED FOR A *REASON*.

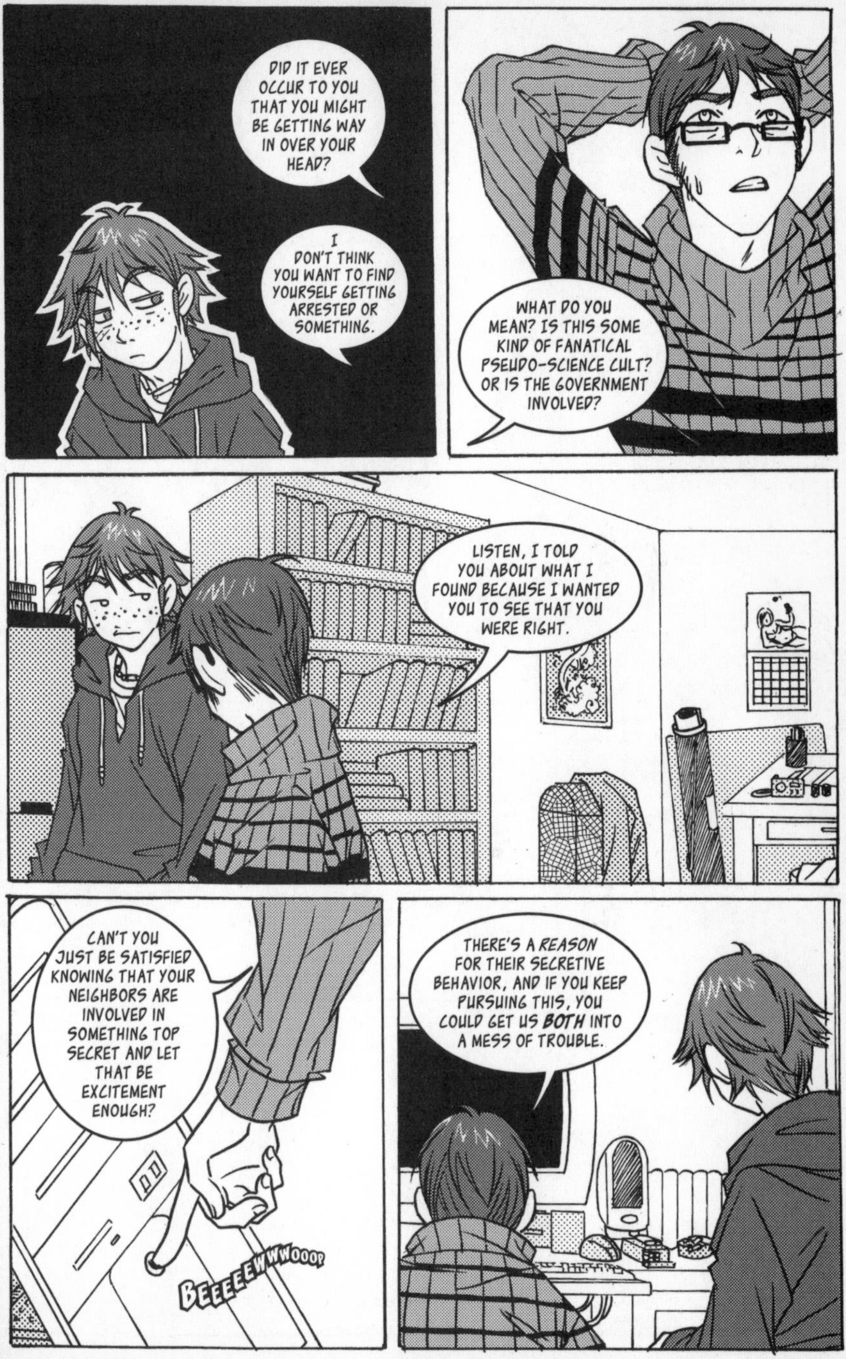
DID IT EVER OCCUR TO YOU THAT YOU MIGHT BE GETTING WAY IN OVER YOUR HEAD?
I DON'T THINK YOU WANT TO FIND YOURSELF GETTING ARRESTED OR SOMETHING.
WHAT DO YOU MEAN? IS THIS SOME KIND OF FANATICAL PSEUDO-SCIENCE CULT? OR IS THE GOVERNMENT INVOLVED?
LISTEN, I TOLD YOU ABOUT WHAT I FOUND BECAUSE I WANTED YOU TO SEE THAT YOU WERE RIGHT.
CAN'T YOU JUST BE SATISFIED KNOWING THAT YOUR NEIGHBORS ARE INVOLVED IN SOMETHING TOP SECRET AND LET THAT BE EXCITEMENT ENOUGH?
BEEEEEWWWOOOP
THERE'S A *REASON* FOR THEIR SECRETIVE BEHAVIOR, AND IF YOU KEEP PURSUING THIS, YOU COULD GET US ***BOTH*** INTO A MESS OF TROUBLE.

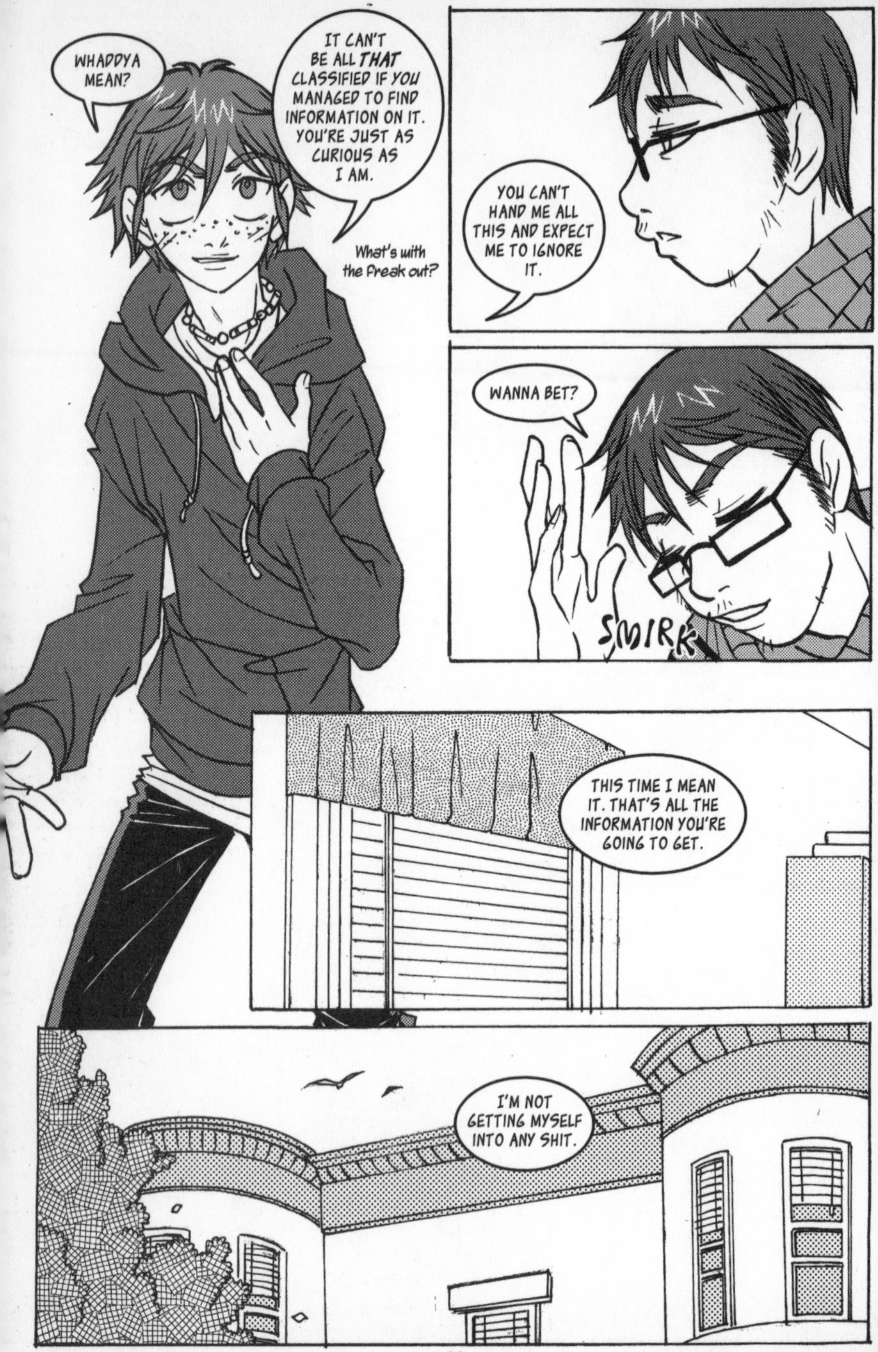
WHADDYA MEAN?
IT CAN'T BE ALL THAT CLASSIFIED IF YOU MANAGED TO FIND INFORMATION ON IT. YOU'RE JUST AS CURIOUS AS I AM.
What's with the freak out?
YOU CAN'T HAND ME ALL THIS AND EXPECT ME TO IGNORE IT.
WANNA BET?
SMIRK
THIS TIME I MEAN IT. THAT'S ALL THE INFORMATION YOU'RE GOING TO GET.
I'M NOT GETTING MYSELF INTO ANY SHIT.

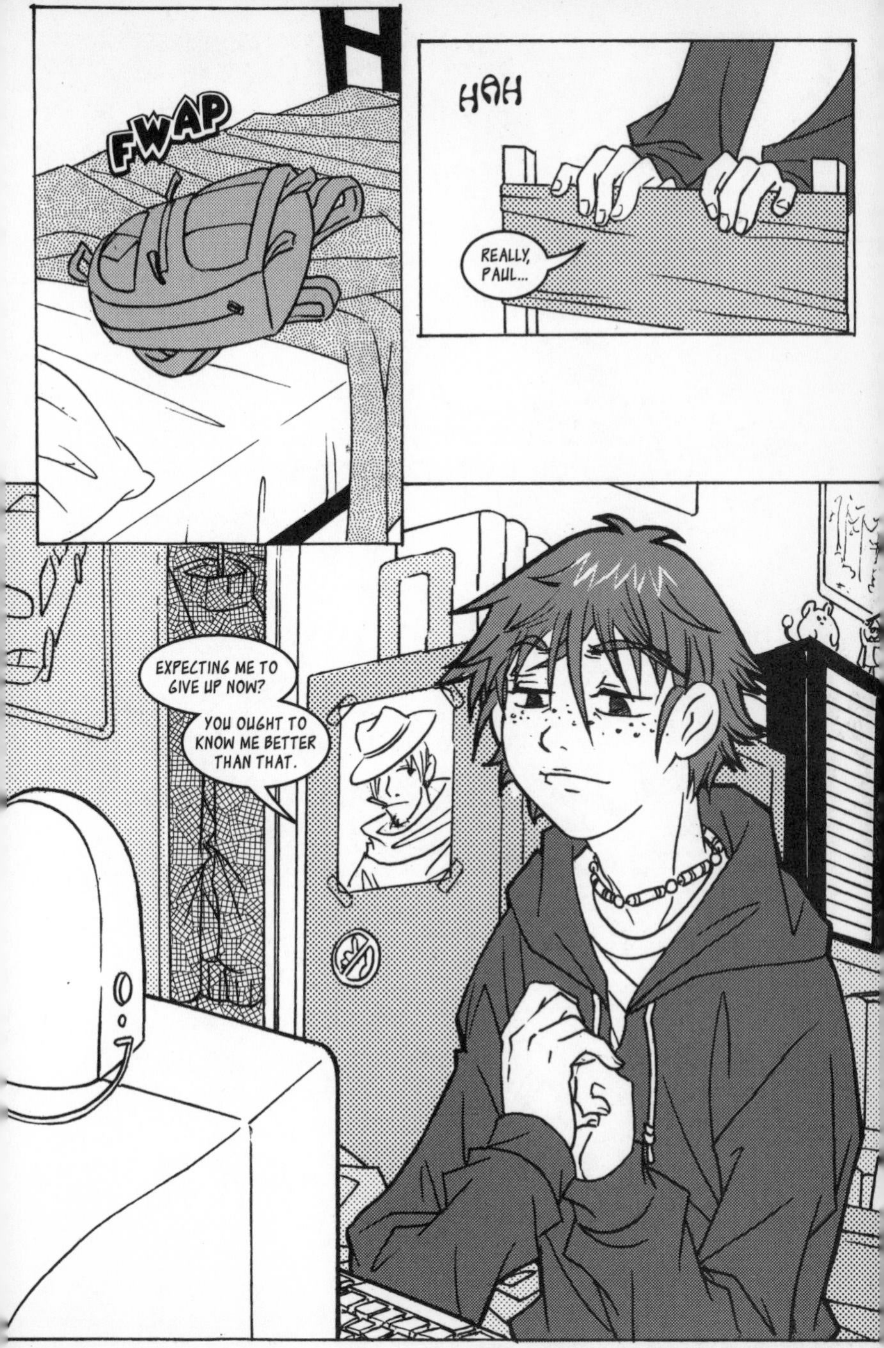
FWAP
HAH
REALLY, PAUL...
EXPECTING ME TO GIVE UP NOW?
YOU OUGHT TO KNOW ME BETTER THAN THAT.

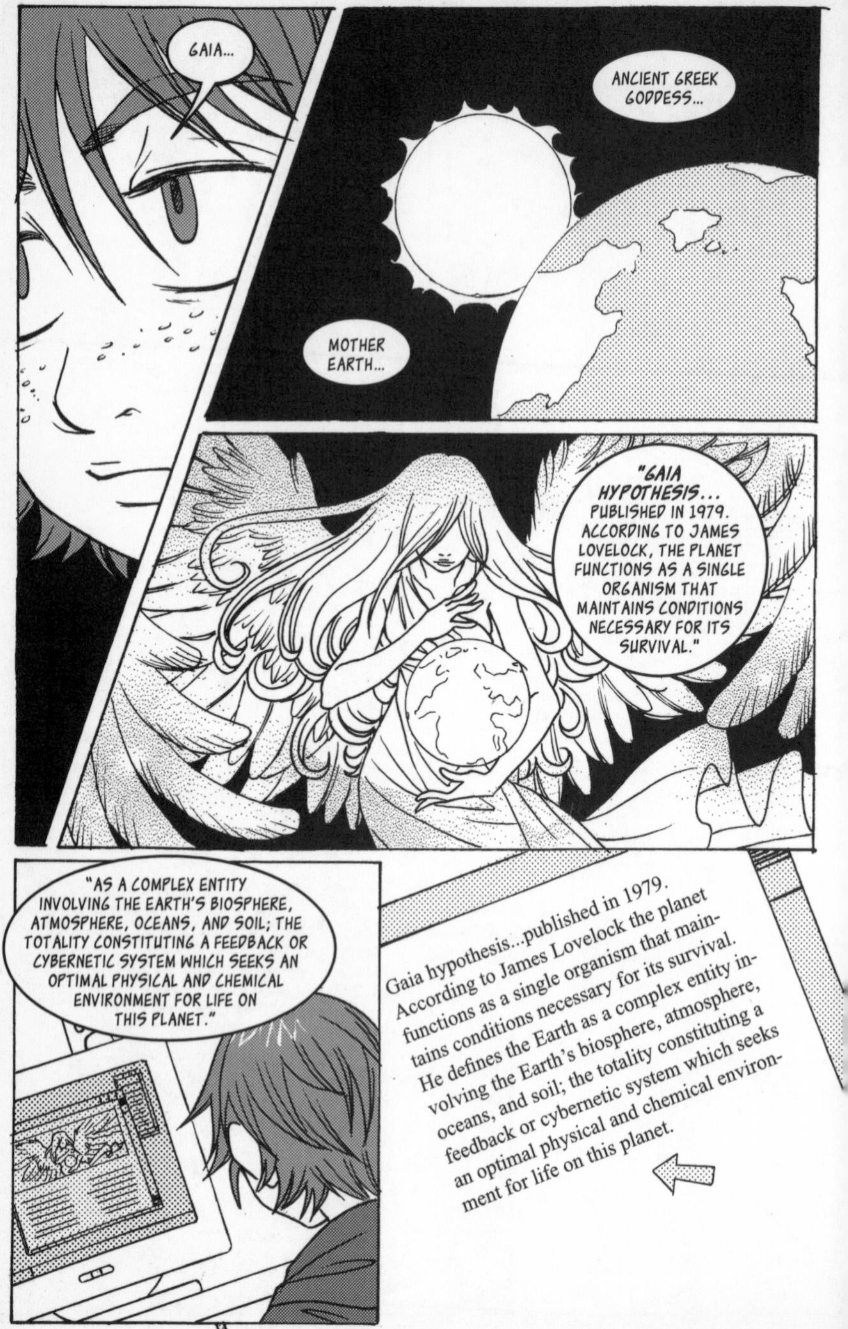
GAIA...
ANCIENT GREEK GODDESS...
MOTHER EARTH...
"GAIA HYPOTHESIS... PUBLISHED IN 1979. ACCORDING TO JAMES LOVELOCK, THE PLANET FUNCTIONS AS A SINGLE ORGANISM THAT MAINTAINS CONDITIONS NECESSARY FOR ITS SURVIVAL."
"AS A COMPLEX ENTITY INVOLVING THE EARTH'S BIOSPHERE, ATMOSPHERE, OCEANS, AND SOIL; THE TOTALITY CONSTITUTING A FEEDBACK OR CYBERNETIC SYSTEM WHICH SEEKS AN OPTIMAL PHYSICAL AND CHEMICAL ENVIRONMENT FOR LIFE ON THIS PLANET."
Gaia hypothesis...published in 1979. According to James Lovelock the planet functions as a single organism that maintains conditions necessary for its survival. He defines the Earth as a complex entity involving the Earth's biosphere, atmosphere, oceans, and soil; the totality constituting a feedback or cybernetic system which seeks an optimal physical and chemical environment for life on this planet.

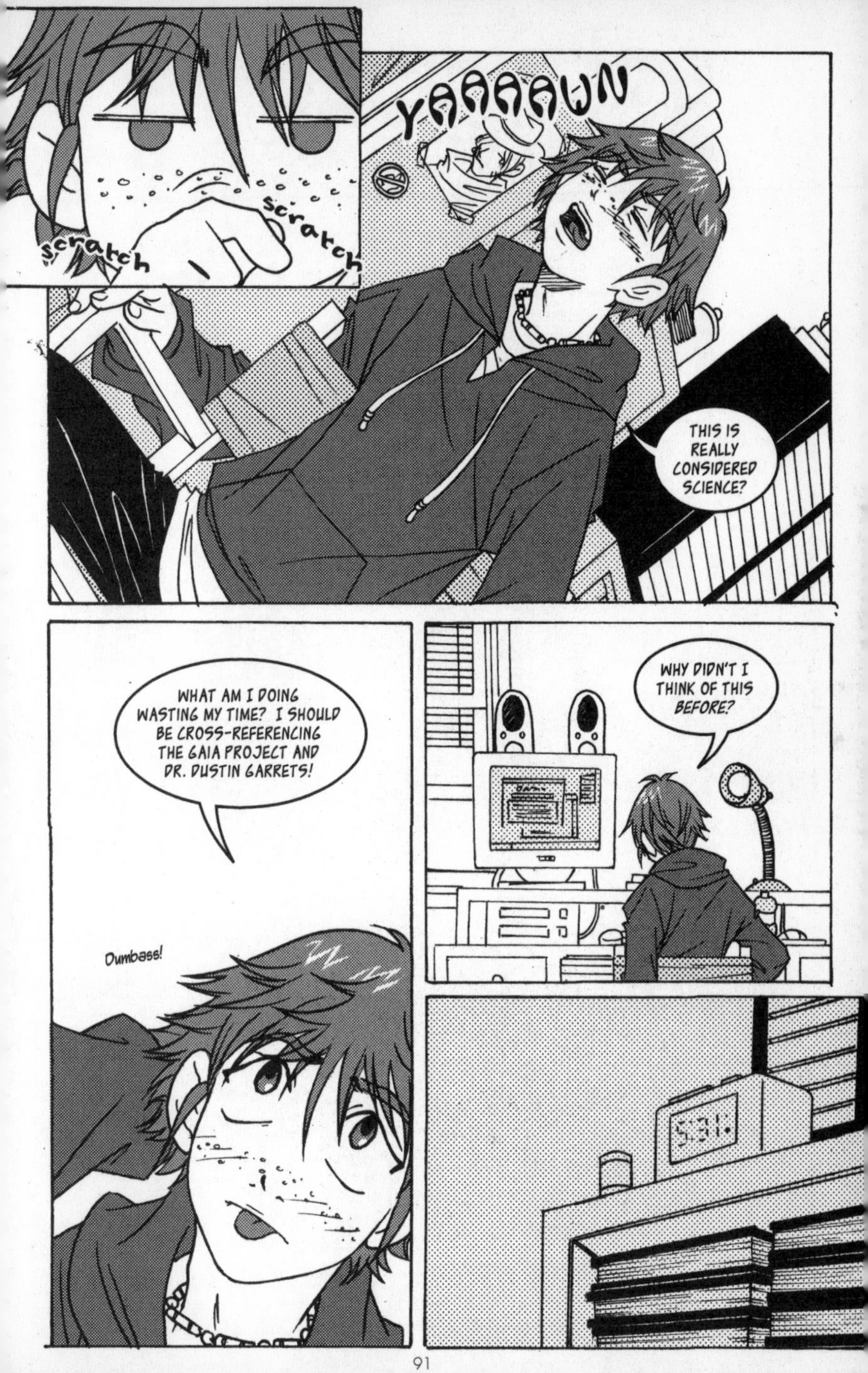
scratch
scratch
YAAAAAWN
THIS IS REALLY CONSIDERED SCIENCE?
WHAT AM I DOING WASTING MY TIME? I SHOULD BE CROSS-REFERENCING THE GAIA PROJECT AND DR. DUSTIN GARRETS!
Dumbass!
WHY DIDN'T I THINK OF THIS *BEFORE?*
5:31

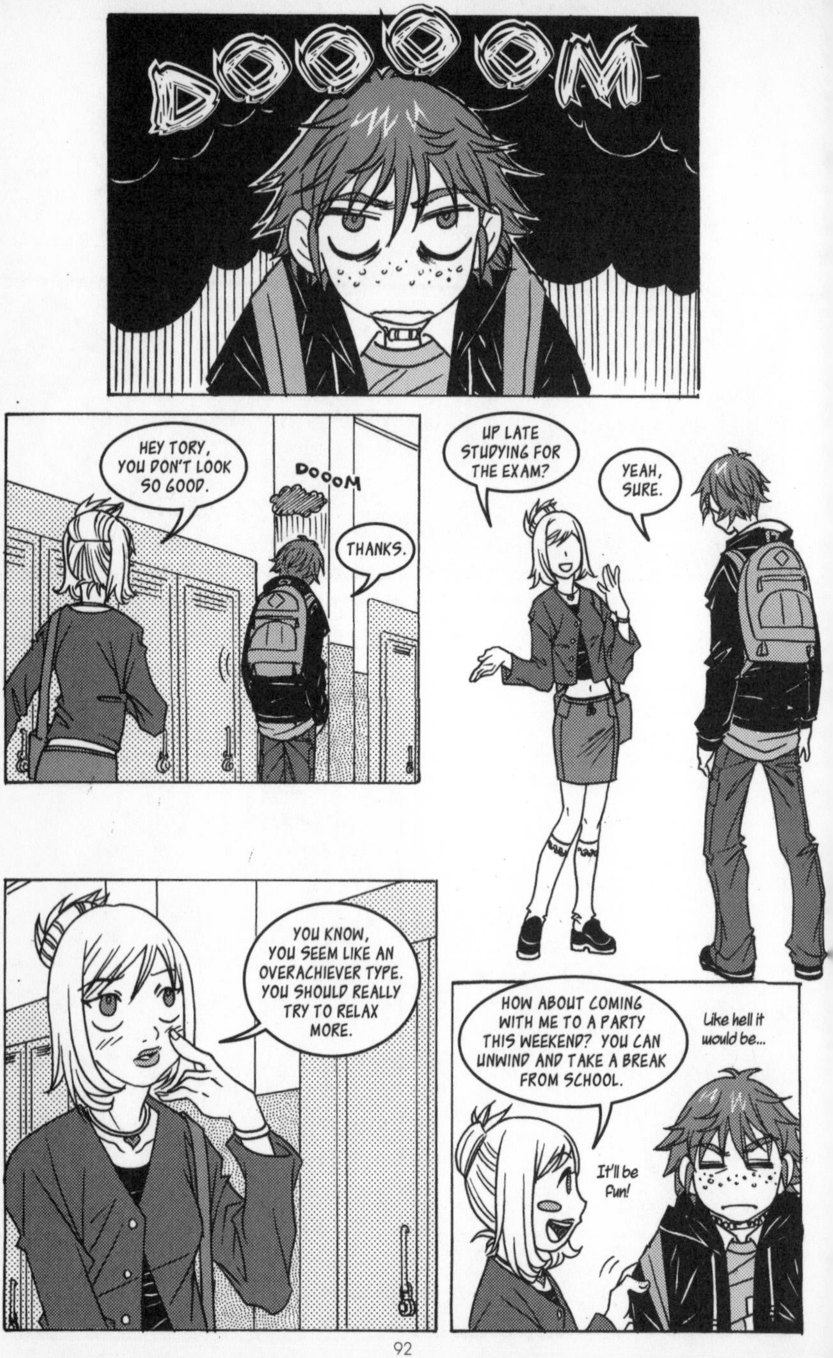
DOOOOOM
HEY TORY, YOU DON'T LOOK SO GOOD.
DOOOM
THANKS.
UP LATE STUDYING FOR THE EXAM?
YEAH, SURE.
YOU KNOW, YOU SEEM LIKE AN OVERACHIEVER TYPE. YOU SHOULD REALLY TRY TO RELAX MORE.
HOW ABOUT COMING WITH ME TO A PARTY THIS WEEKEND? YOU CAN UNWIND AND TAKE A BREAK FROM SCHOOL.
It'll be fun!
Like hell it would be...

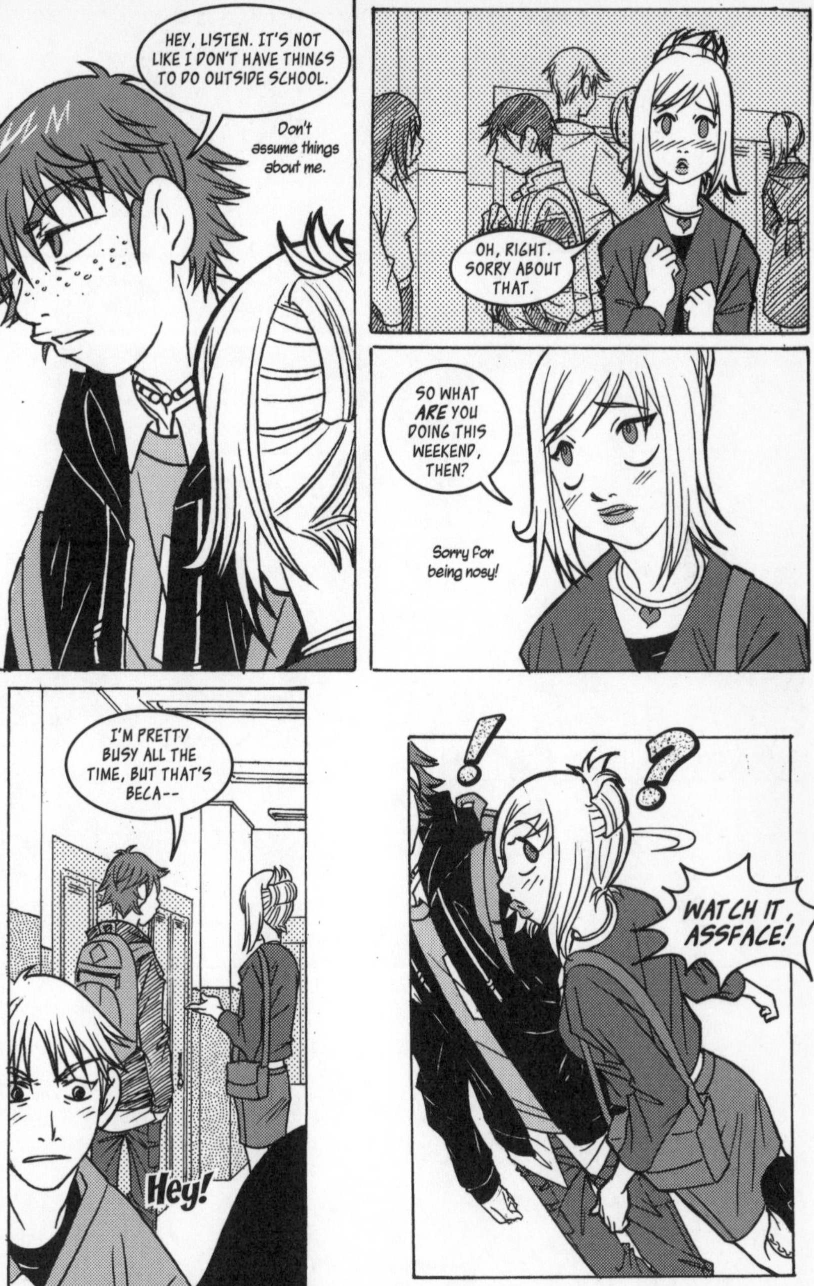
HEY, LISTEN. IT'S NOT LIKE I DON'T HAVE THINGS TO DO OUTSIDE SCHOOL.
Don't assume things about me.
OH, RIGHT. SORRY ABOUT THAT.
SO WHAT **ARE** YOU DOING THIS WEEKEND, THEN?
Sorry for being nosy!
I'M PRETTY BUSY ALL THE TIME, BUT THAT'S BECA--
Hey!
!
?
WATCH IT, ASSFACE!

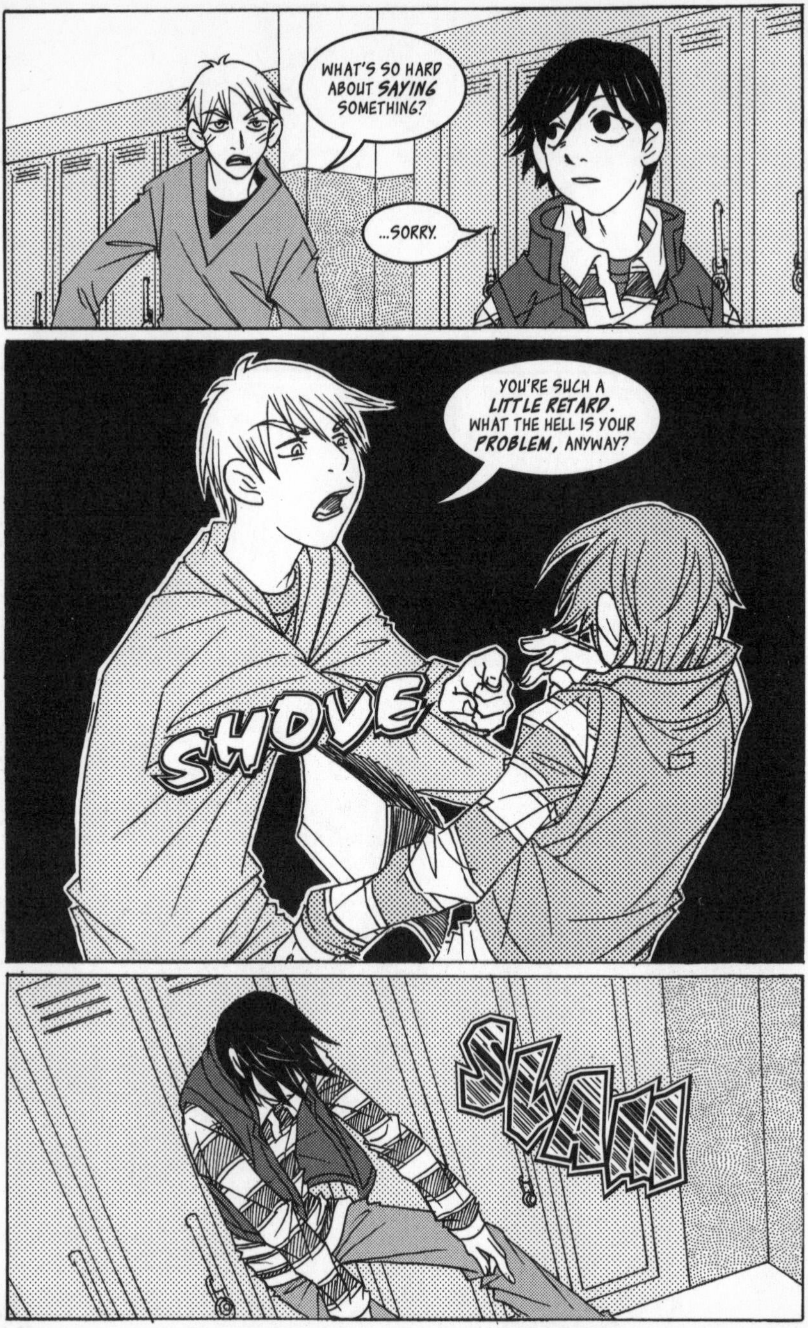
WHAT'S SO HARD ABOUT SAYING SOMETHING?
...SORRY.
YOU'RE SUCH A LITTLE RETARD. WHAT THE HELL IS YOUR PROBLEM, ANYWAY?
SHOVE
SLAM

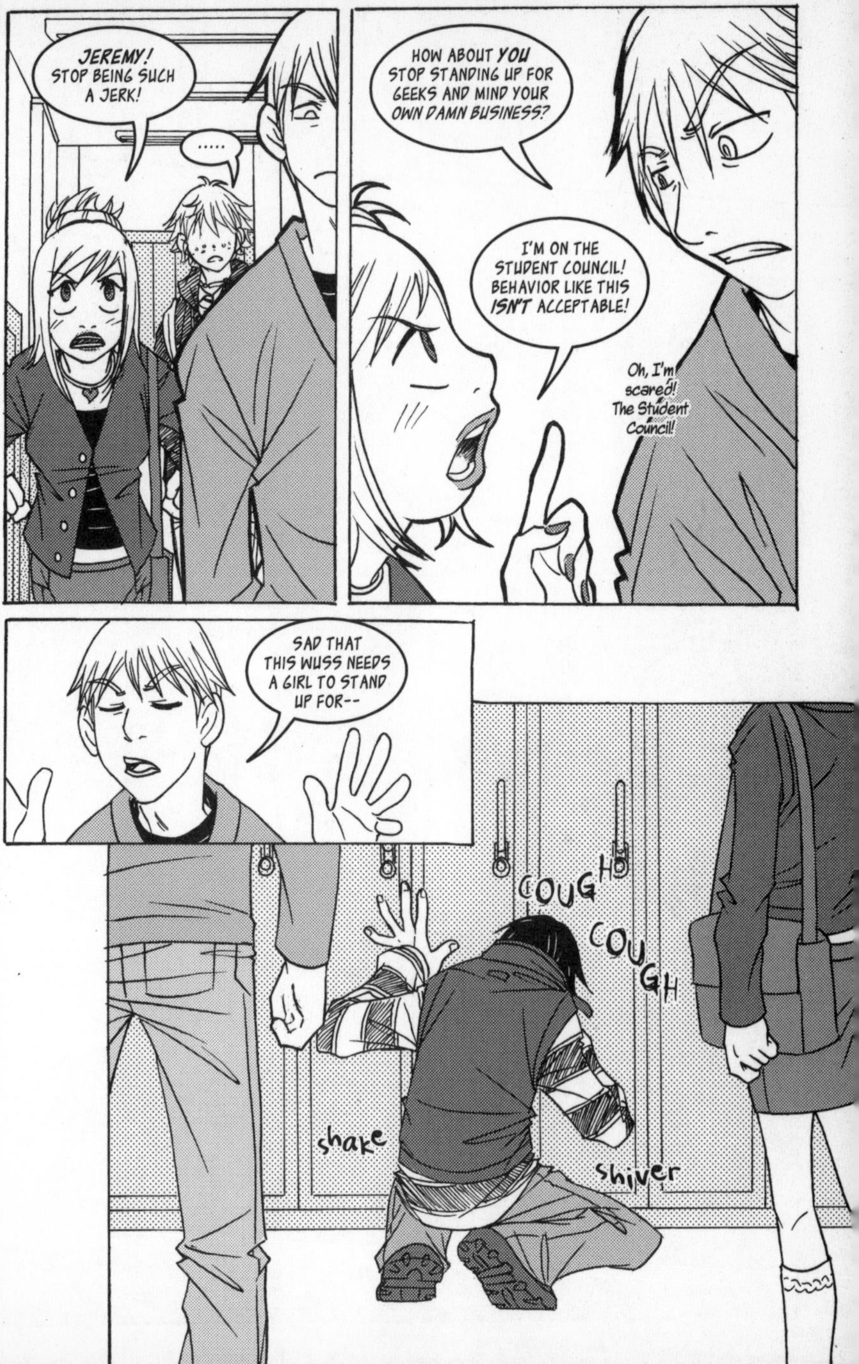
JEREMY! STOP BEING SUCH A JERK!
......
HOW ABOUT YOU STOP STANDING UP FOR GEEKS AND MIND YOUR OWN DAMN BUSINESS?
I'M ON THE STUDENT COUNCIL! BEHAVIOR LIKE THIS ISN'T ACCEPTABLE!
Oh, I'm scared! The Student Council!
SAD THAT THIS WUSS NEEDS A GIRL TO STAND UP FOR--
COUGH
COUGH
shake
shiver

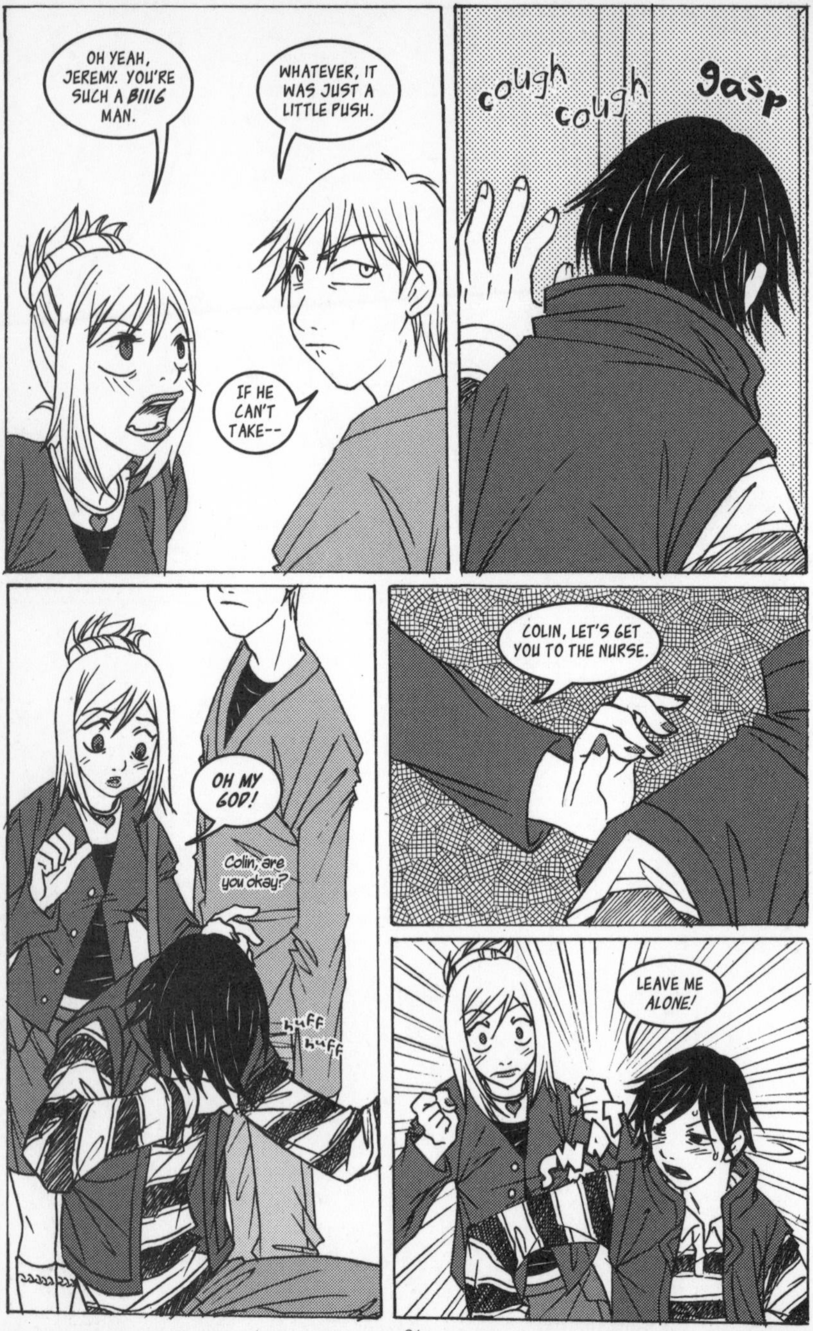
OH YEAH, JEREMY. YOU'RE SUCH A BIIIG MAN.
WHATEVER, IT WAS JUST A LITTLE PUSH.
IF HE CAN'T TAKE--
cough cough
gasp
OH MY GOD!
Colin, are you okay?
huff huff
COLIN, LET'S GET YOU TO THE NURSE.
LEAVE ME ALONE!
SWAT

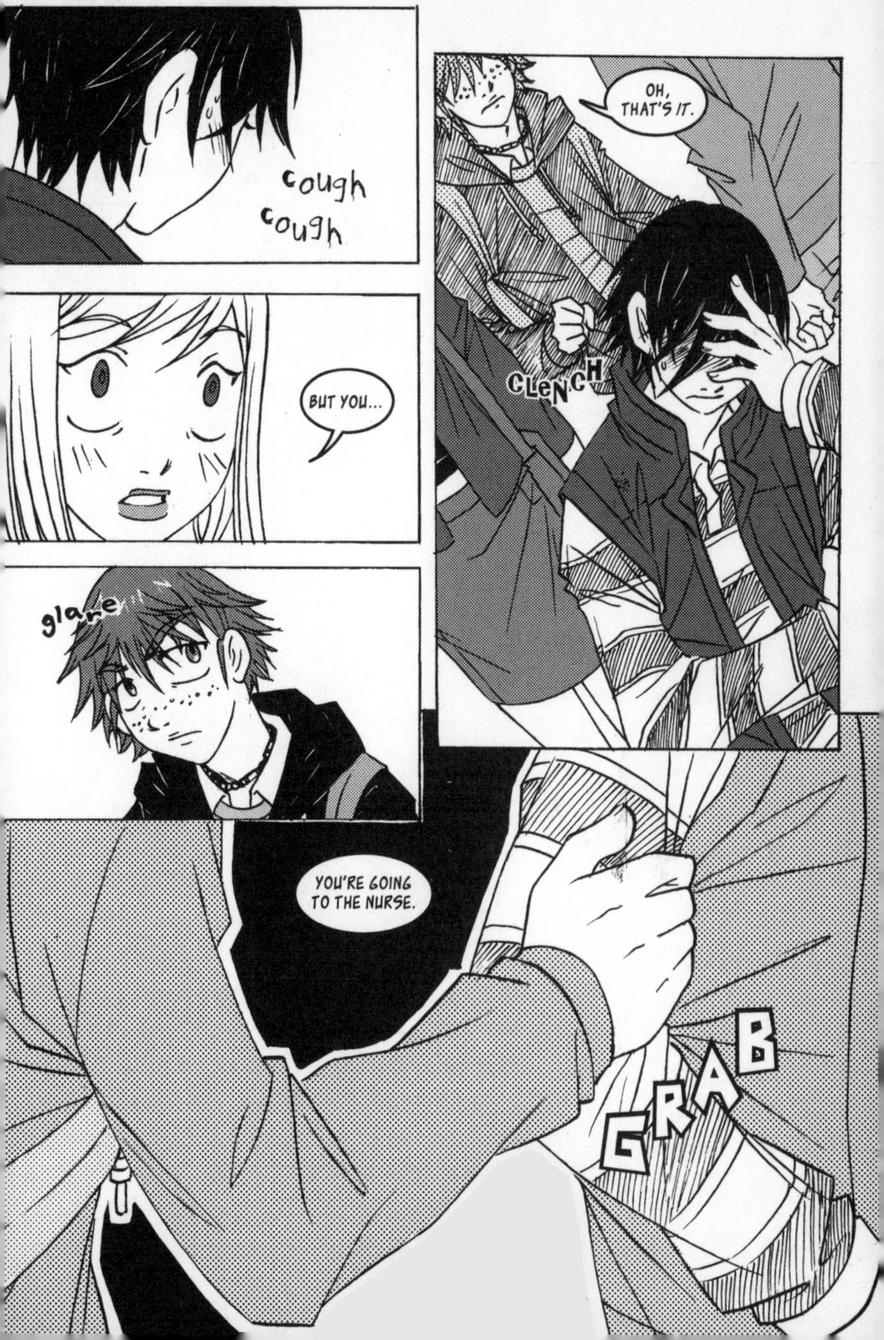
cough
cough
BUT YOU...
glare
OH, THAT'S IT.
CLENCH
YOU'RE GOING TO THE NURSE.
GRAB

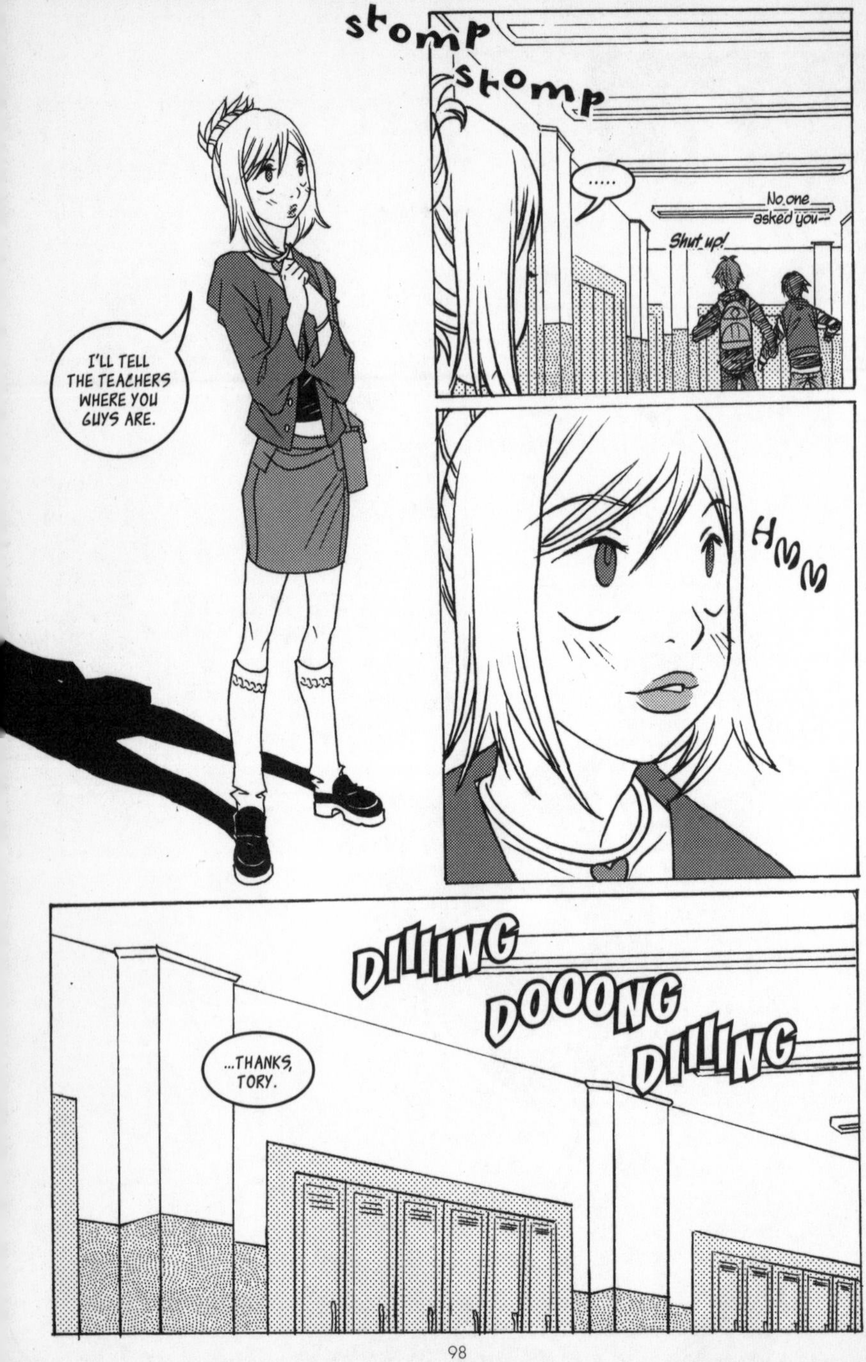
I'LL TELL THE TEACHERS WHERE YOU GUYS ARE.
stomp stomp
.....
No one asked you--
Shut up!
HMM
...THANKS, TORY.
DIIIING DOOONG DIIING

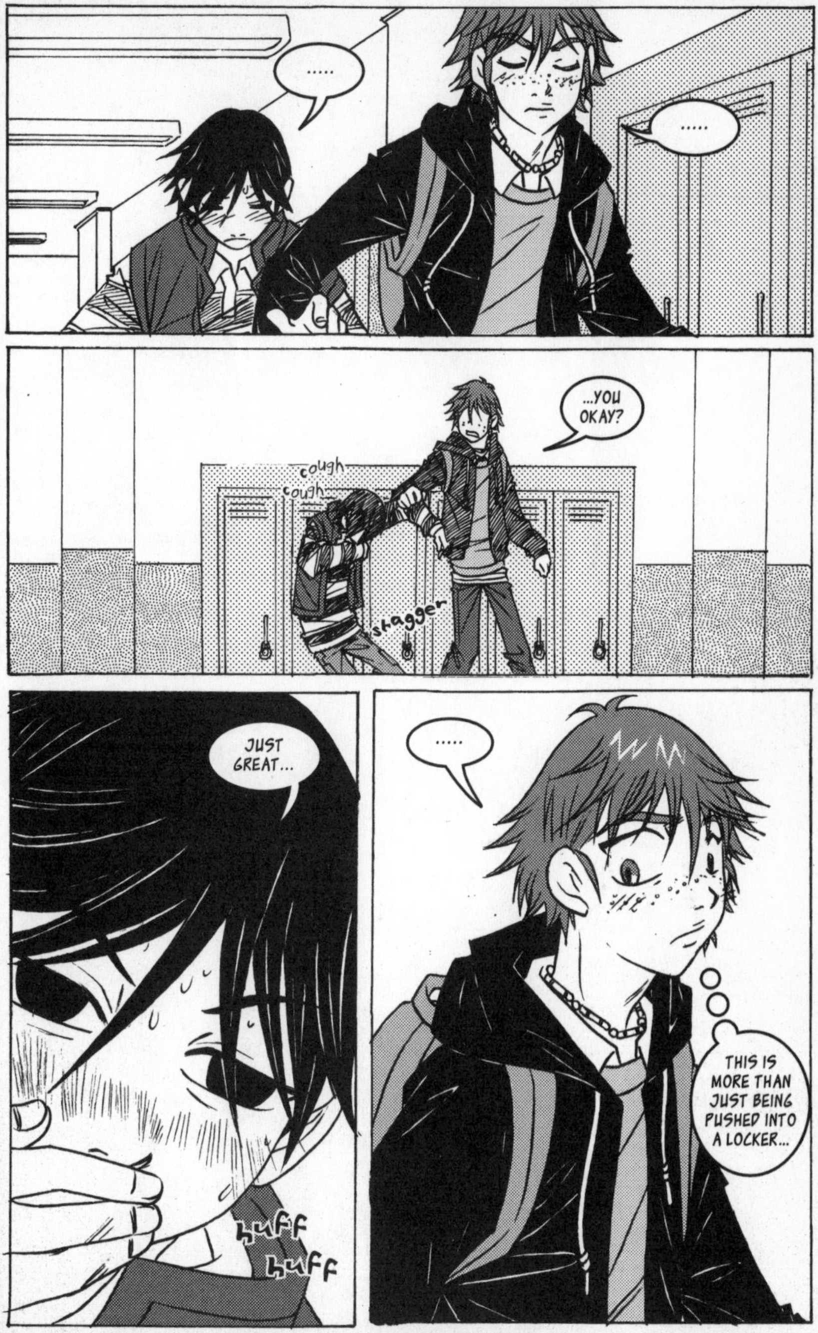
.....
.....
...YOU OKAY?
cough
cough
stagger
JUST GREAT...
huff
huff
.....
THIS IS MORE THAN JUST BEING PUSHED INTO A LOCKER...

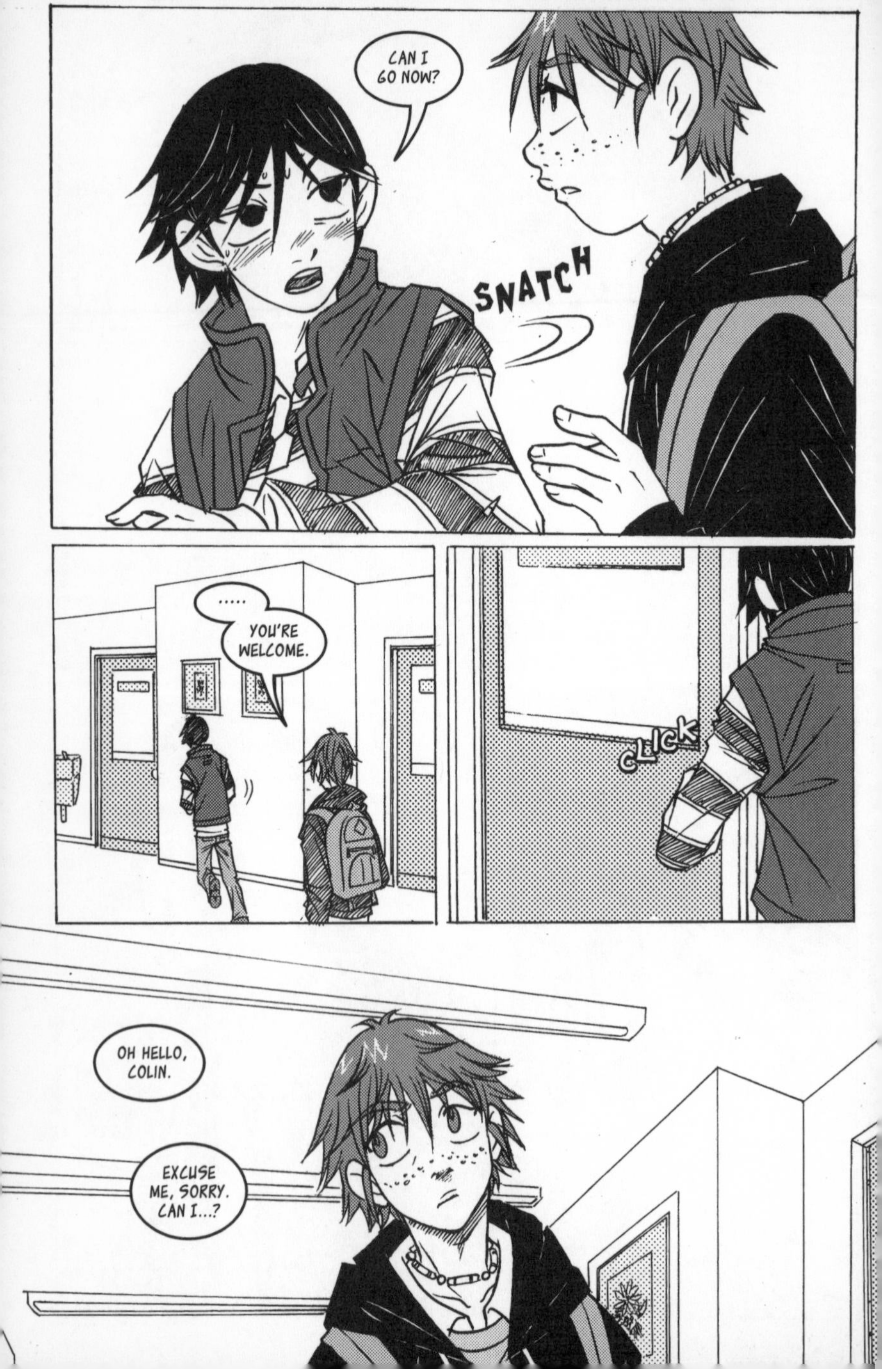
CAN I GO NOW?
SNATCH
......
YOU'RE WELCOME.
CLICK
OH HELLO, COLIN.
EXCUSE ME, SORRY. CAN I...?

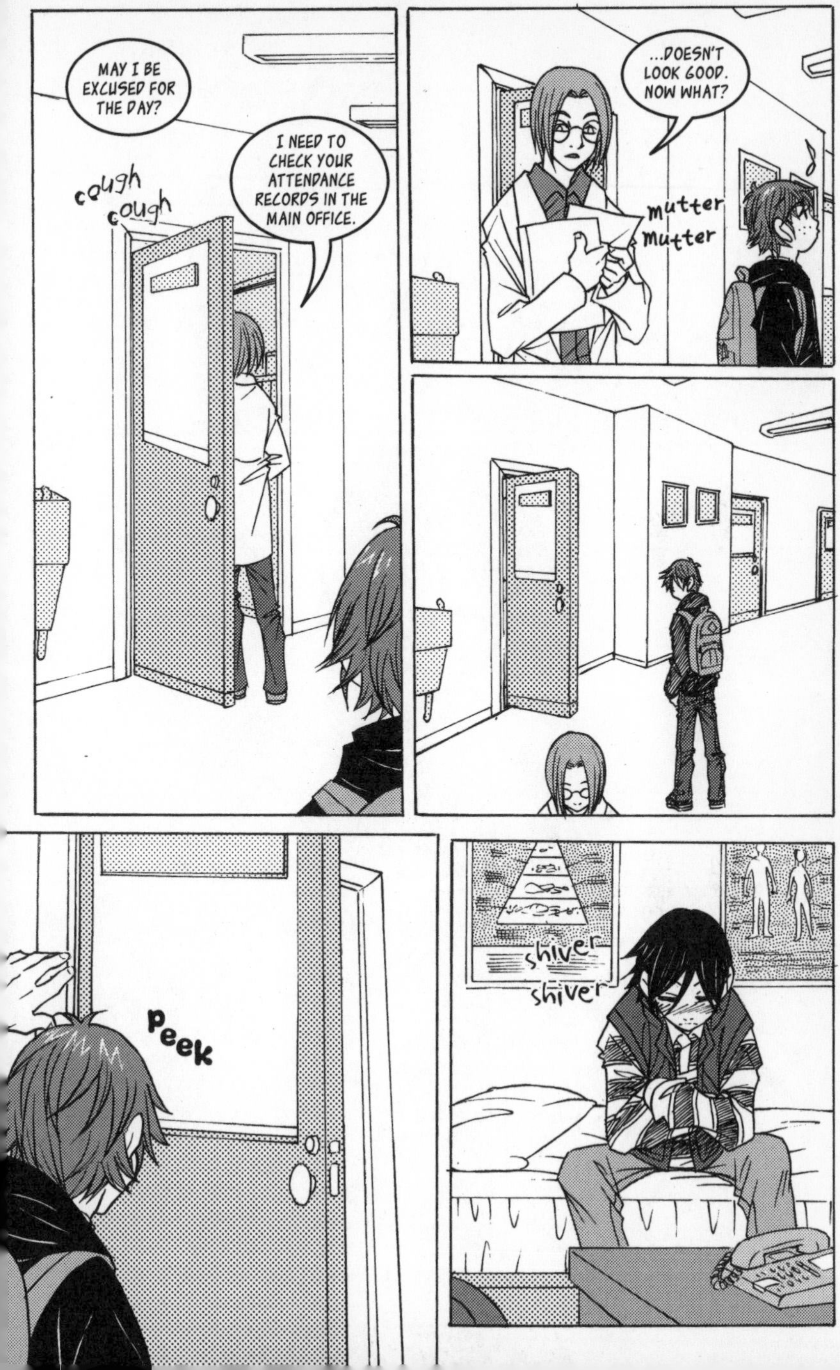
MAY I BE EXCUSED FOR THE DAY?
I NEED TO CHECK YOUR ATTENDANCE RECORDS IN THE MAIN OFFICE.
cough cough
...DOESN'T LOOK GOOD. NOW WHAT?
mutter mutter
Peek
shiver shiver

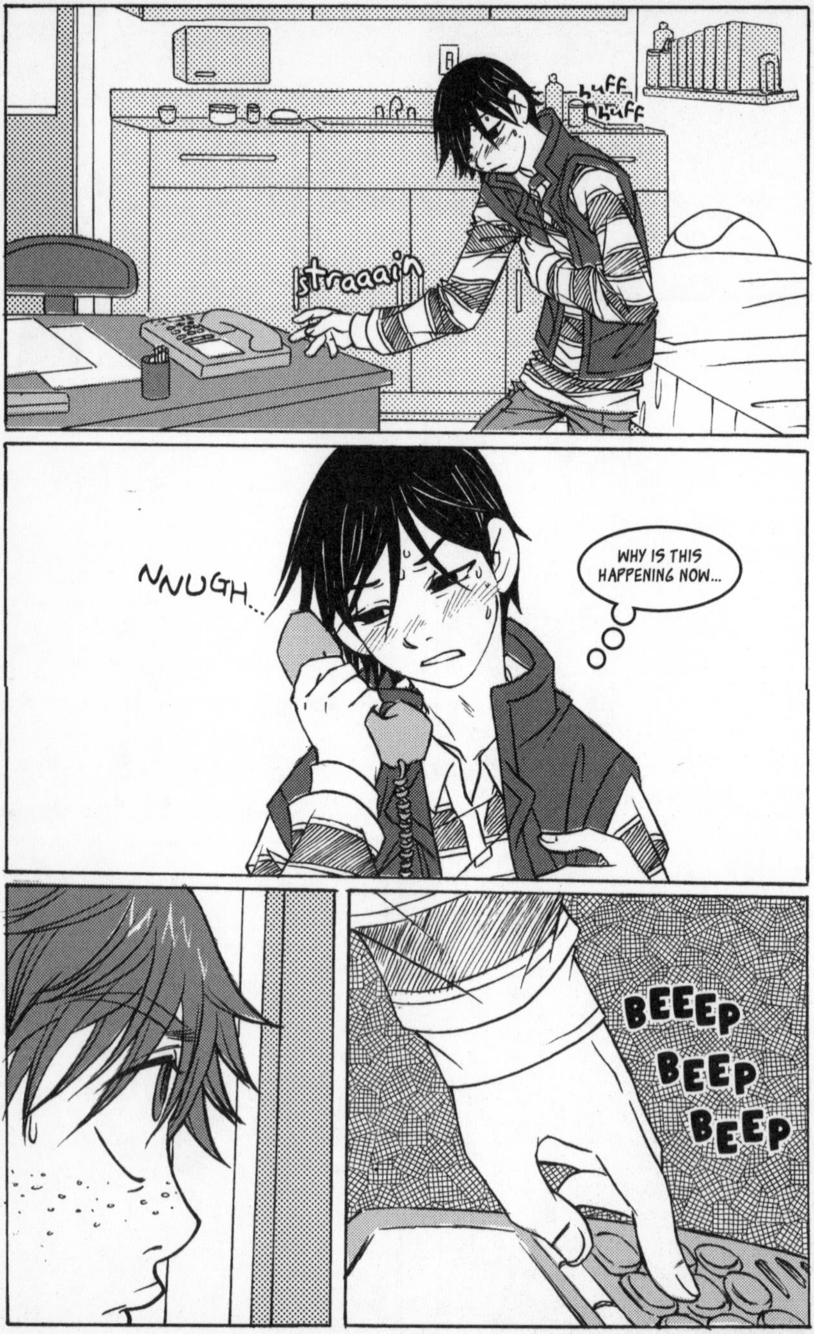
huff
huff
straaain
NNUGH...
WHY IS THIS HAPPENING NOW...
BEEEP
BEEP
BEEP

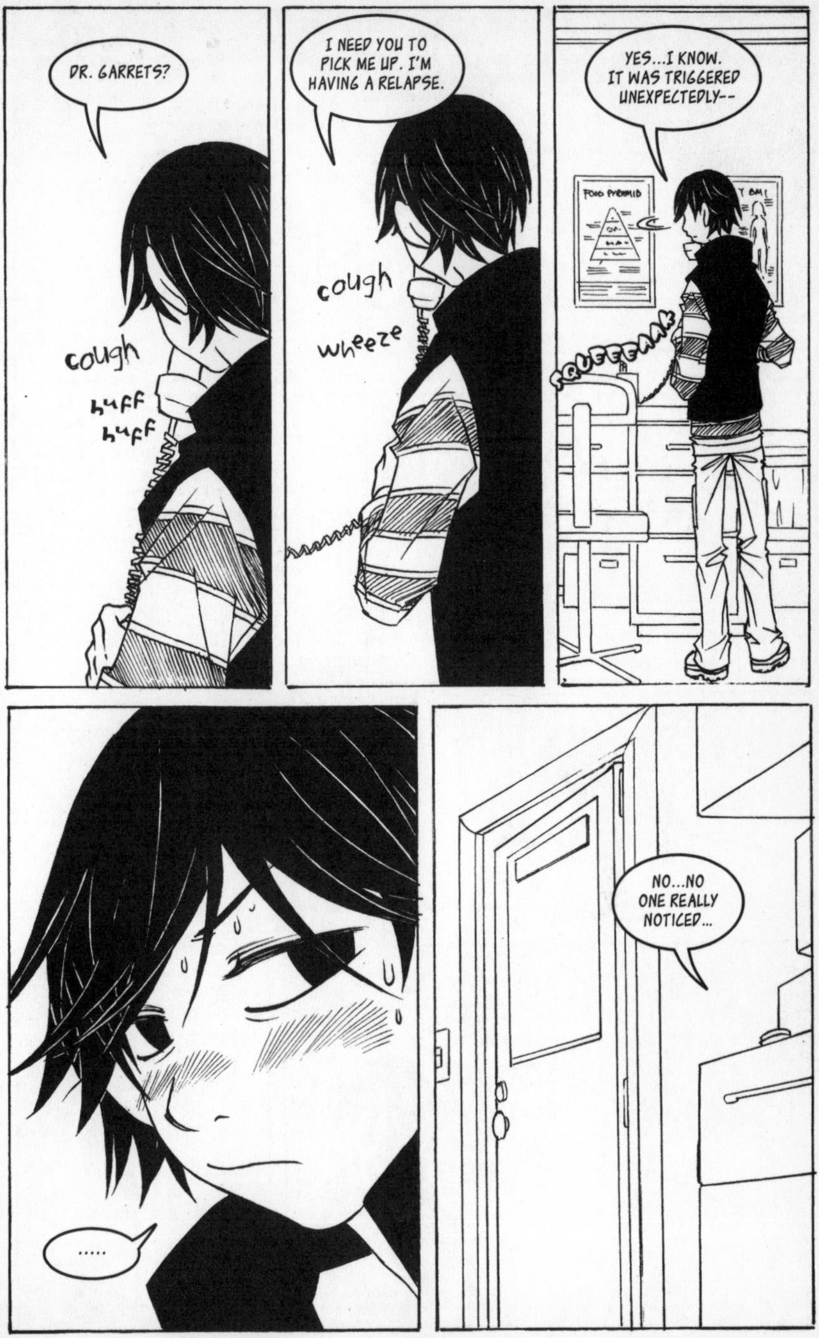
DR. GARRETS?
cough
huff
huff
I NEED YOU TO PICK ME UP. I'M HAVING A RELAPSE.
cough
wheeze
YES...I KNOW. IT WAS TRIGGERED UNEXPECTEDLY--
FOOD PYRAMID
SQUEEEAAK
.....
NO...NO ONE REALLY NOTICED...

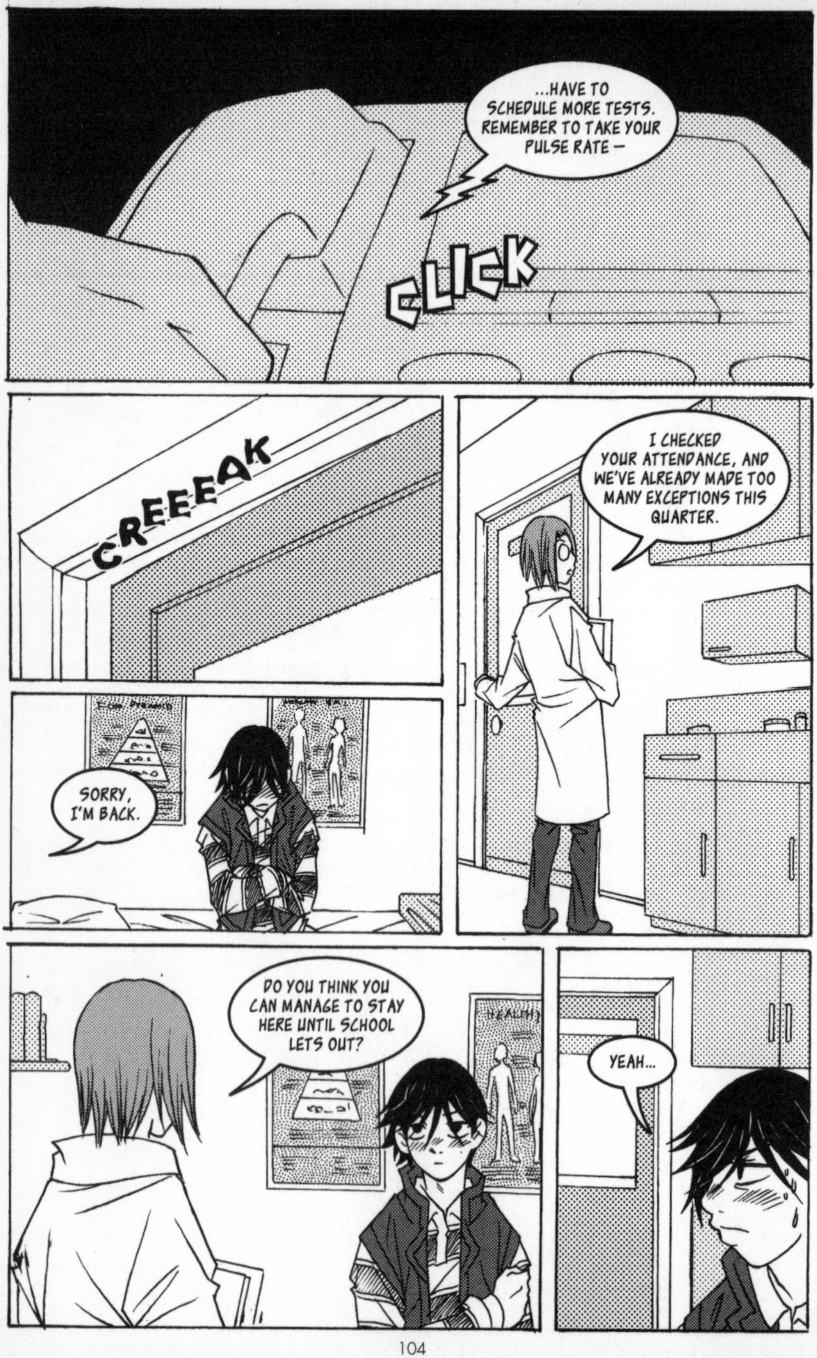
...HAVE TO SCHEDULE MORE TESTS. REMEMBER TO TAKE YOUR PULSE RATE –
CLICK
CREEEAK
I CHECKED YOUR ATTENDANCE, AND WE'VE ALREADY MADE TOO MANY EXCEPTIONS THIS QUARTER.
SORRY, I'M BACK.
DO YOU THINK YOU CAN MANAGE TO STAY HERE UNTIL SCHOOL LETS OUT?
YEAH...

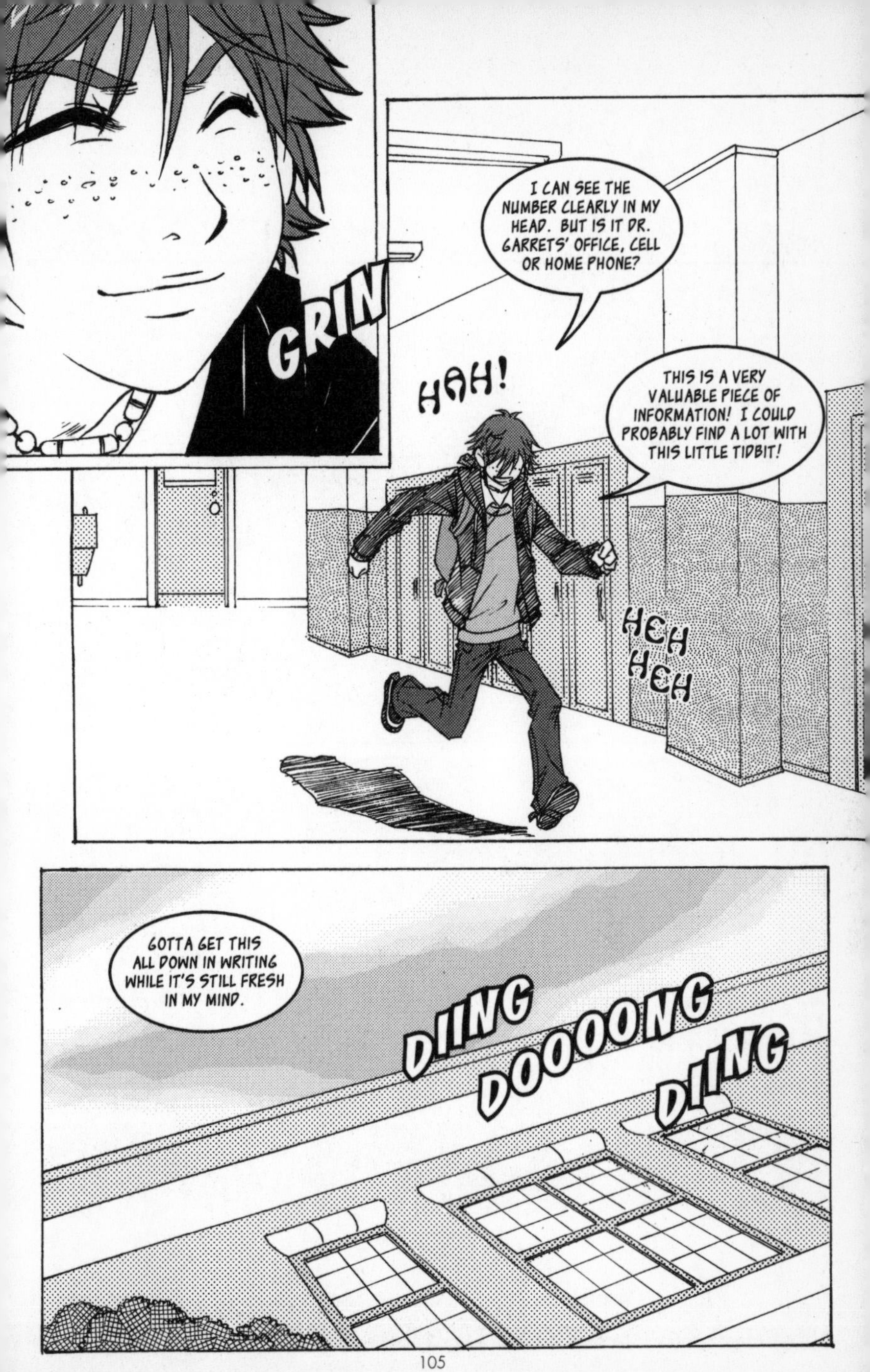
GRIN
I CAN SEE THE NUMBER CLEARLY IN MY HEAD. BUT IS IT DR. GARRETS' OFFICE, CELL OR HOME PHONE?
HAH!
THIS IS A VERY VALUABLE PIECE OF INFORMATION! I COULD PROBABLY FIND A LOT WITH THIS LITTLE TIDBIT!
HEH HEH
GOTTA GET THIS ALL DOWN IN WRITING WHILE IT'S STILL FRESH IN MY MIND.
DIING
DOOOONG
DIING

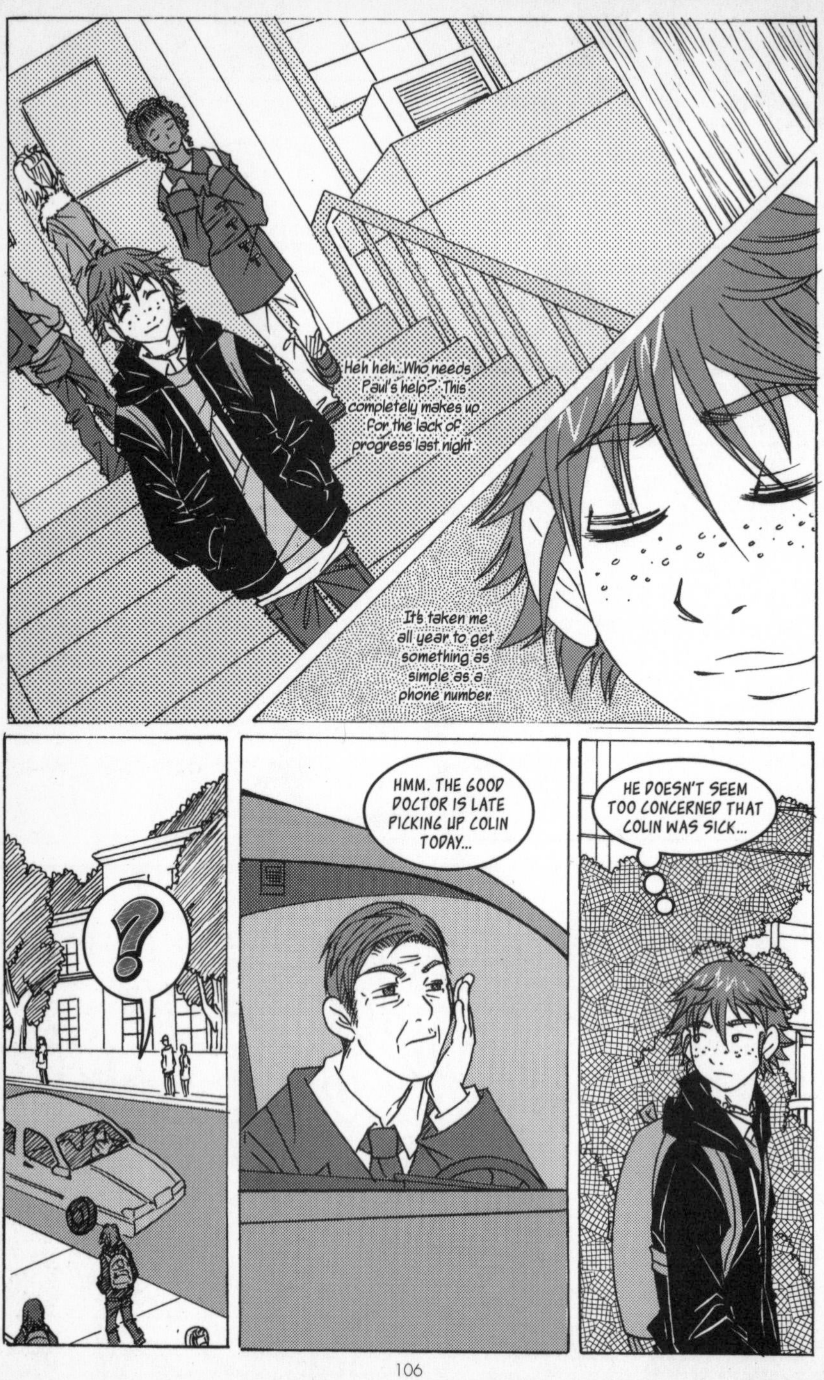
Heh heh...Who needs Paul's help? This completely makes up for the lack of progress last night.
It's taken me all year to get something as simple as a phone number.
?
HMM. THE GOOD DOCTOR IS LATE PICKING UP COLIN TODAY...
HE DOESN'T SEEM TOO CONCERNED THAT COLIN WAS SICK...

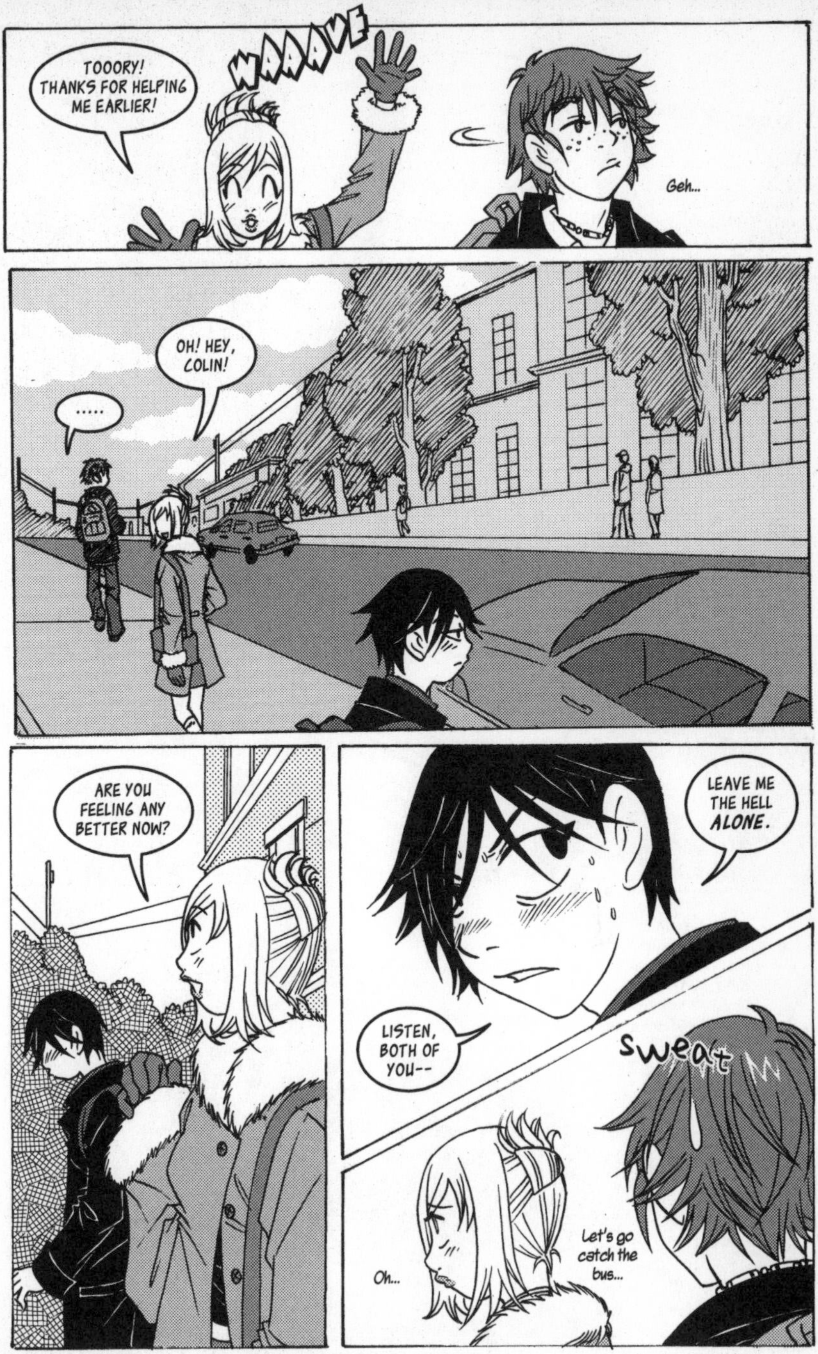
TOOORY!
THANKS FOR HELPING ME EARLIER!
WAAAVE
Geh...
.....
OH! HEY, COLIN!
ARE YOU FEELING ANY BETTER NOW?
LEAVE ME THE HELL **ALONE**.
LISTEN, BOTH OF YOU--
SWEAT
Oh...
Let's go catch the bus...

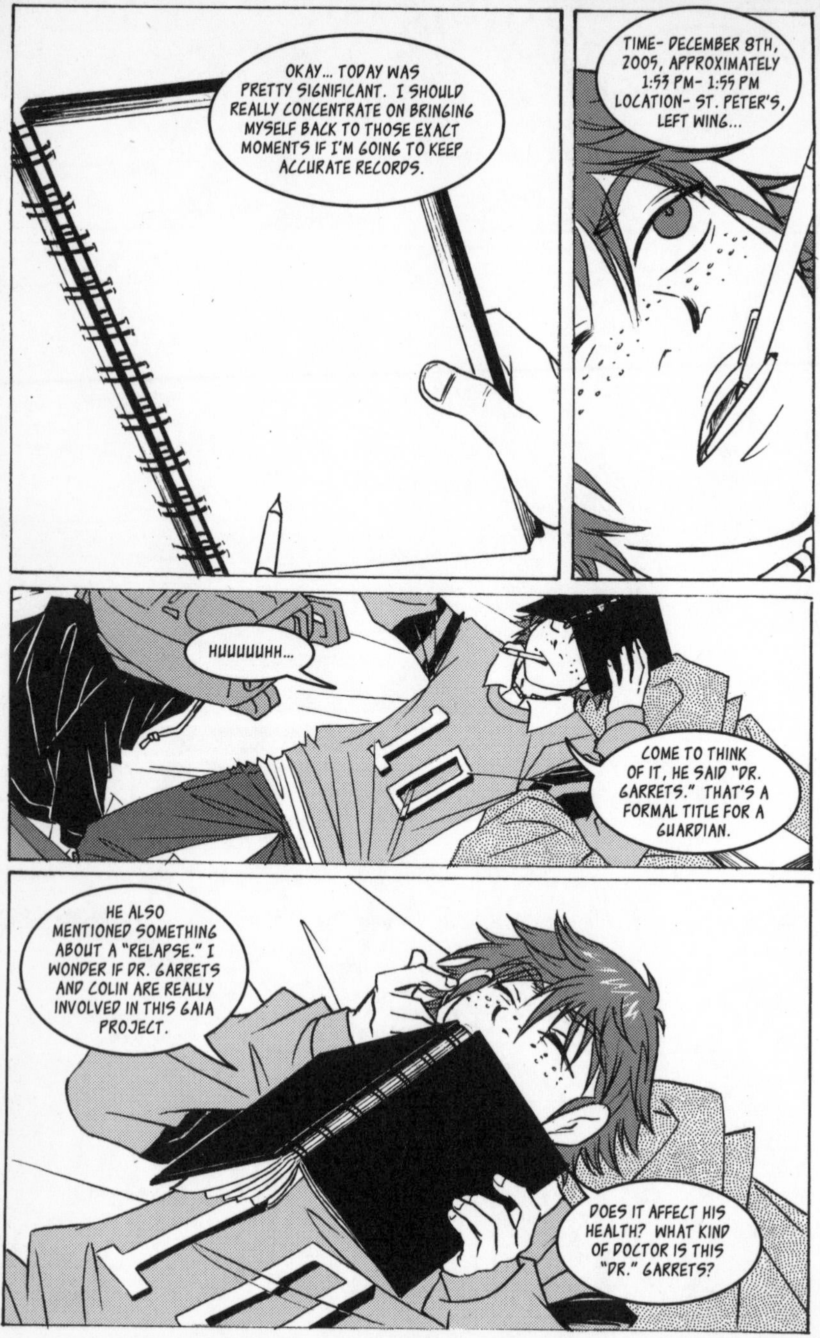
OKAY... TODAY WAS PRETTY SIGNIFICANT. I SHOULD REALLY CONCENTRATE ON BRINGING MYSELF BACK TO THOSE EXACT MOMENTS IF I'M GOING TO KEEP ACCURATE RECORDS.
TIME- DECEMBER 8TH, 2005, APPROXIMATELY 1:53 PM- 1:55 PM LOCATION- ST. PETER'S, LEFT WING...
HUUUUUHH...
COME TO THINK OF IT, HE SAID "DR. GARRETS." THAT'S A FORMAL TITLE FOR A GUARDIAN.
HE ALSO MENTIONED SOMETHING ABOUT A "RELAPSE." I WONDER IF DR. GARRETS AND COLIN ARE REALLY INVOLVED IN THIS GAIA PROJECT.
DOES IT AFFECT HIS HEALTH? WHAT KIND OF DOCTOR IS THIS "DR." GARRETS?

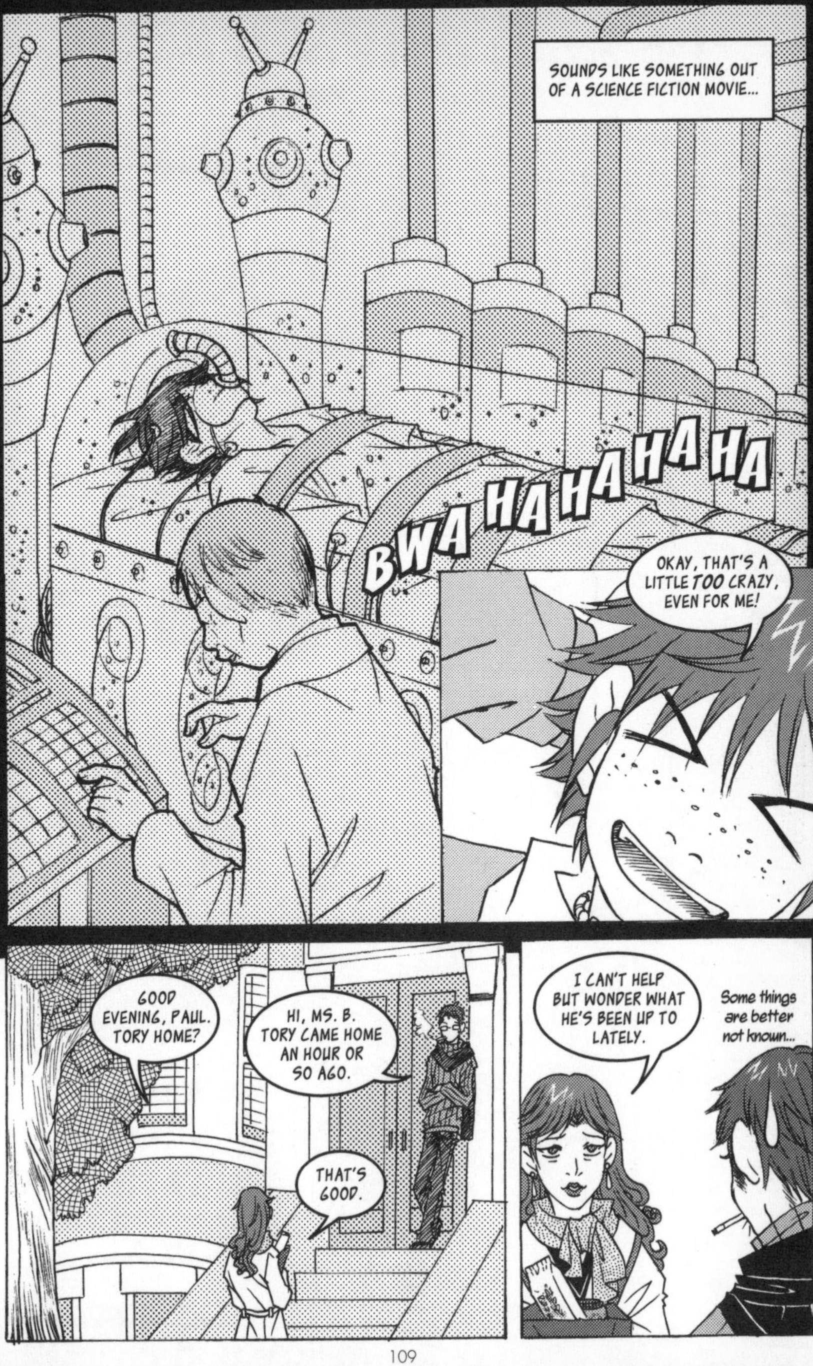
SOUNDS LIKE SOMETHING OUT OF A SCIENCE FICTION MOVIE...
BWA HA HA HA HA HA
OKAY, THAT'S A LITTLE *TOO* CRAZY, EVEN FOR ME!
GOOD EVENING, PAUL. TORY HOME?
HI, MS. B. TORY CAME HOME AN HOUR OR SO AGO.
THAT'S GOOD.
I CAN'T HELP BUT WONDER WHAT HE'S BEEN UP TO LATELY.
Some things are better not known...

Off*Beat

Chapter 5: The Opportunity

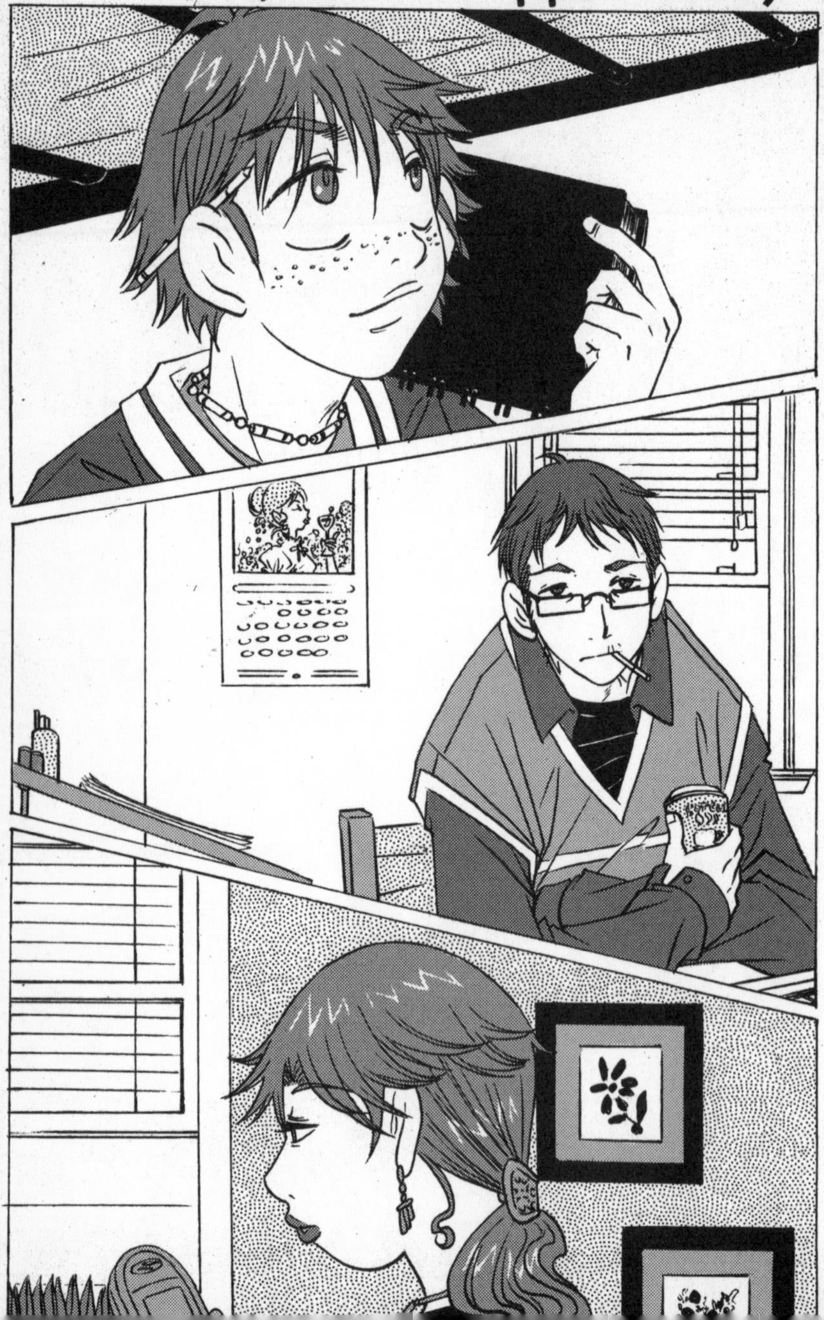

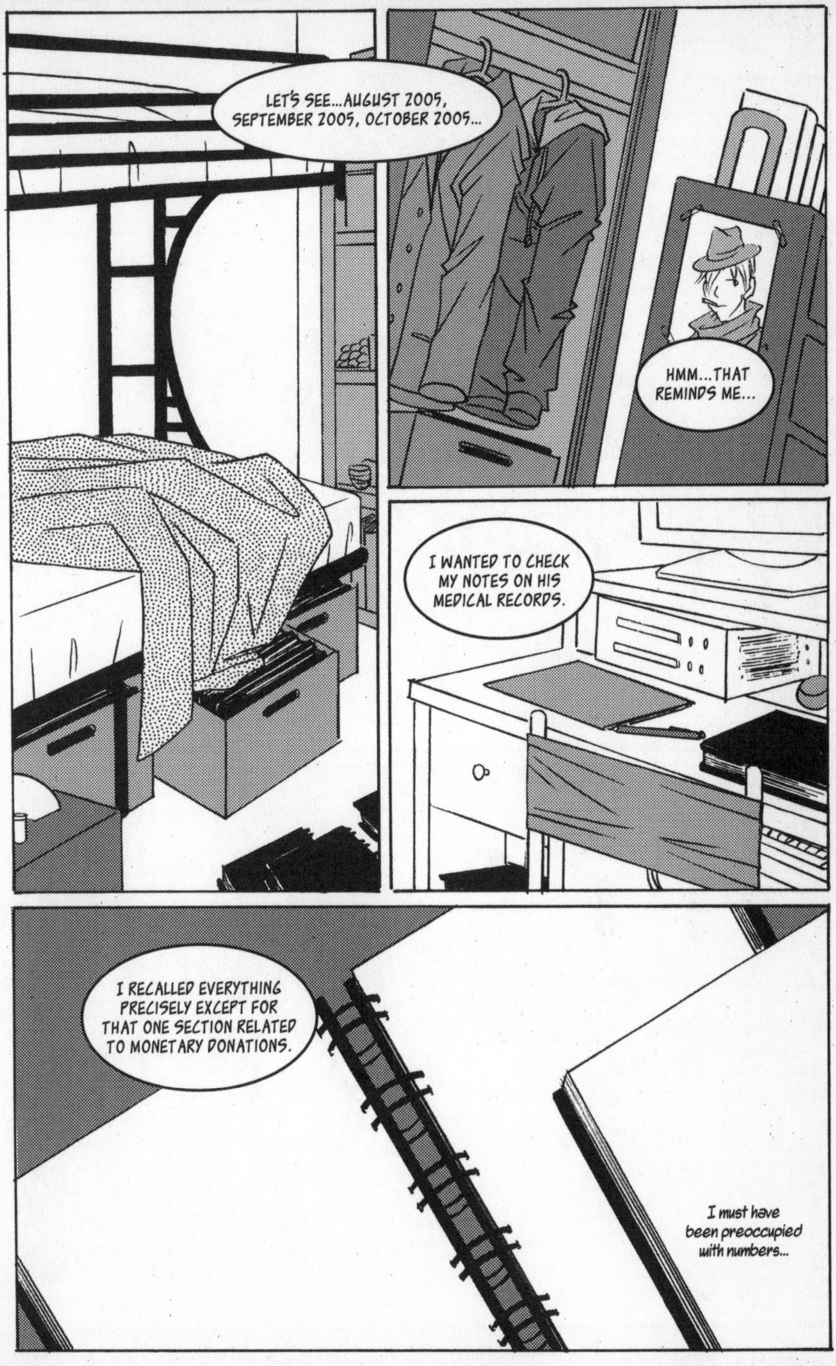
LET'S SEE...AUGUST 2005, SEPTEMBER 2005, OCTOBER 2005...
HMM...THAT REMINDS ME...
I WANTED TO CHECK MY NOTES ON HIS MEDICAL RECORDS.
I RECALLED EVERYTHING PRECISELY EXCEPT FOR THAT ONE SECTION RELATED TO MONETARY DONATIONS.
I must have been preoccupied with numbers...

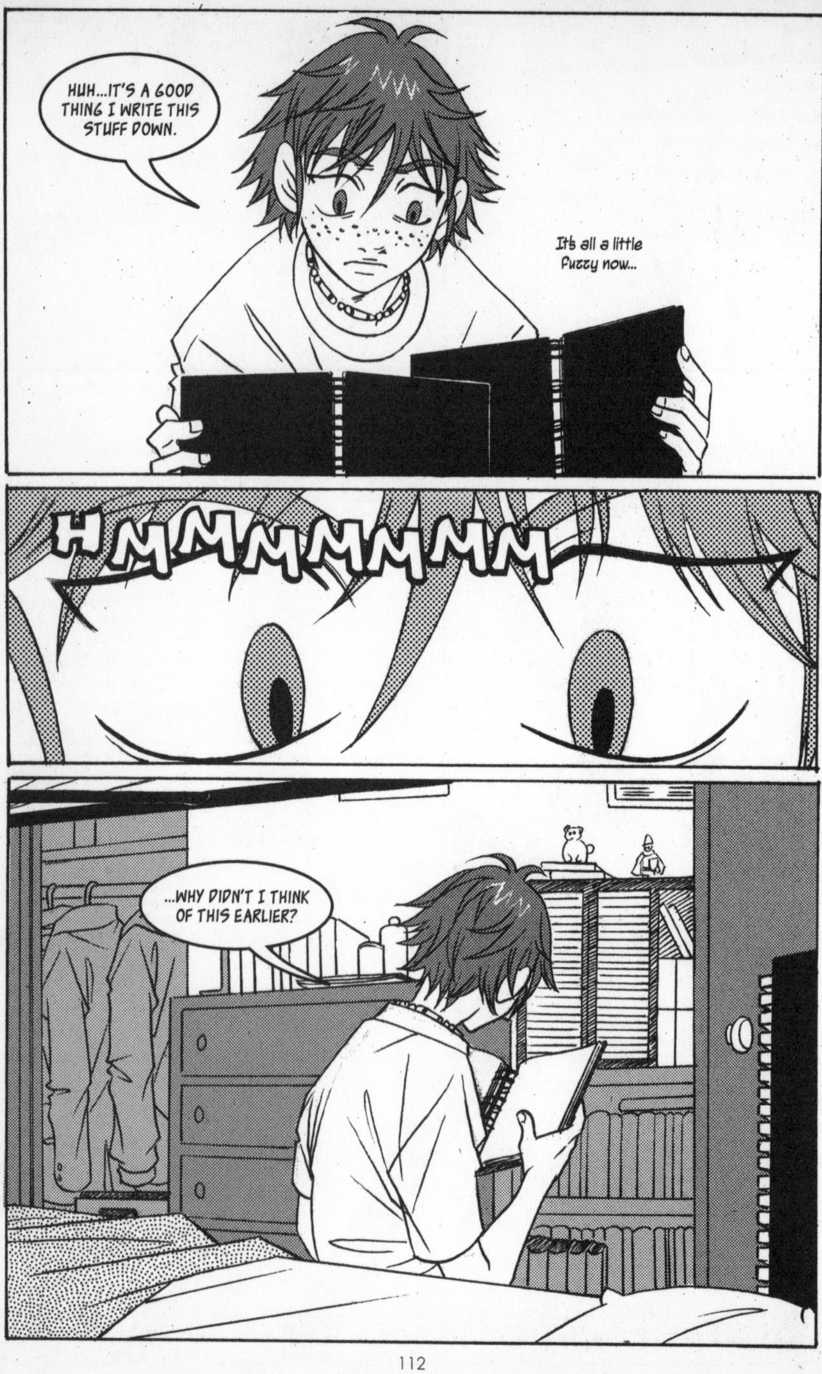
HUH...IT'S A GOOD THING I WRITE THIS STUFF DOWN.
It's all a little fuzzy now...
HMMMMMMMM
...WHY DIDN'T I THINK OF THIS EARLIER?

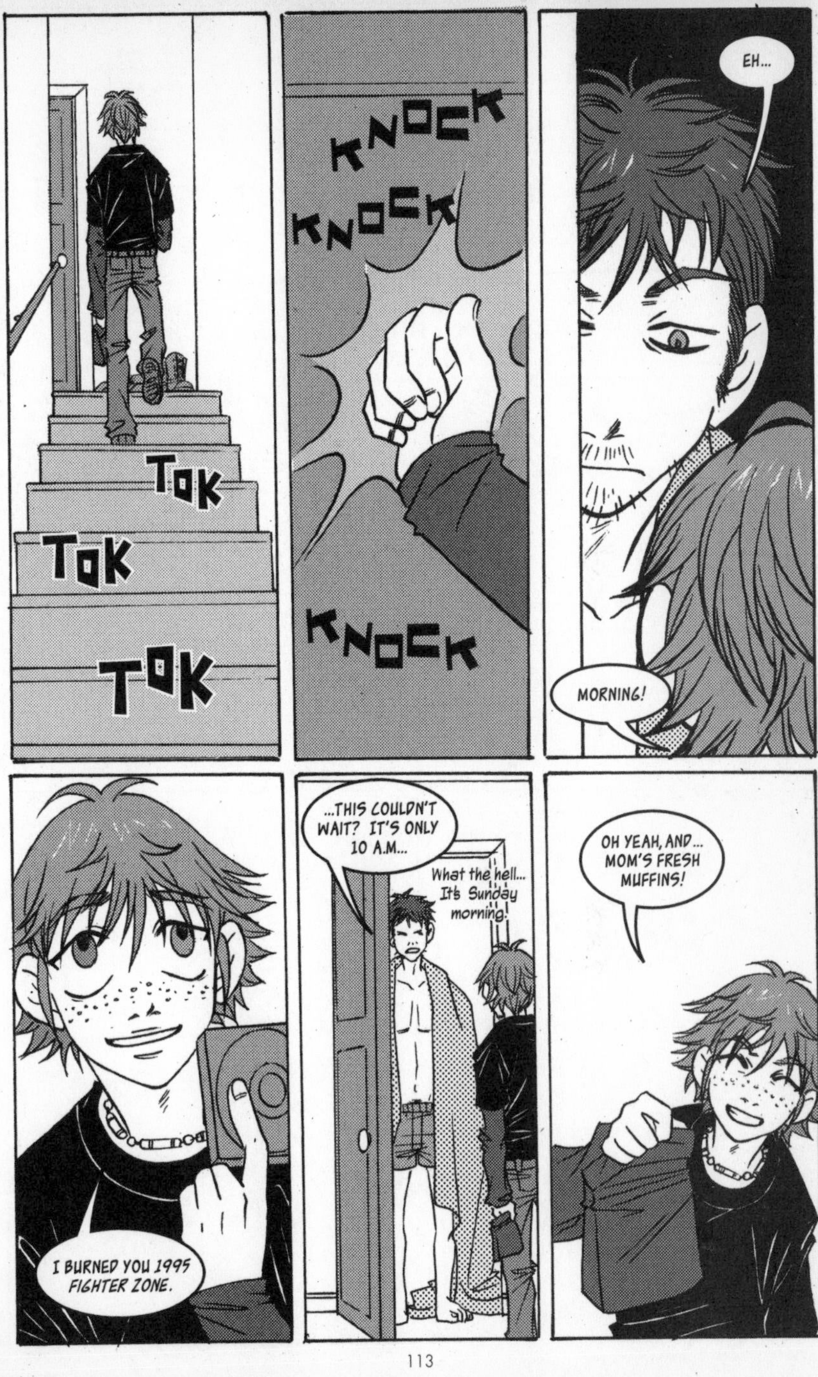
TOK
TOK
TOK
KNOCK
KNOCK
KNOCK
EH...
MORNING!
I BURNED YOU 1995 FIGHTER ZONE.
...THIS COULDN'T WAIT? IT'S ONLY 10 A.M...
What the hell... It's Sunday morning!
OH YEAH, AND... MOM'S FRESH MUFFINS!

EXCUSE THE MESS.

I WASN'T EXPECTING COMPANY.

WELL, UH... I DON'T SUPPOSE YOU STILL HAVE ANY MATERIAL RELATED TO THAT *LICENSE PLATE* STILL ON YOUR COMPUTER?

uurk

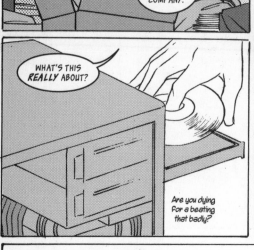

WHAT'S THIS *REALLY* ABOUT?

Are you dying for a beating that badly?

OUT!!

SHOVE

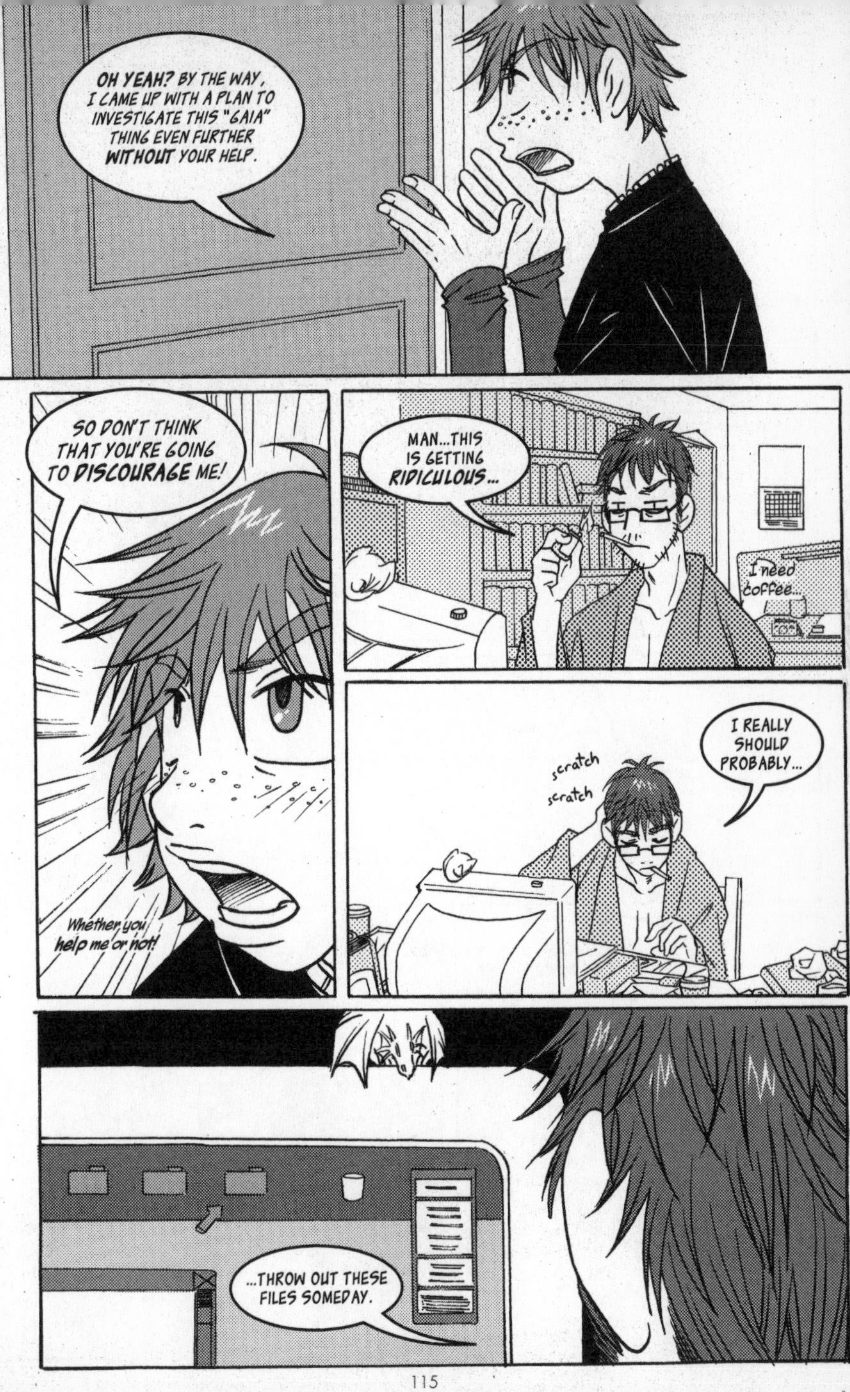
OH YEAH? BY THE WAY, I CAME UP WITH A PLAN TO INVESTIGATE THIS "GAIA" THING EVEN FURTHER WITHOUT YOUR HELP.
SO DON'T THINK THAT YOU'RE GOING TO DISCOURAGE ME!
Whether you help me or not!
MAN...THIS IS GETTING RIDICULOUS...
I need coffee...
scratch
scratch
I REALLY SHOULD PROBABLY...
...THROW OUT THESE FILES SOMEDAY.

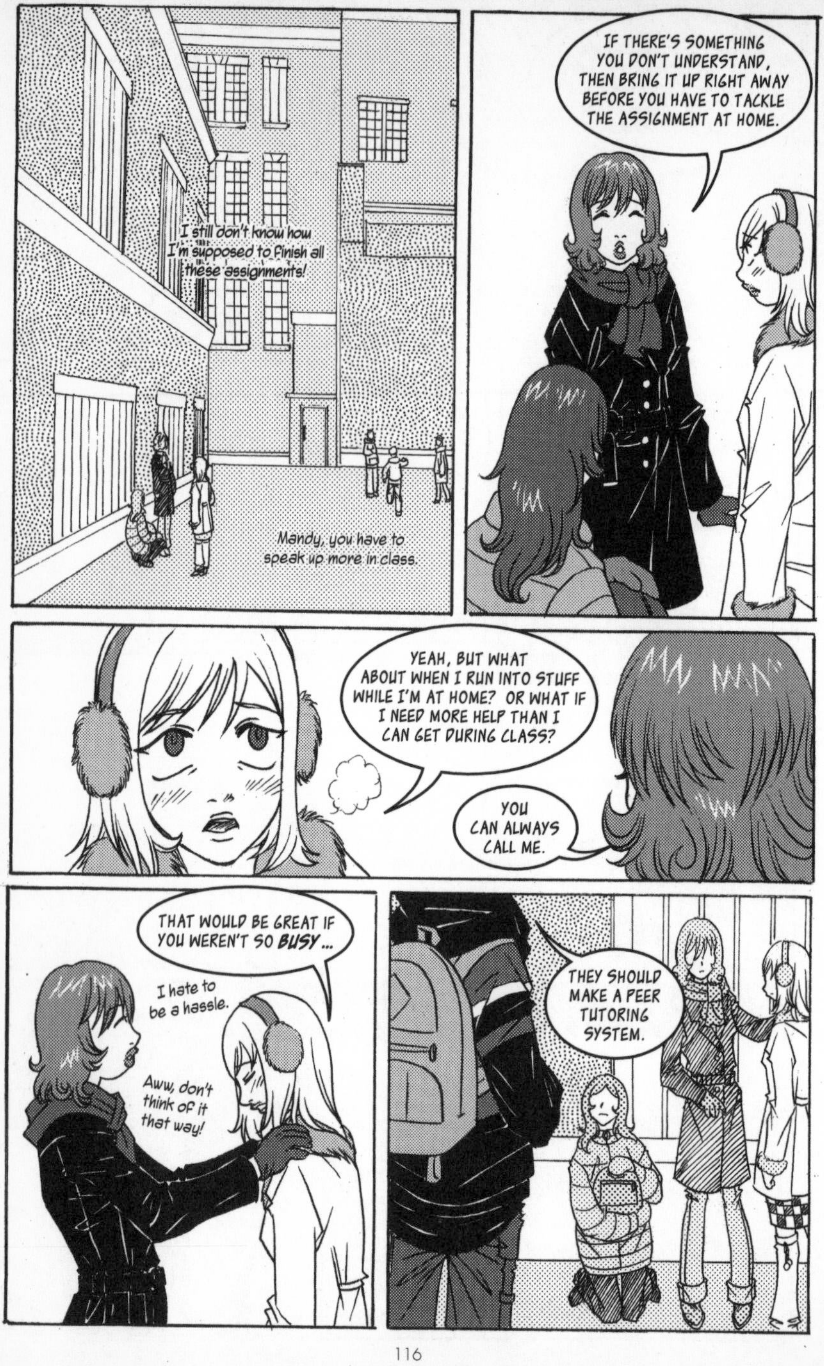
I still don't know how I'm supposed to finish all these assignments!
Mandy, you have to speak up more in class.
IF THERE'S SOMETHING YOU DON'T UNDERSTAND, THEN BRING IT UP RIGHT AWAY BEFORE YOU HAVE TO TACKLE THE ASSIGNMENT AT HOME.
YEAH, BUT WHAT ABOUT WHEN I RUN INTO STUFF WHILE I'M AT HOME? OR WHAT IF I NEED MORE HELP THAN I CAN GET DURING CLASS?
YOU CAN ALWAYS CALL ME.
THAT WOULD BE GREAT IF YOU WEREN'T SO ***BUSY*** ...
I hate to be a hassle.
Aww, don't think of it that way!
THEY SHOULD MAKE A PEER TUTORING SYSTEM.

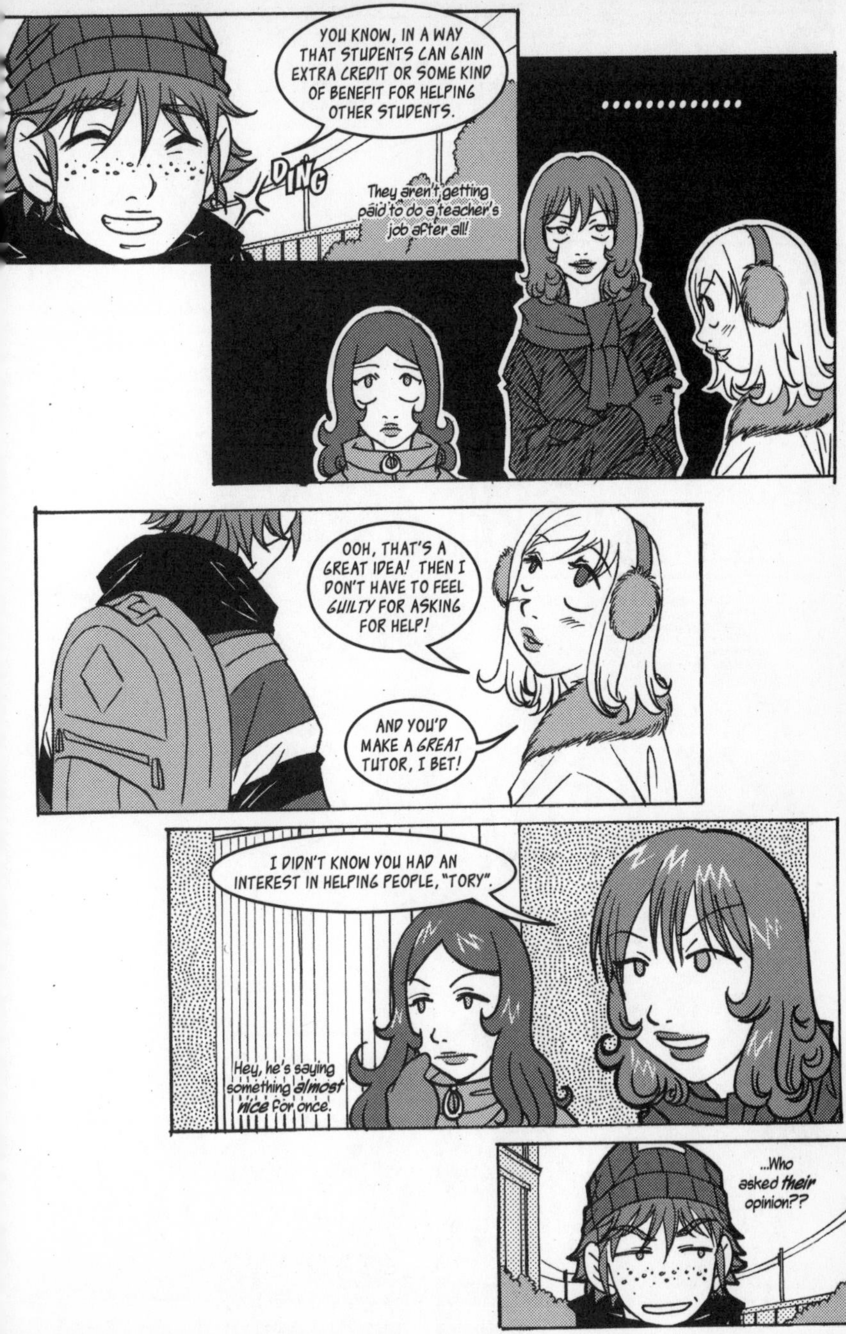
YOU KNOW, IN A WAY THAT STUDENTS CAN GAIN EXTRA CREDIT OR SOME KIND OF BENEFIT FOR HELPING OTHER STUDENTS.
DING
They aren't getting paid to do a teacher's job after all!
....
OOH, THAT'S A GREAT IDEA! THEN I DON'T HAVE TO FEEL GUILTY FOR ASKING FOR HELP!
AND YOU'D MAKE A GREAT TUTOR, I BET!
I DIDN'T KNOW YOU HAD AN INTEREST IN HELPING PEOPLE, "TORY".
Hey, he's saying something almost nice for once.
...Who asked their opinion??

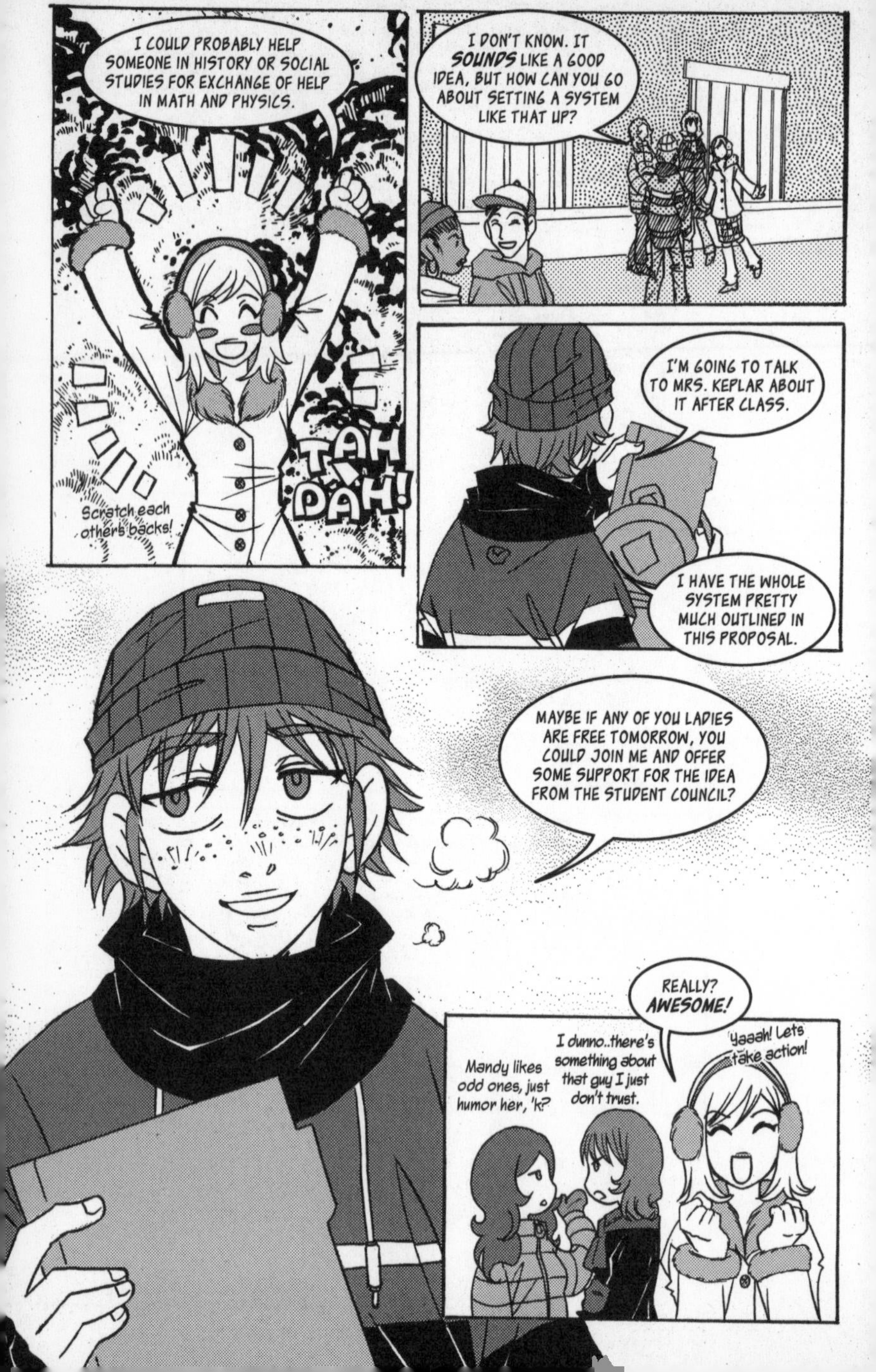
I COULD PROBABLY HELP SOMEONE IN HISTORY OR SOCIAL STUDIES FOR EXCHANGE OF HELP IN MATH AND PHYSICS.
TAH DAH!
Scratch each others backs!
I DON'T KNOW. IT SOUNDS LIKE A GOOD IDEA, BUT HOW CAN YOU GO ABOUT SETTING A SYSTEM LIKE THAT UP?
I'M GOING TO TALK TO MRS. KEPLAR ABOUT IT AFTER CLASS.
I HAVE THE WHOLE SYSTEM PRETTY MUCH OUTLINED IN THIS PROPOSAL.
MAYBE IF ANY OF YOU LADIES ARE FREE TOMORROW, YOU COULD JOIN ME AND OFFER SOME SUPPORT FOR THE IDEA FROM THE STUDENT COUNCIL?
Mandy likes odd ones, just humor her, 'k?
I dunno..there's something about that guy I just don't trust.
REALLY? AWESOME!
Yaaah! Lets take action!

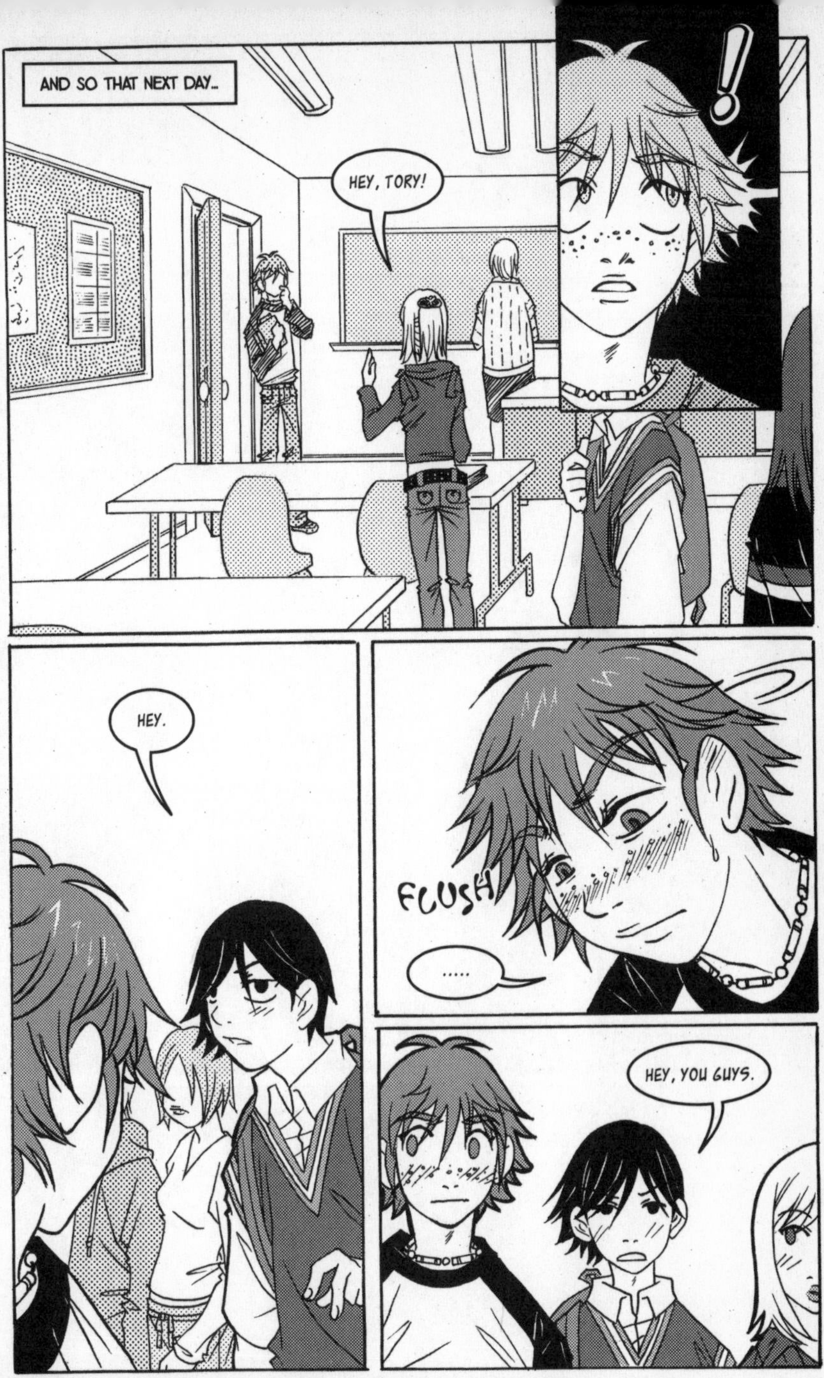
AND SO THAT NEXT DAY..
HEY, TORY!
!
HEY.
FLUSH
.....
HEY, YOU GUYS.

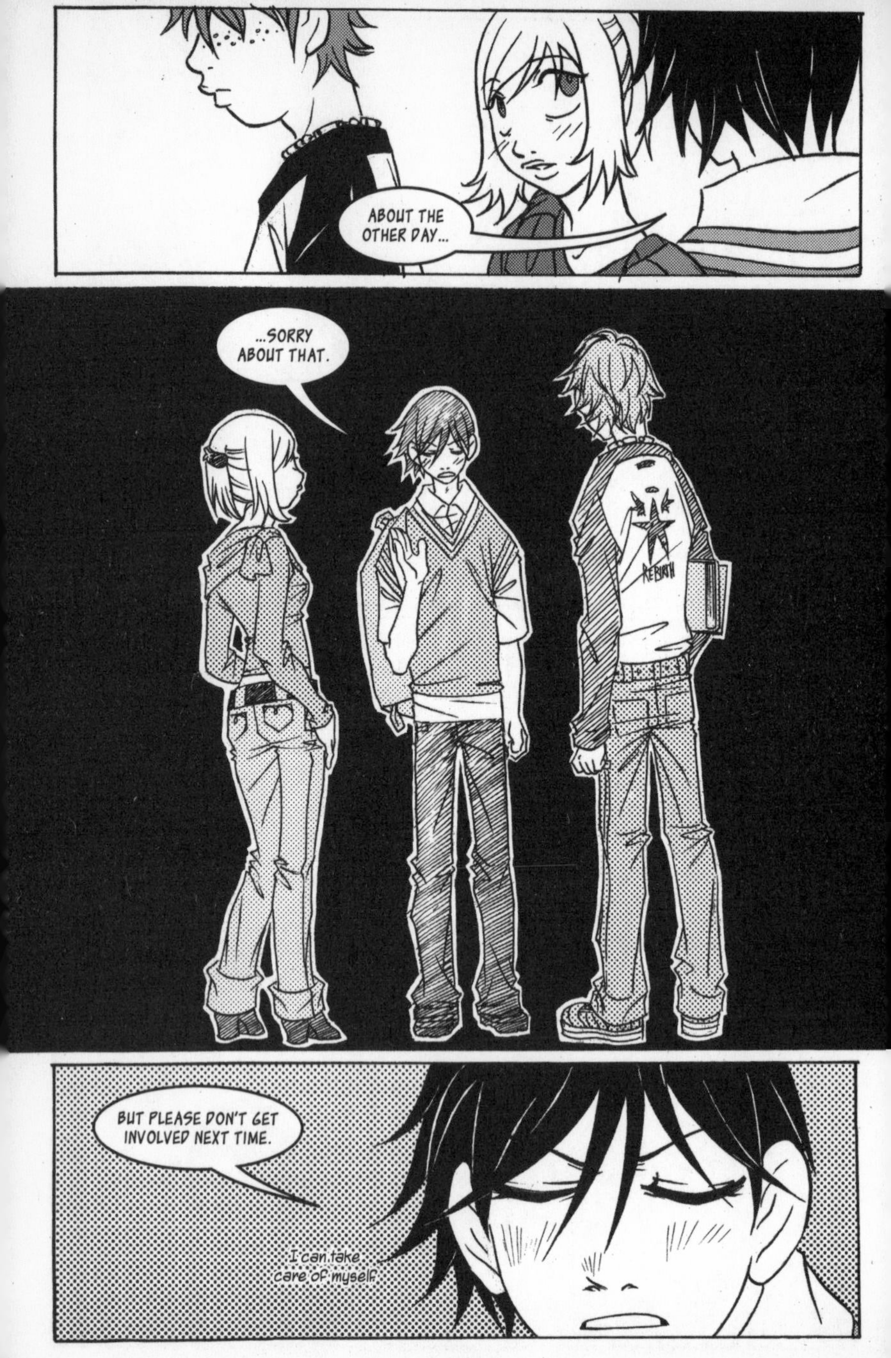
ABOUT THE OTHER DAY...
...SORRY ABOUT THAT.
REBIRTH
BUT PLEASE DON'T GET INVOLVED NEXT TIME.
I can take care of myself.

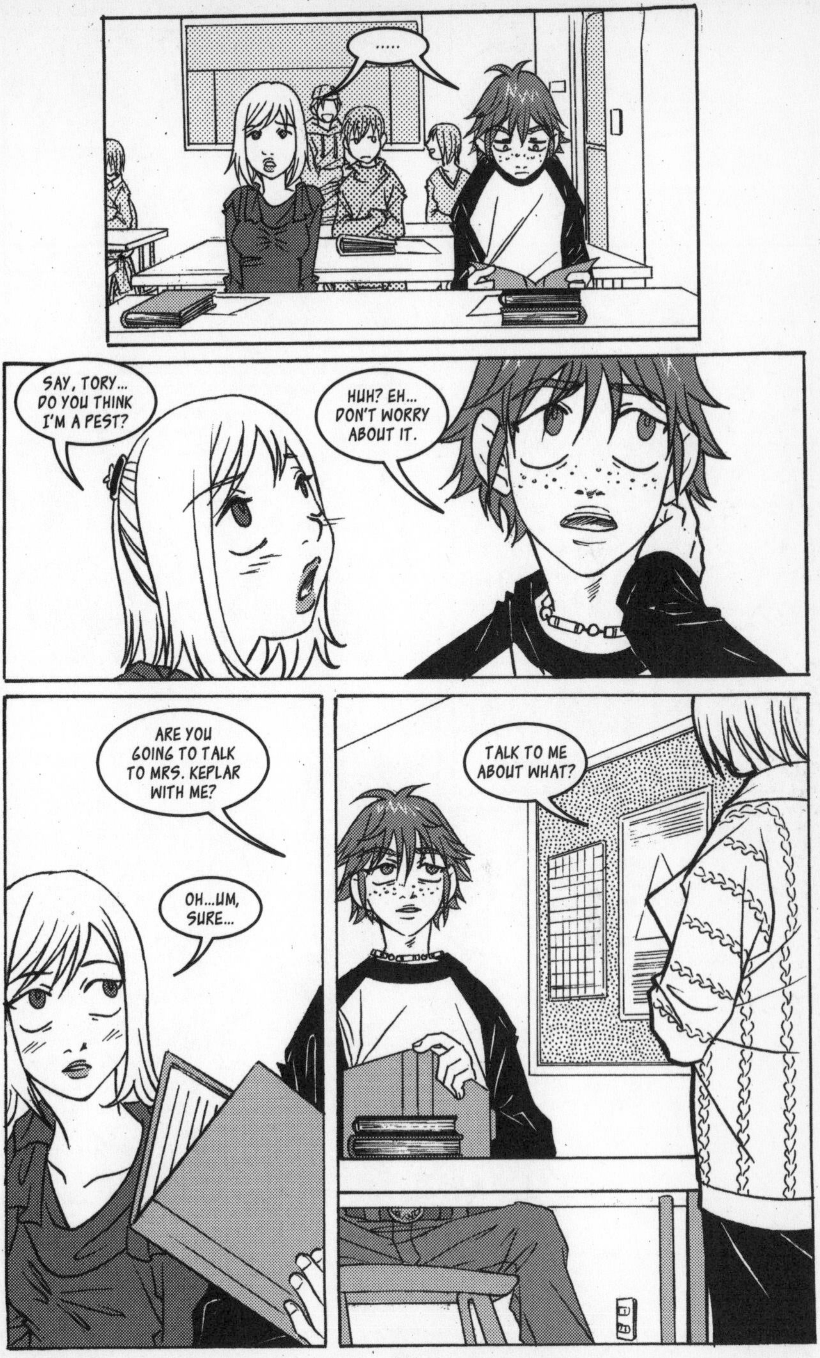
......
SAY, TORY... DO YOU THINK I'M A PEST?
HUH? EH... DON'T WORRY ABOUT IT.
ARE YOU GOING TO TALK TO MRS. KEPLAR WITH ME?
OH...UM, SURE...
TALK TO ME ABOUT WHAT?

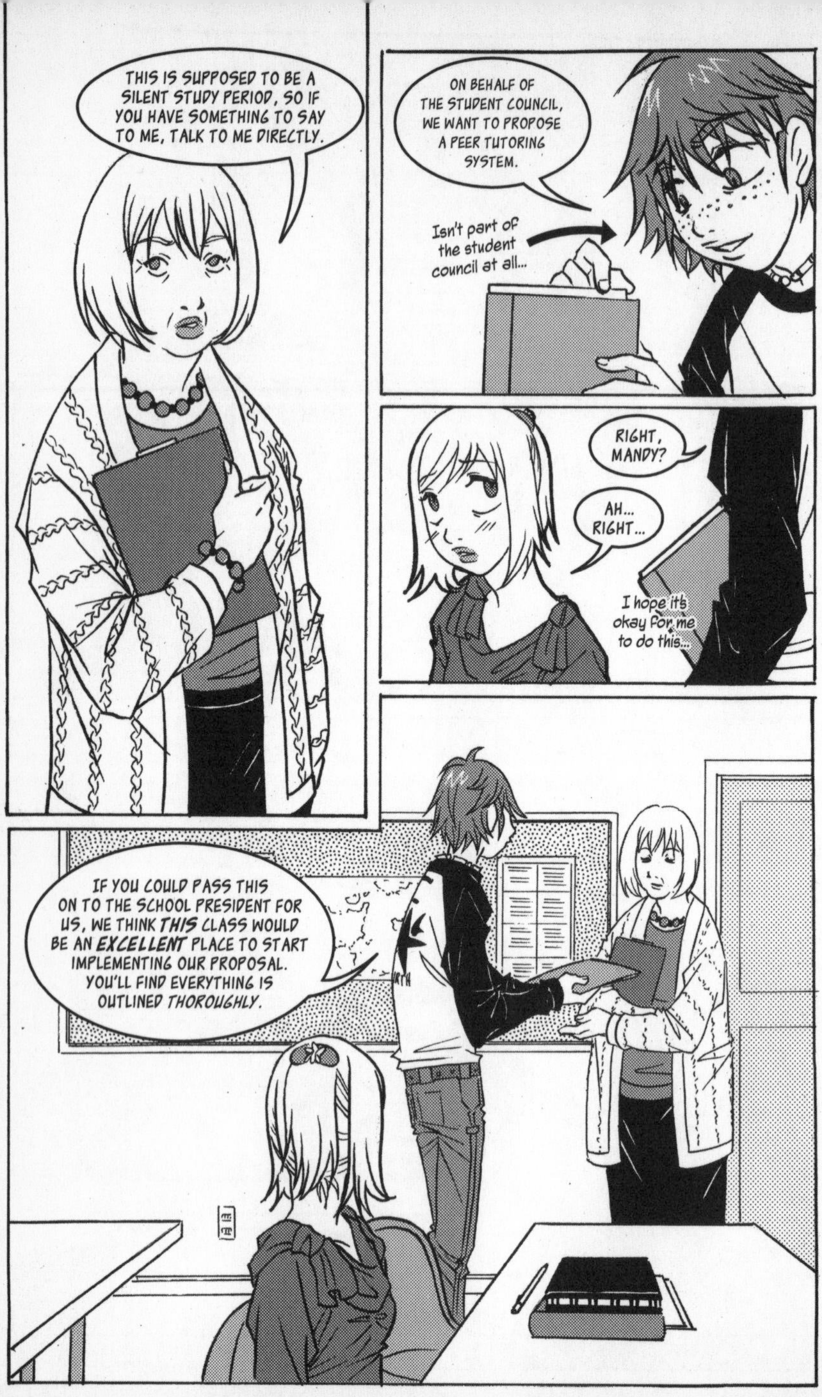
THIS IS SUPPOSED TO BE A SILENT STUDY PERIOD, SO IF YOU HAVE SOMETHING TO SAY TO ME, TALK TO ME DIRECTLY.
ON BEHALF OF THE STUDENT COUNCIL, WE WANT TO PROPOSE A PEER TUTORING SYSTEM.
Isn't part of the student council at all...
RIGHT, MANDY?
AH... RIGHT...
I hope it's okay for me to do this...
IF YOU COULD PASS THIS ON TO THE SCHOOL PRESIDENT FOR US, WE THINK *THIS* CLASS WOULD BE AN *EXCELLENT* PLACE TO START IMPLEMENTING OUR PROPOSAL. YOU'LL FIND EVERYTHING IS OUTLINED *THOROUGHLY*.

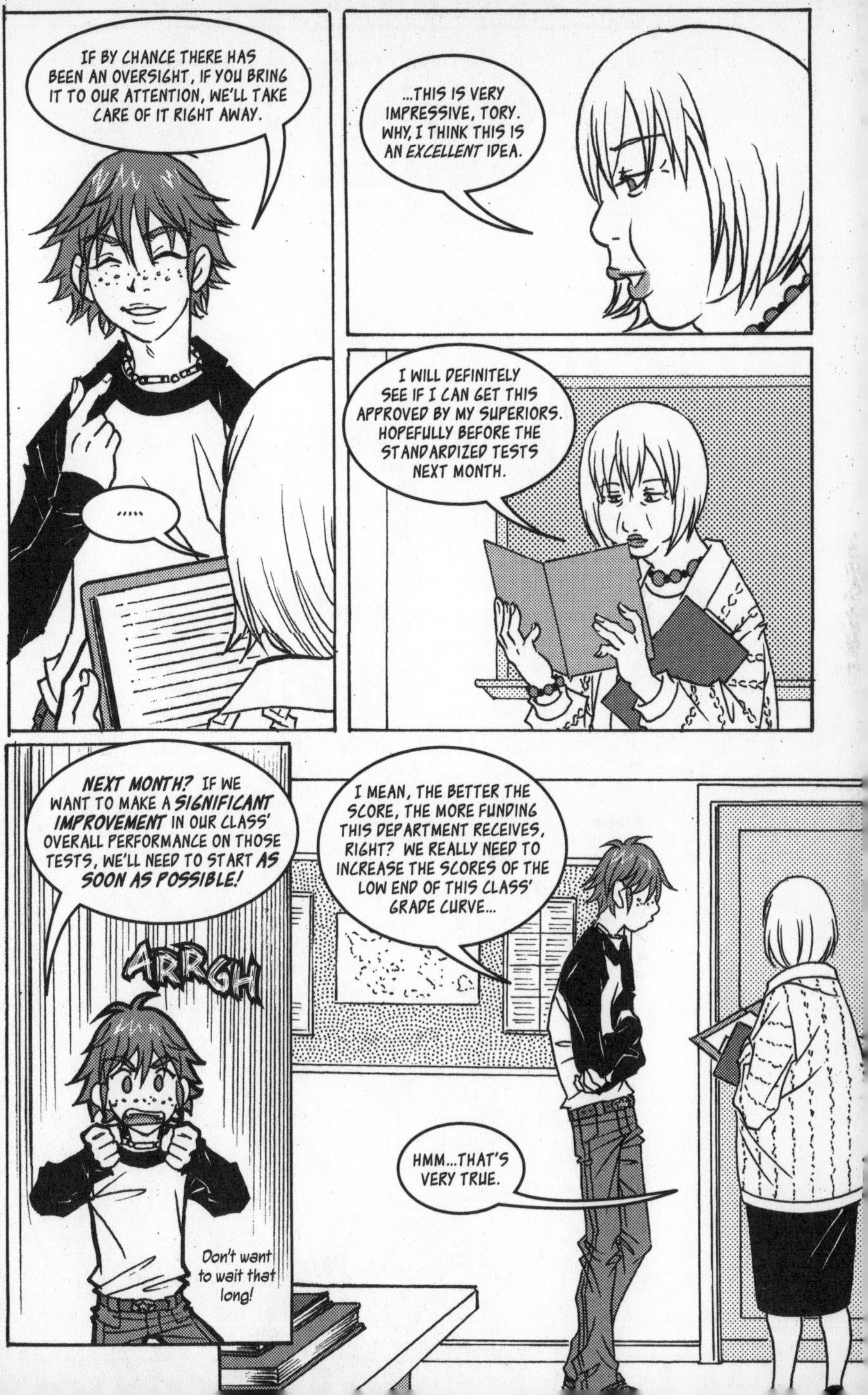
IF BY CHANCE THERE HAS BEEN AN OVERSIGHT, IF YOU BRING IT TO OUR ATTENTION, WE'LL TAKE CARE OF IT RIGHT AWAY.
.....
...THIS IS VERY IMPRESSIVE, TORY. WHY, I THINK THIS IS AN *EXCELLENT* IDEA.
I WILL DEFINITELY SEE IF I CAN GET THIS APPROVED BY MY SUPERIORS. HOPEFULLY BEFORE THE STANDARDIZED TESTS NEXT MONTH.
NEXT MONTH? IF WE WANT TO MAKE A ***SIGNIFICANT IMPROVEMENT*** IN OUR CLASS' OVERALL PERFORMANCE ON THOSE TESTS, WE'LL NEED TO START ***AS SOON AS POSSIBLE!***
ARRGH
Don't want to wait that long!
I MEAN, THE BETTER THE SCORE, THE MORE FUNDING THIS DEPARTMENT RECEIVES, RIGHT? WE REALLY NEED TO INCREASE THE SCORES OF THE LOW END OF THIS CLASS' GRADE CURVE...
HMM...THAT'S VERY TRUE.

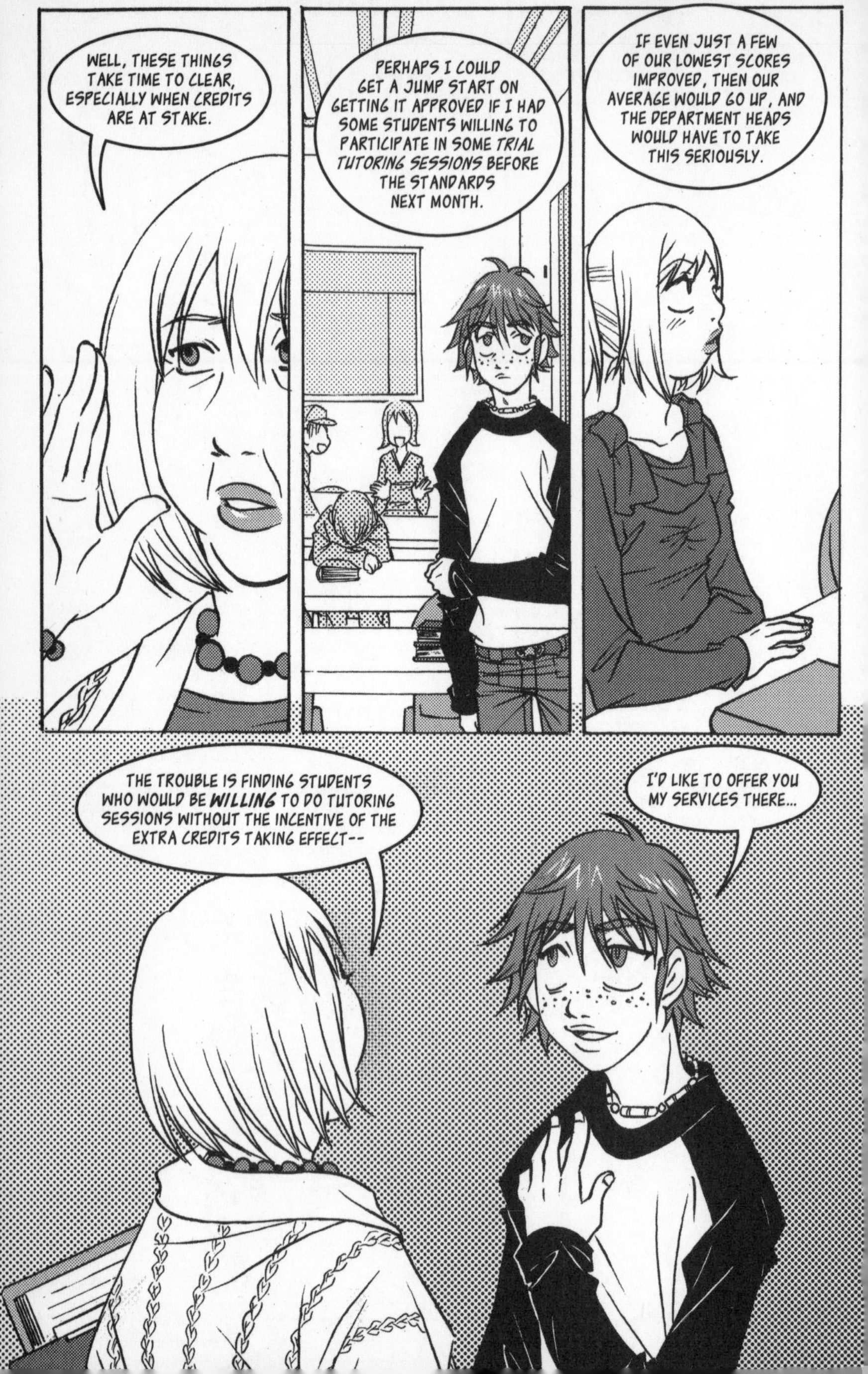
WELL, THESE THINGS TAKE TIME TO CLEAR, ESPECIALLY WHEN CREDITS ARE AT STAKE.
PERHAPS I COULD GET A JUMP START ON GETTING IT APPROVED IF I HAD SOME STUDENTS WILLING TO PARTICIPATE IN SOME *TRIAL TUTORING SESSIONS* BEFORE THE STANDARDS NEXT MONTH.
IF EVEN JUST A FEW OF OUR LOWEST SCORES IMPROVED, THEN OUR AVERAGE WOULD GO UP, AND THE DEPARTMENT HEADS WOULD HAVE TO TAKE THIS SERIOUSLY.
THE TROUBLE IS FINDING STUDENTS WHO WOULD BE ***WILLING*** TO DO TUTORING SESSIONS WITHOUT THE INCENTIVE OF THE EXTRA CREDITS TAKING EFFECT--
I'D LIKE TO OFFER YOU MY SERVICES THERE...

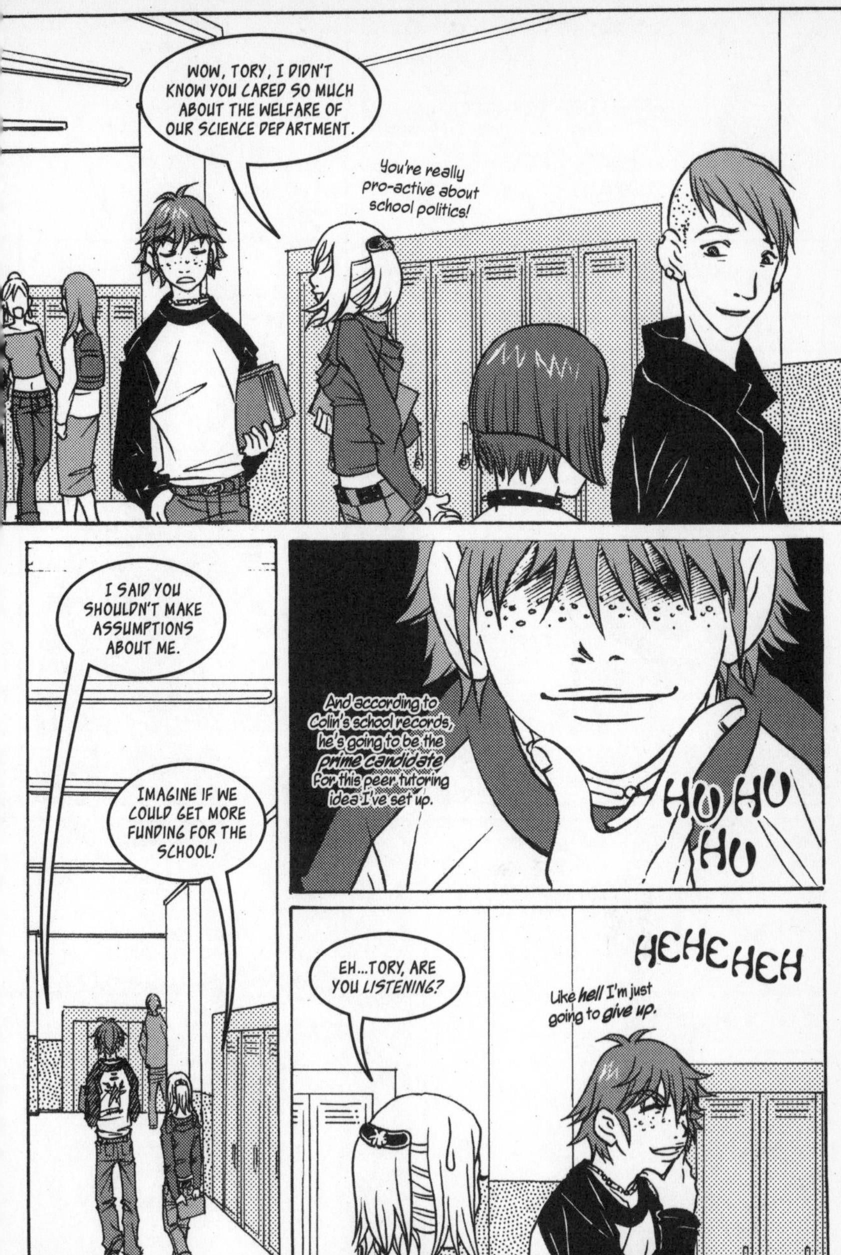
WOW, TORY, I DIDN'T KNOW YOU CARED SO MUCH ABOUT THE WELFARE OF OUR SCIENCE DEPARTMENT.
You're really pro-active about school politics!
I SAID YOU SHOULDN'T MAKE ASSUMPTIONS ABOUT ME.
IMAGINE IF WE COULD GET MORE FUNDING FOR THE SCHOOL!
And according to Colin's school records, he's going to be the *prime candidate* for this peer tutoring idea I've set up.
HU HU HU
EH...TORY, ARE YOU *LISTENING?*
HEHEHEH
Like *hell* I'm just going to *give up.*

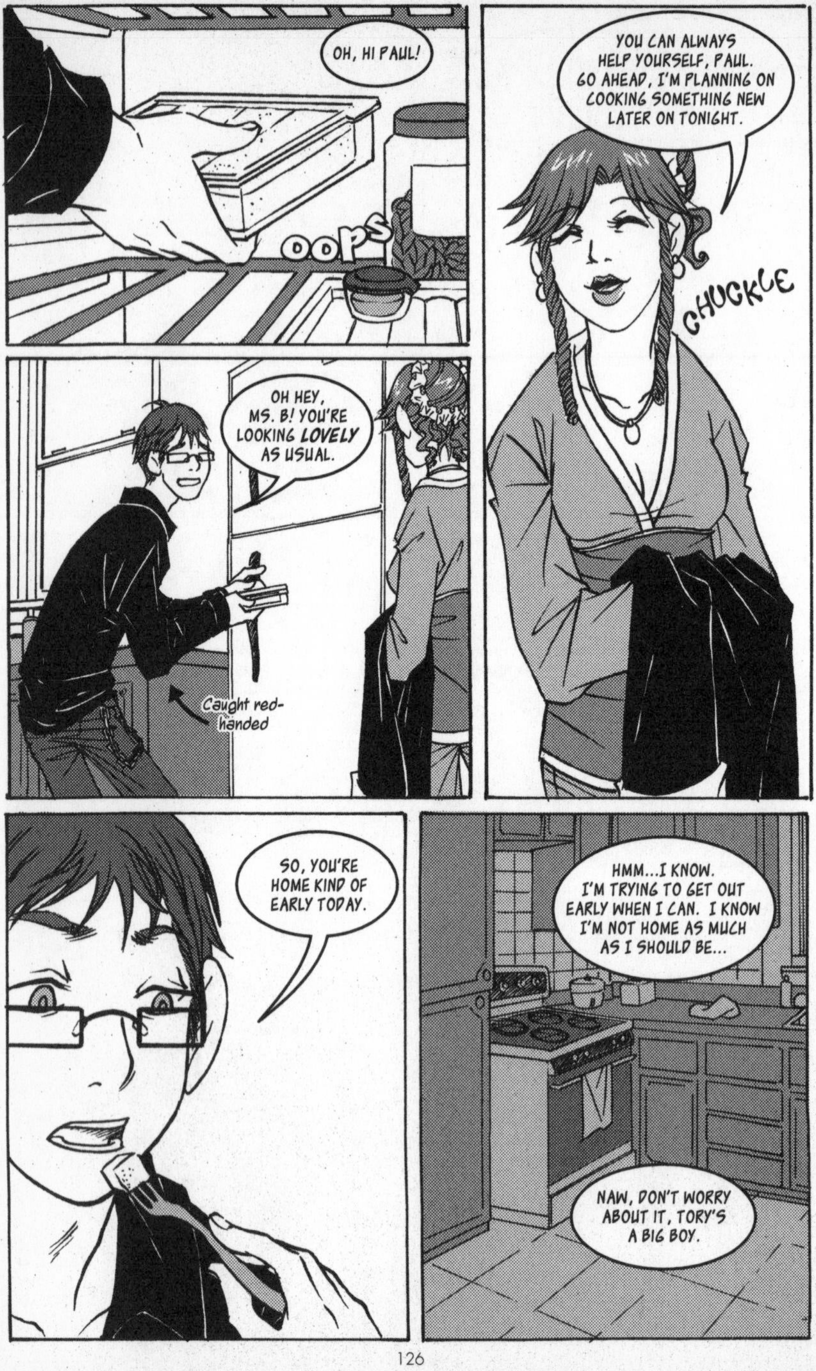
OH, HI PAUL!
OOPS
OH HEY, MS. B! YOU'RE LOOKING LOVELY AS USUAL.
Caught red-handed
YOU CAN ALWAYS HELP YOURSELF, PAUL. GO AHEAD, I'M PLANNING ON COOKING SOMETHING NEW LATER ON TONIGHT.
CHUCKLE
SO, YOU'RE HOME KIND OF EARLY TODAY.
HMM...I KNOW. I'M TRYING TO GET OUT EARLY WHEN I CAN. I KNOW I'M NOT HOME AS MUCH AS I SHOULD BE...
NAW, DON'T WORRY ABOUT IT, TORY'S A BIG BOY.

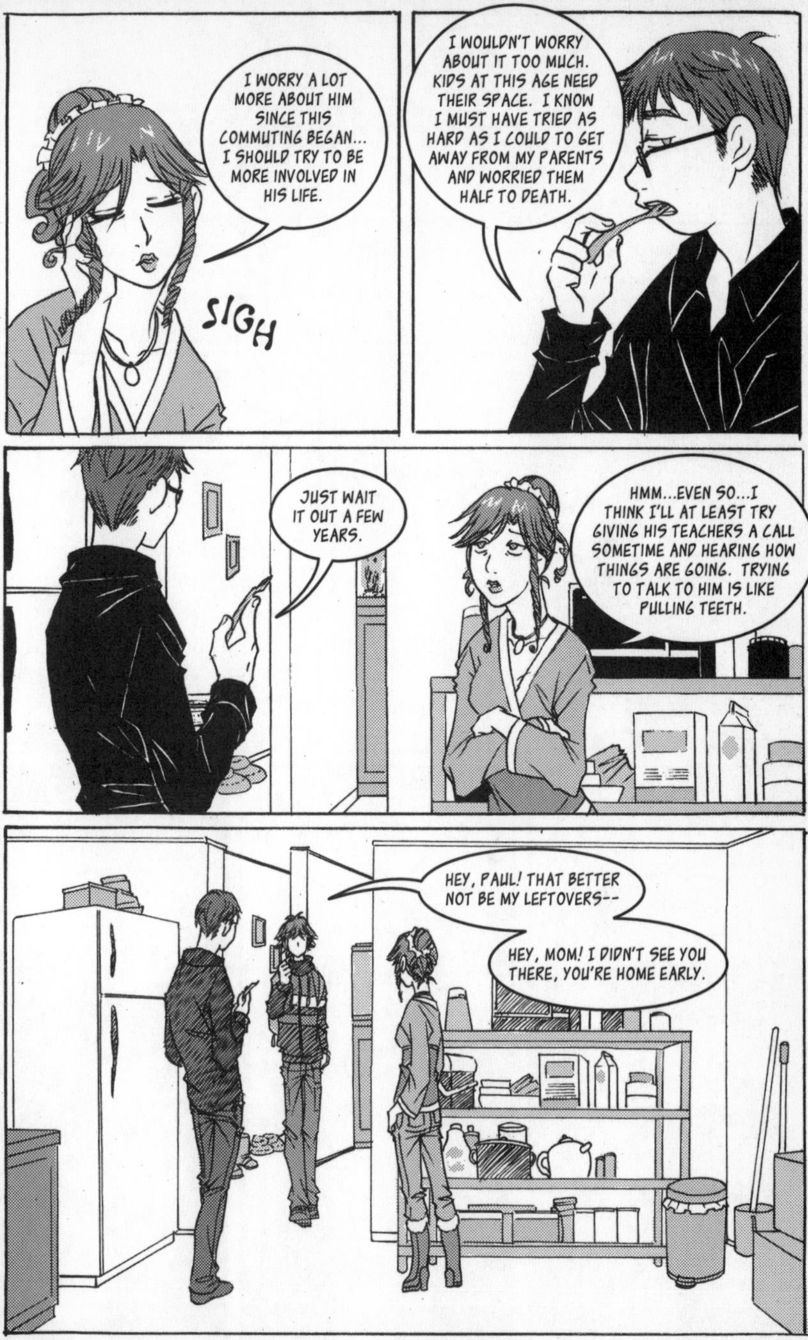
I WORRY A LOT MORE ABOUT HIM SINCE THIS COMMUTING BEGAN... I SHOULD TRY TO BE MORE INVOLVED IN HIS LIFE.
SIGH
I WOULDN'T WORRY ABOUT IT TOO MUCH. KIDS AT THIS AGE NEED THEIR SPACE. I KNOW I MUST HAVE TRIED AS HARD AS I COULD TO GET AWAY FROM MY PARENTS AND WORRIED THEM HALF TO DEATH.
JUST WAIT IT OUT A FEW YEARS.
HMM...EVEN SO...I THINK I'LL AT LEAST TRY GIVING HIS TEACHERS A CALL SOMETIME AND HEARING HOW THINGS ARE GOING. TRYING TO TALK TO HIM IS LIKE PULLING TEETH.
HEY, PAUL! THAT BETTER NOT BE MY LEFTOVERS--
HEY, MOM! I DIDN'T SEE YOU THERE, YOU'RE HOME EARLY.

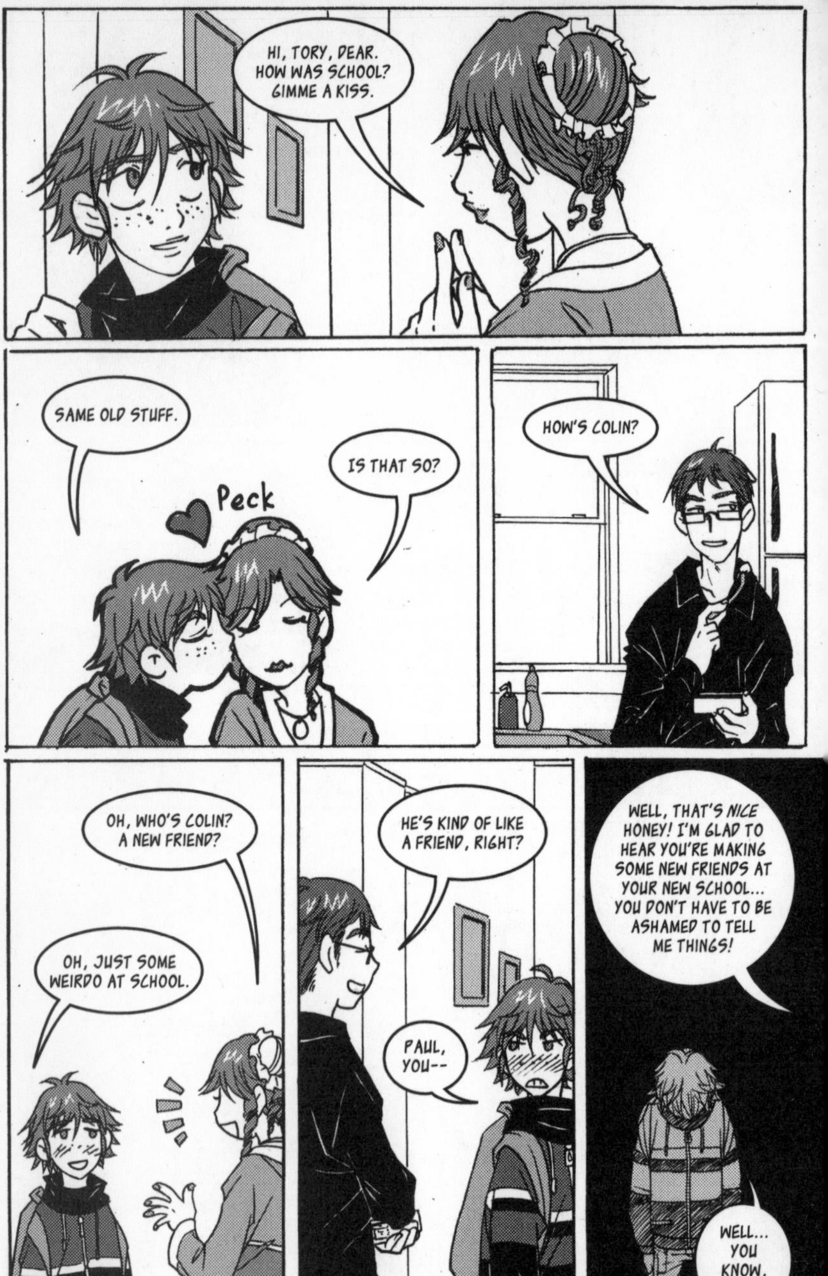
HI, TORY, DEAR. HOW WAS SCHOOL? GIMME A KISS.
SAME OLD STUFF.
Peck
IS THAT SO?
HOW'S COLIN?
OH, WHO'S COLIN? A NEW FRIEND?
OH, JUST SOME WEIRDO AT SCHOOL.
HE'S KIND OF LIKE A FRIEND, RIGHT?
PAUL, YOU--
WELL, THAT'S *NICE* HONEY! I'M GLAD TO HEAR YOU'RE MAKING SOME NEW FRIENDS AT YOUR NEW SCHOOL... YOU DON'T HAVE TO BE ASHAMED TO TELL ME THINGS!
WELL... YOU KNOW, STUFF...

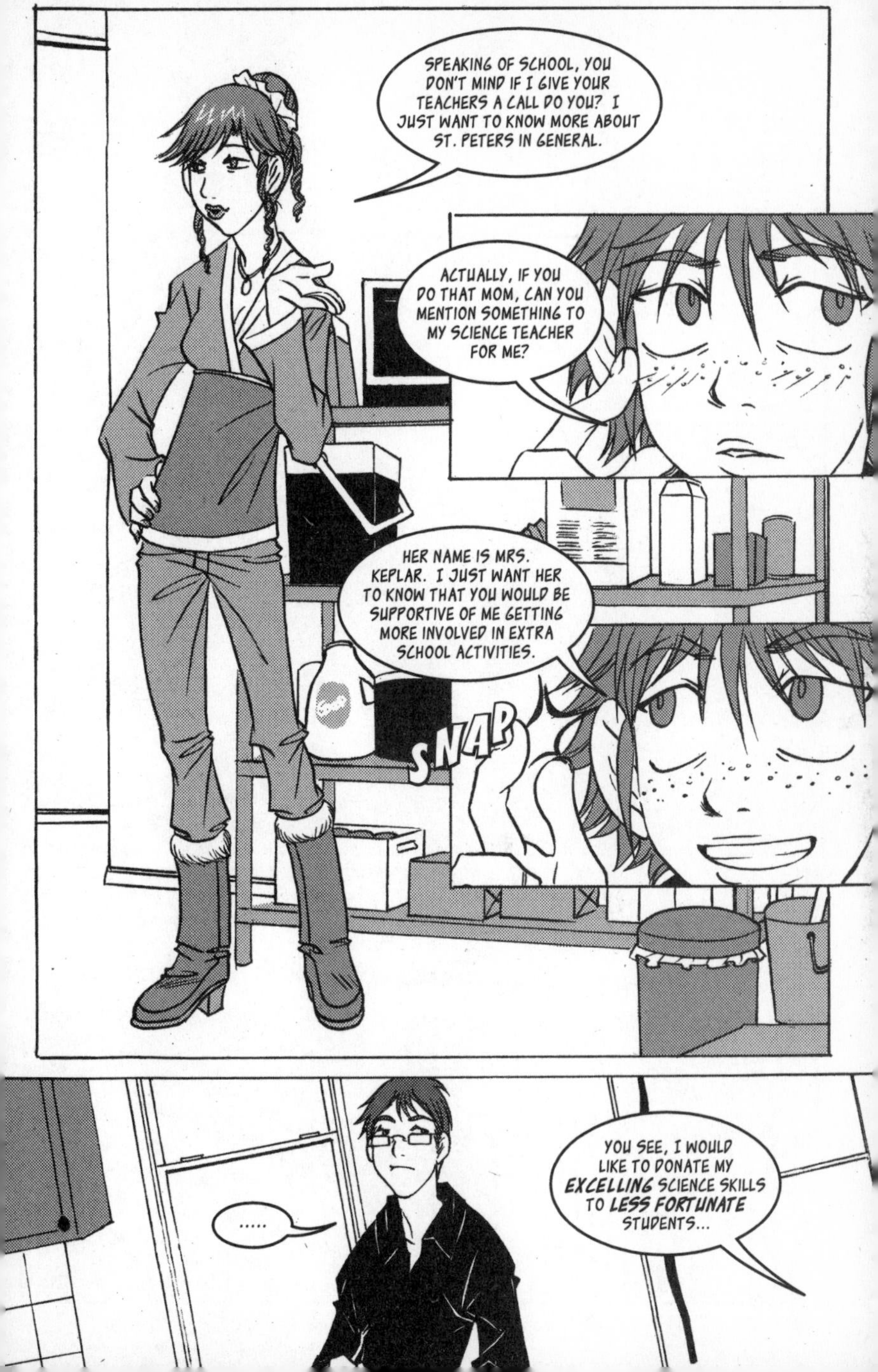

SPEAKING OF SCHOOL, YOU DON'T MIND IF I GIVE YOUR TEACHERS A CALL DO YOU? I JUST WANT TO KNOW MORE ABOUT ST. PETERS IN GENERAL.
ACTUALLY, IF YOU DO THAT MOM, CAN YOU MENTION SOMETHING TO MY SCIENCE TEACHER FOR ME?
HER NAME IS MRS. KEPLAR. I JUST WANT HER TO KNOW THAT YOU WOULD BE SUPPORTIVE OF ME GETTING MORE INVOLVED IN EXTRA SCHOOL ACTIVITIES.
SNAP
.....
YOU SEE, I WOULD LIKE TO DONATE MY ***EXCELLING*** SCIENCE SKILLS TO ***LESS FORTUNATE*** STUDENTS...

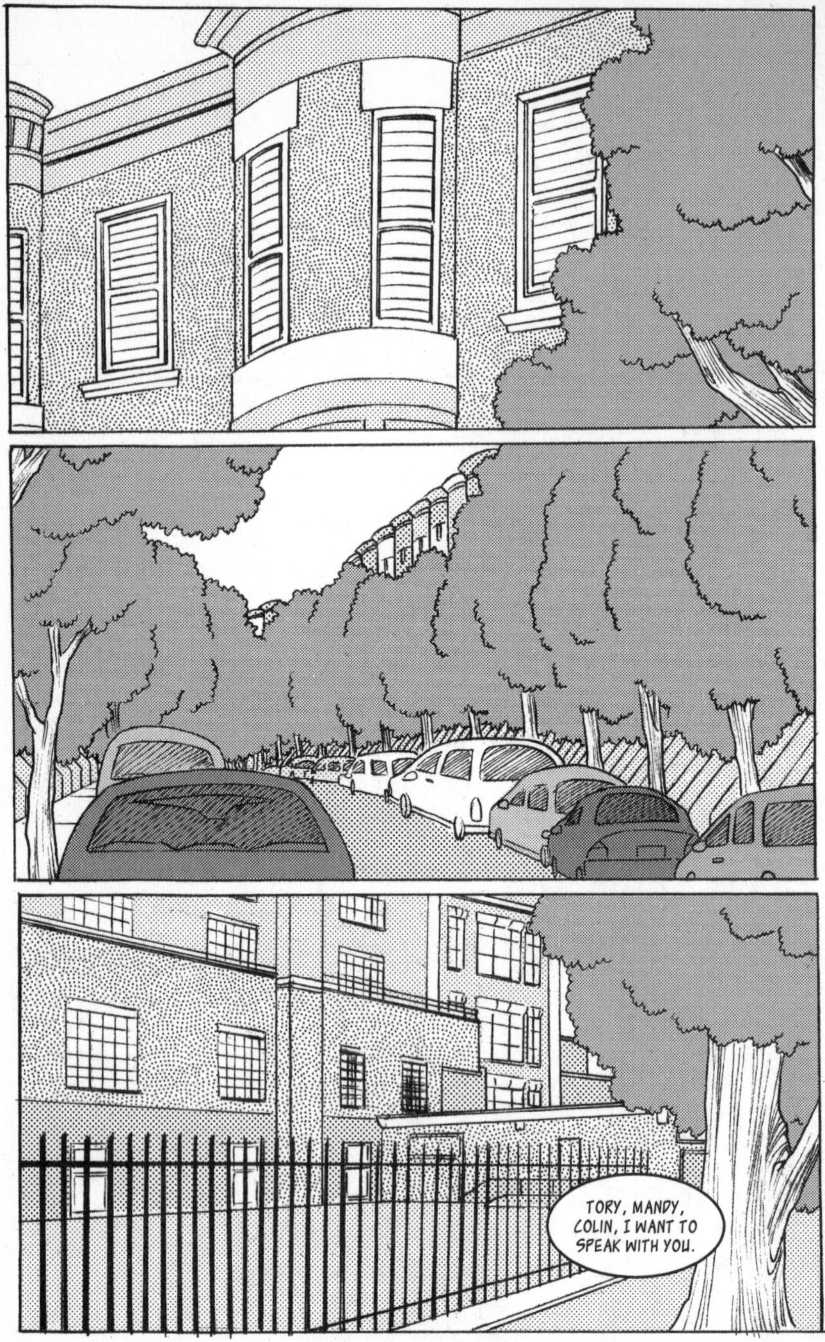
TORY, MANDY, COLIN, I WANT TO SPEAK WITH YOU.

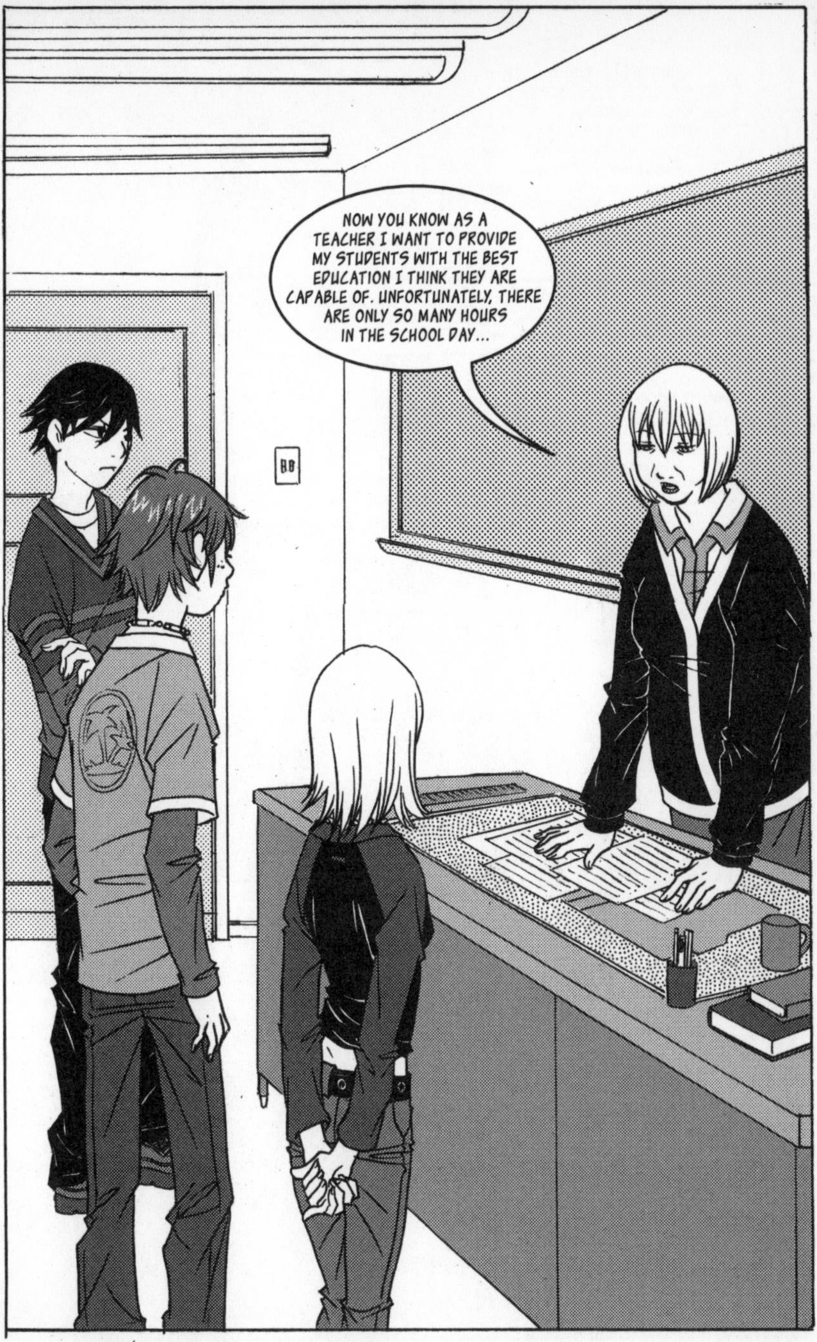
NOW YOU KNOW AS A TEACHER I WANT TO PROVIDE MY STUDENTS WITH THE BEST EDUCATION I THINK THEY ARE CAPABLE OF. UNFORTUNATELY, THERE ARE ONLY SO MANY HOURS IN THE SCHOOL DAY...

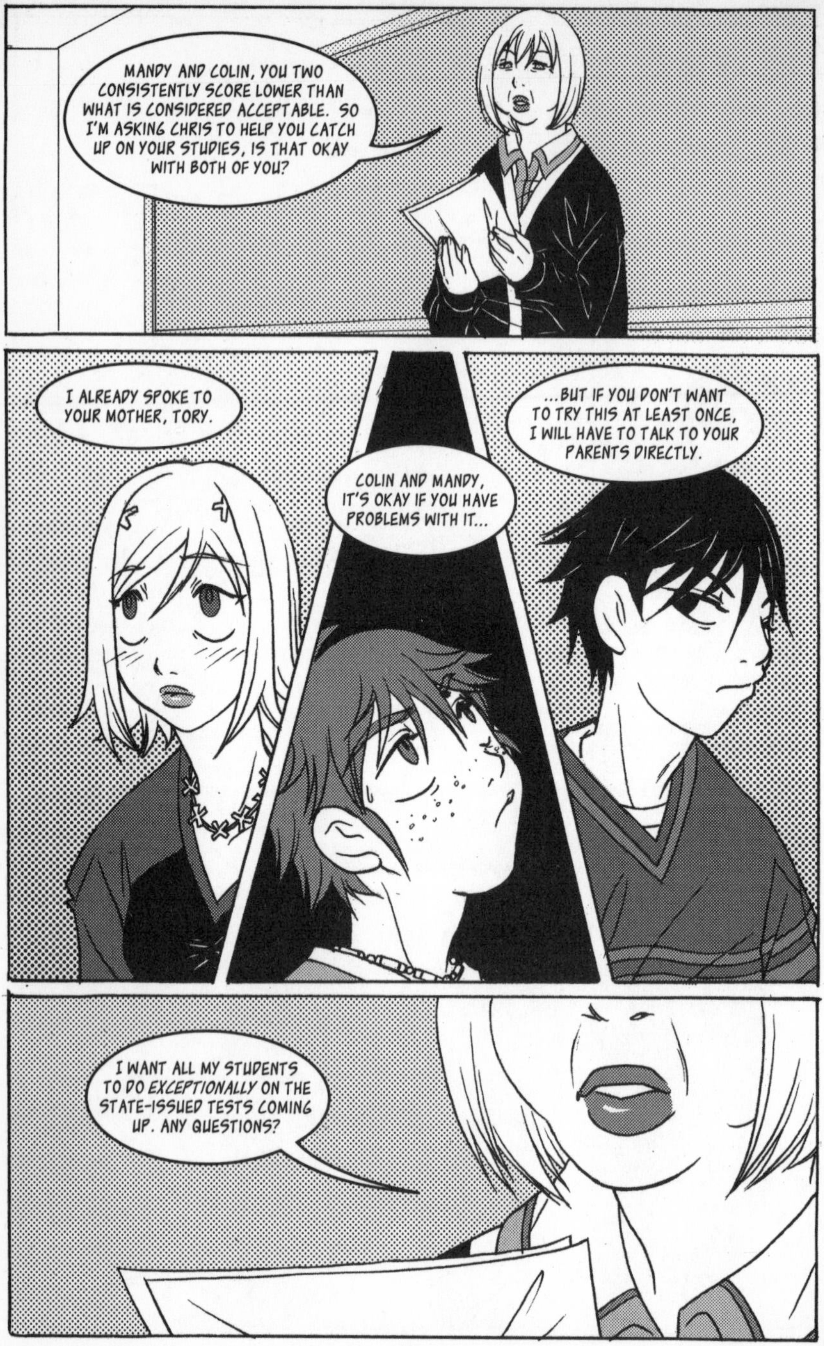
MANDY AND COLIN, YOU TWO CONSISTENTLY SCORE LOWER THAN WHAT IS CONSIDERED ACCEPTABLE. SO I'M ASKING CHRIS TO HELP YOU CATCH UP ON YOUR STUDIES, IS THAT OKAY WITH BOTH OF YOU?
I ALREADY SPOKE TO YOUR MOTHER, TORY.
COLIN AND MANDY, IT'S OKAY IF YOU HAVE PROBLEMS WITH IT...
...BUT IF YOU DON'T WANT TO TRY THIS AT LEAST ONCE, I WILL HAVE TO TALK TO YOUR PARENTS DIRECTLY.
I WANT ALL MY STUDENTS TO DO *EXCEPTIONALLY* ON THE STATE-ISSUED TESTS COMING UP. ANY QUESTIONS?

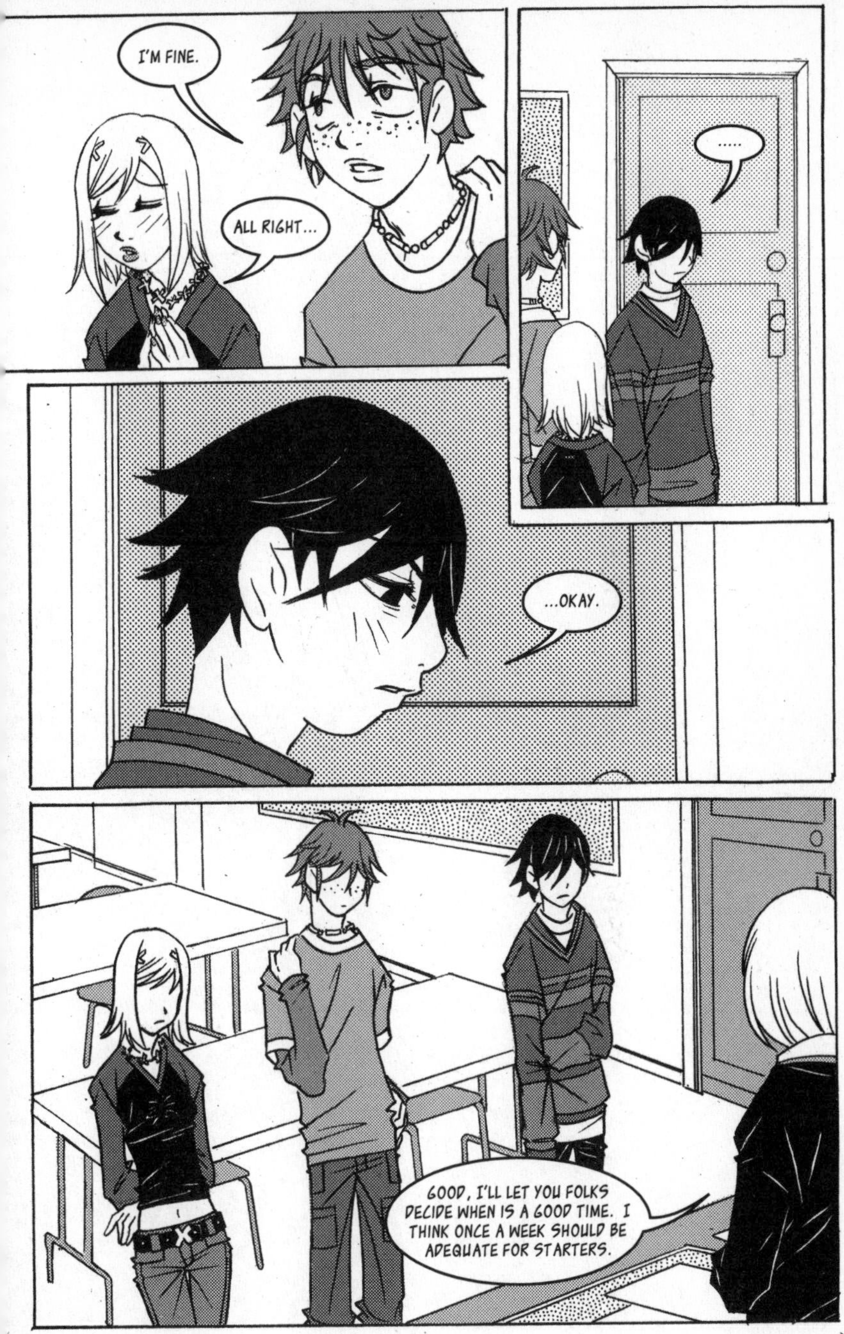
I'M FINE.
ALL RIGHT...
......
...OKAY.
GOOD, I'LL LET YOU FOLKS DECIDE WHEN IS A GOOD TIME. I THINK ONCE A WEEK SHOULD BE ADEQUATE FOR STARTERS.

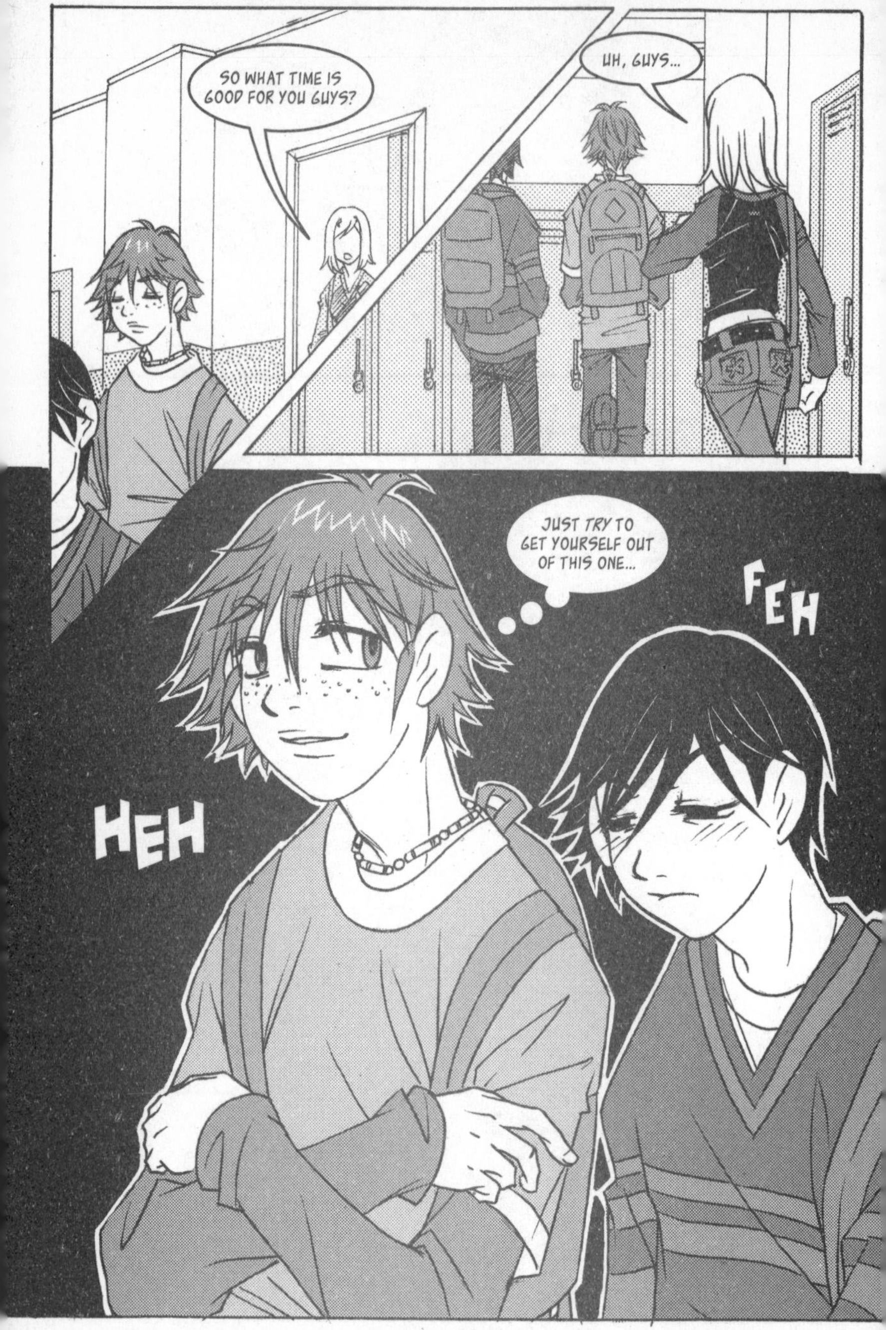

SO WHAT TIME IS GOOD FOR YOU GUYS?
UH, GUYS...
JUST TRY TO GET YOURSELF OUT OF THIS ONE...
FEH
HEH

Off*Beat

Chapter 6: The Meeting

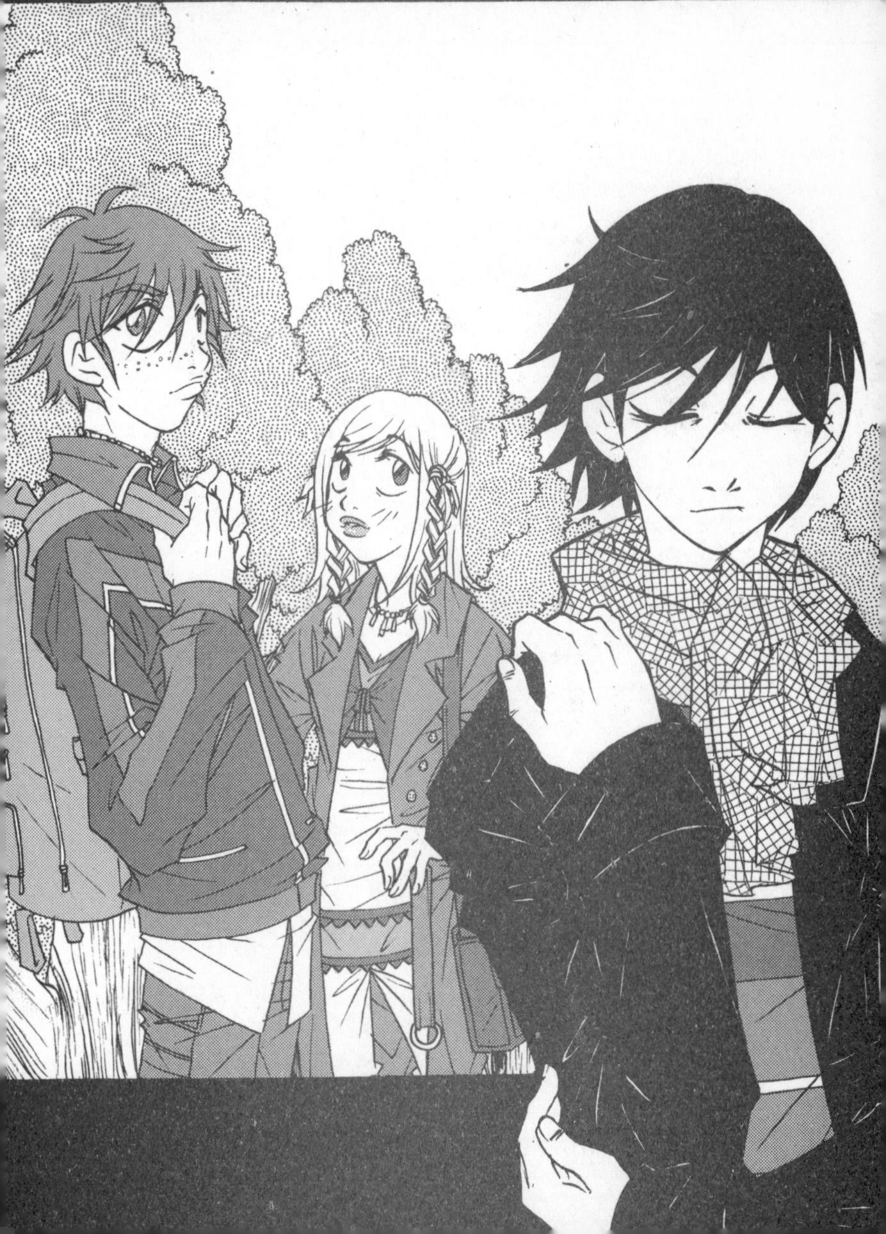

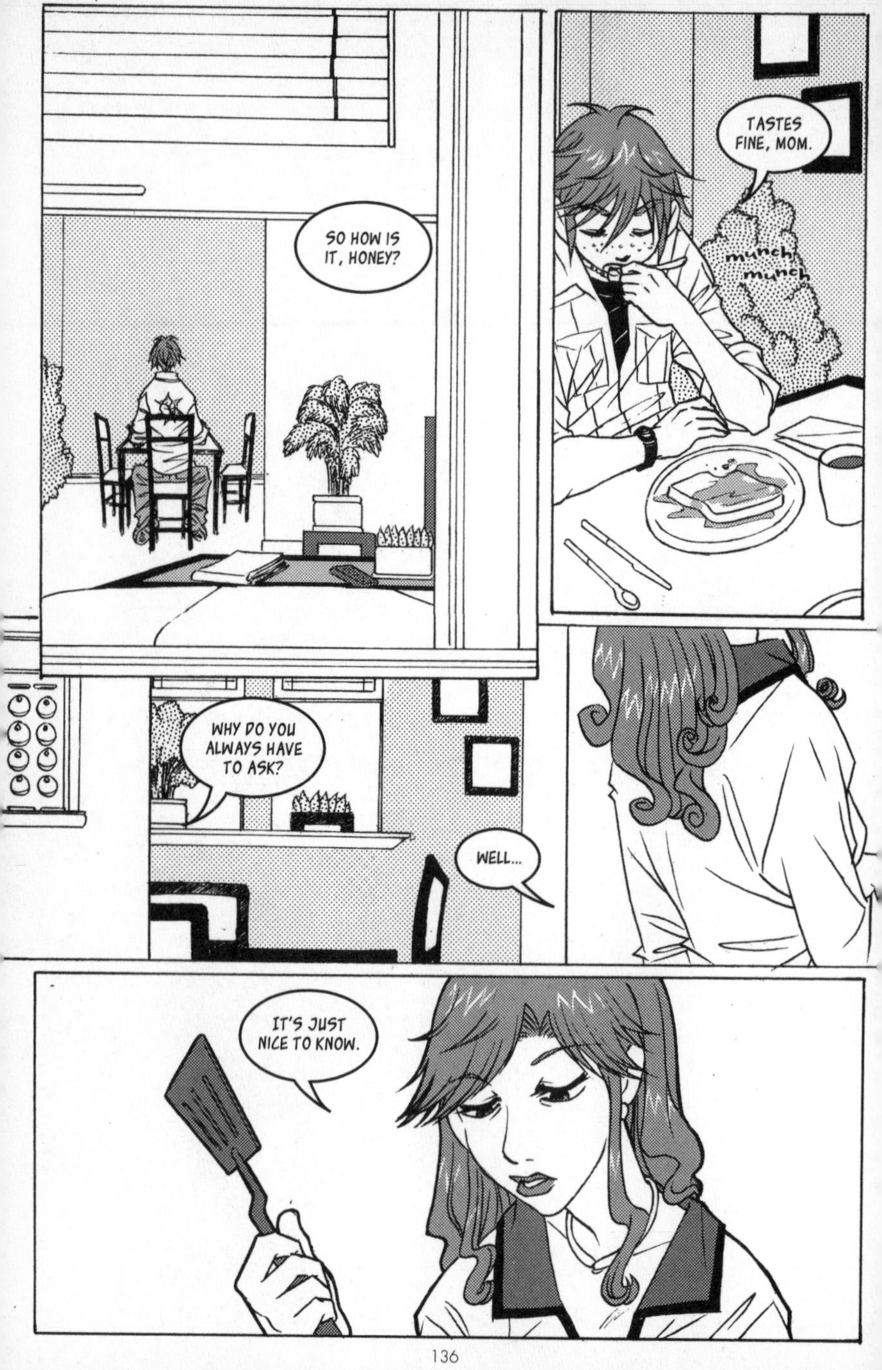
SO HOW IS IT, HONEY?
TASTES FINE, MOM.
munch munch
WHY DO YOU ALWAYS HAVE TO ASK?
WELL...
IT'S JUST NICE TO KNOW.

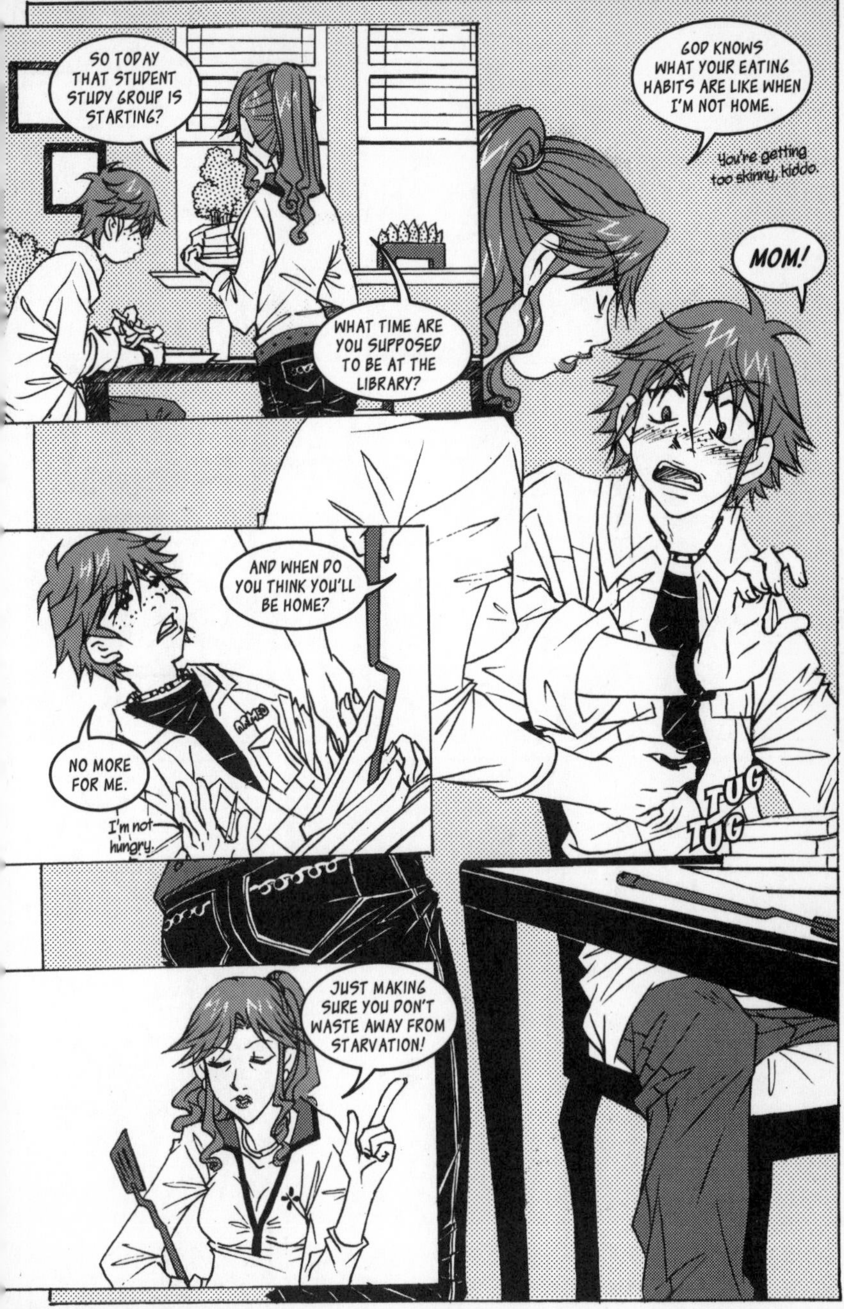
SO TODAY THAT STUDENT STUDY GROUP IS STARTING?
WHAT TIME ARE YOU SUPPOSED TO BE AT THE LIBRARY?
GOD KNOWS WHAT YOUR EATING HABITS ARE LIKE WHEN I'M NOT HOME.
You're getting too skinny, kiddo.
MOM!
AND WHEN DO YOU THINK YOU'LL BE HOME?
NO MORE FOR ME.
I'm not hungry.
TUG
TUG
JUST MAKING SURE YOU DON'T WASTE AWAY FROM STARVATION!

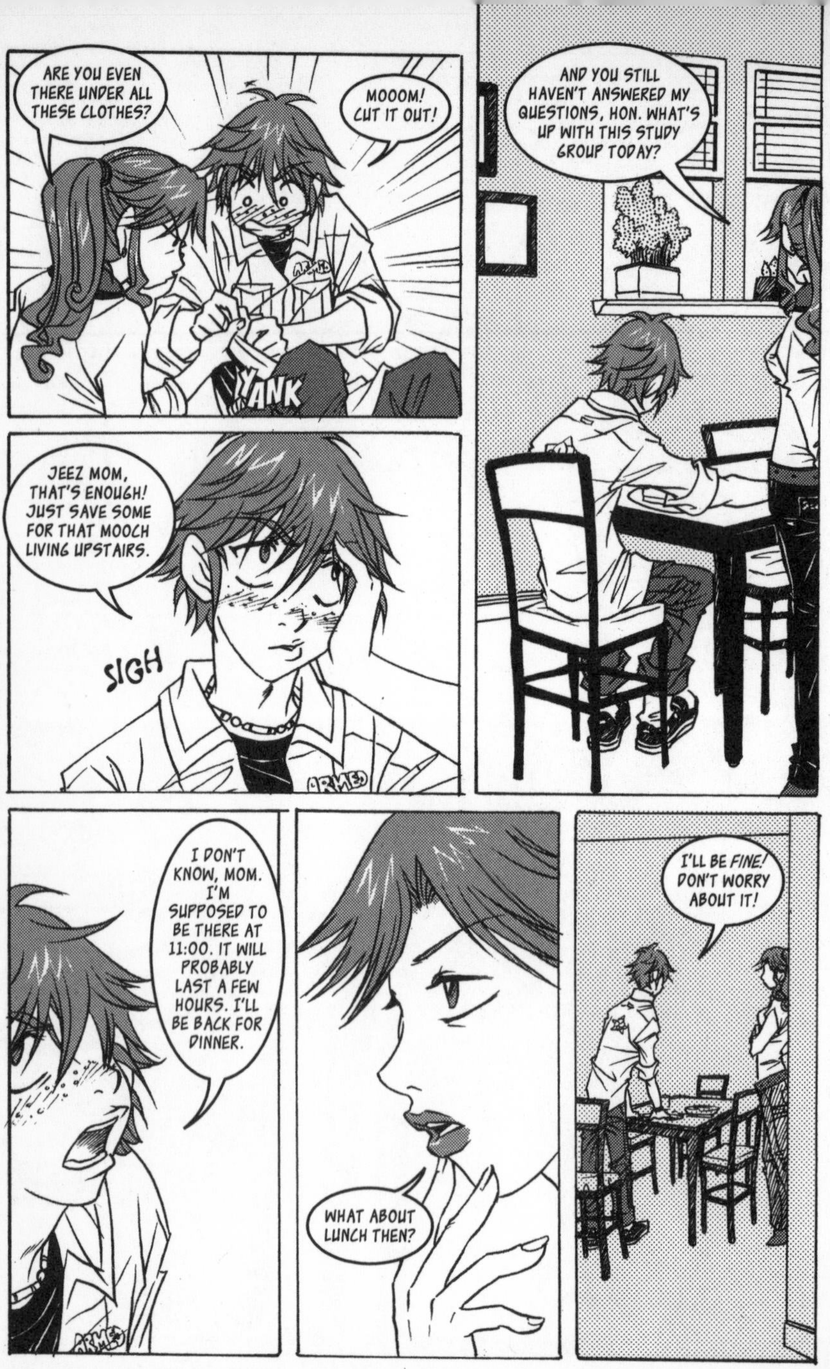
ARE YOU EVEN THERE UNDER ALL THESE CLOTHES?
MOOOM! CUT IT OUT!
YANK
AND YOU STILL HAVEN'T ANSWERED MY QUESTIONS, HON. WHAT'S UP WITH THIS STUDY GROUP TODAY?
JEEZ MOM, THAT'S ENOUGH! JUST SAVE SOME FOR THAT MOOCH LIVING UPSTAIRS.
SIGH
I DON'T KNOW, MOM. I'M SUPPOSED TO BE THERE AT 11:00. IT WILL PROBABLY LAST A FEW HOURS. I'LL BE BACK FOR DINNER.
WHAT ABOUT LUNCH THEN?
I'LL BE *FINE!* DON'T WORRY ABOUT IT!

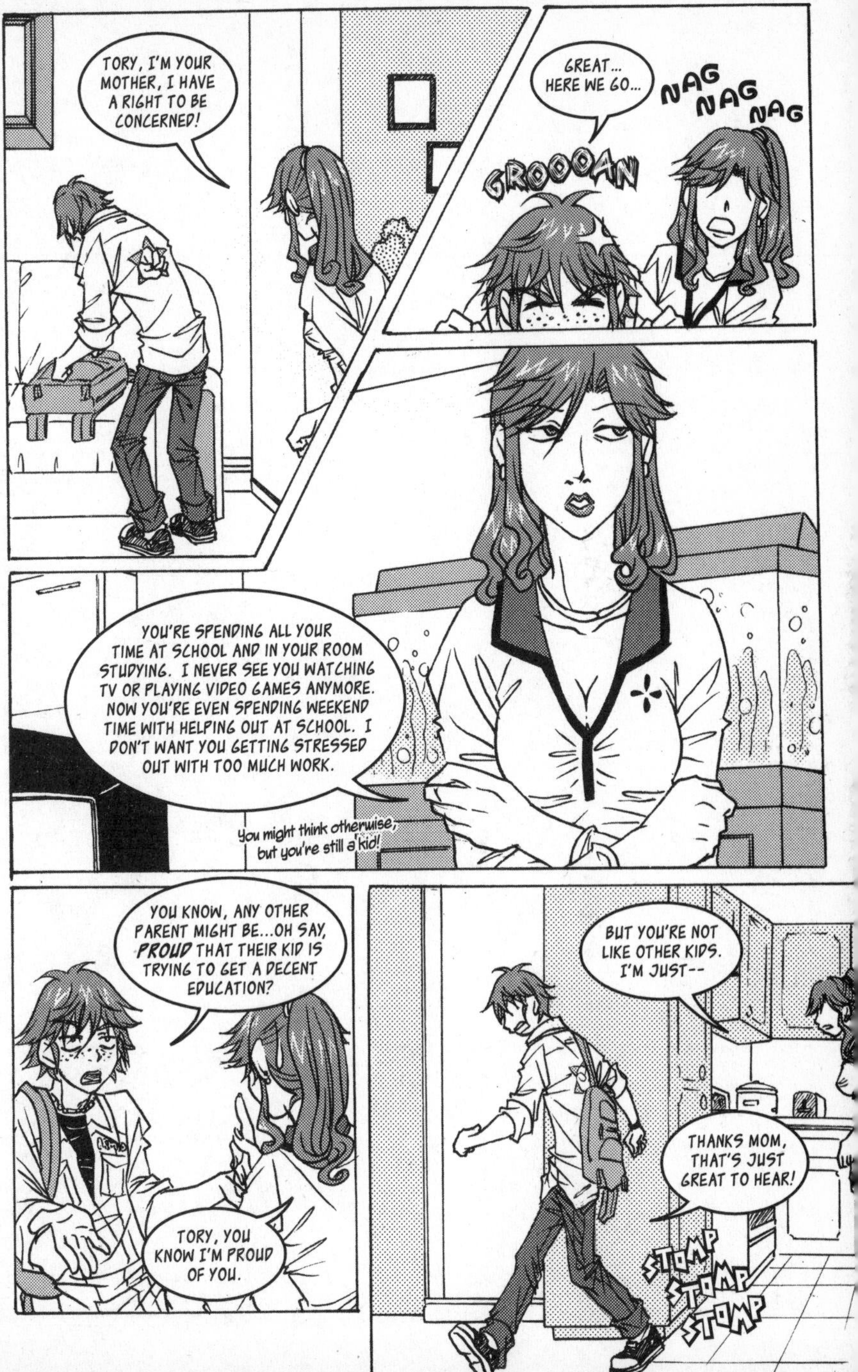
TORY, I'M YOUR MOTHER, I HAVE A RIGHT TO BE CONCERNED!
GREAT... HERE WE GO...
NAG NAG NAG
GROOOAN
YOU'RE SPENDING ALL YOUR TIME AT SCHOOL AND IN YOUR ROOM STUDYING. I NEVER SEE YOU WATCHING TV OR PLAYING VIDEO GAMES ANYMORE. NOW YOU'RE EVEN SPENDING WEEKEND TIME WITH HELPING OUT AT SCHOOL. I DON'T WANT YOU GETTING STRESSED OUT WITH TOO MUCH WORK.
You might think otherwise, but you're still a kid!
YOU KNOW, ANY OTHER PARENT MIGHT BE...OH SAY, PROUD THAT THEIR KID IS TRYING TO GET A DECENT EDUCATION?
TORY, YOU KNOW I'M PROUD OF YOU.
BUT YOU'RE NOT LIKE OTHER KIDS. I'M JUST--
THANKS MOM, THAT'S JUST GREAT TO HEAR!
STOMP STOMP STOMP

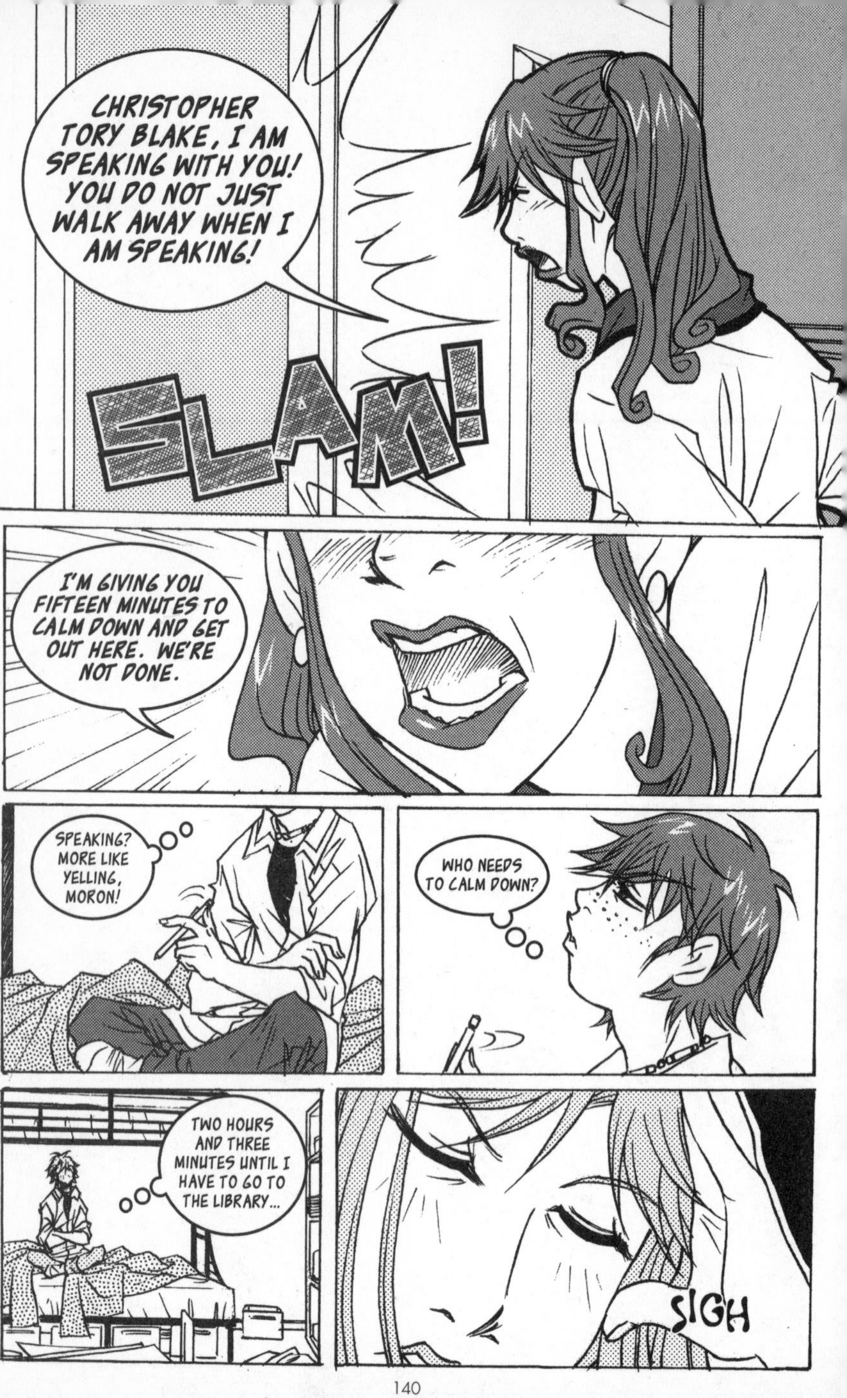
CHRISTOPHER TORY BLAKE, I AM SPEAKING WITH YOU! YOU DO NOT JUST WALK AWAY WHEN I AM SPEAKING!
SLAM!
I'M GIVING YOU FIFTEEN MINUTES TO CALM DOWN AND GET OUT HERE. WE'RE NOT DONE.
SPEAKING? MORE LIKE YELLING, MORON!
WHO NEEDS TO CALM DOWN?
TWO HOURS AND THREE MINUTES UNTIL I HAVE TO GO TO THE LIBRARY...
SIGH

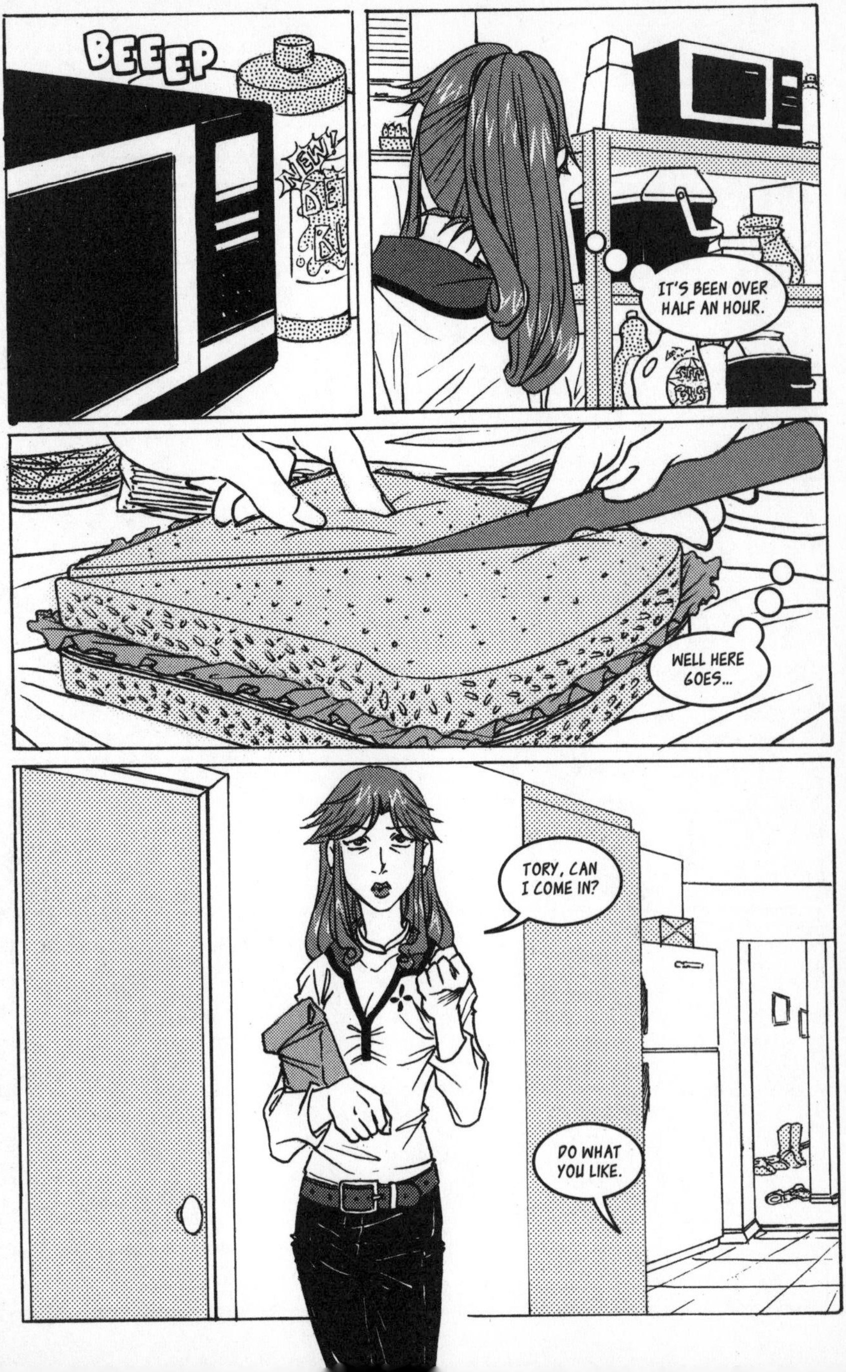
BEEEP
NEW!
IT'S BEEN OVER HALF AN HOUR.
WELL HERE GOES...
TORY, CAN I COME IN?
DO WHAT YOU LIKE.

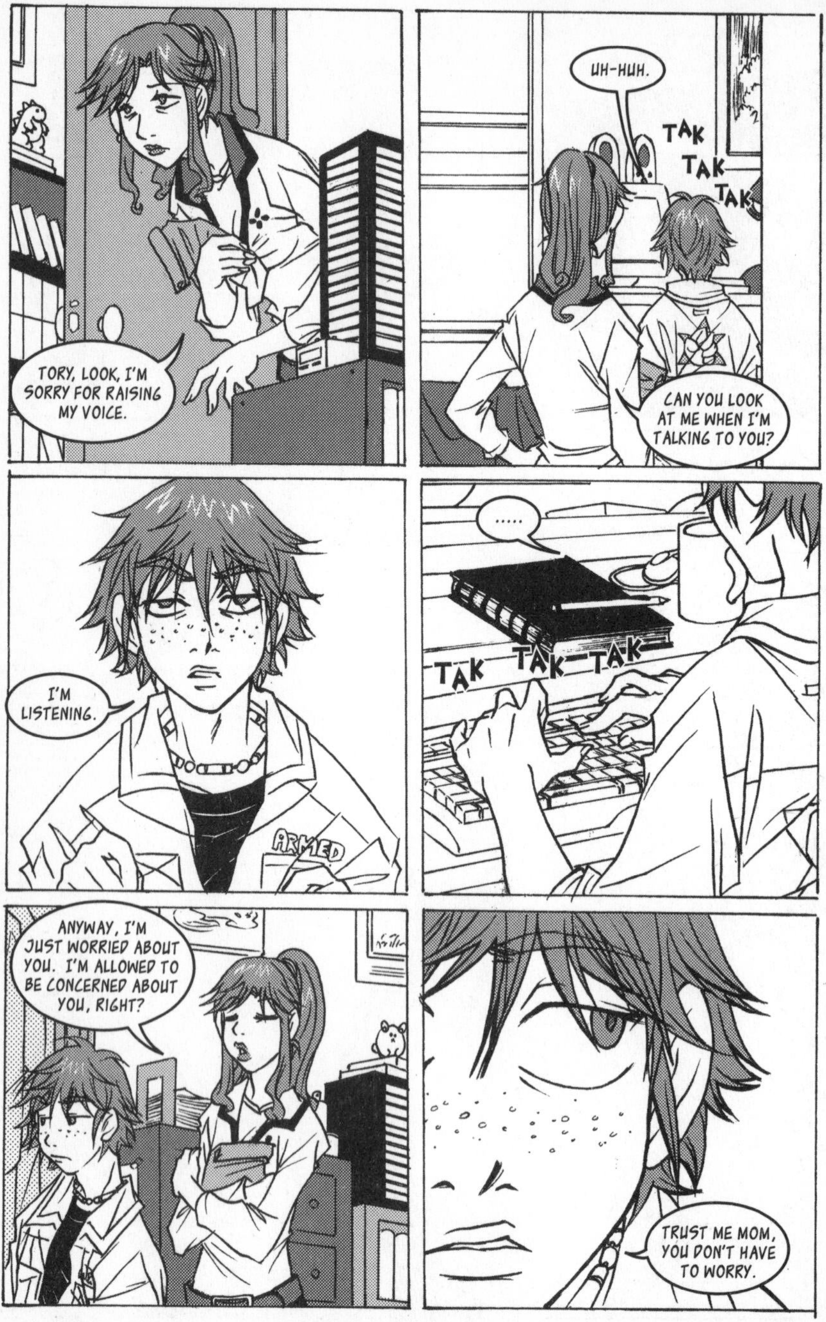
TORY, LOOK, I'M SORRY FOR RAISING MY VOICE.
UH-HUH.
TAK
TAK
TAK
CAN YOU LOOK AT ME WHEN I'M TALKING TO YOU?
I'M LISTENING.
ARMED
......
TAK TAK TAK
ANYWAY, I'M JUST WORRIED ABOUT YOU. I'M ALLOWED TO BE CONCERNED ABOUT YOU, RIGHT?
TRUST ME MOM, YOU DON'T HAVE TO WORRY.

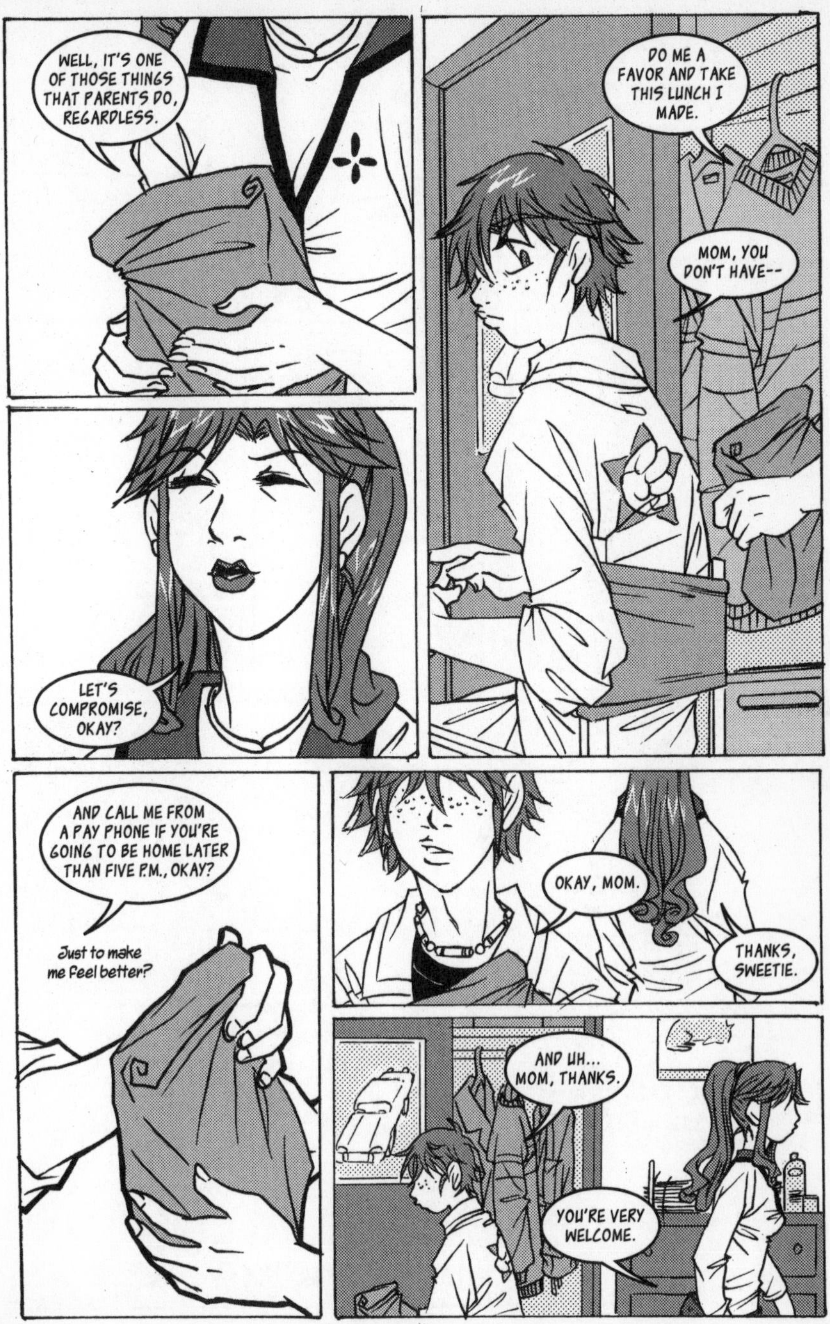
WELL, IT'S ONE OF THOSE THINGS THAT PARENTS DO, REGARDLESS.
DO ME A FAVOR AND TAKE THIS LUNCH I MADE.
MOM, YOU DON'T HAVE--
LET'S COMPROMISE, OKAY?
AND CALL ME FROM A PAY PHONE IF YOU'RE GOING TO BE HOME LATER THAN FIVE P.M., OKAY?
Just to make me feel better?
OKAY, MOM.
THANKS, SWEETIE.
AND UH... MOM, THANKS.
YOU'RE VERY WELCOME.

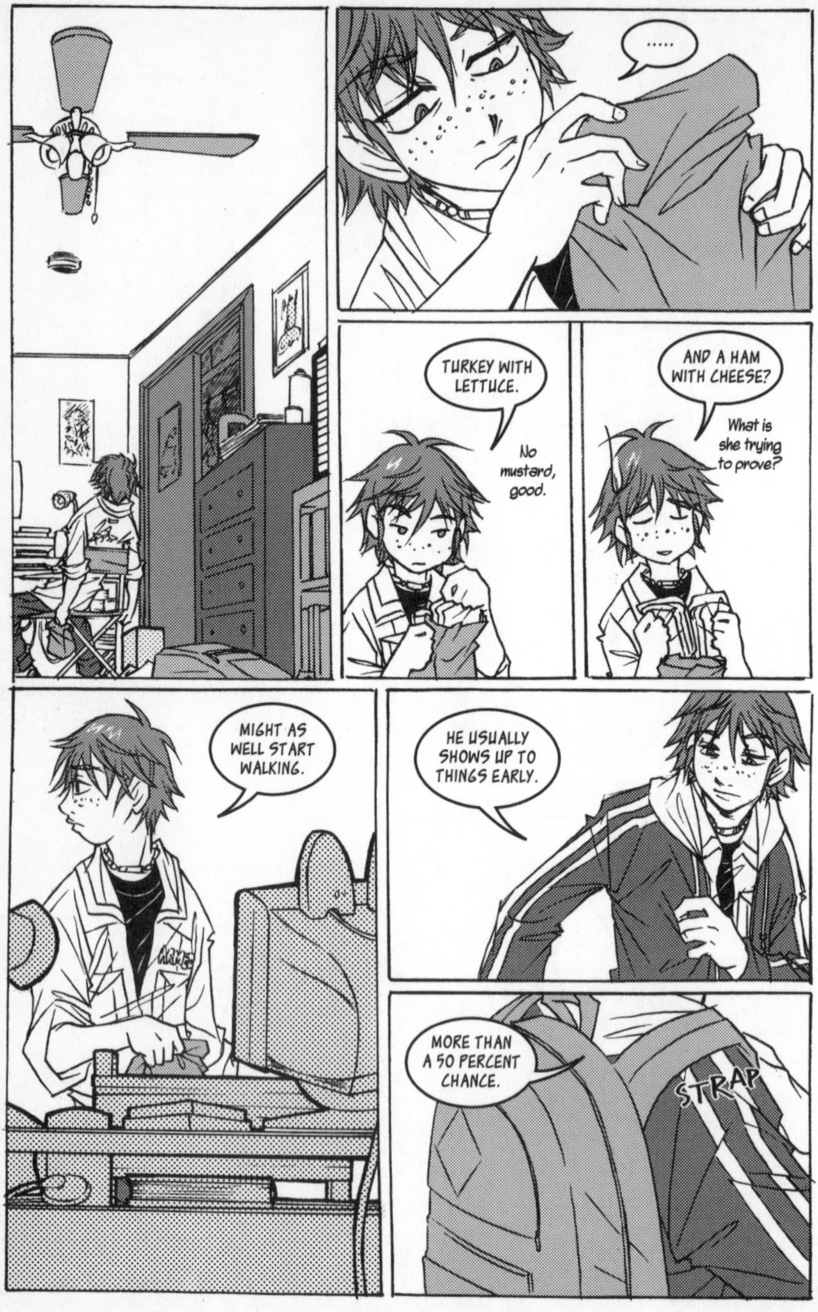
.....
TURKEY WITH LETTUCE.
No mustard, good.
AND A HAM WITH CHEESE?
What is she trying to prove?
MIGHT AS WELL START WALKING.
HE USUALLY SHOWS UP TO THINGS EARLY.
MORE THAN A 50 PERCENT CHANCE.
STRAP

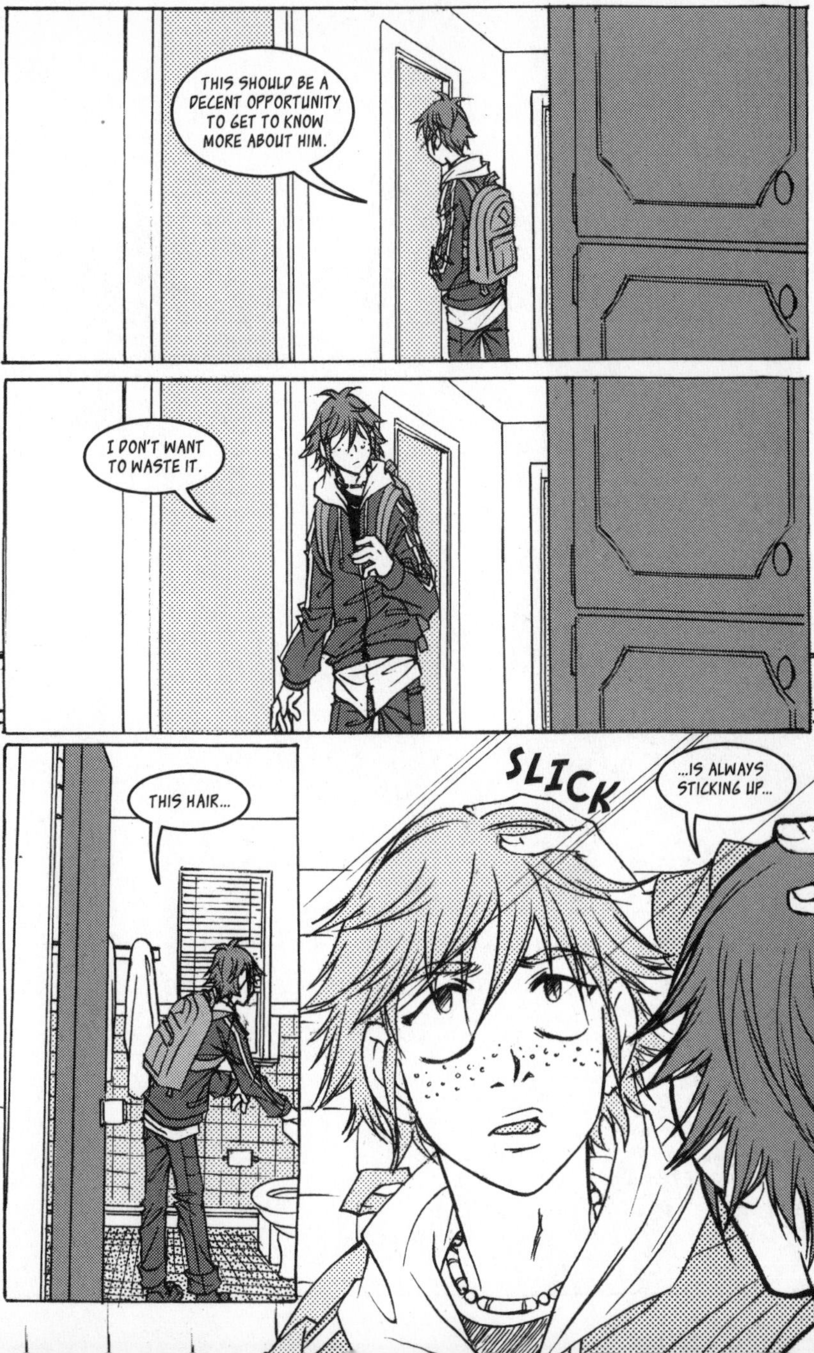
THIS SHOULD BE A DECENT OPPORTUNITY TO GET TO KNOW MORE ABOUT HIM.
I DON'T WANT TO WASTE IT.
THIS HAIR...
SLICK
...IS ALWAYS STICKING UP...

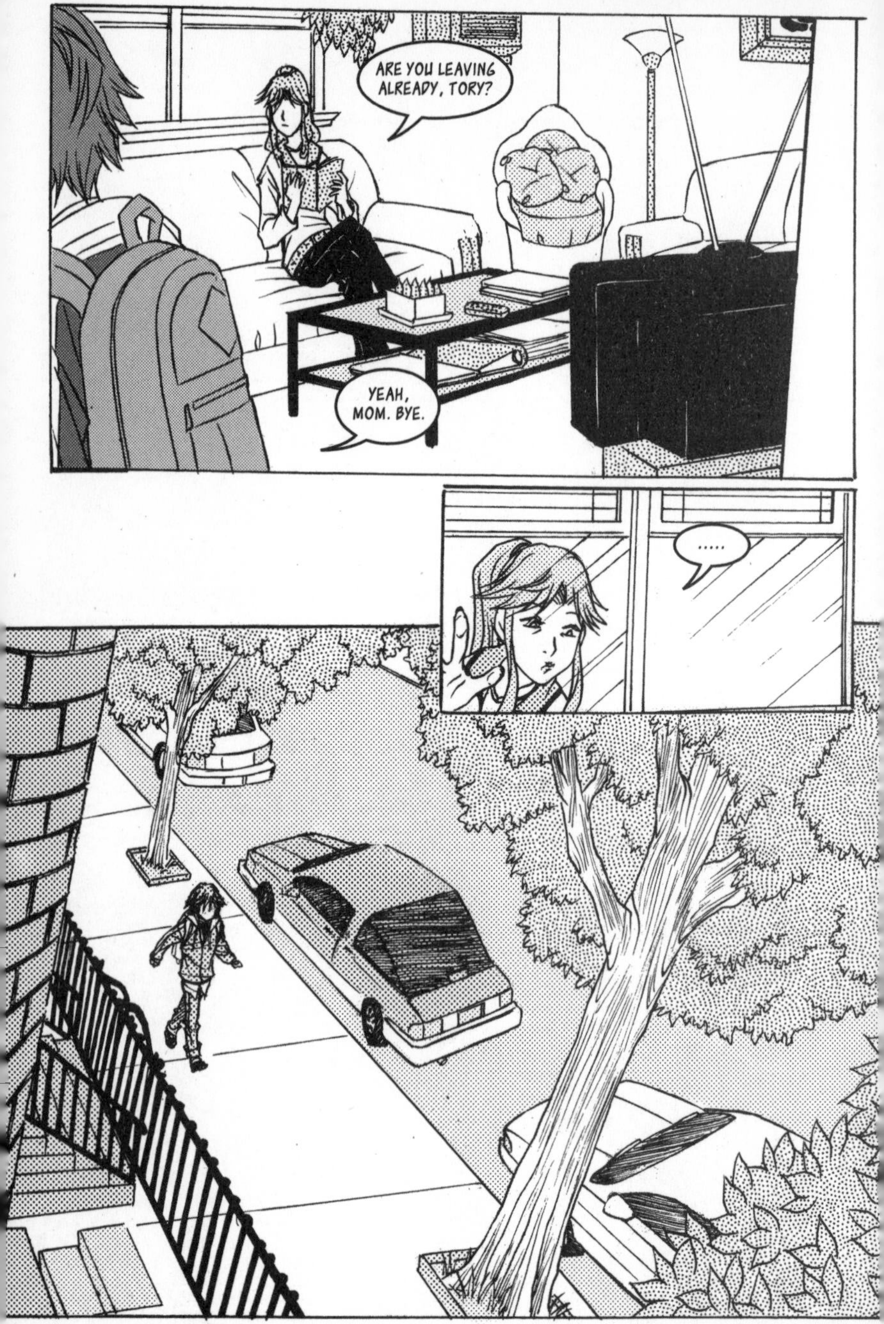
ARE YOU LEAVING ALREADY, TORY?
YEAH, MOM. BYE.
.....

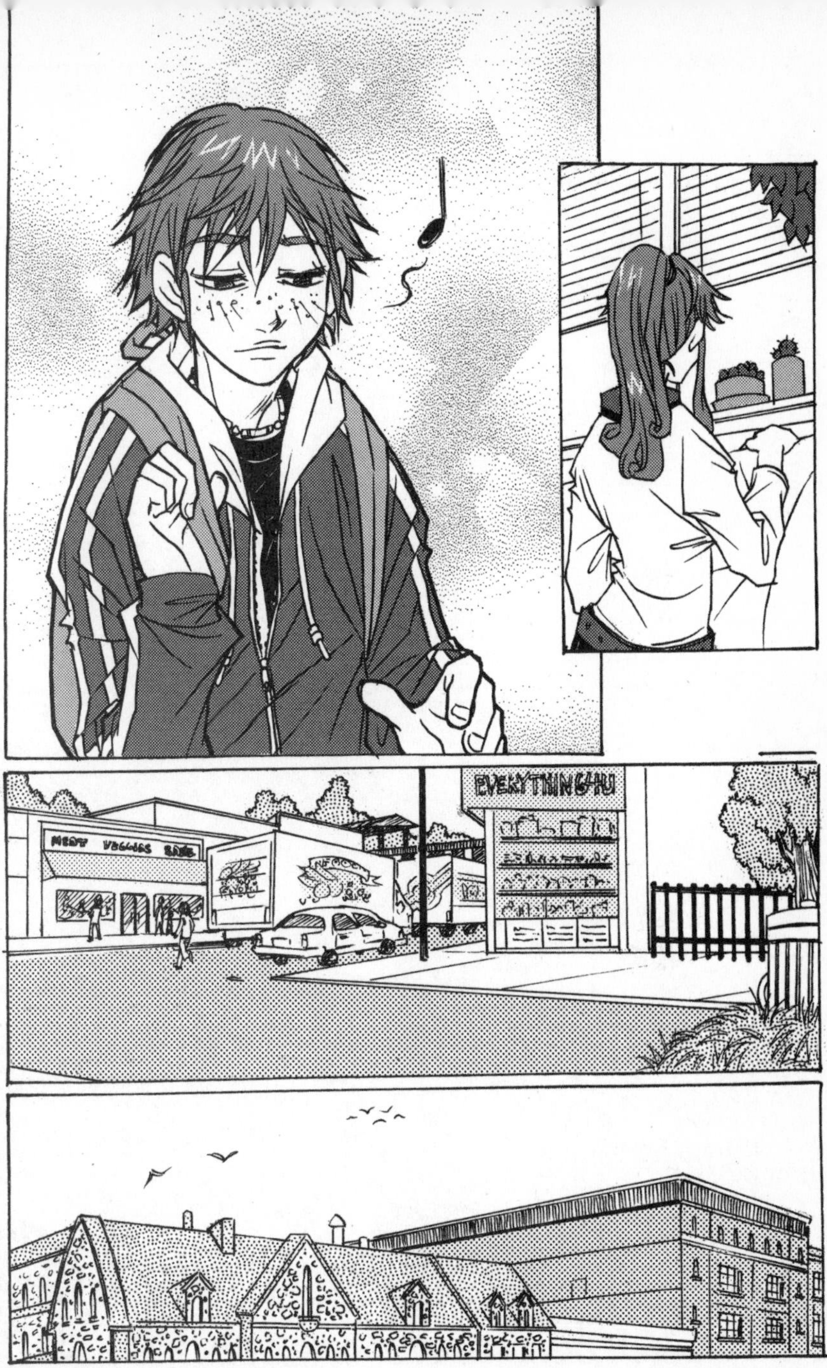
MEAT VEGGIES
EVERYTHING4U

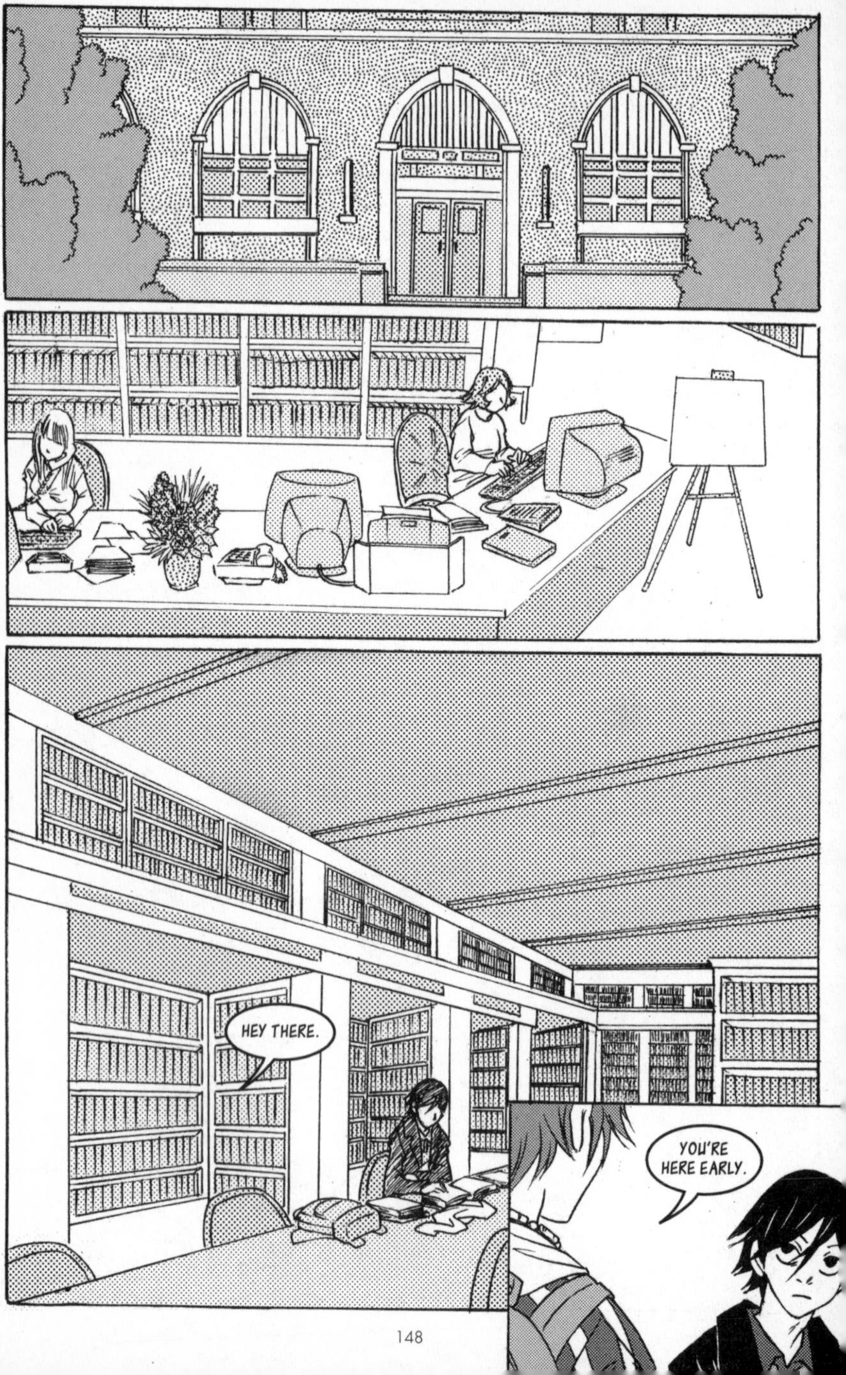
HEY THERE.
YOU'RE HERE EARLY.

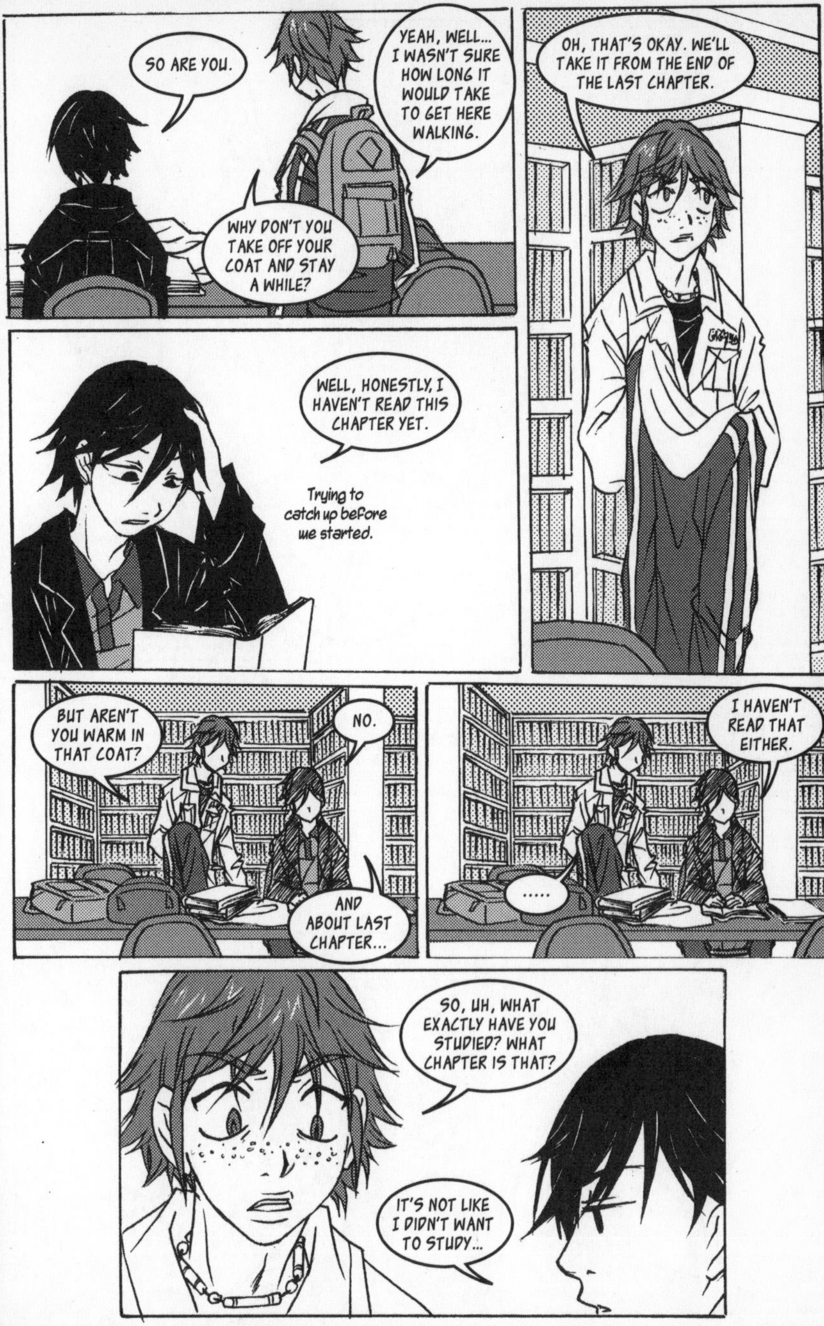
SO ARE YOU.
YEAH, WELL... I WASN'T SURE HOW LONG IT WOULD TAKE TO GET HERE WALKING.
WHY DON'T YOU TAKE OFF YOUR COAT AND STAY A WHILE?
OH, THAT'S OKAY. WE'LL TAKE IT FROM THE END OF THE LAST CHAPTER.
WELL, HONESTLY, I HAVEN'T READ THIS CHAPTER YET.
Trying to catch up before we started.
BUT AREN'T YOU WARM IN THAT COAT?
NO.
AND ABOUT LAST CHAPTER...
I HAVEN'T READ THAT EITHER.
.....
SO, UH, WHAT EXACTLY HAVE YOU STUDIED? WHAT CHAPTER IS THAT?
IT'S NOT LIKE I DIDN'T WANT TO STUDY...

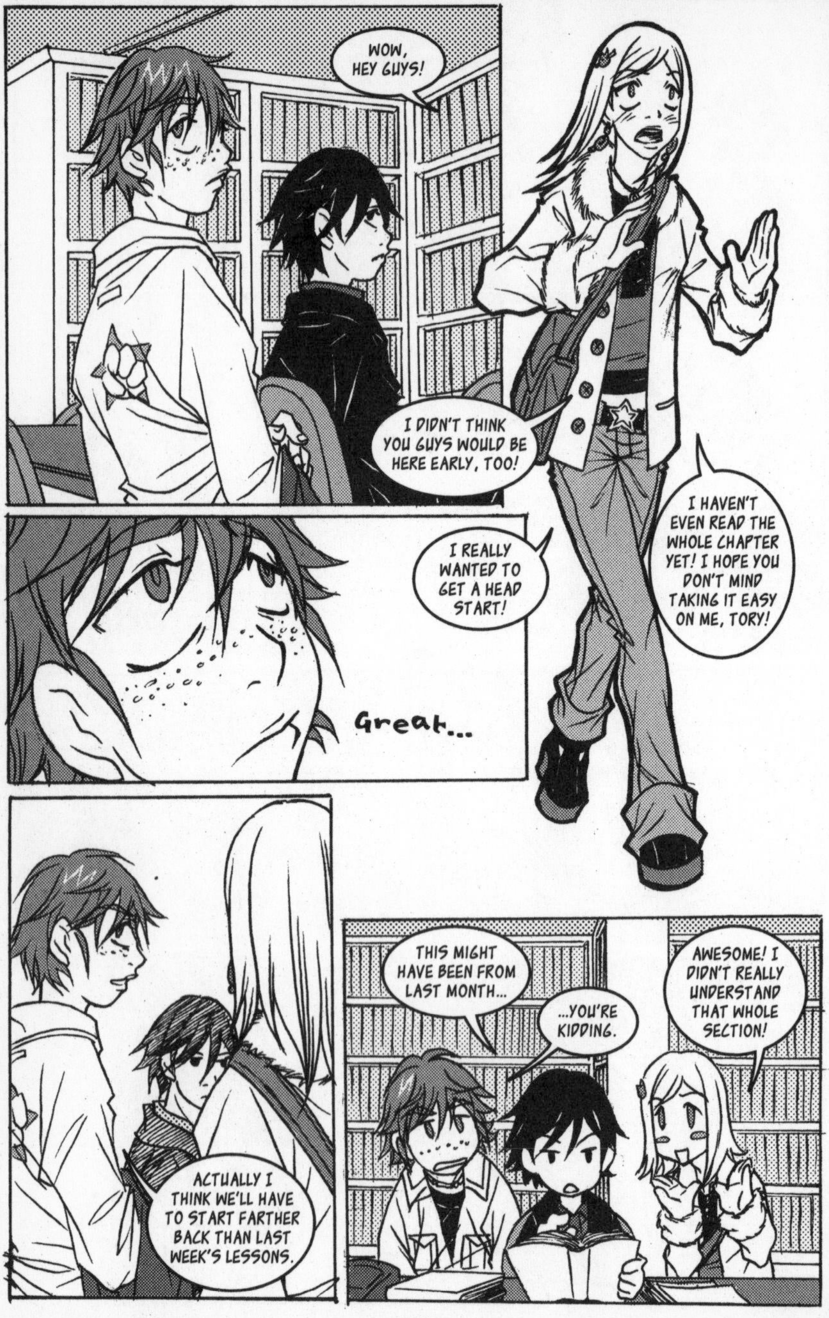
WOW, HEY GUYS!
I DIDN'T THINK YOU GUYS WOULD BE HERE EARLY, TOO!
I REALLY WANTED TO GET A HEAD START!
Great...
I HAVEN'T EVEN READ THE WHOLE CHAPTER YET! I HOPE YOU DON'T MIND TAKING IT EASY ON ME, TORY!
ACTUALLY I THINK WE'LL HAVE TO START FARTHER BACK THAN LAST WEEK'S LESSONS.
THIS MIGHT HAVE BEEN FROM LAST MONTH...
...YOU'RE KIDDING.
AWESOME! I DIDN'T REALLY UNDERSTAND THAT WHOLE SECTION!

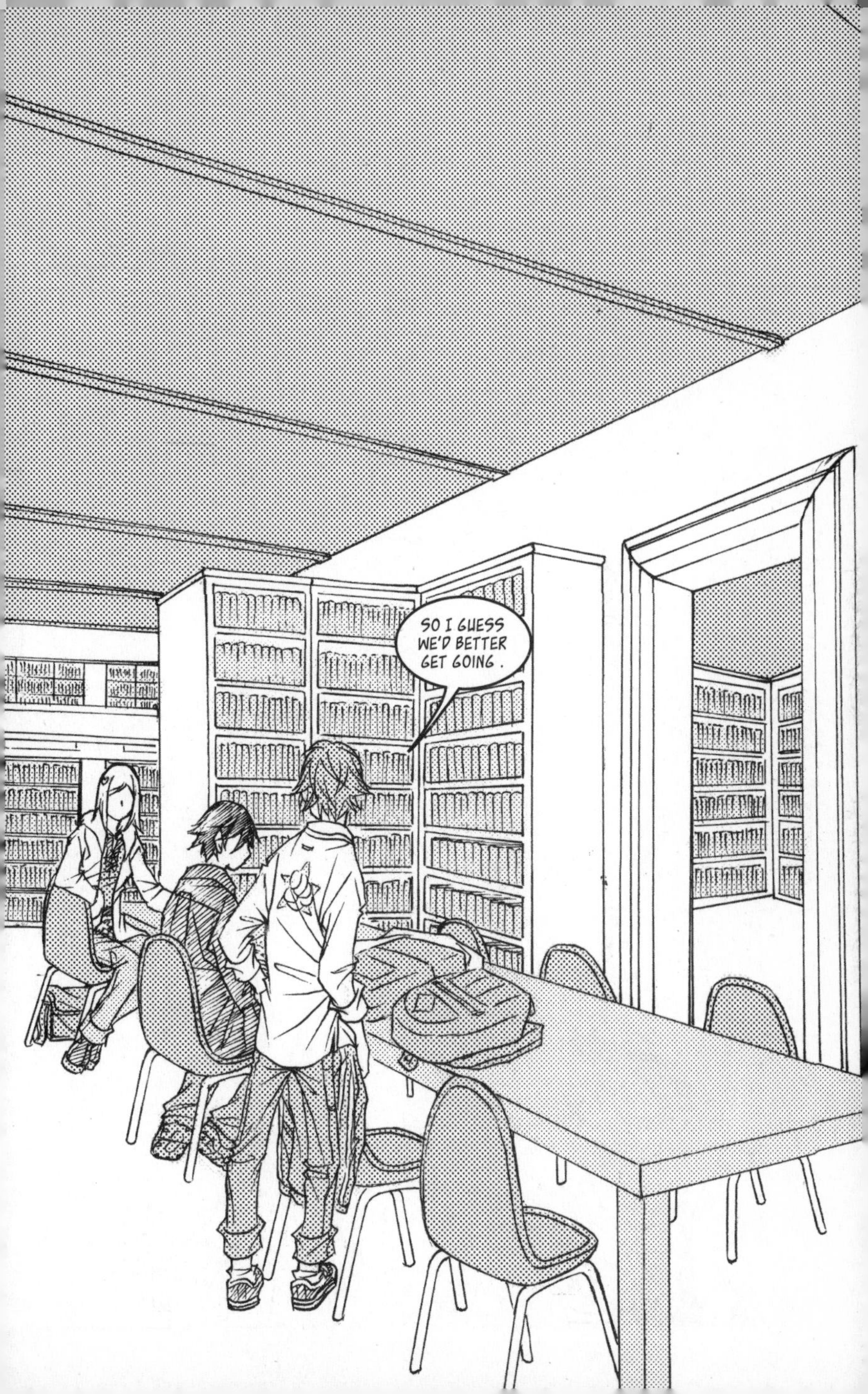
SO I GUESS WE'D BETTER GET GOING.

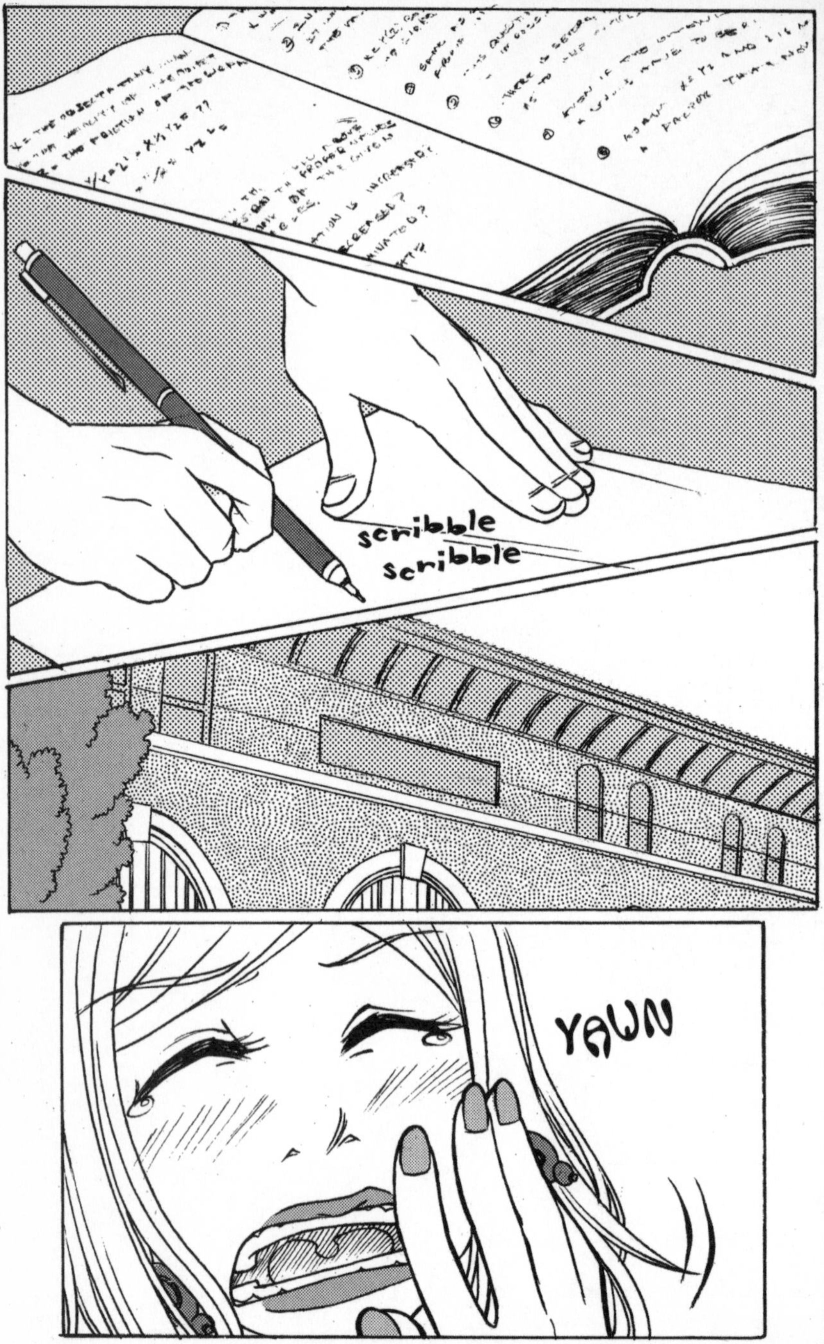

scribble
scribble
YAWN

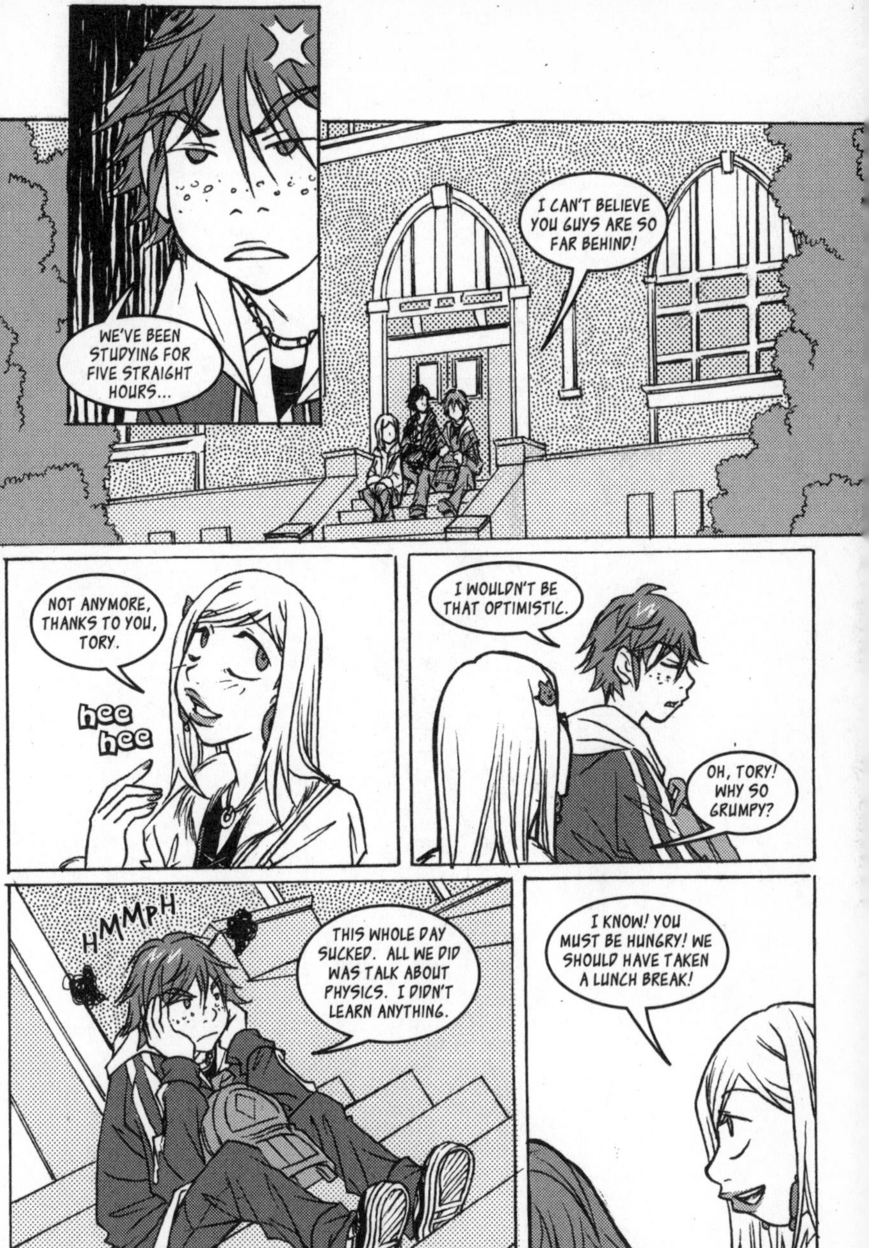
WE'VE BEEN STUDYING FOR FIVE STRAIGHT HOURS...
I CAN'T BELIEVE YOU GUYS ARE SO FAR BEHIND!
NOT ANYMORE, THANKS TO YOU, TORY.
hee hee
I WOULDN'T BE THAT OPTIMISTIC.
OH, TORY! WHY SO GRUMPY?
HMMPH
THIS WHOLE DAY SUCKED. ALL WE DID WAS TALK ABOUT PHYSICS. I DIDN'T LEARN ANYTHING.
I KNOW! YOU MUST BE HUNGRY! WE SHOULD HAVE TAKEN A LUNCH BREAK!

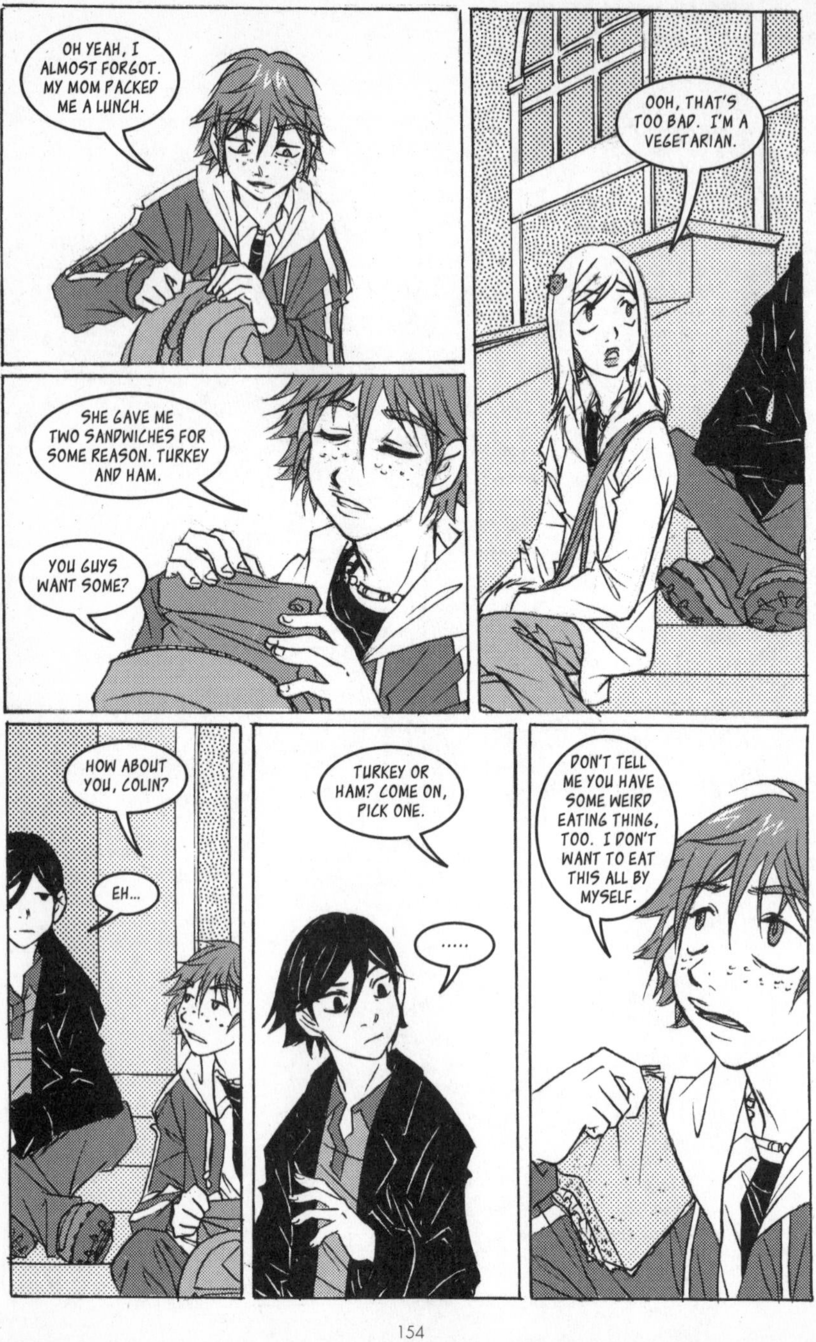
OH YEAH, I ALMOST FORGOT. MY MOM PACKED ME A LUNCH.
SHE GAVE ME TWO SANDWICHES FOR SOME REASON. TURKEY AND HAM.
YOU GUYS WANT SOME?
OOH, THAT'S TOO BAD. I'M A VEGETARIAN.
HOW ABOUT YOU, COLIN?
EH...
TURKEY OR HAM? COME ON, PICK ONE.
.....
DON'T TELL ME YOU HAVE SOME WEIRD EATING THING, TOO. I DON'T WANT TO EAT THIS ALL BY MYSELF.

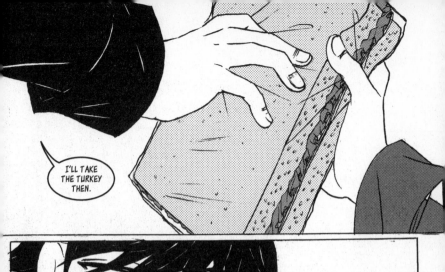

I'LL TAKE THE TURKEY THEN.

SMICE

HMM

YOU KNOW TORY, BEING A VEGETARIAN IS NOT A "WEIRD EATING THING!"

Y-YEAH? WHATEVER, OKAY!

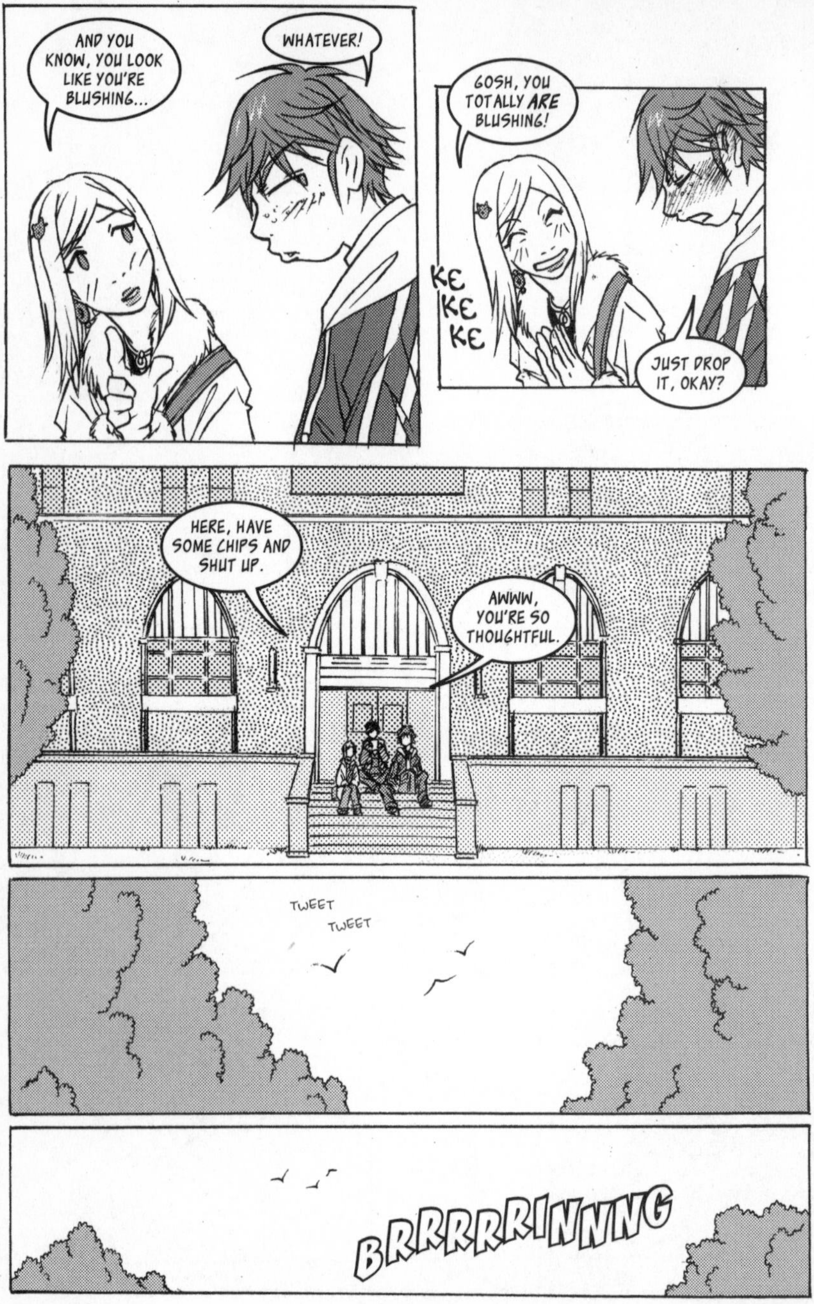
AND YOU KNOW, YOU LOOK LIKE YOU'RE BLUSHING...
WHATEVER!
GOSH, YOU TOTALLY **ARE** BLUSHING!
KE KE KE
JUST DROP IT, OKAY?
HERE, HAVE SOME CHIPS AND SHUT UP.
AWWW, YOU'RE SO THOUGHTFUL.
TWEET TWEET
BRRRRRINNNG

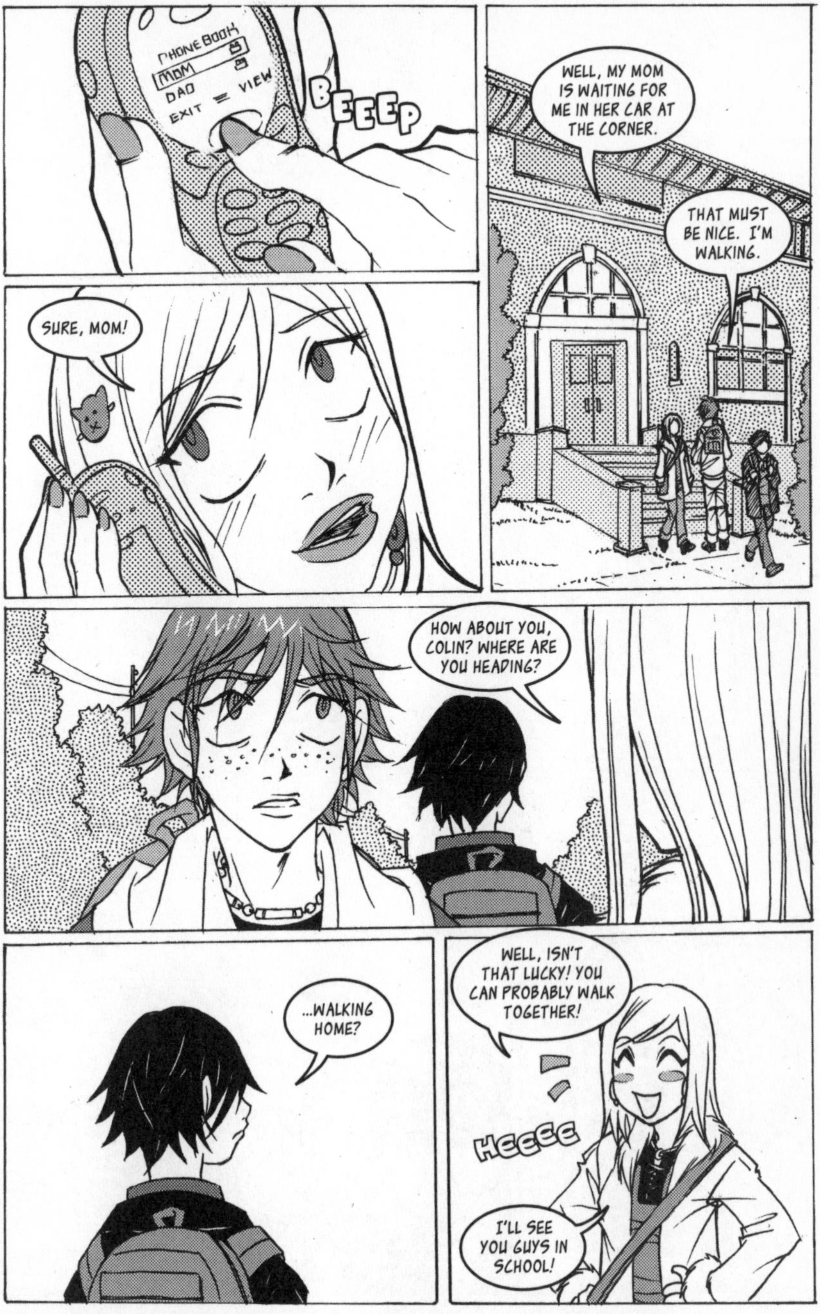
PHONE BOOK
MOM
DAD
EXIT = VIEW
BEEEP
WELL, MY MOM IS WAITING FOR ME IN HER CAR AT THE CORNER.
THAT MUST BE NICE. I'M WALKING.
SURE, MOM!
HOW ABOUT YOU, COLIN? WHERE ARE YOU HEADING?
...WALKING HOME?
WELL, ISN'T THAT LUCKY! YOU CAN PROBABLY WALK TOGETHER!
HEEEE
I'LL SEE YOU GUYS IN SCHOOL!

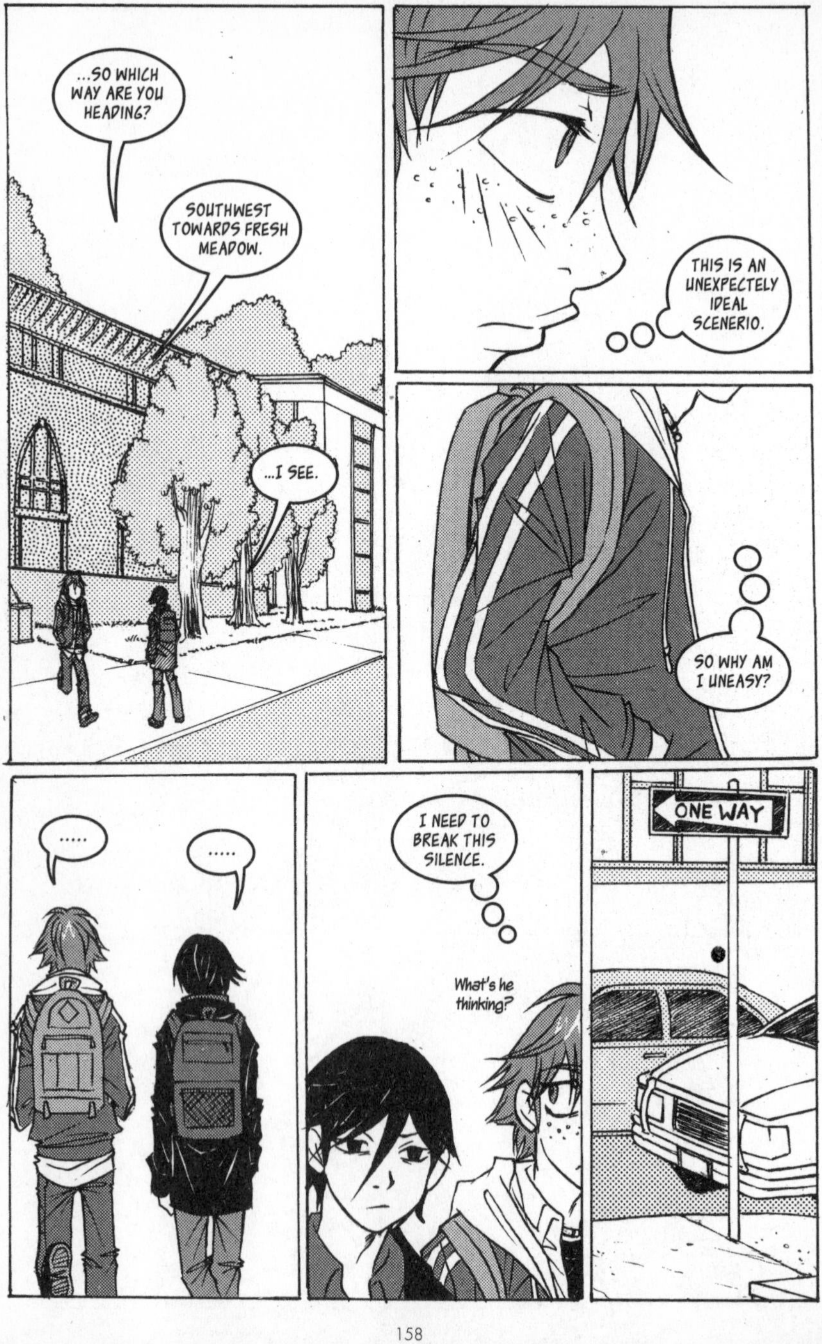
...SO WHICH WAY ARE YOU HEADING?
SOUTHWEST TOWARDS FRESH MEADOW.
...I SEE.
THIS IS AN UNEXPECTELY IDEAL SCENERIO.
SO WHY AM I UNEASY?
.....
.....
I NEED TO BREAK THIS SILENCE.
What's he thinking?
ONE WAY

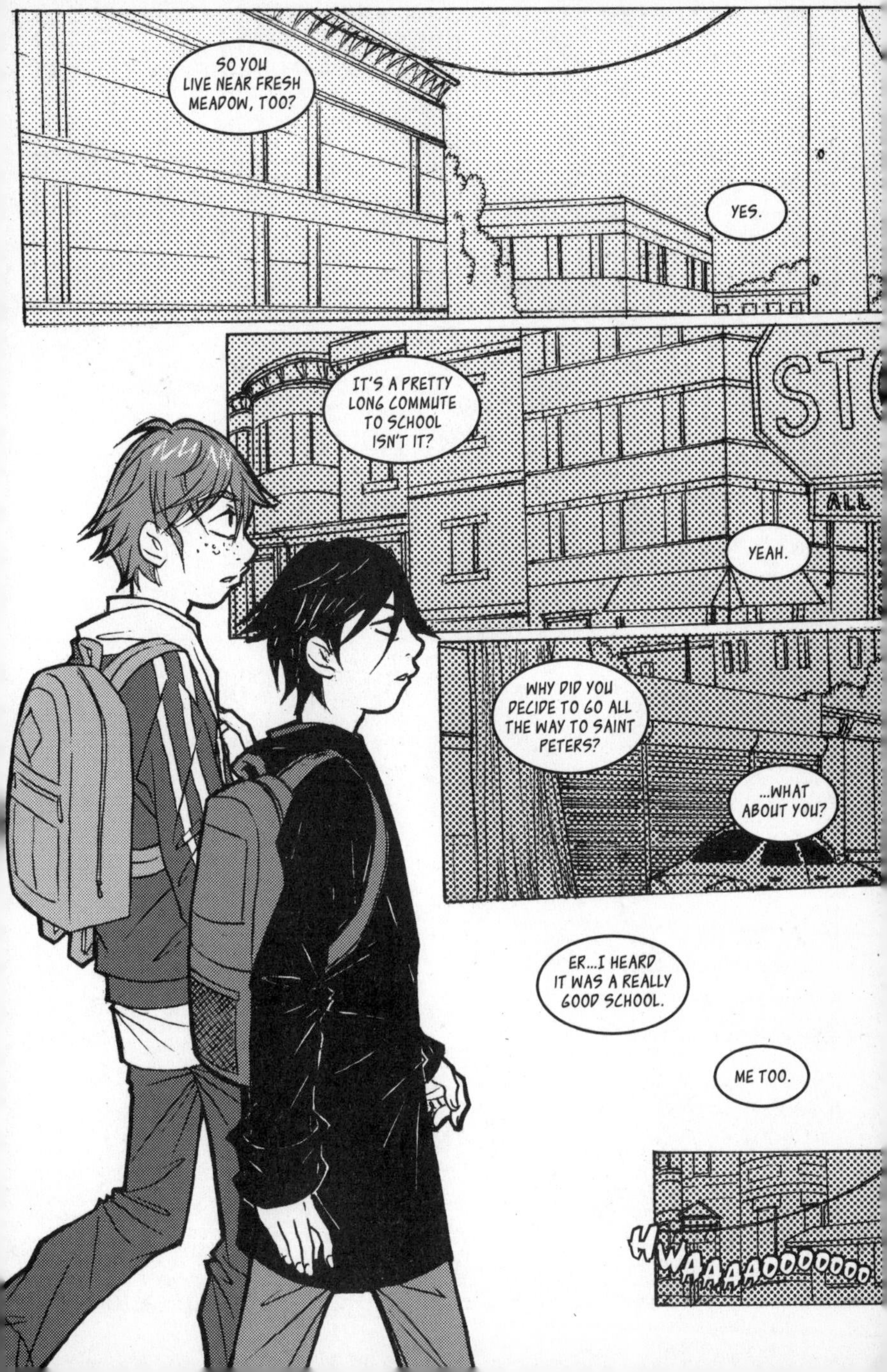
SO YOU LIVE NEAR FRESH MEADOW, TOO?
YES.
IT'S A PRETTY LONG COMMUTE TO SCHOOL ISN'T IT?
STO
ALL
YEAH.
WHY DID YOU DECIDE TO GO ALL THE WAY TO SAINT PETERS?
...WHAT ABOUT YOU?
ER...I HEARD IT WAS A REALLY GOOD SCHOOL.
ME TOO.
HWAAAAOOOOOOO

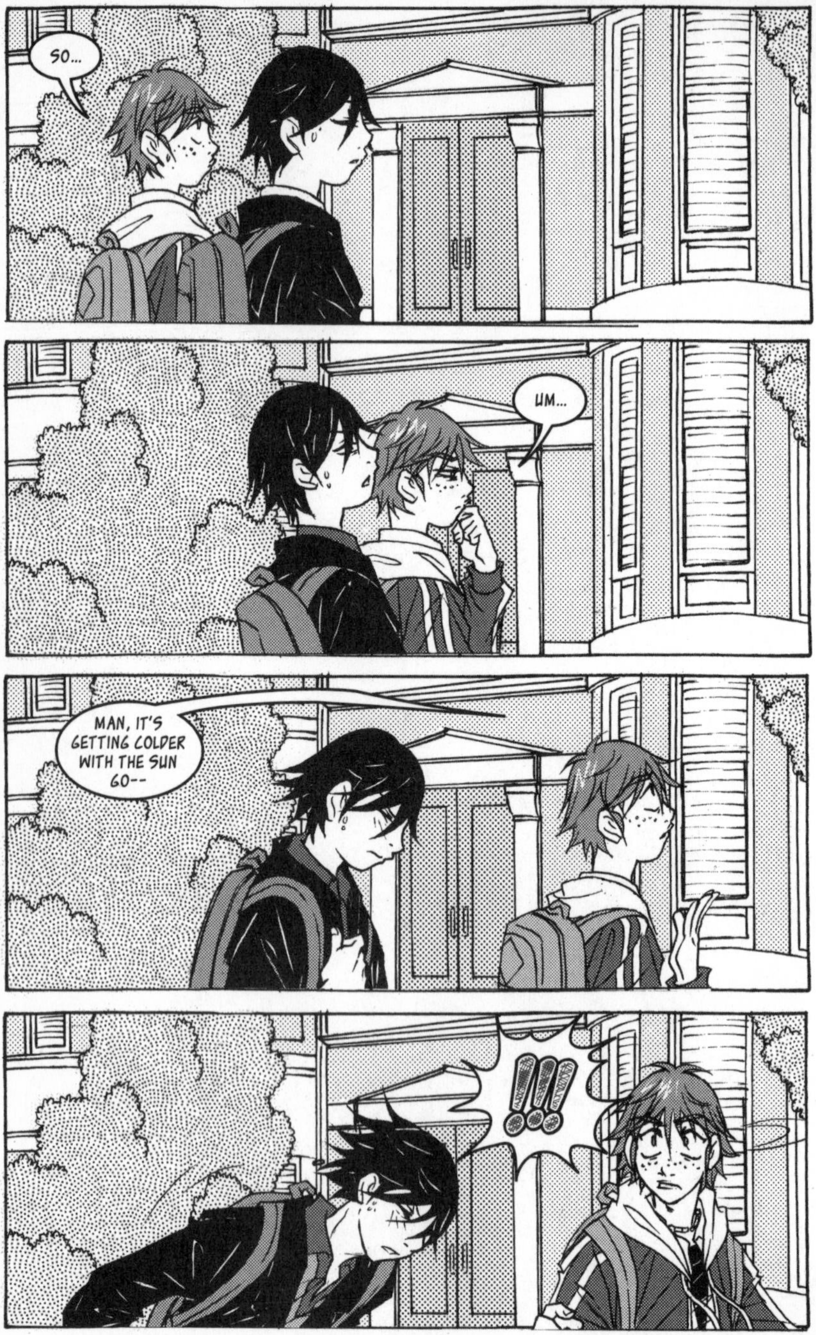
SO...
UM...
MAN, IT'S GETTING COLDER WITH THE SUN GO--
!!!

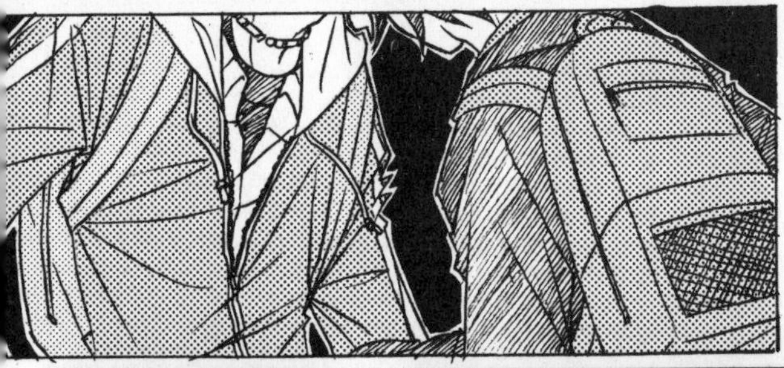

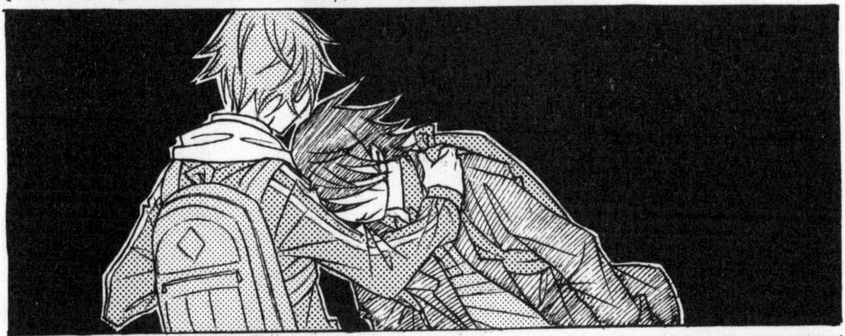

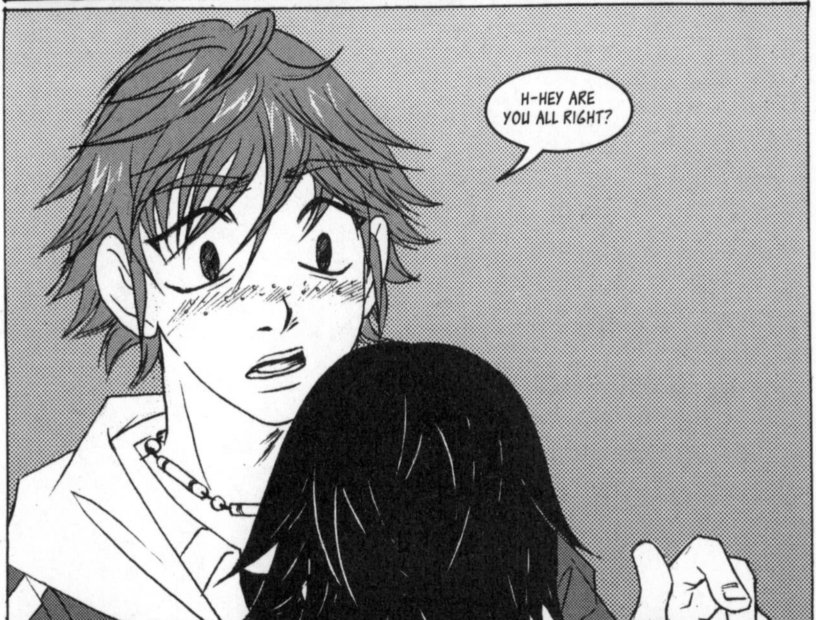
H-HEY ARE YOU ALL RIGHT?

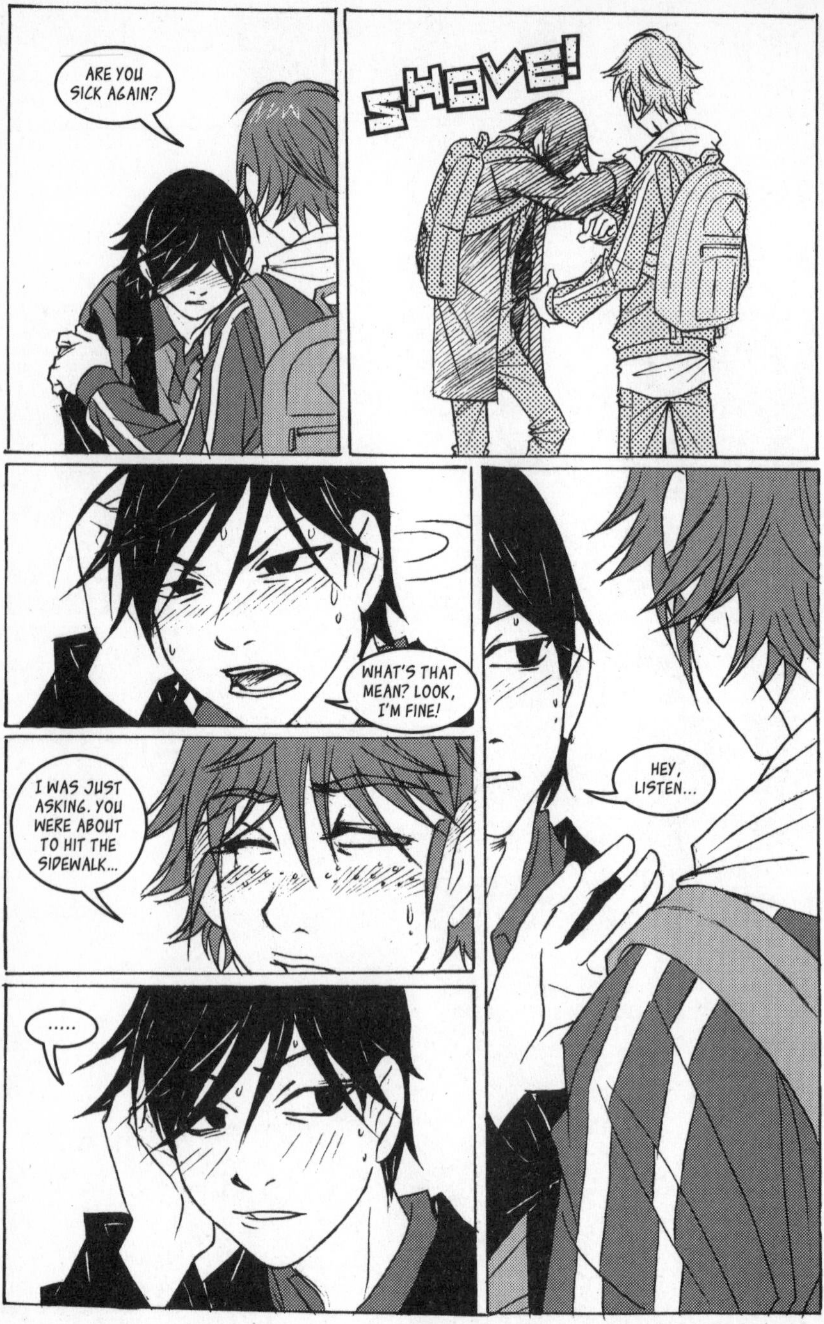
ARE YOU SICK AGAIN?
SHOVE!
WHAT'S THAT MEAN? LOOK, I'M FINE!
I WAS JUST ASKING. YOU WERE ABOUT TO HIT THE SIDEWALK...
......
HEY, LISTEN...

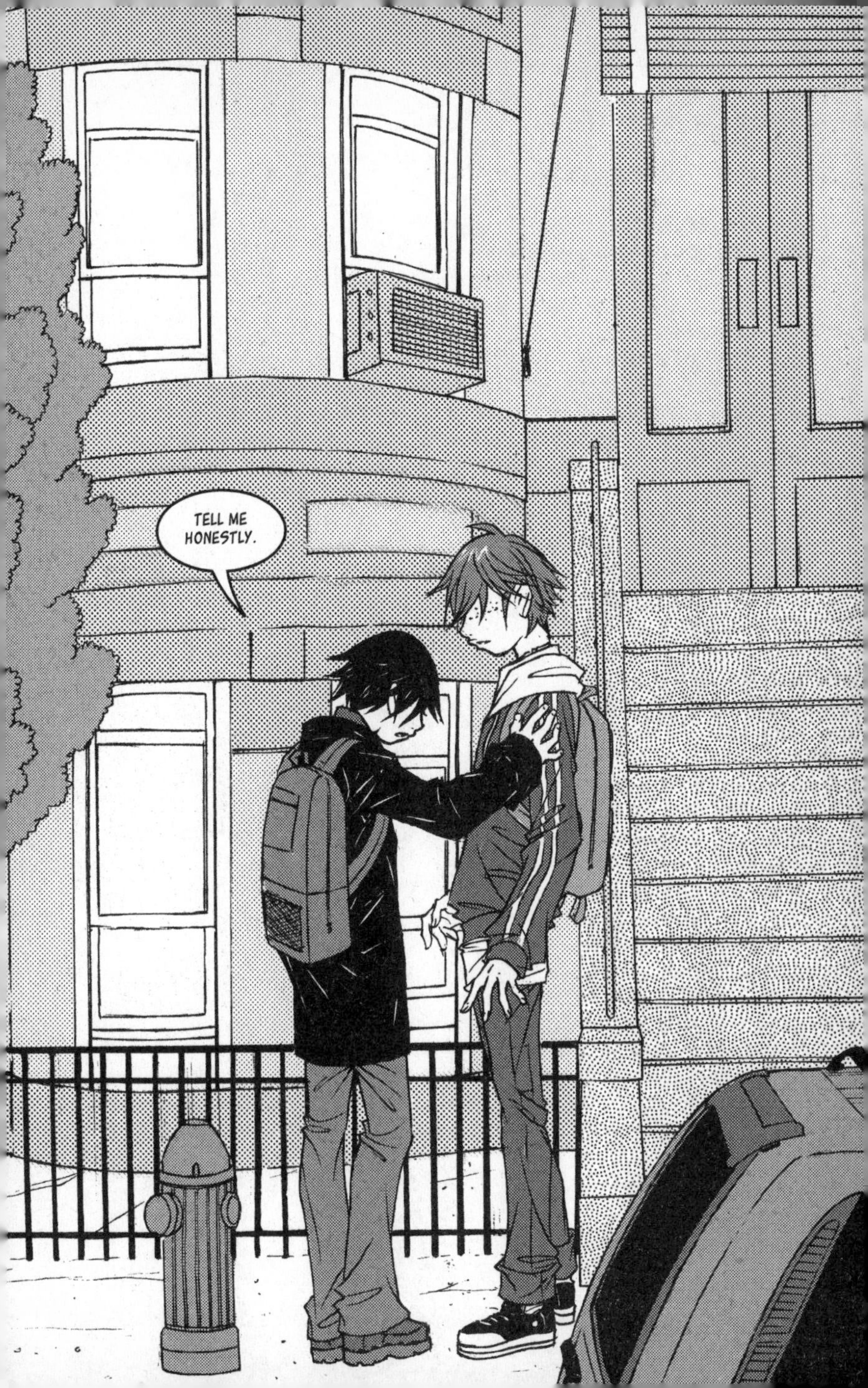
TELL ME HONESTLY.

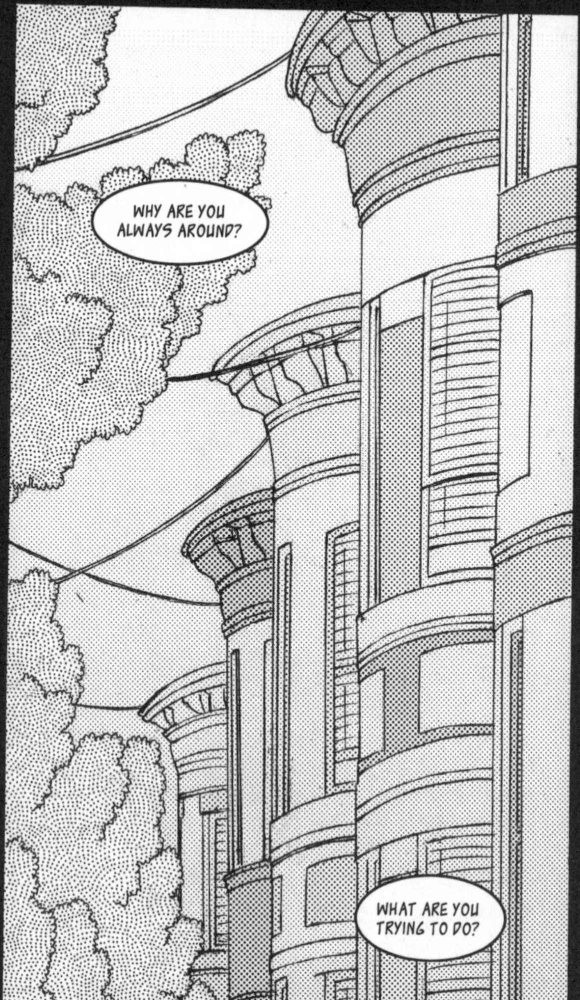
WHY ARE YOU ALWAYS AROUND?
WHAT ARE YOU TRYING TO DO?

**Next
time in**

offbeat

★

Colin has called Tory on just
what exactly he's up to, but
can Tory admit the truth to
him when he can't even admit
it to himself? Friendships
begin to grow and flower
as the connection between
the two boys deepens, and
Mandy becomes a real friend
to rely on. But Colin's not
the only one with secrets
to protect. Just what is
Tory willing to sacrifice
to satisfy his curiosity
about the mysterious
Gaia Project? What if
the cost may be his
relationship with
Colin?

Congratulations, lucky reader!

You've just turned the page into one of the most insightful and flat-out FUNNY manga ever produced on our shores!

Fasten your seatbelts for Svetlana Chmakova's

DRAMACON!

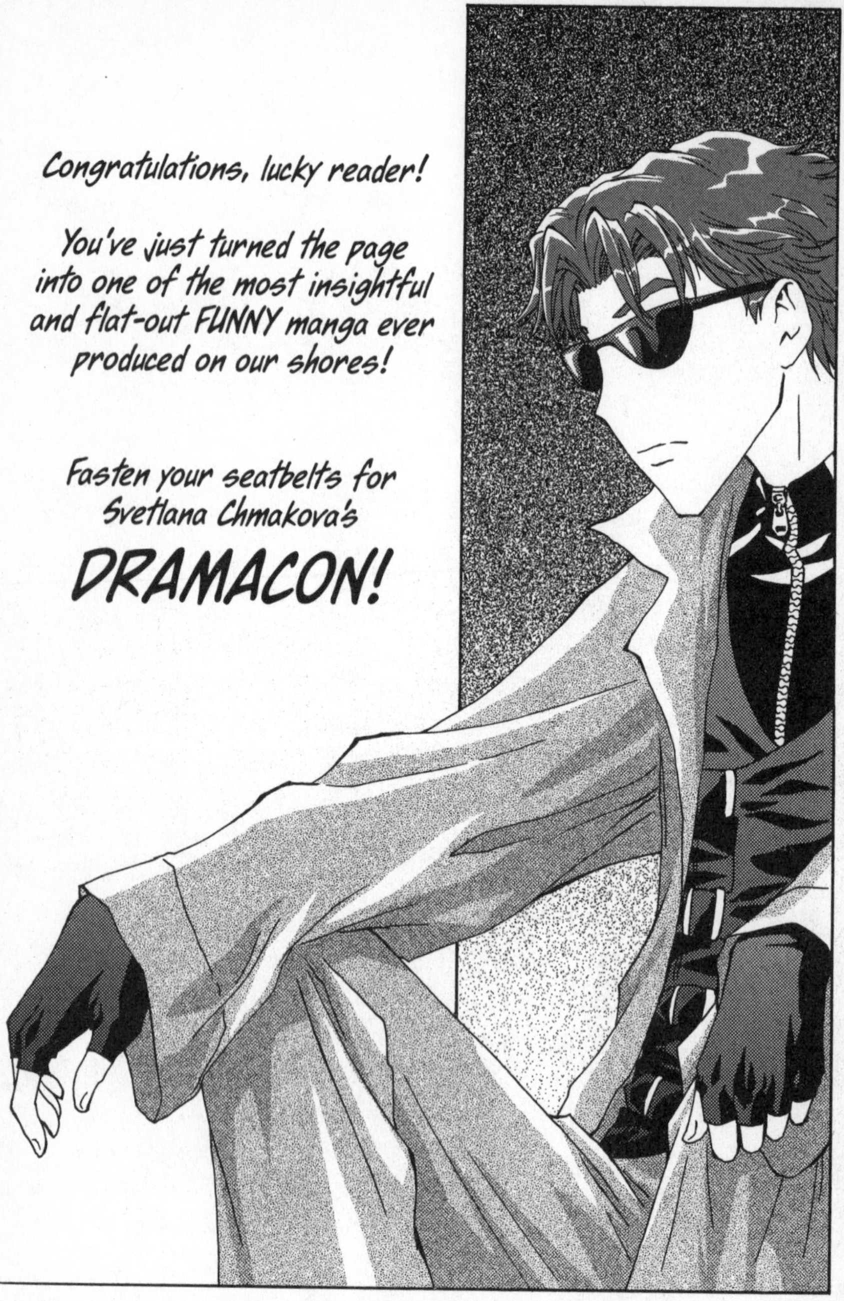

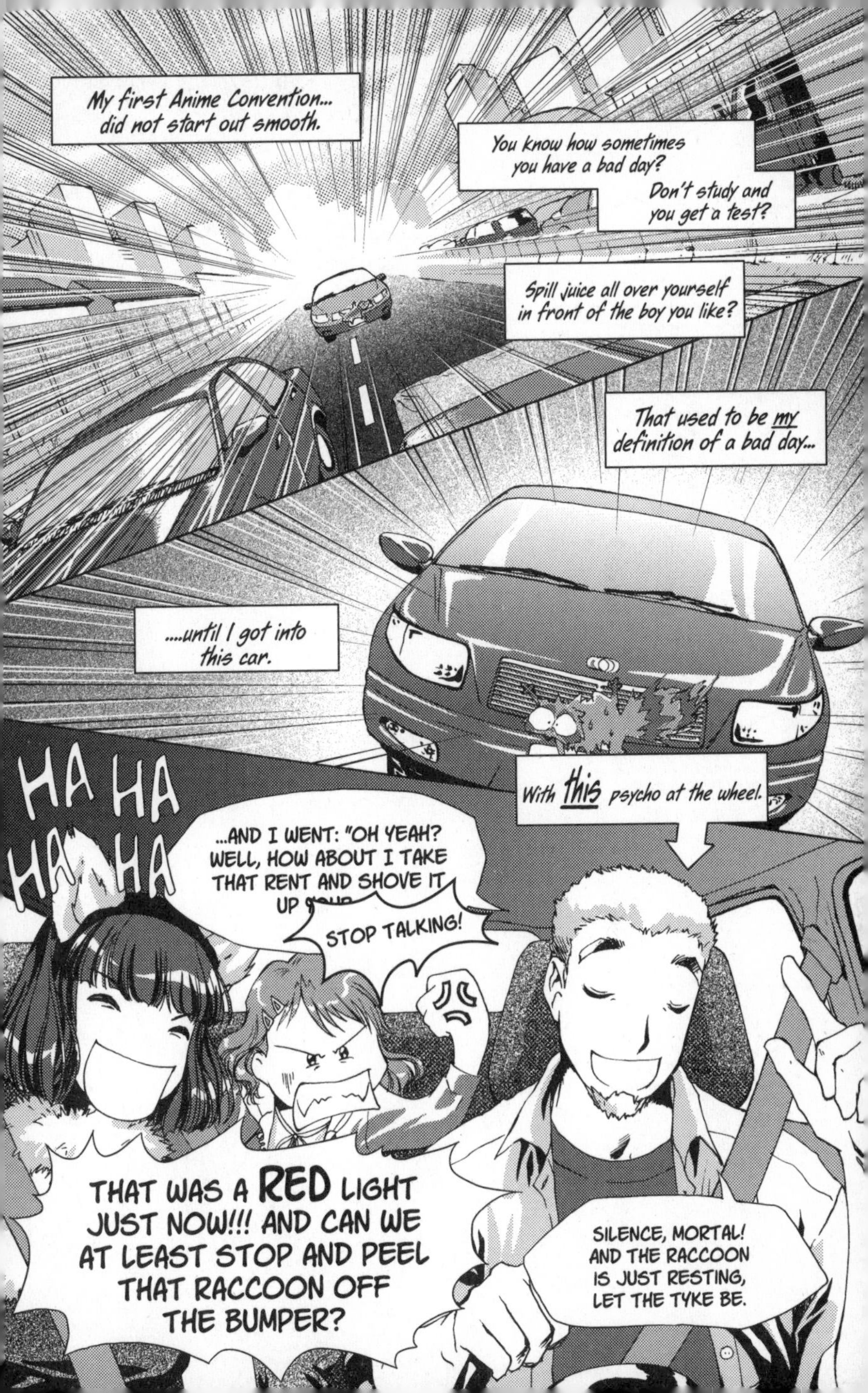
My first Anime Convention... did not start out smooth.
You know how sometimes you have a bad day?
Don't study and you get a test?
Spill juice all over yourself in front of the boy you like?
That used to be my definition of a bad day...
...until I got into this car.
With this psycho at the wheel.
HA HA HA HA
...AND I WENT: "OH YEAH? WELL, HOW ABOUT I TAKE THAT RENT AND SHOVE IT UP
STOP TALKING!
THAT WAS A RED LIGHT JUST NOW!!! AND CAN WE AT LEAST STOP AND PEEL THAT RACCOON OFF THE BUMPER?
SILENCE, MORTAL! AND THE RACCOON IS JUST RESTING, LET THE TYKE BE.

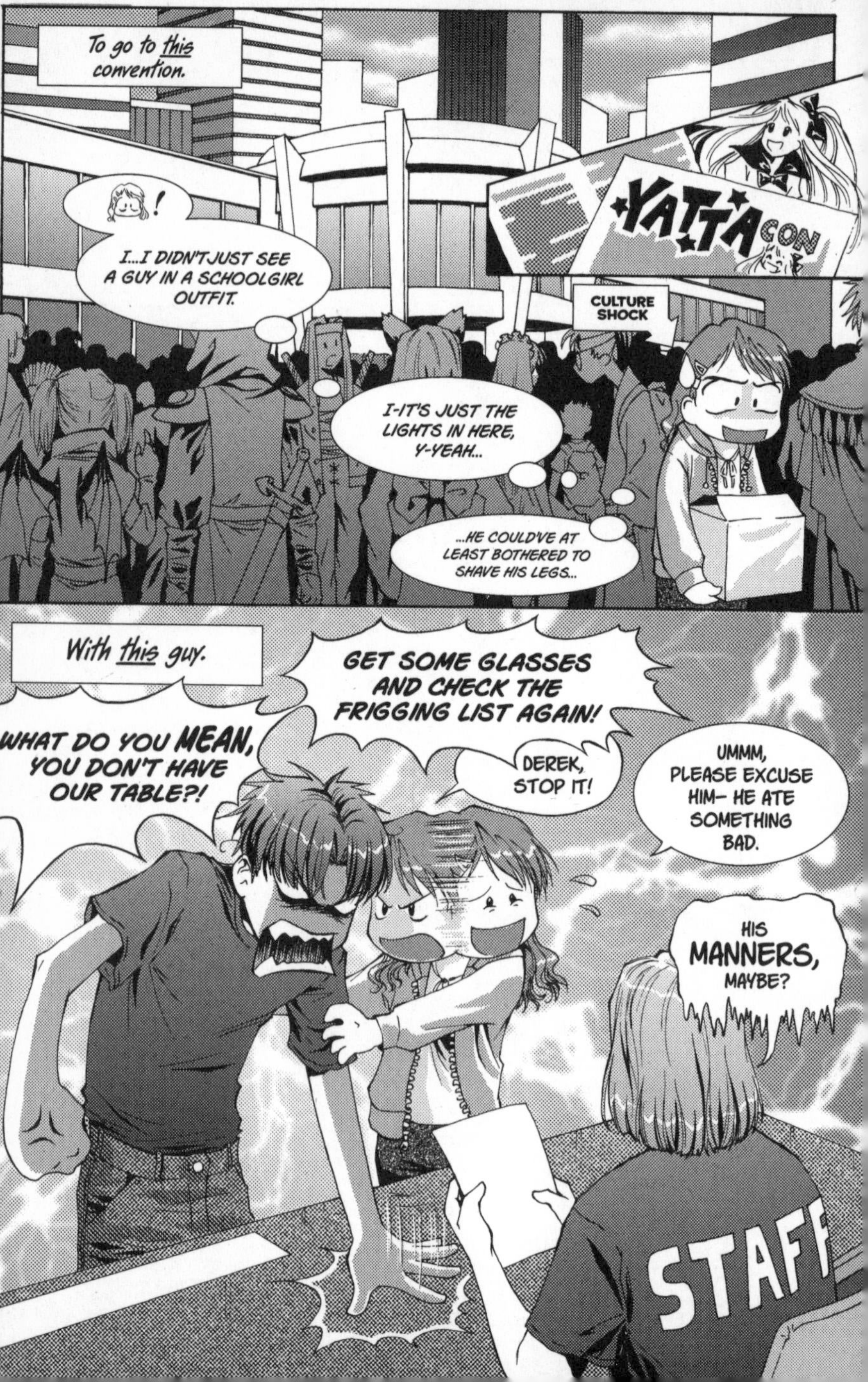
To go to this convention.
YATTA CON
!
I...I DIDN'T JUST SEE A GUY IN A SCHOOLGIRL OUTFIT.
CULTURE SHOCK
I-IT'S JUST THE LIGHTS IN HERE, Y-YEAH...
...HE COULD'VE AT LEAST BOTHERED TO SHAVE HIS LEGS...
With this guy.
WHAT DO YOU MEAN, YOU DON'T HAVE OUR TABLE?!
GET SOME GLASSES AND CHECK THE FRIGGING LIST AGAIN!
DEREK, STOP IT!
UMMM, PLEASE EXCUSE HIM– HE ATE SOMETHING BAD.
HIS MANNERS, MAYBE?
STAFF

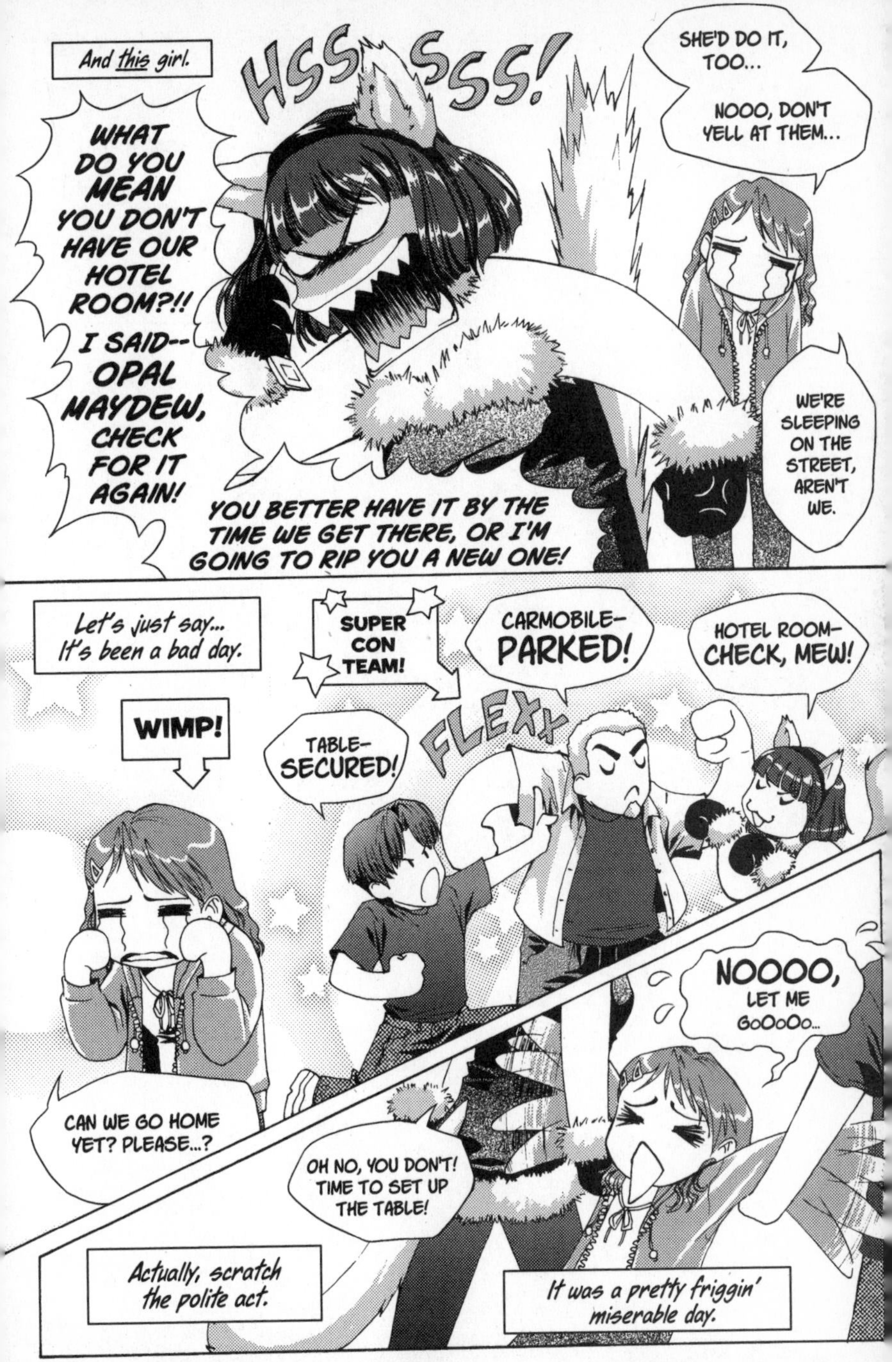

And this girl.
HSS SSS!
WHAT DO YOU MEAN YOU DON'T HAVE OUR HOTEL ROOM?!! I SAID-- OPAL MAYDEW, CHECK FOR IT AGAIN!
YOU BETTER HAVE IT BY THE TIME WE GET THERE, OR I'M GOING TO RIP YOU A NEW ONE!
SHE'D DO IT, TOO...
NOOO, DON'T YELL AT THEM...
WE'RE SLEEPING ON THE STREET, AREN'T WE.
Let's just say... It's been a bad day.
SUPER CON TEAM!
CARMOBILE- PARKED!
HOTEL ROOM- CHECK, MEW!
WIMP!
TABLE- SECURED!
FLEXX
CAN WE GO HOME YET? PLEASE...?
NOOOO, LET ME GoOoOo...
OH NO, YOU DON'T! TIME TO SET UP THE TABLE!
Actually, scratch the polite act.
It was a pretty friggin' miserable day.

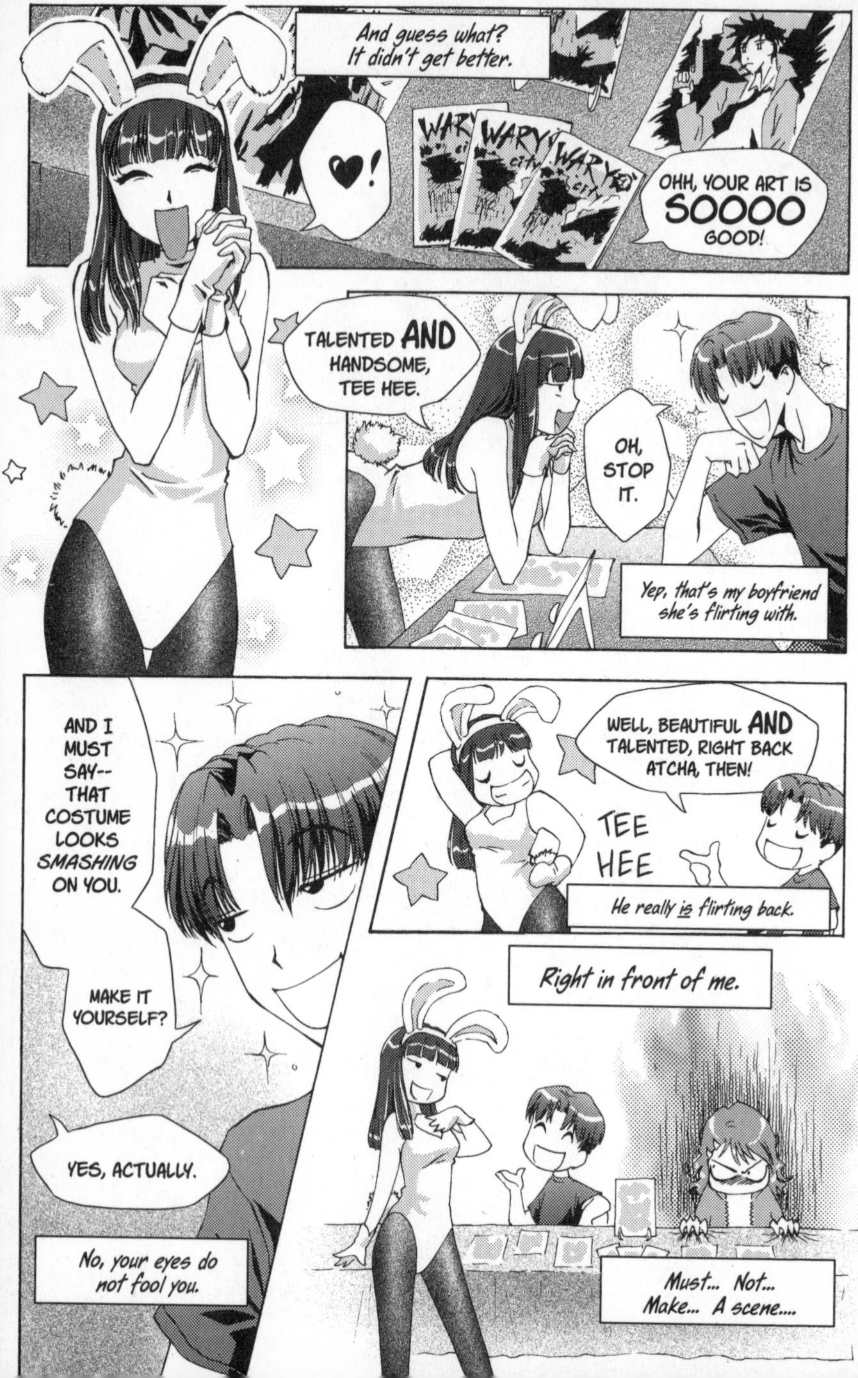

And guess what? It didn't get better.
♥!
OHH, YOUR ART IS SOOOO GOOD!
TALENTED AND HANDSOME, TEE HEE.
OH, STOP IT.
Yep, that's my boyfriend she's flirting with.
AND I MUST SAY-- THAT COSTUME LOOKS SMASHING ON YOU.
MAKE IT YOURSELF?
YES, ACTUALLY.
No, your eyes do not fool you.
WELL, BEAUTIFUL AND TALENTED, RIGHT BACK ATCHA, THEN!
TEE HEE
He really is flirting back.
Right in front of me.
Must... Not... Make... A scene....

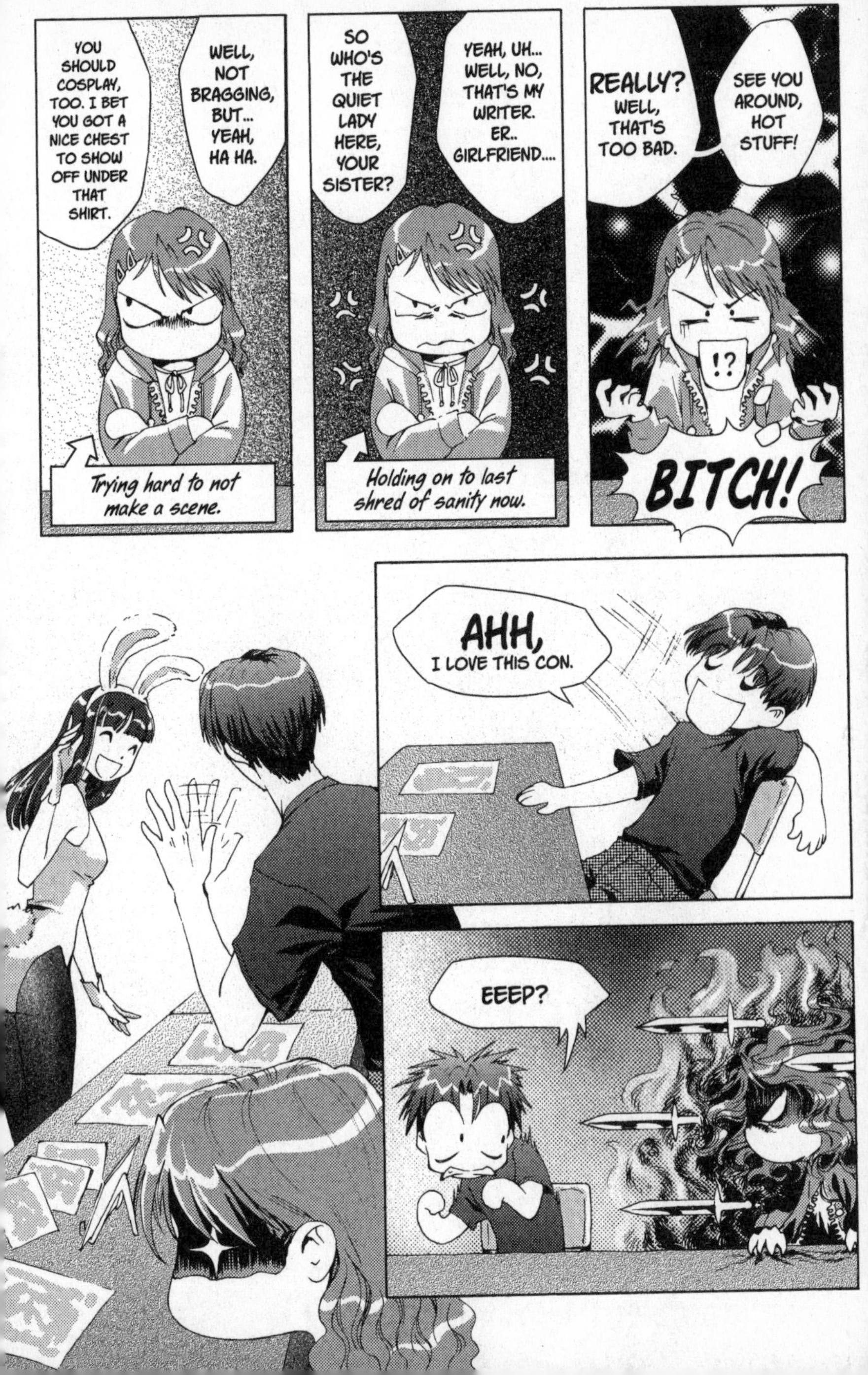
YOU SHOULD COSPLAY, TOO. I BET YOU GOT A NICE CHEST TO SHOW OFF UNDER THAT SHIRT.
WELL, NOT BRAGGING, BUT... YEAH, HA HA.
Trying hard to not make a scene.
SO WHO'S THE QUIET LADY HERE, YOUR SISTER?
YEAH, UH... WELL, NO, THAT'S MY WRITER. ER.. GIRLFRIEND....
Holding on to last shred of sanity now.
REALLY? WELL, THAT'S TOO BAD.
SEE YOU AROUND, HOT STUFF!
!?
BITCH!
AHH, I LOVE THIS CON.
EEEP?

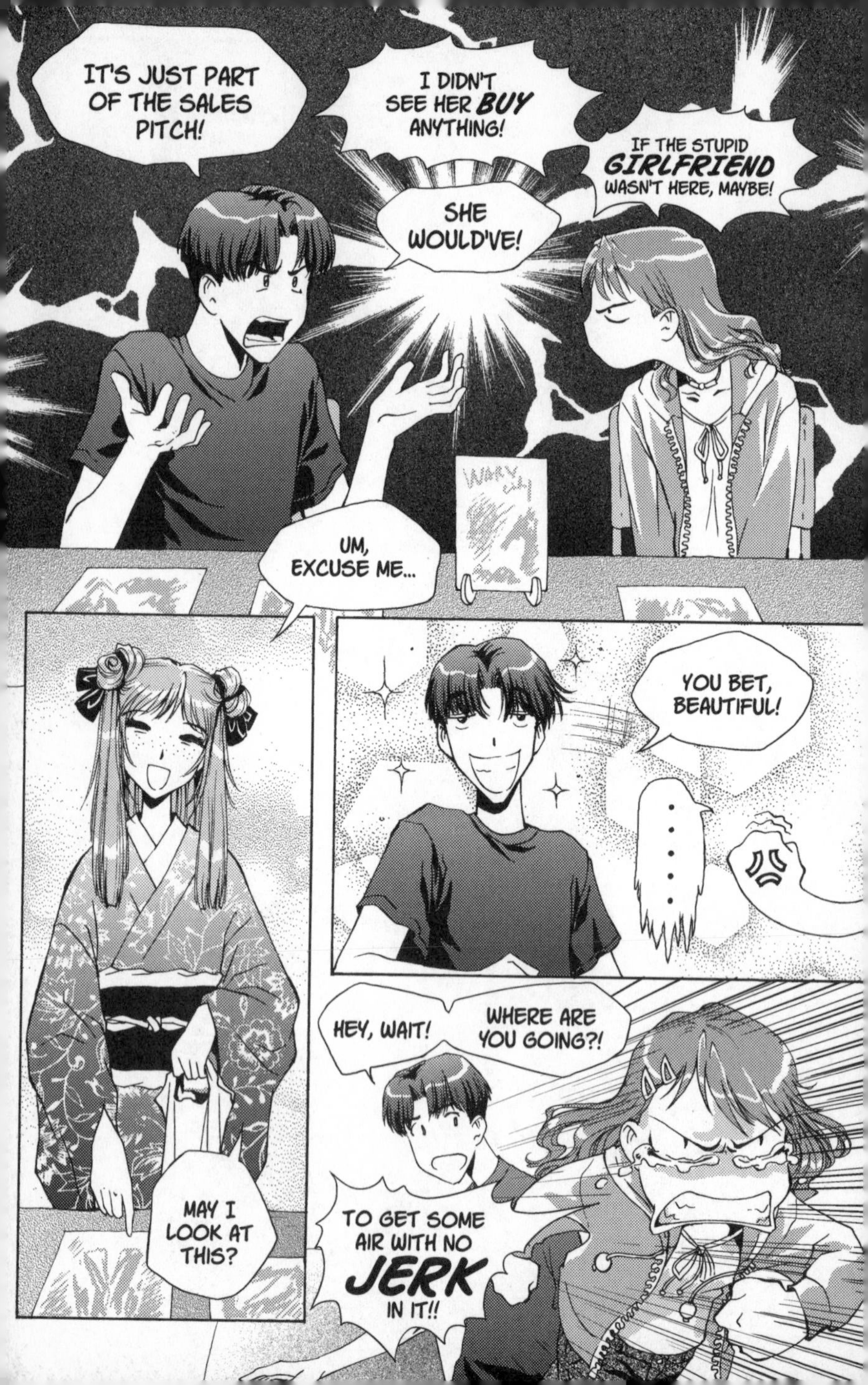
IT'S JUST PART OF THE SALES PITCH!
I DIDN'T SEE HER BUY ANYTHING!
IF THE STUPID GIRLFRIEND WASN'T HERE, MAYBE!
SHE WOULD'VE!
UM, EXCUSE ME...
MAY I LOOK AT THIS?
YOU BET, BEAUTIFUL!
HEY, WAIT!
WHERE ARE YOU GOING?!
TO GET SOME AIR WITH NO JERK IN IT!!

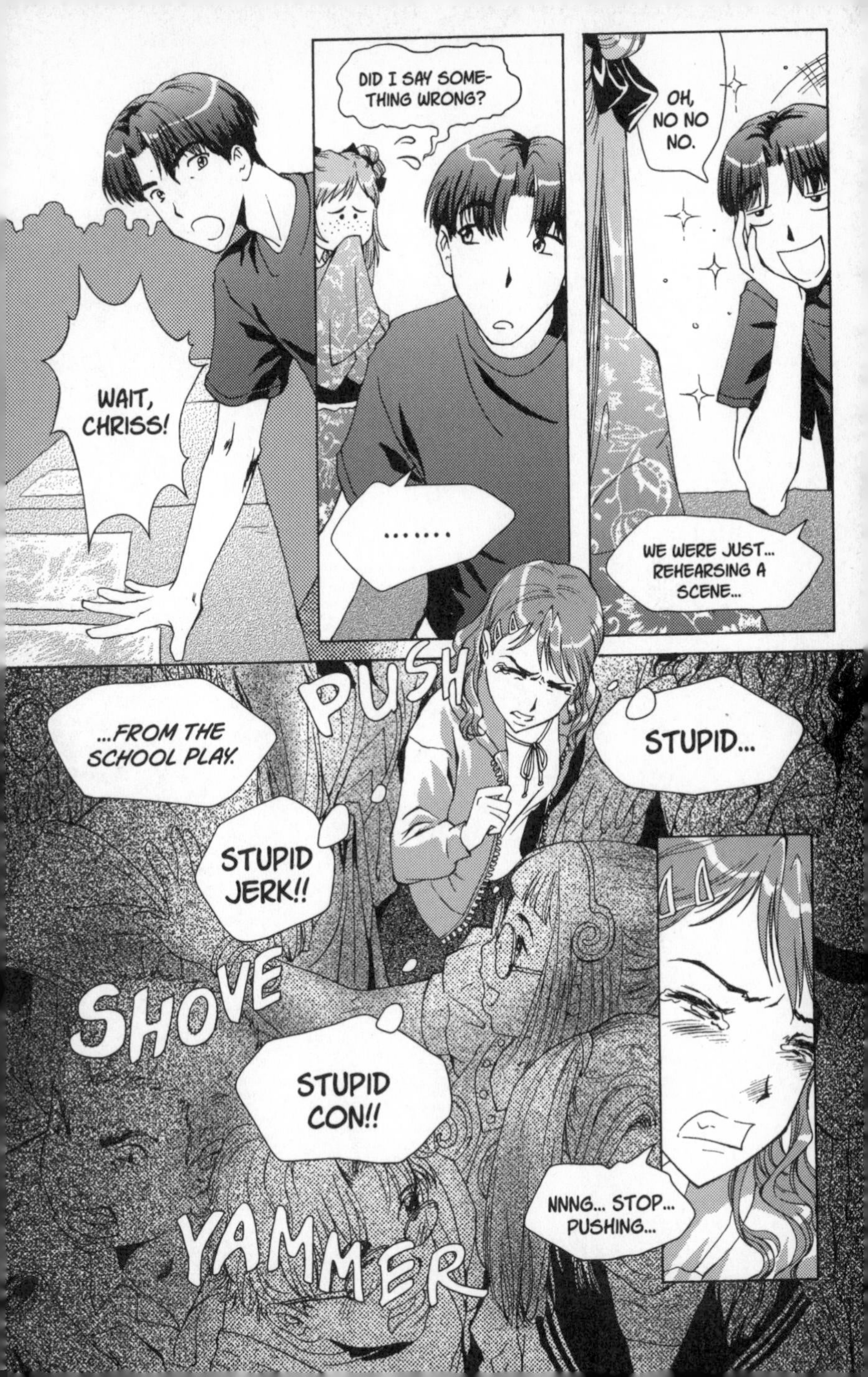
WAIT, CHRISS!
DID I SAY SOME-THING WRONG?
....
OH, NO NO NO.
WE WERE JUST... REHEARSING A SCENE...
...FROM THE SCHOOL PLAY.
PUSH
STUPID...
STUPID JERK!!
SHOVE
STUPID CON!!
NNNG... STOP... PUSHING...
YAMMER

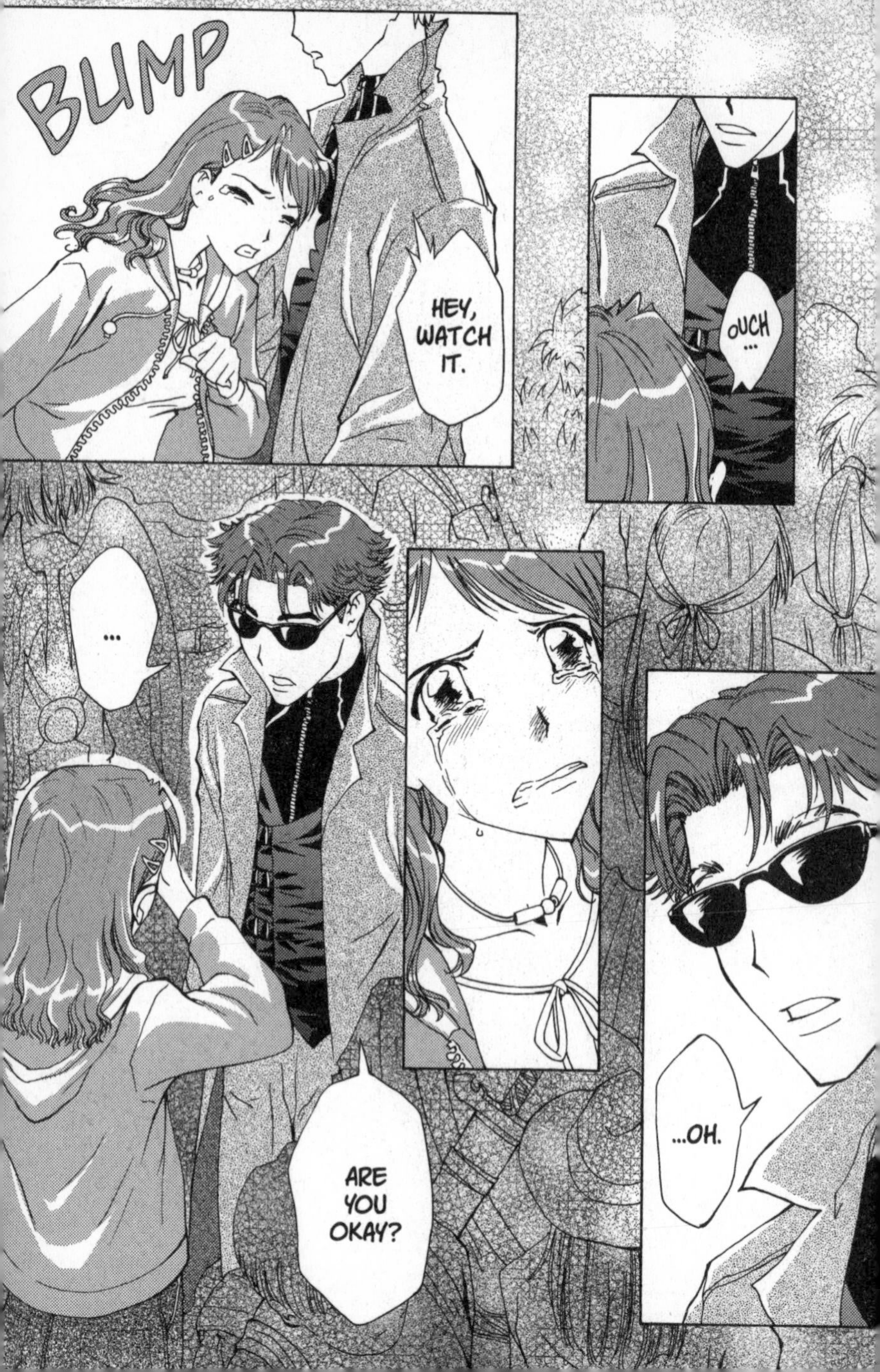
BUMP
HEY, WATCH IT.
OUCH ...
...
ARE YOU OKAY?
...OH.

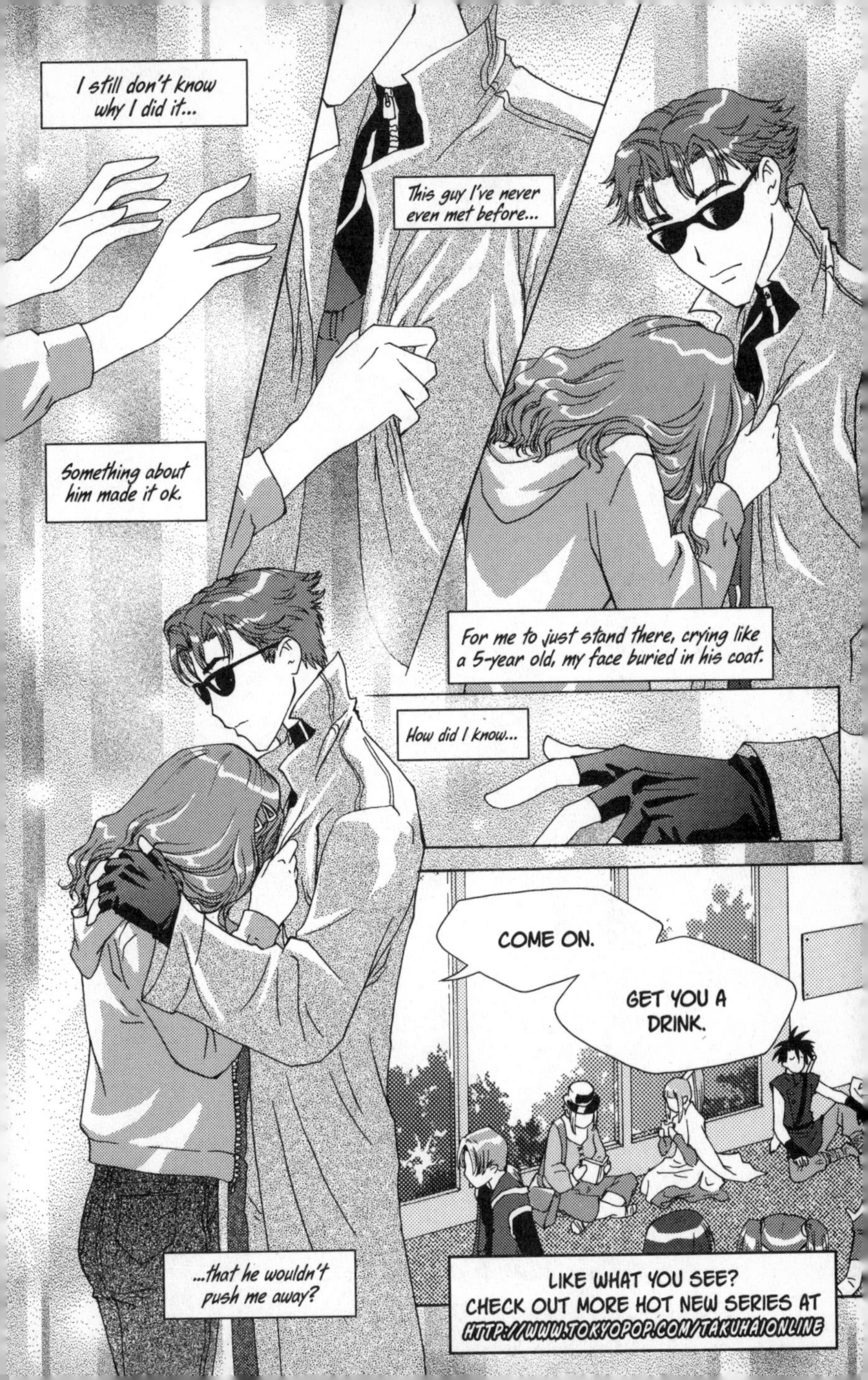
I still don't know why I did it...
Something about him made it ok.
This guy I've never even met before...
For me to just stand there, crying like a 5-year old, my face buried in his coat.
How did I know...
...that he wouldn't push me away?
COME ON.
GET YOU A DRINK.
LIKE WHAT YOU SEE?
CHECK OUT MORE HOT NEW SERIES AT
HTTP://WWW.TOKYOPOP.COM/TAKUHAIONLINE

Princess Ai © & TM TOKYOPOP Inc. and Kitty Radio, Inc.
TAKUHAI 宅配
WANNA DO TAKUHAI?
THE NEW SIZZLING HOT MANGA MAGAZINE
SIGN UP FOR FREE
WWW.TOKYOPOP.com
Ai from Princess Ai

TOKYOPOP SHOP

i luv halloween

Written by Keith Giffen, comic book pro and English language adapter of *Battle Royale* and *Battle Vixens*.

Join the misadventures of a group of particularly disturbing trick-or-treaters as they go about their macabre business on Halloween night. Blaming the apples they got from the first house of the evening for the bad candy they've been receiving all night, the kids plot revenge on the old bag who handed out the funky fruit. Riotously funny and always wickedly shocking—who doesn't *love* Halloween?

OT
OLDER TEEN
AGE 16+

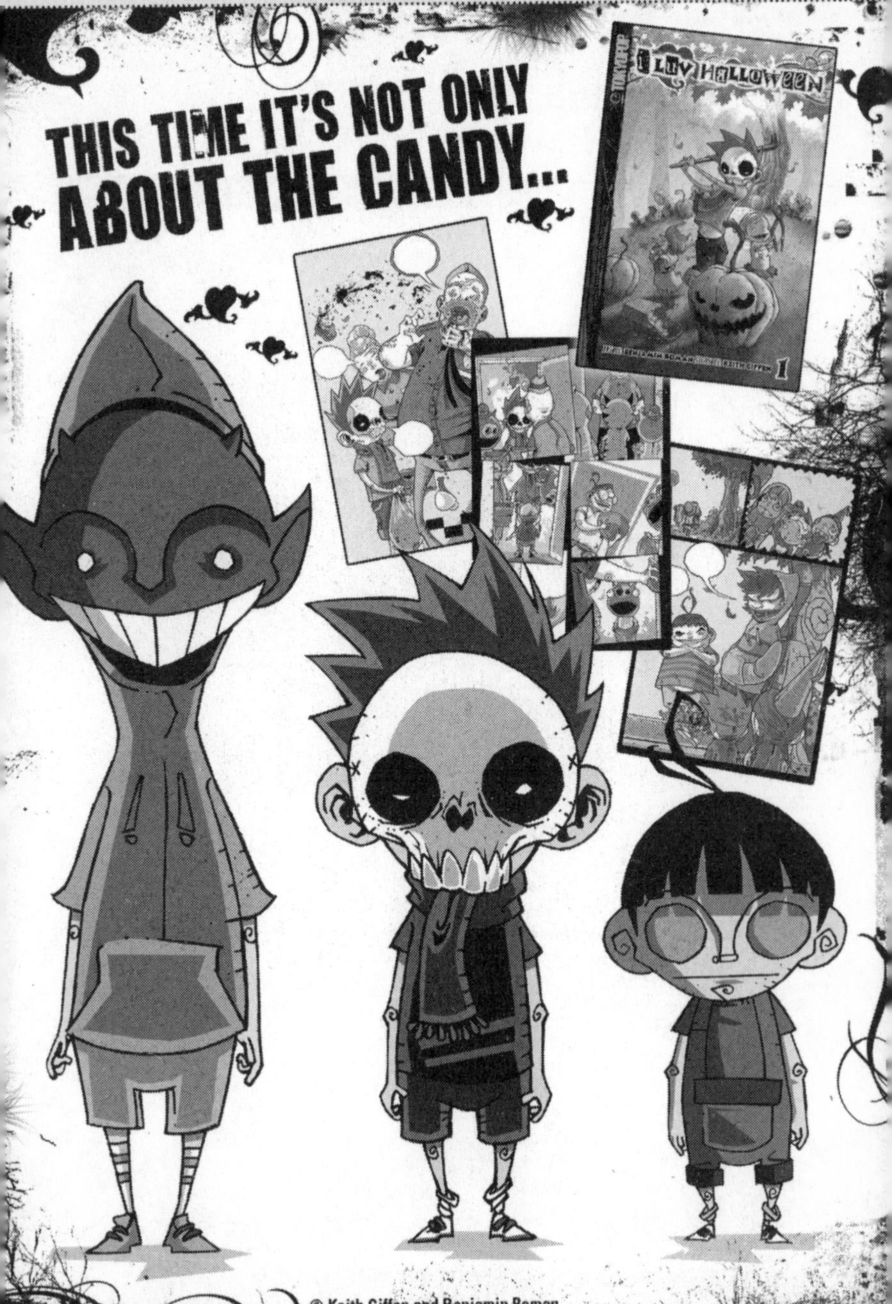
THIS TIME IT'S NOT ONLY ABOUT THE CANDY...
I LUV HALLOWEEN
1

SPOTLIGHT

TOKYOPOP MANGA SUPPLEMENT

SCRAPPED PRINCESS

BY GO YABUKI, ICHIRO SAKAKI, AND YUKINOBU AZUMI

HER BIRTH FORETOLD THE DESTRUCTION OF THE WORLD!

Fifteen years ago, a set of twins—a girl and a boy—was born to the king of Linevan. Shortly after their birth, a prophecy foretold that when the girl turned 16, she would bring about the end of humanity. To avoid this terrible fate, the king ordered the girl disposed of—scrapped! She miraculously survived and was raised away from the kingdom that would kill her. But now she has turned 15, the king's guards have caught wind that she's still alive...and they set out to finish the job!

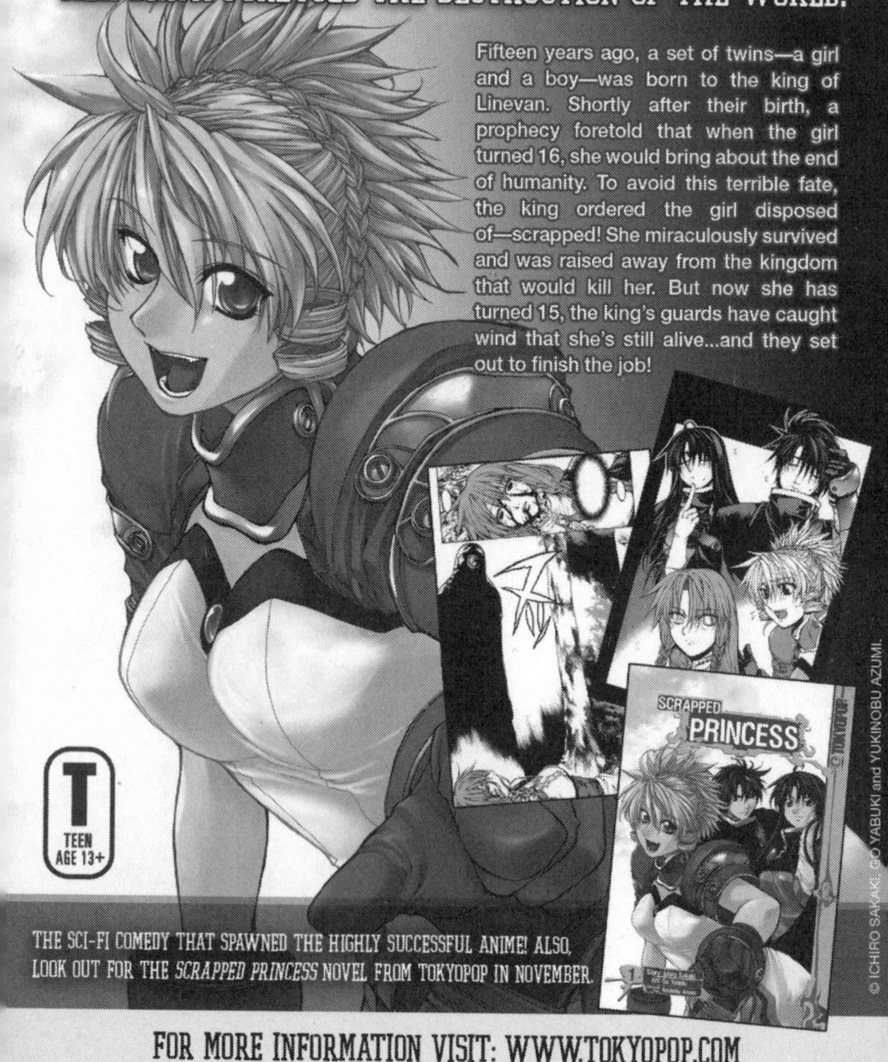
SCRAPPED PRINCESS
T
TEEN AGE 13+

THE SCI-FI COMEDY THAT SPAWNED THE HIGHLY SUCCESSFUL ANIME! ALSO, LOOK OUT FOR THE *SCRAPPED PRINCESS* NOVEL FROM TOKYOPOP IN NOVEMBER.

FOR MORE INFORMATION VISIT: WWW.TOKYOPOP.COM

KAMICHAMA KARIN
BY KOGE-DONBO

Karin is an average girl...at best. She's not good at sports and gets terrible grades. On top of all that, her parents are dead and her beloved cat Shi-chan just died, too. She is miserable. But everything is about to change—little does Karin know that her mother's ring has the power to make her a goddess!

From the creator of *Pita-Ten* and *Digi-Charat!*

Y YOUTH AGE 10+

© Koge-Donbo.

KANPAI!
BY MAKI MURAKAMI

Yamada Shintaro is a monster guardian in training—his job is to protect the monsters from harm. But when he meets Nao, a girl from his middle school, he suddenly falls in love...with her neckline! Shintaro will go to any lengths to prevent disruption to her peaceful life—and preserve his choice view of her neck!

A wild and wonderful adventure from the creator of *Gravitation!*

T TEEN AGE 13+

© MAKI MURAKAMI.

MOBILE SUIT GUNDAM ÉCOLE DU CIEL
BY HARUHIKO MIKIMOTO

École du Ciel—where aspiring pilots train to become Top Gundam! Asuna, daughter of a brilliant professor, is a below-average student at École du Ciel. But the world is spiraling toward war, and Asuna is headed for a crash course in danger, battle, and most of all, love.

From the artist of the phenomenally successful *Macross* and *Baby Birth!*

T TEEN AGE 13+

© Haruhiko Mikimoto and Sostu Agency · Sunrise.

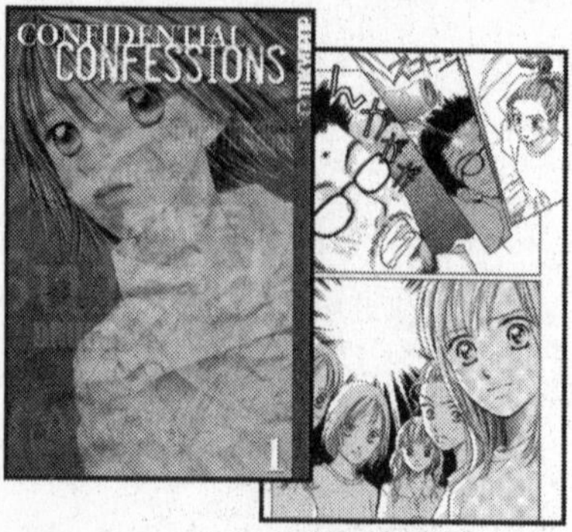
CONFIDENTIAL CONFESSIONS
1

BY REIKO MOMOCHI

CONFIDENTIAL CONFESSIONS

If you're looking for a happy, rosy, zit-free look at high school life, skip this manga. But if you're jonesing for a real-life view of what high school's truly like, *Confidential Confessions* offers a gritty, unflinching look at what really happens in those hallowed halls. Rape, sexual harassment, anorexia, cutting, suicide...no subject is too hardcore for *Confidential Confessions*. While you're at it, don't expect a happy ending.

~Julie Taylor, Sr. Editor

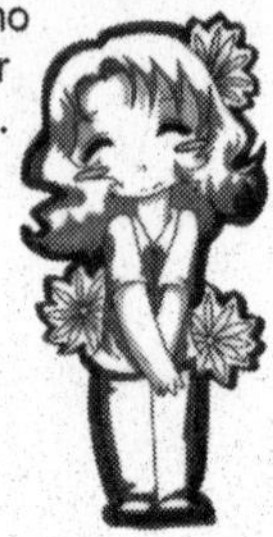

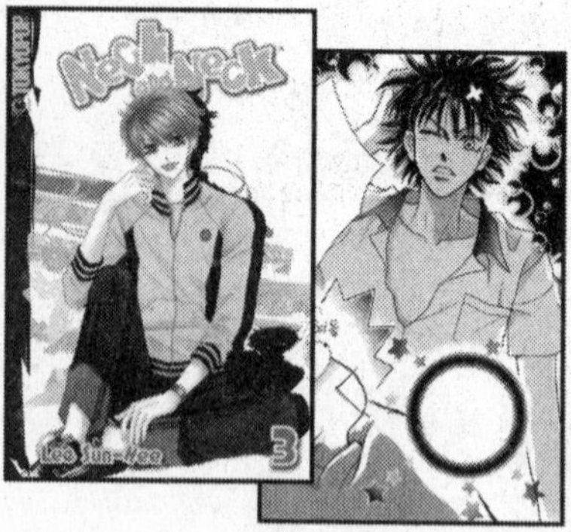
Neck and Neck
3

BY LEE SUN-HEE

NECK AND NECK

Competition can bring out the best or the worst in people...but in *Neck and Neck*, it does both! Dabin Choi and Shihu Myoung are both high school students, both children of mob bosses, and each is out to totally humiliate the other. Dabin and Shihu are very creative in their mutual tortures and there's more than a hint of romantic tension behind their attacks. This book's art may look somewhat shojo, but I found the story to be very accessible and very entertaining!

~Rob Tokar, Sr. Editor

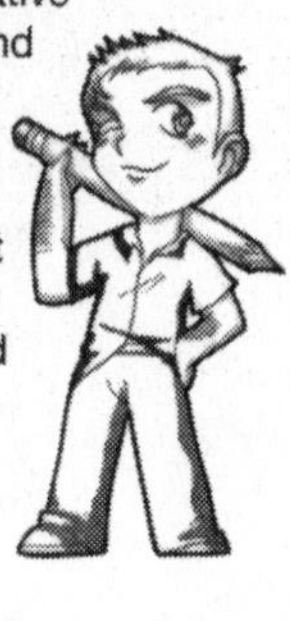

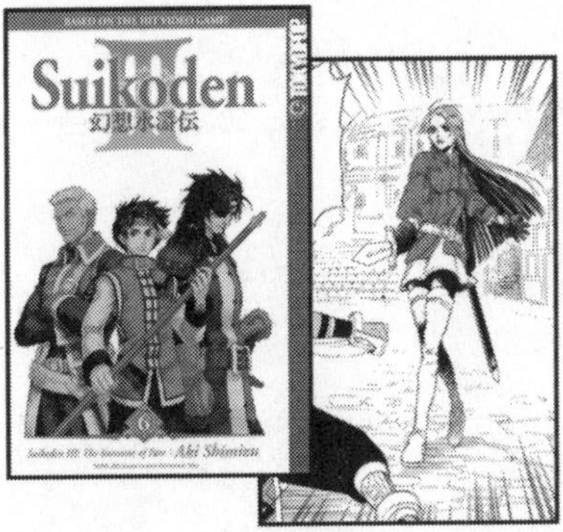
Suikoden
Aki Shimizu

BY AKI SHIMIZU

SUIKODEN III

I'm one of those people who likes to watch others play video games (I tend to run into walls and get stuck), so here comes the perfect manga for me! All the neat plot of a great RPG game, without any effort on my part! Aki Shimizu, creator of the delightful series *Qwan*, has done a lovely, lovely job of bringing the world of Suikoden to life. There are great creatures (Fighting ducks! Giant lizard people!), great character designs, and an engaging story full of conflict, drama and intrigue. I picked up one volume while I was eating lunch at my desk one day, and was totally hooked. I can't wait for the next one to come out!

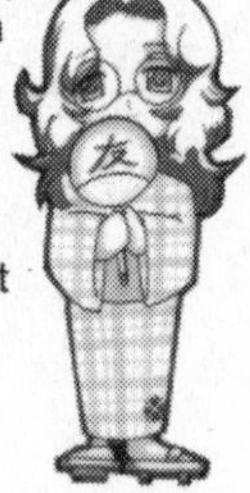

~Lillian Diaz-Przybyl, Editor

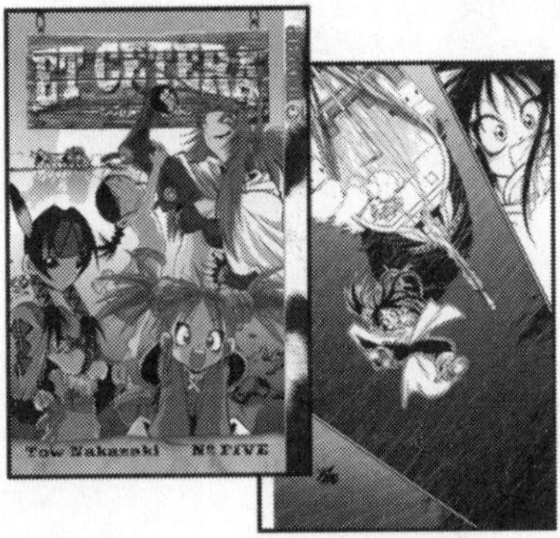
Tow Nakazaki
Nº FIVE

BY TOW NAKAZAKI

ET CETERA

Meet Mingchao, an energetic girl from China who now travels the deserts of the old west. She dreams of becoming a star in Hollywood, eager for fame and fortune. She was given the Eto Gun—a magical weapon that fires bullets with properties of the 12 zodiac signs—as a keepsake from her grandfather before he died. On her journey to Hollywood, she meets a number of zany characters...some who want to help, and others who are after the power of the Eto Gun. Chock full of gun fights, train hijackings, collapsing mineshafts...this East-meets-wild-West tale has it all!

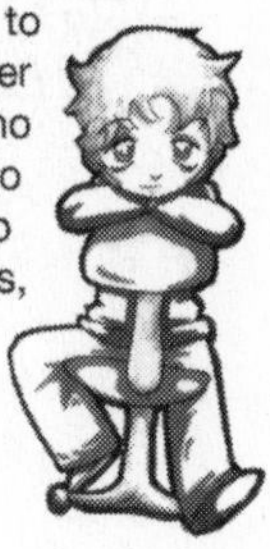

~Aaron Suhr, Sr. Editor